FLOOD
OF
FORTUNE

DAN WHITE

GOLDEN ARROW PRESS

ISBN-13: 978-1540756794

ISBN-10: 1540756793

Golden Arrow Press
P. O. Box 442
Versailles, KY 40383

Typeset by Marsha Swan
Cover designed by Carl Graves at Extended Imagery
Printed in the United States of America

This book is dedicated to my friends and family who have been closely involved in my life and have helped to shape my past.

I would like to extend a special thanks to my son Shane, who inspires me daily to be creative and strive for greatness.

Flood of Fortune is a fictional novel inspired by true events. Names (unless used by permission), characters, and places are either the products of the author's imagination or are used fictitiously. Any resemblance to actual persons, living or dead, or to actual events or locales is unintentional and coincidental.

In life, other than our birth, there are seldom clear-cut beginnings, those moments when we can, in looking back, say for certain that our life's story began here. Yet there are moments when fate intersects with our daily lives, setting in motion a sequence of events with an outcome so Machiavellian it could never have been foreseen, therefore changing the course of our life's fortune, with fortune being defined simply as chance or luck as an external, arbitrary force affecting the outcome of human affairs.

—BOOK ONE—

It was the year 1947, in a rural part of Arkansas, on an island surrounded on three sides by the Arkansas River and cut off from land by a muddy creek, filled with poisonous snakes and snapping turtles, called Big Creek. This island was home to about thirty-five families, most living in poorly constructed homes and others living in caves dug out of the creek banks and covered with willow branches. These last were known as willow twisters and were the poorest of families, living on what they could grow or catch out of the river. The island was called Arbuckle Island and there was a major flood sweeping down the river that would forever change history and the family fortunes of Sam and Jack Mantooth.

PROLOGUE

Sam Mantooth sat in a wooden chair on the front porch of his father's old house on Mill Creek Road. His brother, Jack, had taken a fishing pole and a sack of grasshoppers down to the creek in hopes of catching a few fish for supper. This was going to be their last night in the house. The bank had foreclosed on the property, and was taking possession tomorrow. Yesterday the brothers had buried their father in Arbuckle Island Cemetery next to their mother, who had passed away the year before. The bank had been kind enough to allow the family to stay in the house while their father was alive, knowing the cancer would take his life soon enough. The brothers had saved a small sum of money while serving in the military, but doctor's bills and the funeral expenses for their father had used up every penny. Doc Bolinger had told the brothers not to worry about the rest of his bill; he felt that it was an honor to help two war veterans in their time of need and it was the War that Sam was now thinking of.

When Germany had invaded Poland in 1939 the brothers were thirteen and fourteen years old—Europe, in their minds, was a million miles away. But over the next four years the War became the focal point of a nation. In February of 1943 the brothers hitched a ride to Camp Chaffee, Arkansas, and joined the Army. They were each given a physical exam and declared fit for combat training. Two days later they were transported to Fort Benning, Georgia, by train for ten weeks of basic combat training. After completing basic training, both brothers went into Columbus, Georgia, for a night on the town. They, along with hundreds of fellow soldiers, crammed themselves into bars and pubs that lined the Chattahoochee River. This was an opportunity for everyone to blow off a little steam, because they all knew that the battlefields in Europe could be their final resting place. The young women that went out that night drew the attention of large groups of men. They laughed, danced, and flirted with the soldiers. They were busy declining marriage proposals but always promised to write. Sam and Jack ended up in a diner with a pair of local girls whose names he no longer remembered. The brothers had treated the girls to burgers, fries and milkshakes. The girls treated the brothers to hugs, kisses and promises to write.

Sam and Jack were assigned to the 4th Infantry Division. Great Britain was in dire need of Allied troops. France had surrendered and was now occupied by Germany. After crossing the Atlantic on a troop transport ship their unit was sent to Thorpe Abbotts, near the North Sea in Suffolk, England. Initially the unit was to support and protect the Eighth Air Force Base and the fleet of B-17 bombers that flew secret missions across the entire European theater of war. These aircraft and the bombs they dropped were helping to slow the rapid advancement of Nazis troops.

The 4th infantry Division was chosen to spearhead the D-Day amphibious landing on the Normandy coast of France. On

June 6, 1944, under the command of Brigadier General Theodore Roosevelt, Jr., the men of the 4th Infantry stormed ashore on a stretch of the French coast known as Utah Beach. Fighting beside his brother Jack, Sam was witness to the death of hundreds of brave American soldiers that day. At the end of the day they had advanced four miles inland, crossing the Cotentin Peninsula en route to the very important Port of Cherbourg.

That night Sam and Jack, totally exhausted from marching and fighting, lay side by side in a foxhole. They took turns sleeping for short periods when they could. Most of the time they were both awake because it was hard to ignore the noise of war.

"Sam, did you ever think that war could be this bad? I sure as hell didn't. I can still smell the breath of that poor bastard I killed with my knife this afternoon," Jack said.

Sam replied, "No, I never believed that I could kill another man without an ounce of regret and today I killed a bunch of the bastards. Whatever you do, little brother, stay focused, it's kill or be killed. Now get some rest, tomorrow may be worse than today."

The division encountered fierce resistance at Cherbourg. The fighting lasted twenty-one days and the American troops sustained heavy losses. After taking control of the Port, the troops rested for one day, and then resumed their march across the French countryside. On August 25, 1944, the 4th Infantry Division, with the help of the French 2nd Armored Division, liberated Paris from four years of Nazi rule.

The brothers were part of the victory parade that marched through the streets of Paris, streets lined with thousands of cheering Parisians. Sam fondly remembered the beautiful young lady named Adelle whom he met that day. She was wearing a white dress decorated with pink flowers and a pink hat that shaded her beautiful green eyes. She was the sexiest woman he had ever seen and she took his breath away.

She had invited him into her home and prepared a delicious home-cooked meal. Afterward they had shared a bottle of wine and laughed at their language barrier. She had taken him into her bedroom and made love to him on a goose-down bed fitted with silk sheets. She had teased him with her naked body and had shown him ways to please her in return. After hours of making love they had laid wrapped in each other's arms, their bodies covered in sweat. The next morning they ate croissants and drank coffee at a street side café near the Seine. He remembered the taste of her tears as he kissed her goodbye. She had written her address on a piece of paper that she stuffed in his pocket and made him promise to write to her. That was a night that Sam would always remember—he believed in his heart that it had given him hope and helped him survive the rest of the War.

On September 11, 1944, the 4th Infantry Division was one of the first units to enter Germany. They fought their way through the Hurtgen Forest, and by December were engaged in the Battle of the Bulge, where they halted the push by the Germans. For the first four months of 1945 their unit had fought its way across Germany, leaving a trail of blood and destruction in their wake. When the War ended on May 8, 1945, the 4th Infantry Division had participated in all of the major battles from Normandy Beach to Berlin. Sam and Jack were returned to France with their unit where they assisted in the packing and shipping of supplies and equipment back to the United States.

Sam made numerous requests for a weekend pass so that he could return to Paris by train and visit Adelle. His requests had been denied; he and Jack were forced to work seven days a week until the thousands of troops were shipped home from the French port of Dunkirk. Sam had written several letters to Adelle before his departure but had not received a reply before they departed France on July 1, 1945. Finally, on July 26, Sam and Jack arrived back in Boston, Massachusetts, on board the troop ship called *Aiken Victory*. It had taken another three months of Stateside service, unloading ships in Boston Harbor, before the military granted the brothers their release.

They had enjoyed their stay in Boston; the city was beautiful and unbroken. The people had been gracious, always thanking them for their service. Their accent was certainly different. It seemed the letter 'R' had been permanently removed from their vocabulary. Jack was always teasing the girls, asking them to say certain words that he found funny. He had met one girl that he liked, but she was from a large Italian family, and her brothers didn't care much for Jack or his country boy ways.

In late November of 1945, the brothers had arrived home to find their mother dead and buried and their father dying of cancer. Their dad had borrowed money against the farm, money he had been unable to pay back. The brothers were moving to Arbuckle Island tomorrow, where there was some work to be had, working in the fields for the local farmers. They were moving into a dirt cave dug into the bank of Big Creek. To most this would have been an unacceptable way of life, but both brothers had seen and survived much worse. Jack came up the hill carrying a string of fish and whistling a merry tune. Jack did not speak much about the War and neither did Sam, but often at night Jack cried out in his sleep, reliving the War in his dreams.

Sam stood and called out to Jack, "Good job, little brother, looks like our last meal here will be a good one."

CHAPTER 1

Sam slowly awoke from a nap to the sounds of Jack's complaint of hunger.

"Sam," Jack groaned, "we have to find something to eat. My damn navel is rubbing on my backbone and my britches are falling off my bony ass. I never in my wildest dreams thought that I would crave roasted woodchuck, but after eating possum stew and boiled turnips for a week which, by the way, caused me awful stomach cramps, I know I've got to have some better food. Oh what I would give for some fried chicken."

Sam had heard these complaints a lot of late; times were hard and money was scarce. The past year had been really rough on both brothers. He stood up and stretched his lean but well-muscled body and replied with a grin, "Jack, why don't you dig us some red worms and we'll bait the throw line and catch some catfish tonight? Remember, tomorrow we're diggin' potatoes for Fred Martin and he'll give us a few, and we can fry those with the catfish. Also, he'll pay us a dollar apiece for a full day's work. How about at the end of the day we hike up to the little store and buy us a loaf of bread, a couple of sweet onions, and a few soda pops?"

Jack took off his straw hat and pushed his dark brown hair out of his eyes before he spoke. "Sam, you're full of good ideas and I'm all for them, but how the hell are we ever gonna get out of this place if we spend all the money we make on food? Living in this damn dirt cave and sleepin' on grain sacks is getting old. We need enough money to buy a couple of bus tickets to California. You know Albert Eubanks and his daughter, Sally, are living out there now in Buttonwillow and working on a vegetable farm. She wrote me and said they were living in a small house and makin' decent money. She also said that the weather is nice, seldom gets cold and hardly ever rains. This damn cave leaks like a sieve when it rains."

Sam looked out over the flat and dusty bottomland and watched a dust-devil dance along the narrow dirt road that bordered the bean fields. He said to Jack, "I've got another idea! Old Jack Dunn has a flat-bottom boat that he uses for running his fish lines. He has sold catfish to the locals and made a decent living. After paying his expenses, he had enough money to live on, and a little to put away for a rainy day. I heard his wife is concerned about his age. He's fallen out of his boat several times lately, and she's put her foot down. She told him in no uncertain terms to hang up his fishing pole and sell the darned boat. We could take over where he's left off if we can buy his boat. We could go downriver to Hoover's Ferry and cut a deal with Mr. Hoover to take fish over to the city of Mulberry once or twice a week and sell it to the town folk. He knows more people in Mulberry than we do and he's got a wagon and mule team. In the summer we could take him watermelons and cantaloupe and he could peddle those too."

"Where are we gonna get the money to buy a dang boat?" Jack

asked. "We're so damn broke and living hand to mouth, day in and day out. We've been up shit creek ever since we got discharged from the Army and buried our pa."

"We've got pa's gold pocket watch, and it's in good shape. Doc Reed is keeping it in his safe along with some of our family records and such. I think Mr. Dunn just might make us a trade for Pa's watch and a personal promise to pay him a little to boot, from the money we make selling fish," Sam answered.

Jack stepped back into the shade of a large cottonwood tree and seemed to be in deep thought. Finally he spoke again, "That's the last thing that we have left from our family and maybe we shouldn't get rid of our last family keepsake. But, if we are going to do that, let's just sell the watch and buy us a couple of bus tickets. I'm ready to get the hell out of these back woods and start a new life in California."

Sam replied, "Jack, you're my little brother and I care about you, but dang it that Eubanks girl has got you thinking with your little head. To make a trip to California we would need traveling money and a new change of clothes, along with a pair of decent shoes. The watch wouldn't bring enough money to buy all of those things. Money's scarce as hen's teeth these days and I don't know anyone around here that could buy the watch. So for now, let's put out those throw lines and catch us some fish. Tomorrow, after we get through diggin' potatoes, we'll get Pa's watch out of Doc's safe. Then, we need to wash some clothes for Sunday church."

"All right, Sam, while I'm digging red worms for bait, you take a file and sharpen the hooks. Some are getting a little rusty on the tips and there's some knots in the lines that need to be fixed."

The next morning, Sam awoke at six o'clock knowing they had to walk a mile and a half to reach the south end of the island. Fred Martin would be there waiting for them. They had caught a couple of catfish during the night and he took them off the hooks and put them in the fish box in the creek to keep the turtles from eating them. Sam was delighted; they were going to have fried fish and potatoes for supper.

"Jack, rise and shine! There's no cab service between here and the potato patch! Get a move on!"

Jack rolled out of the makeshift bed, dipped some water into a washbasin, and rinsed the sleep off before he spoke. "Sam, I've thought about what you said about us buying the boat and I guess that's a pretty good idea if ole man Dunn will go for it. After we got off the ship that brought us home from France, I decided I wasn't ever gonna get on another boat. But after thinking about it most of the night, I asked myself, 'Just how dangerous can the Arkansas River be?' Hell, it ain't nothing compared to the Atlantic Ocean and we survived that plus the English Channel."

"Welcome aboard, little brother, I'm glad you like my idea! I've got a feeling that this is going to be an adventure that leads us to a better life. We'll save up some money, get a place of our own, and who knows? If we're lucky, we'll both find a wife. Come on, we've got to get to work."

They walked down the dusty road that separated the fields planted in row crops. After reaching the end of the island, they came upon Fred Martin, their employer for the day. He was sitting on his old Case tractor with his felt hat pulled down, shading his eyes. When the brothers each greeted him, he snapped alert.

"Good morning, Mr. Martin."

"We're here and ready to work."

"Hope you and Mrs. Martin are doing well."

"Morning, boys!" Martin exclaimed in his deep, kind voice. "Glad you made it! Thanks for asking about the wife, she's doing good, she's too damn ornery and mean to be sick. I get home yesterday, and she'd shot and killed a deer. She sent y'all some shoulder meat. I've got it in a bucket with ice in the front of the truck."

Sam said as he shook Martin's hand, "That's real nice of you and your missus! Maybe we can return the favor soon and send you home with a mess of catfish."

As Martin pushed in the clutch on the tractor, he said, "Sounds good. Let's get to work. We can dig about half an acre before dark. Just put the taters in those five-gallon cans and dump them in the trailer behind the truck."

Jack raised his hand to halt the starting of the tractor, "Mr. Martin, just one more quick question, how is your brother Rob? I haven't seen or heard from him since we got off the army bus at Camp Chaffee."

Fred slowly shook his head, "Well, to tell you the truth, the family is a little worried. Rob is living in Fort Smith. He's spending too much time drinking in the bars with some ole boys that don't have his best interest in mind. As I see it, the War took a toll on his mind and soul. He says he drinks to forget about all the pain and suffering that he witnessed over there. Did the War have the same effect on you boys?"

Sam shook his head no and quickly replied, "We were lucky I guess. We saw our fair share of combat, but Jack and I were always together, and that helped us keep our sanity." Wanting to avoid further discussions of the casualties of war and wishing Jack hadn't even brought it up, Sam quipped, "I guess we better get started on this tater patch so we can finish before dark, me and my brother need to see a man about a boat."

Nine hours later, tired and dirty from a hard day's work, the brothers arrived back at camp and started a cook fire. They melted some lard in an iron skillet and broiled some of the deer meat so kindly shared by Mrs. Martin. Jack fried a mess of catfish along with sliced potatoes that Fred Martin had given them at the end of the workday. Sharing with others was a sign of kindness instinctively displayed by country folk during hard times. Many Arkansans were poor, but had learned from one generation to the next how to make do. The widespread poor economy, most realized, was the direct result of the ending of a World War that, at a great cost, had been fought in order to avoid world dominance by Adolf Hitler's German dictatorship. The War effort was over, causing an influx of soldiers back into the American work force and a significant decrease in American exports. The result was a much weaker economy that many feared could reach a depth comparable to that of Hoover's Great Depression. There were others who believed the economy was failing due to poor decisions made by Harry Truman and his current administration. Regardless of the cause, the effect was widespread poverty in eastern Oklahoma and western Arkansas. The roads were bad and transportation scarce, forcing many to use the rivers as a means of transportation.

Job opportunities were rare and making money was very hard around Arbuckle Island. Even illegal businesses had fallen on hard times. During Prohibition in the 1920s and early 1930s, making moonshine whiskey had become an important industry for the people along the Arkansas River. But Prohibition ended in 1933 and cheap booze became readily available. Bootlegging virtually dried up overnight and the market for moonshine was at an all-time low. By the early 1940s most of the notorious bank robbers from Oklahoma were either dead or in jail. Only a few of the gangs remained at large and they were feeling the effects of a poor economy. They were having trouble finding money to steal.

The Mantooth family had always been considered an honest and hard-working family, but never would anyone consider them entrepreneurs. But something had to change for the two young men. Sam, aged 22 years, and Jack, who had just turned 21, both of whom possessed plenty of native intelligence, just needed one positive turn of events. The often-quoted adage, "It takes money to make money," was a reality standing in the way of progress for the Mantooth brothers. It was Sunday morning and both Sam and Jack were sitting on the back pew in Riverdale Freewill Baptist Church. They decided to attend services in hope of seeing Jack Dunn and trading him out of his boat. It appeared that luck was on their side for he was sitting in the first row with his wife and there was going to be a church picnic after the pastor dismissed his congregation.

Sam and Jack were invited by their parents' old neighbors Mack and Alice Underwood to share their table and the food prepared by Mrs. Underwood. The brothers had known and spent time with the Underwood family since they were little children. After eating their fill of Mrs. Underwood's fried chicken, pinto beans and homemade biscuits, they indulged themselves with a slice of her chocolate cake. Her cake was especially good and known throughout the community for its prize-winning quality. After expressing their heartfelt thanks and giving Mrs. Alice a big hug, they went looking for Jack Dunn and his wife.

Hoping to make an amicable trade, the brothers walked up to Dunn and exchanged handshakes with him and pleasantries with his wife. Mrs. Dunn then excused herself to visit some of the ladies of the church, leaving them alone with a soon-to-be-retired fisherman. Sam took the lead in the negotiation by simply stating, "Mr. Dunn, I hear that you might have an interest in selling or trading your flat-bottom boat, and if that's true, Jack and I would have a strong interest in being the proud new owners."

Dunn eyed the brothers warily and said, "What you heard is true, my wife has laid down the law and if I don't park that old boat she's threatened to leave me and move in with her sister. Just what kind of deal do you boys have in mind?"

Sam removed the gold watch from his pocket and unwrapped the small flannel cloth that kept it safe.

"Mr. Dunn, this was my dad's watch and it keeps good time. I believe that he bought the watch when he worked for the Union Pacific Railroad, which was around 1930. My brother and I would like to trade you this watch for your boat with the understanding that if you ever sell it we would like first chance to buy it back."

Dunn examined the watch carefully and said, "I have always wanted a gold pocket watch and with this being an Elgin brand, it sounds like a deal too good to pass up. However, I feel bad about taking your daddy's watch and depriving you boys of it and the memories that go along with it... So here is what I'm willing to do. I will keep this watch as collateral and give you two years to pay me $175 plus $20 interest. When you have paid me all the money, I'll return the watch. I would like permission to wear it to church and on special occasions while it is in my possession. If that sounds fair to you then let's shake on it and call it a Dunn deal," he said, laughing at his own joke.

Jack was the first to shake his hand and, with a tear in his eye, he said, "Mr. Dunn, I can't thank you enough, my brother and I will always be grateful for what you've done for us and for the faith that you've placed in us. We will take extra good care of our new boat and be happy for any advice that you might give us for catching fish."

Sam also shook Dunn's hand and expressed his gratitude as well.

After making arrangements to have the boat delivered down to Big Creek, both boys headed back toward their camp, feeling exhilarated that they had a chance for a better future. As they walked they became silent as each thought about how they would approach their new business and the work it would take to make it a success. When they reached their camp they took an inventory of the fishing supplies they had on hand and determined that they had enough fishing line and hooks to get started and enough lead to make sinkers.

After a cold supper of leftovers that the church ladies had sent home with them, they called it a good day and went to bed. Little did they know as they drifted off to a pleasant sleep that within just a couple a weeks their lives would change again and that all their dreams would be altered in ways they had never imagined. There was a major storm brewing out West and it was going to challenge everything that they had learned in life so far; their army training would finally pay off in dividends much greater than the $50 a month the U.S. Army had paid them during the War.

CHAPTER 2

Dr. George Ingram stood in his office on the second floor of the National Weather Service Forecast Center in Tulsa, Oklahoma. The date was April 1, 1947, but the weather information on Dr. Ingram's desk was far from an April fool's joke. He was looking at the weather data sheets that helped him predict the extent of spring flooding for the lower half of the Arkansas River Valley.

Dr. Ingram was head of the Storm Prediction Center, a job that he had held for the past ten years and he took his job very seriously, as he should, because thousands of lives along the Arkansas and Mississippi rivers depended on his warnings.

In 1937, his first year on the job as chief meteorologist, he had dealt with the second-worst flooding of the Arkansas River in recorded history. That year thousands of homes and farms were damaged or destroyed and hundreds of lives were lost. Even if it had been an improvement compared to the worst flood in recorded history in 1927, it had not been enough of an improvement to satisfy Dr. Ingram.

The data sheets on his desk indicated that all of the factors were in place for another major flood on the lower Arkansas River. The Colorado Weather Service Center was already reporting higher than normal snowmelt and predicting an increase over the next 30 days. The Kansas Weather Center was reporting saturated soils from previous rains and predicting above-average rainfall over the next two weeks. The additional rain would result in the flooding of tributary rivers that would eventually flow full force into the Arkansas River. Ingram's home state of Oklahoma was very similar to Kansas. There was a low-pressure system moving into the state from the West. This would result in heavier than normal rainfall across the entire state over the next two weeks. All of this surface water had to go somewhere and that somewhere was the Arkansas River.

Dr. Ingram decided it was time to call in his assistant, Bob Tate, and get emergency procedures initiated. First he needed his secretary to bring him the file on basic emergency protocol. He needed to give Bob the list of agencies, both in Oklahoma and Arkansas, that required notification. "Shirley, get in here!" he yelled to his secretary.

Shirley entered the office. "Yes Dr. Ingram, what may I help you with?" she asked.

Dr. Ingram took a deep breath before beginning, "I believe that we have an impending crisis on our hands and I want to get on top of this as quickly as possible. I need you to bring me all of the appropriate files for dealing with major flooding in the lower Arkansas River, then send Bob Tate to my office, please."

"I'll get right to it," she replied as she headed for her office, soon returning with an office cart full of emergency files.

Dr. Ingram met with Bob Tate in his office, sharing his data and seeking confirmation from his co-worker. Working together through the lunch hour, two minds became as one and Tate was also now convinced there was a serious situation at hand. Tate and Dr. Ingram worked feverishly throughout the afternoon and by the end of the day phone calls had been made to the other National Weather Service Centers in Norman, Oklahoma, and Little Rock, Arkansas, explaining the findings of Dr. Ingram. With the help of his entire staff, all media outlets and other appropriate government agencies had been contacted as well. Within 48 hours, flood warnings would be issued up and down the Arkansas River.

On Monday, April 4, 1947, George Domerese, a radio news broadcaster for KFDF in Fort Smith, Arkansas, sat down in the newsroom and began to prepare his evening report. He usually began his live show with a recap of national events but tonight he would start with the emergency weather alert. Rain had plagued the river valley for the last two days. His drive into work had been a challenge. It was raining cats and dogs and the same was predicted again for tomorrow. The station had received a telegram from the National Weather Center that stated that flooding of the Arkansas River Valley was a certainty and should be taken seriously. In Kansas the Arkansas River had already reached flood stage and the water level was twenty-one feet and rising. His radio station had a significant share of the local audience and George was pretty popular himself. He felt his show tonight might save the lives of people he had never met. Thirty minutes later he began his broadcast with, "Ladies and gentleman, this is George Domerese of KFDF radio. Tonight we start the news with an emergency weather alert and a severe flood warning issued by the National Weather Service Center out of Tulsa, Oklahoma."

Twenty-eight miles downriver, a group of farmers were sitting around the pot-belly stove in Reed's country store listening to Doc's Silvertone battery-powered radio. Electric power had yet to reach Arbuckle Island. Men came to Reed's store for many reasons. Groceries, gasoline and gossip were a few of the reasons and gossip was the clear leader. The main reason they were there today was to get out of the weather and listen for any news on when the rain might stop. So when George Domerese came on the radio with his weather bulletin and flood warning it quickly became the main topic of conversation.

Curtis Wright, the largest land owner on Arbuckle Island, and Tom White, who farmed across the creek in Oliver Bottom, had both seen the floods of 1927 and 1937. They were singled out for advice on what to expect when the river reached flood stage. White spoke of caution—he advised those that would listen to notify the families to pack up their belongings, round up their livestock, take their pets and get the hell off the island. Wright, whose livelihood depended on the tenant farmers and sharecroppers, took a different approach. His advice was to wait and see what happened upriver, stating that weather forecasters were wrong as much as they were right. He further stated, as a matter of fact, that the houses on the island were located near the middle of the island, at its highest point, and would be safe from the floodwaters. He did take a more cautionary tone when he suggested stocking up on food, water and kerosene. The rest of the group was worried but indecisive as they left the store and headed home to spend the evening with their families.

CHAPTER 3

Tom White, his wife Annie, and his teenage son Tommy or little Tom as some called him, piled into their 1946 Chevy truck after lunch on April 6, 1947 and drove down toward Arbuckle Island to see how the residents were reacting to the news of the upcoming flood. They observed several cars parked in front of the country store as they turned to head down the hill and across the bridge that spanned Big Creek. It was a beautiful spring day with few clouds in the sky.

The first people they saw were the Mantooth brothers skinning catfish that they had hung on a low limb of a maple tree. The number of fish hanging in the tree indicated that the brothers' new business was thriving. Tom pulled over under an oak shade tree, parked the truck, and he and his family got out to talk to Sam and Jack.

Sam greeted the visitors with a heartfelt hello. He had always admired Tom White, whom he perceived to be a very honest and hard-working man. He tipped his hat to Mrs. Annie, a very fine lady and one of the best cooks in the county.

Tom approached the young fishermen. "Hi, Sam, Jack," Tom called out, "looks like the fish are biting!"

Jack spoke up, "These darn catfish are some kind of hungry, act like they're afraid to miss a meal! There was a fish on every other hook. It took us dang near all morning to run the lines. Would you like to buy some for your family's supper? We've got us a regular buffet. There's blue cat, yellow cat, channel cat and flatheads. Also there are a couple of drum, a sturgeon, and four or five fresh water eel. Take your pick and we'll clean 'em and cut 'em up for you."

Annie suggested to Tom that she would like enough fish for two meals. They could eat a mess of channel cat tonight and put a mess of flathead in the icebox for tomorrow night. Tom turned to Jack, "You heard the lady, what do I owe you?"

"That will be a dollar and thirty cents," said Sam. "Mr. White, the weather sure was nice today—do you think it's still gonna flood?"

Tom pushed his hat back with his forearm and reset it before he spoke in a serious but knowledgeable tone. "The majority of the water is coming from up North. I heard the river was out of its banks around Tulsa and still rising. Between here and Tulsa the largest tributaries, the Canadian River, and the Poteau River, both northwest of Fort Smith, are at flood stage now. By tomorrow night the high water on those two rivers will join the Arkansas River. I predict that the day after tomorrow this island will start to flood. The National Weather Service says the river will reach twenty-eight feet in the next three or four days. When that happens, this whole dang island is gonna be underwater." He went on to say, "You fellas need to tell everybody you see to get off this island tomorrow. Tell 'em to take their livestock and as much gear as they can carry. That boat of yours will be put to good use over the next week if it doesn't wash down the river. If I don't miss my guess, this one will be worse than the flood of 1937. Tell everyone to make camp up on the ridge, either east of the cemetery or west of the store, then they should be safe."

Sam and Jack promised Mr. White that they would do their best to help the people of Arbuckle Island make it to safety.

After the Whites left, the brothers finished cleaning the fish. Jack made deliveries on the island and Sam took the rest of the fish up to Reed's country store. They would meet back at camp and make a plan for the next day.

Doc had started buying fish from day one. He sold mostly fresh fish to his customers; fish that was left over he cooked the next day and sold as a hot lunch, and that had proven to be an overnight success.

When the brothers met back at camp, they prepared their own meal. Since buying the boat Jack had stopped complaining about his hunger. They had all of the fresh fish that they could eat every night. They usually added some fresh vegetables and had started making sun tea, something they learned in Europe. After they ate and completed the clean up, they each rolled a smoke, an old habit they could once again afford. This evening, Jack was the first to break the silence.

"We've gotta make some important decisions about tomorrow. We need a plan. We've got fish lines to take up. We need to pull our boat out of the creek and I want to move our camp up by the cemetery. The view of the island and river are much better there."

"You're right, little brother, we're running out of time, that's for sure. Our new business is going to be put on hold for a few days and I really regret that, we're bringing in around fifteen dollars a day and after expenses we've got ten dollars to split between the two of us. That's a five hundred percent increase over what we were making. I figure by the end of the summer we could afford a real roof over our heads."

"By the way, what did the islanders say about moving to higher ground?"

"Well, I'd say about half are gonna leave, the rest are a 'wait and see.' None are moving their livestock, except for the old lady, Nannie Williams, who's taking her herd of goats. Bob Brewer said he would probably take his milk cow and his two hounds. The majority of the ones leaving have little kids to care for."

"Do you reckon we might have to row our boat out there and save some of those folks that are staying put?" Jack asked.

Sam pondered what Jack had told him and answered, "Yes, Jack, I think that's a real possibility—according to what I'm hearing, the water may not recede for a week or more. There will be some danger involved with this adventure. We need to use those old army life jackets that Mr. Dunn threw in when he delivered the boat. Some of the houses are a mile or more from the bridge. Going downriver won't be a problem, but rowing back will be something short of a good time. In the morning, after we take the fish off the hooks, we'll roll up the fish lines, and bring it all back to camp. After we clean the fish, we'll pack up our gear and move our camp to higher ground. I believe we can use the long rope to tie the boat to that big cottonwood tree, from there we'll make it available for emergencies."

Yawning and stretching, Sam went on to say, "We better turn in for the night. I feel sure tomorrow will be a very long day. Jack, be sure to say your prayers before you sleep tonight. We're going to need some divine intervention before this is over. Goodnight, little brother."

The following morning, the brothers took the boat down to the mouth of Big Creek to run their trotlines. Immediately they noticed the river had risen over a foot during the night and was moving faster than the day before. The rising of the river had affected the fish as well. From the five lines, which had ten hooks each, there were only six fish worth keeping. As planned, the lines were pulled from the river and carefully wrapped top to bottom on 18-inch 2x4 planks.

With their tasks completed, Sam and Jack rowed back up the creek to their camp. The only bridge leading to the island was visible from their camp, and a few cars and several wagons could be seen moving off the island. The brothers broke their cave camp and carried their belongings to the top of the hill and claimed a small patch of land under a large oak tree. This would be home for a while; no one knew when life would return to normal. Events beyond human control would soon take place here at Arbuckle Island and fate would play a major role in the lives of many people over the next several days.

* * *

Meanwhile, thirty miles to the west, Bobby Pascal was sitting on a rock beside the Arkansas River and contemplating his own fate. He was located about seven miles south of Sallisaw, Oklahoma, where he had arrived the night before. He was waiting on Frank Farmer to bring him a couple of suitcases filled with money obtained from various bank robberies around the state.

Frank and his wife, Esther, operated a safe house on Black Horse Mountain, just a couple of miles from the river and a mile off Highway 59. Frank had a cave near his home where he hid the stolen money until it could be shipped downriver and given legitimacy through various investments. This had been the plan of action for the last fifteen years, and it had worked well for everyone involved. Frank had earned the trust of the gang members because he had been one of them. He had been the getaway driver for years until he lost the sight in his left eye from a shotgun blast. A piece of shattered glass from the driver's window had sliced through his cornea, rendering him virtually blind in that eye. Esther was Bobby Pascal's aunt, his mother's younger sister.

Bobby's family lived in New Orleans, from where he had just arrived and was anxious to return. The trip took five days up but only three days back because of the current flowing downriver and Bobby didn't stop along the way. He had plenty of fuel cans, boxes of food and jugs of water. Bobby liked to think of his family as investment bankers. They took stolen bank money from Oklahoma and invested it in property in New Orleans. The property was held in multiple trusts, each assigned to a particular family. Bobby's family received 20 percent of the money for their efforts, with Frank and Esther receiving 10 percent. Bobby was aware that the river was flooding and he needed to leave, but he wasn't worried, he had a great boat with plenty of speed and power. He would travel all night and stay ahead of the flood. There would be a full moon tonight and he was an experienced boatman who was paid well for his boating skills. Suddenly he heard the sound of Frank's Ford coming down the dirt road toward the river, probably still a half mile away. This secluded spot had always worked well—Frank brought the money and supplies, Bobby avoided being seen, and the county sheriff turned a blind eye and stayed far away. A few minutes later Frank slid to a stop.

"Hello, Frank," Bobby said, as Frank got out of his Ford.

"Hi Bobby," Frank replied. "How was the trip?"

"The trip up was a piece of cake—a little rain, not much else.

It's the trip home that's got me worried. This damn river is up almost two feet since I got here last night. I just need to get my ass out of here and head south. How much money am I taking back?" Bobby asked.

"It's the most that you've ever taken at one time." Frank handed Bobby two suitcases, and said, "There's fifty thousand and change in there. That's from three bank heists over the last four months. Thirty-two thousand belongs to the Barker family and the rest belongs to the Davis family. Curly Davis is working again. The times are changing—the local cops are about to clamp down because the Feds are breathing down their necks. Most of the gang members are either dead or in the pen. I believe this could be the end of a good run. Esther and me are thinking about calling it quits and moving out West, maybe Arizona. Esther will send your mom a telegram in July and let her know whether you need to come back for a visit."

"Grab a couple of those fuel cans and put 'em on your boat, I'll get the rest, and you can get the hell out of here."

Bobby asked Frank to push him off the beach. Once he was in the current he started the boat and headed for the deepest part of the river. It was well past noon and Bobby wanted to get as far downriver as a possible before darkness became a factor. After an hour on the river he came to the mouth of the Poteau River and saw a lot of debris in the water. He began watching for larger objects, both on top of the water and partly submerged. Large trees were apt to be mostly under the water and could wreak havoc on a speeding boat. Bobby made it past Fort Smith and Van Buren without any problems, but he knew that over the next 20 miles the land was flat and the river would be out of its banks. Bobby pulled out his map of the Arkansas River. He wanted to familiarize himself with the tributaries that he would encounter just after dark, before the moon was high enough to give him light.

The currents were shifting back and forth, creating whirlpools that grabbed the boat like some invisible hand and shook it from side to side. The waves were getting bigger and the boat was hopping up and down. Bobby had never ridden a rodeo bull, but he was sure it had to be similar. For the first time in his life, after operating a boat on the river for thousands of miles, Bobby was scared. This intense fear caused his heart rate to increase, his breathing quickened, and he felt light-headed. He was past Arbuckle Island now. He had made it well into the stretch of lowlands. Then, suddenly, in the distance he heard a low rumble. The eerie sound made a tingle pass down his spine and a chill run through his entire body. Goosebumps popped out on his arms, and he wondered, "What the hell...?"

Then he knew. It was the Big Mulberry River, and it was rockin' like a Southern Baptist preacher on Sunday morning. It was clear to the left, but on the right was a large dark shadow. Quickly he pulled back on the throttle and spun the steering wheel to the left, but it was too late. The boat hit the tree at an angle, but hard enough to hurl Bobby forward. His head slammed into the outside corner of the cabin. He heard a sharp crack and his mouth swam with the metallic taste of blood. His head filled with bright points of light, then there was a feeling of weightlessness, like he was flying. Then he hit the water.

Semi-conscious, he thought to himself, "Wow! There goes the boat and all of that money, somebody is going to be pissed they lost it and somebody is going to be happy they found it." Amazingly, he no longer felt fear. He felt warm and tranquil. Then he felt nothing at all. His body had returned to the water and earth from which it came and his soul had crossed over the realm into the hereafter.

CHAPTER 4

It was 5:30 in the morning on April 8, 1947 when Sam threw back his blankets. It was cool and windy and he felt the chill of early spring. He stood and stretched, pulled on his homespun shirt and wool trousers, laced up his shoes and grabbed his army pea coat that the military had allowed him to keep. He then gathered a handful of sticks and headed for the fire pit to rekindle the fire that had been reduced to ashes. Sam filled the coffee pot with water and added an extra large scoop of Community coffee. A good, strong, hot cup of Joe was just what he needed to start the day.

Sam heard Jack roll out of bed and step behind the oak tree to relieve himself. While waiting for his brother he took a seat by the fire, poured them both a cup of coffee and rolled his first smoke of the day. Halfway through the cigarette, he finally spoke to Jack. "I just saw two sets of headlights going toward the island. I believe one was Curtis Wright's truck, but I never heard 'em cross the bridge. That must mean the river is over the road on the other side. If that's the case, there ain't anyone else getting off that island without a boat. Grab the life jackets, I'll get a jug of fresh water, and let's go check on our boat."

The brothers walked across the top of the ridge, and to their amazement, when looking at the river with the early-morning sun reflecting its golden hue across the surface, they were eerily reminded of the English Channel. The creek and the river had become as one—water stretched as far as the eye could see. There was only a small part of the island still visible with houses dotting the landscape. Upon closer examination, it was revealed that houses on the northern end of the island were partially to completely underwater with objects outlined on the rooftops. Curtis Wright had walked up and had a pair of field glasses that he handed to Sam.

Curtis, who appeared shaken, said, "Sam, I underestimated this damn river. Those are people on the rooftops and some are waving pillowcases or something trying to get our attention. If you boys still have a boat, and are interested, I'll pay you a dollar apiece for every man, woman and child that you can bring off the island to safety."

Jack spoke first, "Mr. Wright, you ain't gotta pay us—it's our civic duty to rescue those people off that island. Why don't you hustle us some help, 'cause me and Sam can't do this all by ourselves. We need people on the bank to meet the ones we bring back. We may need some strong men to row if we get tired and we need the ladies to keep us supplied with food and water. That you can pay for. First things first, we need to check on our boat. Come on Sam, let's go!"

Thankfully, the boat was still afloat. It had washed against the bank with the bow facing upriver and the rope was taught but holding steady against the fast-moving water. Sam told Jack to put on a life jacket and he did the same. He climbed into the boat, sat on the rowing seat and grabbed the oars. Jack sat in the front of the boat, picked up a paddle, untied the rope and tossed it to Curtis Wright. The boat shot down the river backwards as soon as it was given its release. Jack waved and yelled, "We'll be back!" Sam turned the boat by using the right oar, while Jack used the paddle like a rudder. They maneuvered away from the shoreline and turned the bow toward the row of houses.

The first four houses they came to were partially submerged, but there weren't any people. The next dozen homes currently sat on dry land with people waving from their porches. Jack shouted as they passed by that they would return. The brothers decided to continue downriver to the northern end of the island, giving immediate attention to the homes that seemed in the most danger. Jim Smith, his wife and two cats were on the roof of their home and were very happy to see the rescuers. Jack grabbed a porch post and swung the front of the boat under the porch. He told Mr. Smith to hand down his wife first, then the two cats. When that task was complete, Sam told Smith to jump into the water and they would pull him on board. Smith hit the water with a splash, went under, but popped up like a cork and was quickly assisted into the boat. Jack pushed the boat away from the house and Sam began rowing against the current and toward the bridge where help waited. The going was slow, and the strain was great on Sam's arms and shoulders, but the trip upriver went smoothly, with the exception of the snake that tried his best to hitch a ride. Jack was able to dissuade the snake from joining the passengers by whacking him a couple of times with the paddle. As soon as the boat touched the bank, the cats leaped to safety and quickly distanced themselves from the river. There were numerous people on the riverbank to assist the Smiths from the boat. A young sharecropper held the boat steady while Sam and Jack switched places.

Curtis Wright had some news to share with the brothers before they pushed off. He informed them that Albert Underwood's boat, the only other boat in the area, was missing and assumed lost. Wright told them, "Fred Patterson of Lavaca sent word that the U.S. Army dispatched several amphibious vehicles from Camp Chaffee to the Mud Town bottoms and he thought that later in the day a couple of those would be sent to assist in the evacuation of Arbuckle Island." Sam thought that was good news if it really happened.

The boat was once again pushed into the river and the second rescue attempt was underway. The water was still rising, a fact that was made obvious by the height of the water surrounding the first four houses they passed. This time the brothers rescued another man, wife and their teenage son. Five people filled the boat to capacity and the boat sat low in the river water. Their trips continued in this manner, taking almost an hour each, until well past noon. Two local men had manned the oars on a couple of trips, giving Jack and Sam some much-needed rest and a chance to eat some lunch. The river continued to rise, raising new concerns— larger trees were now washing downriver, which, at any moment, could hit one of the houses, knocking it off its foundation. This could cause a domino effect, sending one house into the next, until all would be gone.

Around four o'clock in the afternoon, two amphibious vehicles arrived to assist in the rescue operation. This was cause for a brief celebration by the locals, most of whom had never seen a vehicle that could function on both land and water. Some vocalized their doubts that it was even possible. But it was possible: the rescue operation was moving much faster and only a few families remained in harm's way. Fate, however, was not to be denied a presence in an event that would be remembered for ages.

Alice Cooper, an elderly lady who had been rescued earlier in the day, approached Sam and Jack with a request: would they return to her home and retrieve her family Bible? She said she would understand if they didn't want to go, although, it would really mean so much. There were family pictures and important papers pressed between the pages in that old Bible. She was sure that her marriage certificate, her sons' birth certificates and social security cards were in the Bible on the top shelf of the old roll-top desk.

Sam and Jack readily agreed to the task. After all, what decent young American man would not come to the aid of a sweet old lady who brought back fond memories of their own dear mother? So, with Sam rowing the boat, the brothers headed downriver to the Cooper home, dodging trees that had been ripped from the riverbanks and buildings that had broken loose from their foundations. They felt sorry for all the chickens and guinea fowl stranded on the rooftops, but saving them was not a part of their mission. Sam rowed the boat around the end of the Cooper house, where Jack grabbed the step railing and steadied the boat until Sam could wade through the doorway and into the house. The water was above his knees and he could feel a strong vibration coursing through the entire structure. He made his way to the desk and retrieved the Bible and returned to the boat as quickly as possible.

He placed the Bible in a canvas knapsack and shoved it safely under his seat. Jack pushed away from the railing and Sam began to row the boat back away from the house. That was when fate intervened in the lives of the two young men and the moment that all hell broke loose, as did the Cooper's house. With a gut-wrenching sound, something between a scream and a boom, the house broke apart. The boat was slammed backward with tremendous force, snapping the left oar into multiple pieces. Both brothers instinctively leaned far to the left to counteract the forces seeking to capsize their boat. The boat was caught in the debris field of the destroyed home, and with only one oar and one paddle, the only option for the Mantooth brothers was to head downstream and pray to God above.

The two brothers were mentally shaken but physically they were fine. They had just survived a very frightening event, an experience that was ongoing. Their boat was being pushed down the river amidst a cavalcade of what previously had been homes and barns, and dead animals that had lived in those barns. There were large trees that had provided shade to playing children, and personal treasures that had belonged to the displaced families. If anything positive was to be gleaned from this tragedy, it was the lack of human casualties. At this time the brothers had not observed any human remains; it was their belief that the island's farm families had all been saved.

Darkness was rapidly approaching, yet an opportunity to reach land had not presented itself. Sam and Jack agreed it was safer to maintain their current position than to attempt an escape from the debris. Sam used the one remaining oar to push away larger debris and Jack acted as scout and used his paddle to keep the bow of the boat straight as possible. When darkness prevailed a plan was made to allow one brother to sleep while the other maintained vigilance over the river. Sooner rather than later the boat would surely wash ashore.

After a long and miserable night Jack awoke to the sound and smell of a flooding river. The predawn light offered Jack a view of his surroundings. He was not sure of their location, but being alive on the river was better than the alternative. He could see Sam at the front of the boat, eyes focused down the river. "Sam, where are we? Do you know?"

"Well, about thirty minutes ago I saw bluffs on the right—that was probably Citadel Bluff, just east of Nichols Bottoms—then ten minutes ago there were lights above a bluff on the left—I think that was Ozark, so I believe we're approximately thirty-five miles downriver from Arbuckle Island," explained Sam. "The channel has narrowed and the river has picked up speed. The larger debris is pretty much behind us now, so when the river widens again we need to do our best to get off the river."

"All right, Sam, I'm feeling nature's call and solid ground will suit me fine."

The sun had risen above the horizon and fog had settled in on the river, partially obscuring the view. Suddenly, there was a large body of water to the left of the main channel—not sure of what they were getting into, the decision was quickly made to go for broke. Jack used the oar as a paddle at the back of the boat and Sam was paddling with all his might in the front. Gradually the boat broke away from the current of the main channel: they were making progress, and after a mighty struggle the brothers found themselves in a large body of calm water. They paddled for another ten minutes or so before they reached the banks of a muddy cove. Sam jumped out and pulled the front of the boat onto the shore and tied a rope around a small tree. Jack brought the jug of water, handed it to Sam and headed into the woods. Sam took a drink of water from the jug and lay back in the grass along the shoreline. He was exhausted and worried about how they would get their boat back home, as well as themselves.

Jack returned, sat down beside Sam, and quipped, "Well we're down the river without a paddle, so to speak. What are we gonna do now? I'm so hungry I could eat one of those dead critters we saw in the river." Then he thought for a second, "Oh hell, we ain't got any dry matches."

Sam advised that they sleep for an hour or so, let the fog burn off, then take a look around and see if they had any options other than walking back to Ozark.

After sleeping for two hours Sam felt much better. The fog was gone and he walked down the shoreline to get a better look at his surroundings. The flood pool took a turn to the left; walking past the point he saw a boat about a quarter of a mile away. He shaded his eyes looking for the boat's occupants, but saw no one and thought maybe they were asleep on the boat. Sam walked back within shouting distance and yelled for Jack to come see what he had found.

Jack shot up and hurried toward Sam. "What have you found?" he asked, as he got closer. "I hope it's something to eat."

Sam showed Jack the boat and together they walked in that direction. When they were closer, Sam shouted, "Halloo the boat!" They waited, but there wasn't any answer. As they approached, Jack noticed that the boat hadn't been secured with a rope. It had run aground and was lodged on top of a newly created sandbar. It was a beautiful cabin craft that looked expensive—the emblem on the side read Chris Craft. The brothers were familiar with the boat's manufacturer; they had seen similar craft used by the U.S. Navy in the War.

Jack waded out to the starboard side of the cruiser to peer inside. "There's no one in the boat. It looks abandoned and the key's in the ignition," he told Sam. "Should I board her?"

Sam was unsure what to do. What if the owners had walked out to find help, and if they came back, what would happen? "Too many questions and not enough answers," thought Sam. He said, "Let's wait a little while and see if anyone comes back."

Jack's hunger was overriding his better judgment; ignoring Sam's advice he climbed aboard the cruiser and immediately noticed the bloodstains on the corner of the cabin. He jerked open the cabin doors to see if anyone was inside, but boxes of food and luggage were all that was there.

"Sam, you had better come up here!" Jack shouted as he opened a box of food. There were cans of sardines, blocks of cheese, and boxes of saltine crackers and ropes of smoked sausage. There was a case of red wine and a carton of domestic beer. He also found a can of coffee and a coffee pot. Jack was ecstatic; he hadn't seen food like that since leaving Europe.

Sam joined Jack on board and his jaw dropped in utter amazement. "What in the world! I can't imagine who would leave all this unguarded. What do you think happened here, Jack?"

Jack was enjoying a link of smoked sausage and a bottle of warm beer. So much for the consideration of other people's property; hunger was acting as the devil's advocate. In between bites, Jack told Sam to check out the blood on the roof of the cabin and the side railing. He was sure that something unfortunate had happened to the boat driver, or otherwise he would have secured the boat to a tree with the coil of rope lying on the deck.

Sam looked at the body of evidence, concurring with Jack's assessment of the situation, then Sam gave into his own hunger, joining his brother in the food fest and free libations. The brothers talked and laughed at length, so overwhelmed with such a reversal of fortune it left them giddy. After their hunger had been satisfied and their thirst quenched, a further search revealed little other than four gas containers, a large jug of water and three suitcases. One suitcase was different than the other two, so it was opened first. Inside were folded shirts, pants, socks, underwear, one shaving kit and a pair of size nine leather shoes. Those were the normal items one would expect to find in the luggage of a traveler. Underneath the normal items, however, were two pistols, a sawed-off shotgun, and a box of shells for each of the weapons. One pistol was a .32 caliber Walther PPK, the other a .45 caliber M1911 Colt and the shotgun was an Ithaca 12-gauge pump. Each of the brothers had a look of quizzical wonder: What else were they about to find?

Jack handed the other two suitcases to Sam, who placed them on the floor of the boat. Jack looked at Sam. "What do you think are in these two?" he asked.

Sam slowly shook his head, "I don't know what we're going find in them suitcases, but this whole deal has a funny smell, the kind of smell that lingers around criminals. Let's get it over with, you open one and I'll open the other." The snaps clicked and both suit-cases were opened. What the brothers saw at that moment would forever be imprinted in their minds. There was more money in one suitcase than the entire Mantooth family had made in a lifetime.

Sam looked around again to make sure they were alone, then said, "Let's count the money in one suitcase, close 'em up, put 'em back in the cabin and get the hell out of here." The money amounted to a little over $26,000; they figured the amount was similar in the other case. They stacked the money neatly back in the suitcase and snapped it shut. All three suitcases were placed back inside the boat's cabin. It was time to see if they could start the boat.

Jack turned the key to start the engine but nothing happened. Two things were quickly apparent: the gas tank was empty and the battery had lost its charge. With four gas cans full of fuel, half of the problem would be easy to solve. Sam, a decent mechanic, felt he could overcome the battery problem. He was pretty sure that he had a metal rod in the other boat. He could turn the boat key to the on position, use the metal rod to touch both the positive and negative terminals on the solenoid switch above the starter, creating an arc that would short-circuit the starter, causing it to turn and allow the engine to fire. There was a downside to this procedure—the person holding the metal rod was going to get the shit shocked out of him unless he could use a couple of sticks to hold the rod in place.

Sam refueled the Chris Craft while Jack went back to the old boat to retrieve the metal rod and the canvas bag with Mrs. Cooper's Bible inside. Sam had an idea, a way he and Jack might keep what they had found. It was going to require drastic changes, a brand-new lifestyle, and he was not sure his brother would agree to the idea. Jack returned, bringing the requested items, plus a small oak tree limb, and climbed back on board. Sam cut the limb in two equal pieces, split the ends of both pieces, inserted the rod and tied it in place with twine. He raised the motor cover, asked Jack to turn the key, and then placed the rod against the solenoid terminals. Fire arced across the terminals, the starter turned, but the engine failed to start. Sam disconnected the lower end of the fuel line and blew gas into the carburetor, then reconnected the fuel line. Once again he placed the rod against the solenoid terminals and the starter turned over. The engine sputtered several times before finally roaring to life. Sam yelled for Jack to add more throttle as he removed the rod from the terminals. The motor was running smoothly now. Sam wiped the sweat from his brow, grabbed two bottles of beer and handed one to Jack. Sam sat down in the rear seat of the boat and said, "Let's let her idle for fifteen to twenty minutes while we enjoy this beer in the luxury of our new boat and by the time we've finished our beer, the battery should be charged."

Twenty minutes later, Jack eased the boat into reverse, slowly adding throttle; the boat grudgingly pulled away from the sandbar and slipped into deeper water. Sam asked Jack to pull over near the old boat and then jumped into the muddy water. He grabbed the oar and paddle and tossed them into the Chris Craft, then pulled the flat-bottom into deeper water, where he secured the towline to the back of the new boat. After climbing back on board the Chris Craft, he told Jack to drive slowly out of the cove into the main channel and head downriver. Jack looked confused, but followed instructions. When they reached the main channel Sam told Jack to slow the boat down. He leaned over the back and pulled Mr. Dunn's old boat forward. Sam closed his eyes and said a prayer of thanks before he untied the old boat and shoved it back toward the riverbank, watching sadly as the current whisked it away.

"Jack, let's head down the river and put some distance behind us," Sam instructed.

"What are we doing and where are we going? I guess you know Arbuckle Island is the other way," Jack pointed out.

"If you trust me, just head down the river. After we're far enough away from here I'll tell you my plan, and if you don't like it we can turn around and go back to a community that no longer exists."

Jack hesitated for a moment, turned, looked downriver and hit the throttle. In his own mind, he knew what Sam was thinking. It would be impossible to explain their newfound wealth to the people back home.

CHAPTER 5

Sam and Jack had traveled about twenty miles downriver, with Sam seated comfortably in the back of the boat listening to the purr of the engine and the sound of the boat hull as it sliced through the river. He was deep in thought when Jack interrupted. "We just passed Altus, where the Wiederkehr family is growing grapes for makin' wine. Johann Wiederkehr and his family moved here from Switzerland. He said this area, with its mountains and valleys, reminded him of Europe's finest wine regions. Do you think he could be right?"

"I don't really know—the wine that I drank in France tasted pretty good and the homemade Muscatine wine that Wayne Martin made got me drunk when we were kids growin' up, but other than that, I know very little about grape-growin' and wine-makin'. I hope it works for them, 'cause that's a long way to travel just to grow grapes," replied Sam. "Jack, I've got some ideas floatin' around in my head about what we can do with this boat and the money we found. But first I'm going to look again at that suitcase with the clothes in it. We need to find some clues and figure out who owned all of this."

Sam pulled the suitcase out of the cabin and popped the latches; he took out one of the shirts and held it between his hands. He thought it looked like a large size, so he removed his own shirt and tried it on. It fit him well, except the sleeves were a tad short. There were three shirts in the case, one apiece and one to keep clean. Next he pulled out a pair of pants, checked the pockets, and held them up to his waist. The pants were big enough around the middle but a little short for Sam's 6'1" frame. Jack was a couple inches shorter than Sam and the pants would fit him just fine. Sam laid the shirts and pants on the boat seat.

He removed the vest and went through the pockets, where he found some coins and a few pieces of paper. One was a receipt from a speakeasy in New Orleans. That was the first clue, but maybe there were more: he had to keep looking. He laid the vest and the men's underwear on top of the other clothes. As Sam was removing the socks he found one pair of wool socks with a surprise inside—stuffed in the folded socks was a switchblade knife and a Louisiana driver's license. Sam read the name on the license. It was Robert Jean Pascal, born August 14, 1924. The address read 103 Chantilly Street, New Orleans, Louisiana. Sam had never been to New Orleans, but he had heard numerous stories from fellow soldiers. The Louisiana bayou held many secrets. Whatever was needed could be found there.

There was one question still unanswered: Where did the money come from? Sam went back to the suitcase to conduct a closer inspection. He ran his hands around the lining, on the left side. Near the back he felt something thin and rectangular in shape. The object of his interest was inside the lining that had been opened and sewn back with needle and thread and hidden away from prying eyes. Sam took the switchblade and slit the lining, unveiling a small black book. Sam opened the book and thumbed through the first few pages; what he saw were names and account numbers. It was the names that drew his attention—some of them he knew from the radio and newspapers, and they were not names of your everyday, law-abiding citizens. There were names that he didn't recognize, but the family names of Barker, Dillinger, Floyd, Farmer and Kelly were names that had terrorized the banking communities across the entire Midwest for the past twenty years.

"Holy shit, Jack, I've found some things that we need to discuss! There's a large cove just this side of Dardanelle—let's pull the boat in there and take a break from the river, besides it will be dark soon. Also, start thinking of another state besides Arkansas that you'd like to live in and I'll do the same.

"Sam, you look like you've seen a ghost. Hell, we got us a dang nice boat and two suitcases full of money. If you can recall, when we woke up this morning we were two hungry, dead-broke farmhands down the river without a paddle. Whatever it is that's got you worried can't be all that bad. This is a once-in-a-lifetime opportunity. The way I see it, we have done for others long enough, and it's time we took care of ourselves. This is a reward for all the sacrifices that we've made. For two years we fought toe-to-toe with the Germans and yesterday we helped save all those people from a major flood. So let's just think of this as our flood of fortune. With this money we can make a new life, and it don't matter to me what damn state we live in. Hey, look ahead. I think it's the cove you were talking about, but today it looks more like a lake. Let's head over toward that hill and find some fresh water. We need to fill our water jugs and I need to take a piss. Besides, I want a bath and a shave before I try on those new duds that you got laid out."

Inside the cove, Sam and Jack found an inlet with a small, clear creek flowing along a hillside surrounded by a forest of hardwood trees. The brothers built a nice fire from wood they gathered along the hillside; they wanted a warm fire before they took a bath in the fresh water of the creek. They shared Bobby Pascal's soap and razor and bathed in a shallow pool they found up the creek from the camp. The pool of water was clear, but cold and bathing took on a sense of urgency, and with their teeth chattering they used a blanket to dry off. A line was tied between two trees and the blanket was hung close to the fire to dry and double as a windbreak. While Jack was changing clothes, Sam grabbed some food items from the boat for their dinner. He returned with cheese, crackers and a bottle of wine.

The two brothers shared the fare and, after eating their fill, Sam went back to the boat. He soon returned carrying the shotgun and a box of shells, these he sat between the two of them. Sam took a seat facing his brother and, in a serious tone, he said, "Jack, from this day forward one of us will always sleep in the cabin of the boat with a loaded pistol, the other will keep the shotgun handy, whether on deck or on shore. Nights like tonight when we make a camp we will keep a gun handy. Tomorrow morning I want us to take turns shooting the two pistols for a couple of reasons. One, we need the practice. Two, we need to be sure both pistols have accurate sighting and smooth action. We'll leave immediately after target practice in case someone comes to check out the noise."

Sam handed the black book to Jack and waited for his brother's interpretation of the names, account numbers, and deposit entries. Jack flipped through the pages, stopping occasionally to study a particular name. Jack finally closed the book and leaned back against a tree. "Sam, I think Bobby Pascal was a money man for the bank robbers or, at the least, a runner that transported the money to New Orleans for someone else to invest for the crime families. After looking at the entry dates, I believe that the money we have in our possession came from two sources, the Barker and Davis families. There are dates from three days ago entered next to their names with amounts that equal a little over $51,000 dollars. When they realize the boat and money are missing, someone may begin a search for the boat. There's the possibility that Bobby Pascal's body could be found, but there's some good news for us. We have his driver's license and his body will wash downriver with the floodwaters. We will have at least a week, maybe more, before anyone starts a search, and by then we'll be long gone."

Sam agreed with what Jack had said, but he had some concerns of his own, and he chose this time to share them. "Someone will probably recognize this boat—after all it ain't your average, everyday fishing boat. This morning I felt the best plan was to go down the Mississippi toward Greenville or Vicksburg, but after finding that black book and Robert Pascal's identification, I believe it would be smart to go north, up the Mississippi, maybe toward Memphis. It's a city with lots of people passing through; there, we would have a better chance of going unnoticed. We need to find a place to live and a place to store this boat. After we get that done we can either find a job or buy a small business that's already in operation. Last but not least, if we decide to change our identity we could use the social security cards and birth certificates in Mrs. Cooper's bible. Her two boys are about our age and we could get us a Tennessee driver's license using their identities. Those are some things we need to decide in the next few days. Jack, you sleep on the boat tonight and we'll switch tomorrow night. For now, why don't we get some sleep and be ready for tomorrow. We've got a long day ahead of us."

The brothers were up early, eager to start a new day. They ate some of the sausage and drank a pot of black coffee before loading the boat. Prior to leaving, Sam grabbed both pistols from the suitcase. He and Jack took turns shooting a knot on a hickory tree, both showing the shooting skills learned in the military. Satisfied with the results and the guns, they boarded the boat and headed downriver. Their goal was to make it to Little Rock before sunset. The distance was a little over ninety miles and without any unforeseen circumstances they would make it easily.

Jack drove the boat and Sam sat near the front, looking for dangerous debris and thinking back over the last few days. Were the people from Arbuckle Island wasting their time conducting a search for the two brothers? Did they think the brothers were dead? Everything had happened so fast, he hoped he had made the right decision. Being the older brother, Sam felt responsible for Jack. They had fought side by side through France and Germany, and survived the horrors of war, but this was different. So far they hadn't broken any laws, but they should have reported the boat and its contents to the sheriff. Then there was the criminal element: Would they come looking for the boat? The choice of whether to change their identity bothered him the most. Changing their last name would be akin to abandoning their family. Maybe there was a compromise. He still had a couple of days to make a final decision, and Jack, perhaps, would come up with a better idea.

Jack pointed to the south. "I believe that's Petit Jean Mountain and that means we're about thirty miles from Little Rock. We need to find some place that sells fuel so we can top off the gas tank and fill the one empty gas can. Most of all, I would really like to eat supper at a café with a pretty waitress serving me a plate lunch and several glasses of sweet iced tea."

"Hopefully there's a marina near downtown where we can buy fuel, and maybe a café within walking distance. I can stay with the boat while you eat and when you come back I'll go. Right now I'm going to get us some money out of the suitcase before we get any closer to town," Sam said.

Near the bridge that spanned the Arkansas River, connecting

Little Rock to North Little Rock, the brothers found an old marina. Jack drove the boat past the marina, then turned and headed upriver as he edged closer to the dock. With little effort he maneuvered the boat up against the rubber tires on the front of the dock and Sam tied off the boat to the well-worn metal cleats. A young, pimple-faced dockhand approached the boat and, to their surprise, asked, "Where's Mr. Pascal? That's his boat, ain't it?"

Jack replied quickly, "Bobby took ill and stayed around Fort Smith. We're just driving the boat back to New Orleans for him. Do you know him?"

The kid replied, "Yeah, he always stops here on his way upriver. I would take care of this boat real good and he would always tip me a few bucks."

Sam spoke up, "Well, we'll do the same if you'll top off the tank with gas, check the oil and fill up that one empty gas can. Is there a place to eat around here?"

"Yes sir, the Frisco Station is up on the hill behind us and serves a mean chicken-fried steak. Tell 'em Clarence Smith sent ya."

Sam stayed with the boat and Jack went up the hill, happy as a lark to know he was fixin' to tie on the feedbag. A full belly and a pretty girl was all that it took to keep Jack happy.

Sam watched as Clarence checked the engine oil. He indicated it needed a half quart and Sam told him to go ahead. After the gas tanks were filled, Clarence added up the bill and Sam paid him for the fuel and added a $3 tip. The kid returned to the marina office and Sam sat down in the boat to await Jack's return. Over an hour passed before Jack showed up with a contented look upon his face.

Sam asked, "How was it? I'm talking about the food, not the waitress."

Jack laughed, "It was pretty dang good, the food, I mean. The waitress was real nice as well. She gave me her address and asked me to write her some time. Man oh man, I had me a piece of their chocolate pie, and it was so damn good, I had a second piece. I'll stay with the boat and you go enjoy your supper. By the way, tell them you don't want Tina to wait on you. You want the other waitress, the brunette. Oh, one other thing, there's a surplus store next door. Why don't you buy us a couple of them army sleeping bags? The mornings have been a little nippy."

Jack had been right about the food, especially the pie. The waitresses were friendly and Sam teased Tina, telling her how smitten Jack appeared to be. The sleeping bags were a good idea as well.

The next morning Sam was lying on the boat seat, still snuggled in the sleeping bag, watching the sunrise in the eastern sky. If they hustled it would be possible to make the Mississippi River by dark. The unanswered question was: Where were they going from there? Maybe stopping around Pine Bluff would be a better idea. Spending one more night on the Arkansas River and reaching the Mississippi during the early-morning hours seemed to make the most sense. Jack crawled out of the cabin, and he and Sam went inside the marina. They took turns tending to their personal business and accepted a free cup of coffee from a grouchy old man that said he owned the damn place. Sam paid cash for one night's docking and a small block of ice. He then thanked the old coot and bid him farewell. The brothers returned to the boat without seeing hide nor hair of Clarence and both wondered what he was up to. Sam put four beers in a bucket and placed the chunk of ice on top, then started the boat while Jack untied the ropes from the cleats and pushed them away from the dock.

The terrain southeast of Little Rock was very flat and the river was wide and out of its banks from the floodwaters. It was obvious they had reached the delta region of eastern Arkansas. The trip downriver was hot and boring. Large flocks of ducks and geese provided the only excitement of the trip. For lunch they shared a can of sardines and some crackers, topped off with a bottle of ice-cold beer. After passing Pine Bluff they found a nice-sized island in the middle of the river and moored the boat at the southern tip, close to a grove of cottonwood trees. Jack gathered firewood and started the cook fire while Sam prepared dinner with the slab of bacon he had purchased from the diner the night before. He sliced off a dozen pieces and placed them in a frying pan. Supper was going to be fried bacon sandwiches, with canned peaches for dessert.

After supper there was a considerable amount of daylight remaining. Jack and Sam each rolled a smoke and began the discussion of which direction to go once they reached the Mississippi River. Jack believed they should head south toward Greenville and get a job working on a farm and hide their money for a while. Sam pointed out several reasons for heading north toward Memphis. One, they had already been farmhands and they both knew how that turned out. But the most compelling part of his argument rested on the idea of taking the boat in a direction where hopefully it would not be recognized by anyone along the river. Based on the information provided by Clarence, Sam believed this boat had made several round trips between New Orleans and Oklahoma.

Jack wanted to take a walk around the island so that he could be alone and think about the points Sam had made. Jack enjoyed a country lifestyle—a quiet, peaceful life. He had heard too much noise and seen too much violence during the War. Memphis, being a big city, would have more of the things that he wanted to avoid. But maybe it would be safer for the both of them, if he could tolerate the city for a while. Sam, as always, had thought things through; he had made good points in favor of Memphis.

Suddenly, Jack stopped; he heard voices somewhere up ahead. He eased forward and peered between the trees. There were three men and a small motorboat. All three were taking turns drinking from a jug of what appeared to be moonshine. One was a large man with a bushy beard, the next one was not as tall but bigger around the middle with a bald head, and the third was skinny with a long, narrow face and a big nose. Mentally, Jack nicknamed them Bear, Pig and Rat, respectively. As a group they looked like trouble just waiting for a place to happen. Jack decided to head back toward the boat to inform Sam of what he had seen. He turned to leave and stepped on a small dry tree branch, snapping it in half. When he looked back, Bear was looking directly toward him. Jack walked away, feeling sure that he had been seen. He walked rapidly and ten minutes later arrived back at camp. Sam was on the boat rolling out his sleeping bag when Jack came out of the trees.

"Sam, we got company, three men up the island a ways. They're drinking moonshine and they don't look like anyone we would want to call friends. Unless I miss my guess they'll be here in a few minutes. I'm gonna climb on board and grab the shotgun—why don't you go in the cabin and stay out of sight with the loaded pistols. When they show up, I'll ask 'em to leave. I'll call you if I need you." Sam followed his instructions without question, and disappeared into the cabin.

Jack soon spotted the river pirates walking along the shore headed his way. He wanted them to think he was alone, to see what their intentions were. When they were close enough to hear him without shouting, he said, "You boys stop right where you are and state your purpose. I'm alone and I ain't real friendly."

Bear, who seemed to be the leader, spoke up with a tone that sounded like a growl, "We come down here to see who was a spyin' on us and just who do you think you are a givin' us orders and such? We're from around here local, and we don't like strangers. Now why don't you tell us what yore carryin' in yore fancy boat?"

Jack decided it was time to fish or cut bait. He raised the ante when he aimed the double-barrel at Bear's chest. He noticed immediately the change in his expression. "Let me tell you something, you overgrown piece of shit, I walked up on you by accident. Who I am and what I've got in my boat is none of your damn business. Now, I'm going to give you an order that you will understand, all three of you get the hell out of my sight or I'm going to blow your ugly, stinking heads right off your damn shoulders. If I didn't make myself clear, then come on down closer and we can start this little shindig right now."

Bear didn't like looking down the twin barrels of the shotgun, so with a look of pure hate and contempt, he turned away and issued his own warning, "This ain't over, stranger, we'll be back and yore gonna be sorry that you talked to us like ya did. We're gonna enjoy drivin' that thar fancy ass boat after we bury you in this here river. Sooner or later you gotta sleep and that's when we're gonna getcha."

The river pirates walked away and Sam rejoined Jack on deck. "Little brother, you talked awful mean to them ole boys, you called their bluff tonight, but I believe we'll see them again early in the morning." Sam put his arm around Jack's shoulder. He could feel the anger running through his brother's body. "I'm proud of you and there's no one that I would rather have on my side. You stay on the boat tonight with the double-barrel and I'll take this pistol and hide in the brush above the campfire." Before Jack could object, Sam jumped off the boat, climbed up the embankment, and lay down between two bushes facing the front of the boat.

The night passed without incident, but neither brother slept much. Their bodies were over-producing adrenaline. This was going to be a battle of life or death and they were relying on previous combat experience to get them through. They had faced similar and worse situations numerous times during the War and were still around to talk about it.

They were up before dawn and drank cups of coffee laced with whiskey to calm their nerves and smoked a couple of cigarettes. They loaded the boat while keeping an eye on their surroundings and departed the island at first light. The sky was covered in a thin layer of silky clouds preventing any reflection on the river. Sam wished now that he had purchased a pair of field glasses from the surplus store. Jack was at the wheel of the boat and Sam was standing vigilante behind the passenger seat, their eyes focused downriver. The shotgun was on the floor at Jack's feet, the .32 caliber pistol stuffed in the waistband of his pants. Sam was holding the .45 caliber pistol in his hand, his finger steady on the trigger. He was the first to see the boat pull away from the shoreline on the left side of the river. The pirates were a quarter of a mile ahead and slowly moving toward the middle of the river to intercept the Chris Craft. Sam hunkered down in the boat, hidden from view. He wanted the element of surprise to remain in his favor.

Jack reported, "They've stopped in the middle of the river; one is steering the boat and the other two have long guns pointed in our direction. Should I ram their damn boat?"

"No, don't. One of us might get shot. Try to stop broadside to their boat, but not too close. At your signal I'll grab the shotgun, stand up and fire both barrels. You use your pistol and disable the motor. Shoot some holes in the hull if you can."

The big pirate, the one Jack had named Bear, fired a warning shot over the bow of the Chris Craft and yelled at Jack to stop the boat. Jack pulled back on the throttle and slowly turned parallel to the other boat. The fat pirate, the one Jack called Pig, yelled, "We gotcha now, you arrogant sum'bitch!"

Jack whispered, "Now!" and Sam came up firing both barrels, one at each of the two pirates holding rifles. Both pirates went down, losing their rifles into the river. The Rat stared in disbelief at his bloody friends lying in the bottom of their boat. Jack and Sam unloaded their pistols toward the rear of the boat, trying to take out the motor. At least one of their bullets struck the gas tank, causing it to explode in a ball of fire. All three pirates screamed horribly as the flesh melted off their bodies. The brutal event reminded the brothers of scenes they had witnessed during the War. Scenes they had hoped never to see again. They watched as the scoundrels' boat slowly sank below the surface of the river, taking the smoking pirates one step closer to hell.

CHAPTER 6

The decision to head north was made soon after their deadly altercation on the lower Arkansas River. They did not believe there were any witnesses, but agreed that blending into a large city was the best choice. To get off the river would be a relief for both brothers. They had made a life-changing decision; for better or worse they now had to deal with the consequences. So, mid-morning on April 15, 1947, Sam and Jack pulled their boat into the Port of Memphis.

Jack changed into Bobby Pascal's clean clothes and walked into town, while Sam remained on the boat. He found a local haberdashery and bought a complete wardrobe for Sam. As usual Jack was starving, so while in town he ate lunch at a barbeque joint. It was highly recommended by the tailor at the clothing store. He had described barbeque as something new and deliciously different, and the smells of the smoked meats made Jack's mouth water. He had two barbeque pork sandwiches and several glasses of iced tea. When he returned to the boat he presented Sam with a sack of smoked ribs and a bottle of soda pop. Sam was equally impressed with the taste of this new style of cooking and he loved the flavor of the sauce.

A short time later, Sam changed into his new attire, asked Jack to remain with the boat, and went ashore to inquire about a place to live and find storage space for the boat. He felt like a new man in his store-bought clothes. The new shoes looked and felt great on his size eleven feet. He honestly couldn't remember the last time that he had worn new shoes that weren't provided by the military.

His first stop, which turned out to be a fortunate one, was at the marina office. He introduced himself as Sam Cooper to David Hinkle, one of the owners. He explained that he had just arrived in town by boat from over in western Arkansas and was looking for a place to live and storage for his boat. Hinkle told Sam about a small warehouse he owned near the river on Front Street, with an apartment in the back. The previous occupants had recently moved their operation to Nashville and the building was now vacant. After telling Mr. Hinkle that it sounded like something he would be interested in, he mentioned that he also needed a boat trailer for his 21-foot v-hull Chris Craft. Hinkle came through again: he knew of a trailer that was for sale and he thought that with a couple of minor modifications, which could be made by his employees, it would fit the boat perfectly. Mr. Hinkle walked over to the warehouse with Sam and unlocked the door. Sam liked what he saw. There were four rooms in the apartment: two bedrooms, a living room and a kitchen with a wood cook-stove and an electric Frigidaire refrigerator. The warehouse was large enough for at least three boats. Maybe the extra space could be used as a source of income. He dickered with Mr. Hinkle about the terms of the rental agreement until he was satisfied that the price was fair. He told Mr. Hinkle that he would be back within the hour to bring the first month's rent.

Sam returned to the boat to tell Jack about the warehouse and the deal that was available. Jack said, "It sounds good to me and if it's got four walls and a roof I'll be happy. I just want to get out of this boat and off this damn river for a while." Sam agreed and got the rent money out of the suitcase. Mr. Hinkle accepted the money, wrote out a receipt and sealed the agreement with a handshake. He told Sam that the used boat trailer would work for certain and it could be purchased for $125. Sam asked Hinkle if he could have his men load the boat on the trailer and deliver it to the warehouse. Hinkle replied that he would, but it would cost an extra 20 bucks since he would have to use a hoist to lift the boat onto the trailer and use one of the company trucks to haul it to the warehouse. Sam agreed to the prices and told Hinkle that he would pay in full when the boat was safe inside the warehouse.

Sam returned to the boat and shared the good news with Jack. The brothers ate a cold supper on the boat. They felt it would be wise for the both of them to spend the night on board with the money and be around in the morning when the boat was being moved. There were two very important suitcases to move as well. They would put the guns back in the clothes bag, where they would be out of sight while moving them to the apartment. What was left of the food and wine could be left in the boat's cabin since the boat would end up in the same building as the brothers.

Jack asked, "How are we going to keep the money safe? It's impossible for one of us to stay with the money all the time."

Sam agreed, so he shared his thoughts. "The interior walls of the apartment are built with well-fitted 1 by 6 boards. We'll remove one and stuff the majority of the money inside the wall and then replace the board. We'll also buy a padlock for the door, with a key for each of us. Finally, for the money we carry with us, we'll each wear a money belt around our waist."

Around nine o'clock the following morning three port employees arrived to move the boat. The brothers removed their suitcases and were assured that the boat would be moved without a scratch. They walked to the warehouse, carrying their future inside the two suitcases. A little over an hour later they were in the apartment and the boat was safe inside as well. They tipped the workers with three bottles of wine and bid them good day. With a hammer and a pry bar they removed a board, stored the money in the wall and replaced the board with care, leaving no telltale signs of entry. The $2,000 that they held out was hidden inside the cook-stove under an old baking pan. The brothers headed into the city to take a look around and purchase a few necessities. They walked into the downtown area, discussing the purchase of a vehicle. Sam thought that they should look at a used Chevy truck, because that was what their family had owned. Jack disagreed: "A used vehicle is gonna have more problems—I think we should buy us a new Ford pickup, then we could take care of it ourselves from day one. After we eat some lunch we can go to a car lot and look around."

Sam replied, "That's fine with me, but right now I want to eat lunch at a barbeque joint and drink an ice-cold beer."

The brothers chose City Pitt Barbeque, located on Beale Street, where they indulged in pulled pork sandwiches and dry rubbed ribs. Just inside the door was a number three washtub full of Pabst Blue Ribbon beer, covered with small chunks of ice. The beer looked too good to pass up, so they had one with their meal and another after. While drinking the second beer Sam started up a conversation with the owner, a jolly fellow named Freddie Clanton, asking him questions about the history of his restaurant.

Freddie was happy for the chance to boast about his successful venture. He told the boys that he had learned the trade from his daddy, who had been instructed in the culinary arts by a slave his father bought from a rancher down in south Texas. Sam asked Freddie if he knew of any business opportunities in Memphis. He explained that he and Jack had just relocated from Arkansas, and their only working experience was military or farm-related. Freddie excused himself and disappeared into the back. Sam was worried that he had insulted their new acquaintance. That was not the case, however. Freddie returned carrying a case of Tennessee sour mash whiskey and pulled the cork on one of the bottles. He poured a shot into three glasses and passed one to each of the brothers.

Then he said, "This here is some fine sipping whiskey that my brother Willy is bringing in by the truckload from Nashville. Willy is looking for someone to make deliveries around Memphis. He's been operating out of his house and making the deliveries himself, but he's tired of it. He wants to continue making the trips to Nashville to buy the whiskey and bring it back to Memphis to sell, but he don't want to make any more deliveries. He would rather spend his time drinking and gambling away the profits."

Jack told him about the warehouse and suggested that they could store the cases of whiskey and deliver them as well. Freddie told them he would talk to his brother and ask if he could go by the warehouse and have a look. "My brother has a nickname and it fits him well, so be fair-warned—everyone calls him Slick, Slick Willy Clanton." Both brothers laughed at Freddie's warning, but assured him they could take care of themselves. After shaking hands and thanking him, the brothers gave him directions to their place and left to attend to their other plans.

Now there was a real possibility they would need a pickup truck, so their next stop was Harp's Ford Motor Company, located just three blocks away. Mr. Harp personally showed them his entire inventory, both new and used. Jack was drooling over a shiny black Ford half-ton pickup with a flathead V-8 engine, chrome hubcaps, white-walled tires and an exterior sun visor. Sam liked it as well, and inquired about the best price available. Harp told him it listed for $1695 but he would take $1500 cash on the barrelhead. Sam told Harp to fill the tank with gas and they would be back the following day to pay for the truck. He wanted the truck title to list Cooper Brothers as owner. Harp agreed to the requests, thanked them for their business, and told them he looked forward to their return in the morning. The brothers were so excited they almost forgot to buy their money belts.

On the way home, they had to stop and turn around to find Farris Mercantile, where they bought the belts, a padlock, a couple of towels and some bed linens. The rest of the necessities could wait until tomorrow, when they would have a truck to drive. "Damn that was exciting, we're going to own a brand new Ford truck," Jack thought to himself.

Sam was also thinking about how quickly their life had changed for the better. He remembered one of his daddy's sayings, "Love makes the world go 'round, but it takes money to grease the wheel." When they arrived at the apartment, they looked around to make sure that no one else had been there. Everything was where they had left it. They quickly transferred the cash to the money belts and strapped them around their waists. They spent the rest of the afternoon cleaning the apartment and moving the supplies from the boat into the kitchen. When their new home was deemed livable, they took two wooden chairs from the kitchen to the front of the warehouse, where they smoked cigarettes and watched the sun set over the Mississippi River. Jack went back to the apartment and returned with a bottle of red wine and two glasses. The brothers spent the rest of the evening drinking wine and reminiscing about their past and planning for the future.

Morning arrived, bringing with it an air of excitement and a bit of a hangover. Sam drew a bucket of water from the well and, with a bar of soap and a washrag, bathed before getting dressed. The cold water was refreshing and he urged Jack to do the same. Later on they could buy a rick of firewood for the kitchen stove so they could make a pot of coffee. Sam enjoyed a cup of coffee and a cigarette in the morning.

Today they would get their coffee and some breakfast at the Dixie Café, located on Union Avenue, four blocks from the Ford dealership. Sam had a plate of ham and eggs with homemade biscuits and redeye gravy. Jack ate a stack of pancakes with fried ham on the side. Sam asked the waitress if she knew where the café bought their ham and sausage. She said both came from Pilgrim's Meat Market, where almost everyone shopped for meat, and deliveries were made twice a week. Sam was thinking about other items that needed to be delivered around town. He asked if there were any other delivery services that they had problems with. She told him there were problems getting fresh produce delivered; the café went to produce stands to buy what they needed.

Jack, who had been flirting with the waitress, turned to Sam and said, "I've waited my entire life for a nice truck and I just can't wait any longer. Let's go pay for our new truck and go for a ride around the city."

Sam was ready as well, and paid for their breakfast. "When we get to the car lot I'll go to Mr. Harp's office to pay and you talk to the mechanic, find out everything you can about maintenance on a new truck. As you said, we want to keep it in tip-top shape, because if my plan works, this truck is going to get a lot of use."

Harp greeted the brothers as they entered the dealership and asked if they still wanted the truck. Jack quipped, "Bout the same as a baby wants a bottle."

Harp laughed as he headed for his office and motioned for Sam to follow. Sam signed the title "Sam Matthew Cooper." He knew this was the first step in changing their identity. He counted out the $1,500 that he had removed from the money belt prior to their arrival and with a handshake the transaction was complete.

Mr. Harp recommended breaking the engine in slowly by driving under the speed limit for the first fifty miles or so. Jack had already taken the truck for a test drive around the block and was waiting with the motor running. He said with a grin, "Hop in, Sam, we've got places to go and a damn fine truck to get us there."

Sam retorted, "Damn it, boy, you done wore all the new off this truck."

The new smell of that truck was something special that would forever be remembered by both brothers. Words failed in their effort to describe the overwhelming joy that had taken root in the souls of both Sam and Jack. Nothing could surpass that moment in time, riding around with the windows down, their hair blowing in the wind, without a care in the world. Thoughts of the past and future were blown away to mingle with the smells of springtime. Feelings of pain and sadness were cleansed from their hearts by the rays of sunshine dancing off the chrome of that beautiful new Ford. This feeling of freedom was unlike anything they had ever known; the financial constraints that they were born with and had always lived under disappeared that afternoon.

After driving around downtown and touring the business district, they headed out of town and ended up in a predominantly black community called Nut Bush. The area had many small farms with large vegetable gardens and fruit orchards. The only business was Jimbo's Grocery, a small grocery store located just off the highway intersection. Jack turned into a gravel parking area in front of the store. They entered the store and were met with wary and suspicious looks from the other patrons. Sam and Jack were thirsty and wanted something cold to drink and maybe a snack to eat. Jack selected a Coca Cola and a Moon Pie, while Sam bought a glass of cold apple cider and a sack of fresh roasted peanuts.

Sam asked the very large and very black man behind the counter his name. The towering man answered simply, "They call me Jimbo."

"Well, Jimbo, my name is Sam and that's my brother, Jack." Sam asked if the cider was made from apples grown in the local orchards.

"Almost everything in this little ole store is grown or produced by the local folk, includin' the milk, meat and apple cider. Why do you want to know?"

Sam replied, "I want to know if you would sell to someone that ain't local, and if so, would you or someone local be interested in selling fresh produce to me and my brother?"

Jimbo answered, "I'll think about it. Come back next week and I'll give you my answer."

The brothers thanked him, paid for their purchases and left the store. Sam drove the truck back into town and was impressed with the speed and handling of the Ford. "Sam, what exactly do you have in mind? I have an idea but I'd like to hear it from you."

As he cruised back into town, Sam outlined his plan: "First, everything hinges on getting the whiskey-delivery business from Slick Clanton. If we work out an agreement with him, then we can store all his cases of whiskey in our warehouse and make deliveries in the afternoon. In the mornings, we could make fresh produce deliveries, if we can work a deal with Jimbo. Eventually we want to be able to offer meat, especially pork. The barbeque business is going to grow and they will need a dependable source of fresh meat. I believe that the community of Nut Bush can help us with that if we can convince each small farm to grow out five to ten pigs per year that we supply to them at no cost. We can buy the hogs back at a fair price after they're grown, butcher the hogs and sell meat to the restaurants in town. The growers would be paid in cash and we would provide them with new pigs twice a year. We could give the Pilgrim's some competition, especially if we can make deliveries. We'd need to look into finding a breeding farm and some good breeding stock."

Before reaching home, they purchased a half of a rick of firewood and loaded it into the truck. They backed the truck into the warehouse and stacked the wood near the door of the apartment. After work, Mr. Hinkle stopped by for a visit. He told them that Willy Clanton had been around looking for them. He had already left, but said he would come back later on. Hinkle also said he knew of Clanton and that he had a bit of a reputation around Memphis.

Jack showed Mr. Hinkle their new truck and asked if he would like something to drink. He said, "No, thanks, my wife is making supper and I had better get on home. But I sure do like your new truck and would like to go for a ride someday soon." The brothers thanked him and bid him a good night.

True to his word, Clanton showed up about an hour later and knocked on the door. His brother had described him well. He was a sharp dresser and had been blessed with the gift of the gab. He came in the door with a bottle of Jack Daniels in one hand and a fat cigar in the other. The brothers had set up a small table and three chairs in the warehouse. Sam and Jack shook hands with Clanton and offered him a seat and all three sat down at the table. After exchanging small talk about the city of Memphis and getting to know each other a little better, Clanton switched to the topic of business. He told them he supplied whiskey to nearly forty different bars, dance halls and restaurants. Every other Monday he drove to Nashville to purchase new stock, usually twenty to twenty-five cases at a time. He said he had a dozen cases in the back of his truck right now. He showed them a list of his clientele, his price list, and copies of purchase tickets from the distillers.

His first offer was 20% of the profits, which included using the warehouse. Sam told him that was not good enough. They wanted 20% of the company and 40% of the profits. Clanton started preaching about all the work he had done to get the business where it was now. How, without his connections, there wouldn't be any business. He said that he could find someone else cheaper.

Jack spoke up, "Look, Clanton I've heard enough—we have a warehouse and a delivery truck and you need us. We'll settle for thirty-three percent of the company and the profits. Take it or leave it."

Clanton replied, "I was just getting warmed up, hell, that's damn near highway robbery, but I guess I can live with that arrangement. Get us some glasses and let's toast our new partnership."

Sam insisted on writing out an agreement, which Clanton signed, while continuing to question the need. He said his handshake had always been good enough. Sam said, "Well, we're new in town and the agreement just makes us feel better. Besides, it will prevent any doubt in case something happens to one of us."

Before Clanton left, Sam and Jack unloaded the whiskey from his truck and moved it into the warehouse. Once again, they all shook hands and Clanton said, "All my friends call me Slick. Why don't y'all do the same?"

After Slick departed, Sam put his arm around Jack's shoulder and said, "Jack, you did good, real good, in my opinion. How about another toast to our new business, Cooper Brothers Distribution?"

"Sam, that sounds impressive, but it still feels wrong not to use the names we were born with. This is gonna take some getting used to." Sam understood, but he still felt they had made the right decision, and after the final toast they called it a night and went to bed. Tomorrow would be the first day of deliveries in a city they weren't familiar with and to customers they had never met, but hoped to impress.

CHAPTER 7

The dog days of summer were in their prime as Jack delivered his last case of whiskey for the day. The distribution business was doing very well. In a little over three months they had almost doubled their sales volume of Tennessee whiskey. Jack and Sam were personable and dependable. They also offered incentive rewards to the buyers that bought and sold the greatest number of cases. The winner and his family would be treated to a barbeque dinner at City Pitt Barbeque, compliments of Cooper Brothers Distribution. Freddie Clanton's barbeque business had benefited from this arrangement, so he only billed the brothers for his cost. Sam was delivering produce in the other truck that they had purchased last month. The brothers had bought a used two-ton Ford, with a flatbed and sideboards that worked better for hauling large sacks of produce. Jimbo had convinced the residents of Nut Bush to form a cooperative and sell their produce exclusively to Cooper Brothers.

The farmers were cultivating and planting larger garden plots and a greater variety of vegetables. The soil was very fertile from generations of flooding and the subsequent deposit of topsoil from upriver. The farmers were very proficient. Their skills had been learned from their fathers and perfected through the years. Sam was amazed at the ease of selling fresh vegetables in the city of Memphis. He offered his fare to restaurants, grocery stores and roadside markets. The list of produce included lettuce, tomatoes, onions, corn, beans, peas, carrots and potatoes. Fruit included several varieties of berries, watermelons, cantaloupe, pears, peaches and apples. He also sold large amounts of eggs. In fact, due to the volume of sales, he was compelled to hire their first employee, Jimbo's youngest son, Jordan, to help him make deliveries. Jordan was a really nice kid with a constant smile that was contagious to others around him. He was strong as an ox and a quick learner. Sam was really pleased with his first hire and it made Jimbo a proud father.

Sam was equally excited about a major breakthrough in his personal life as well. He had written to Adelle in May, expressing his feelings for her and his desire to receive news of her wellbeing. Without going into detail, he told her of the move to Memphis and the business they had started. When Sam included his return address, he told Adelle that he and Jack were using the last name of Cooper and that he would explain further if she wrote him back.

In July he finally received the letter he had been waiting for. Adelle wrote that she was doing well and had sorely missed her handsome Yankee gentleman. She told him about writing him at least a dozen letters, all of which were returned as undeliverable. Adelle, however, had never given up hope that they would make contact again. She had sublet her apartment in Paris to move back to the countryside with her family, leaving instructions with the lessee to forward all her mail. Adelle's family, she explained, was also in the business of selling alcoholic beverages. They owned a vineyard south of Paris, where they produced a variety of blended grape wines. Much of the vineyard had been destroyed and numerous casks of wine pilfered by the Germans during the War. She had moved back home to help the family restore the winery, which was only now nearing completion.

She hinted that she would be able to travel to the U.S. around Christmas and wondered if it would it would be possible for Sam to meet her in New York. She closed her letter with several French words that Sam had to have interpreted. He was pleased to find that she loved him with all of her heart. When Sam arrived back at the warehouse he found Jack outside cooking steaks on the grill that he and Sam had built with the permission of Mr. Hinkle. Sam stood for a moment with a feeling of déjà vu. He could remember not so long ago watching Jack roast woodchuck over an open fire on the creek bank of Arbuckle Island. How far they had come in such a short time was almost beyond belief. He yelled at his brother as he grabbed a beer from a bucket of ice, "What's for supper?"

Jack replied, "Beef steak and fried taters, I also got us a plate of cornbread from the Dixie Café."

Sam helped himself to a slice of the cornbread and took a seat in the shade.

"Sam, tomorrow I'm gonna hire me a helper. There was a young feller came by earlier looking for work, and I told him to come back in the mornin'. He's the younger brother of one of the dock workers and seems honest and reliable."

"That's fine by me. Maybe I'll get to meet him if he comes before I leave." Jack put the steaks and fried potatoes on plates and handed one to Sam.

Over dinner, Sam told Jack he was going to First National Bank in the morning and was going to take another thousand bucks out of one of the safety deposit boxes they had rented and put it in their business account. Sam had deposited a thousand in cash each week since starting their business. There was still $15,000 hidden in the wall that they did not intend to put in the bank. They remained a little wary of the banking business because something could happen and they might need immediate access to cash.

The next morning Jack's new helper arrived early, ready to work. He introduced himself as Charles Lacella, and asked to be called Chuck. He helped Jack load the cases of whiskey and the two left to start their deliveries. Sam went to the port office to pay rent to Dave Hinkle. Hinkle offered a cup of coffee and asked him to take a seat.

Sam wanted to ask an important question but decided to wait until they had exchanged pleasantries and small talk. Hinkle had moved to Memphis from Lexington, Kentucky, and he had a love for racehorses. He kept up with the top runners by reading the newspapers that were brought downriver from Kentucky. He had been to the Kentucky Derby several times and said repeatedly that everyone should go at least once. The only thing Sam knew about a horse was how his ass looked while pulling a plow. To him they were all pretty much alike, but he enjoyed listening to Mr. Hinkle and thought maybe he might go to the Derby one day. The one thing Sam had on his mind today was to inquire about buying the warehouse they were leasing. After hearing all the latest news on horse racing, Sam spoke of his desire to purchase the warehouse they were living in. Right off the bat, he asked Hinkle to name a price. Hinkle responded, "Well, Sam, you and Jack have been real good tenants and I like you boys. I am in need of some new equipment here on the dock. Our business is growing. Give me time to speak to my partners and I'll let you know something in a day or two."

Sam thanked him and headed for the bank to make his weekly deposit. When Sam reached the bank he made his deposit and asked to speak to someone about a loan. After a short wait, he was shown into the office of C.R. Dunn, the bank's vice president. Dunn stood and shook hands with Sam. Introductions were made and Dunn asked, "How might we be of service to you?"

Sam explained how the business of Cooper Brother's Distribution worked and the growth that had taken place since the start up. He told Mr. Dunn that he wanted to buy the warehouse that they were currently leasing and gave him the business address. Sam went on to say that, if the purchase price was manageable, Cooper Brothers could pay down half of the money and would need a loan for the other half. Dunn excused himself and went into a different office. Sam knew that this was another step in establishing their new identity. He and Jack could have paid for the building, but he worried that too much cash might arouse Dave Hinkle's suspicions. No one had asked any questions about their past, and he wanted to keep it that way. Dunn returned and said, "Sam, you and your brother have a substantial balance in our bank and we value your business. So when you get a contract to purchase from Mr. Hinkle, come back and we will loan you half of the purchase price." Sam thanked the man and headed for Nut Bush to talk to Jimbo.

Sam parked his truck in back of Jimbo's Grocery, where Jordan was waiting to load today's produce. Sam told Jordan to go ahead and load the truck while he spoke with his daddy. Jimbo was working at the meat counter, slicing baloney, when Sam asked him if he could spare a few minutes. Jimbo wiped his hands on a towel, removed his apron, and the two men walked outside. Sam told Jimbo how pleased he was with their business arrangement, and that he had another idea that could work well for the entire community. Sam outlined his plan. First, they would need a farm that could be used for breeding purposes. Cooper Brothers would supply the breeding stock and would buy the piglets after they were weaned. They would then need multiple farms to grow the pigs until they were large enough to slaughter. The grower could keep one pig for every five they grew for the company, and Cooper Brothers would supply the pigs. When the hogs were ready to slaughter, the grower would be paid a reasonable price per pound. He further explained that Cooper Brothers would build a slaughterhouse in Nut Bush. They would need to hire local men to erect the building and also to work in the slaughterhouse when it was completed. Sam said they would discuss the sales plan at a later date. He wanted to sell every part of the hog but its squeal. Jimbo said that he would explain the plan to the locals to get their opinions.

Jordan had loaded the truck in the order of the deliveries. First stops were loaded last. The first stop was a regular customer and the delivery was quick and easy. The second delivery of the day went to a new client, a burger joint called Mack's Burgers. Their order consisted of several heads of lettuce, a crate of tomatoes and ten pounds of onions, a simple delivery that was made difficult by a big ole redneck employee that hated all blacks. Jordan started through the back door carrying the tomato crate, but his path was blocked. The large sweaty arm, belonging to the redneck cook, prohibited his passage. The redneck yelled in his face, "Niggas ain't allowed in here, and that means you, boy!"

Jordan stopped and turned to look at Sam, his ever-present smile gone. Sam quickly said, "Come on, Jordan. Let's go. We can live without their business."

The redneck didn't know when to quit. He said, "Hey, bring them damn vegetables in here yourself, nigga lover, 'cause if'n you don't I'm gonna kick your ass!"

Sam turned slowly and, with the graceful move of a big cat, he spun and kicked the redneck in his gut. As the man doubled over,

Sam broke his nose with a left uppercut, followed by a right cross that broke his jaw. Sam leaned over the fallen redneck and said, "I do care for that young man and you will never be half the man that he is. What you need to understand, here and now, is that he is quicker and stronger than me and I just kicked your sorry ass."

Sam was sure he had lost that account and he was equally sure that the redneck would be drinking his meals through a straw for a while. He and Jordan continued the rest of their deliveries without incidence. Jordan didn't say any more about the fight, but looked at Sam with great admiration and respect.

The next few weeks were a blur. Everything Sam had set in motion came to pass. Dave Hinkle agreed to sell the warehouse at a fair price, so Jack and Sam signed the contract and paid him half of the money down. The bank fulfilled its commitment and loaned the other half of the purchase price with payments due every three months. Jimbo reported that he had the support of the locals for the hog-growing operation. Sam asked Mr. Hinkle if he knew anyone he could recommend that raised hogs. He said there was a German named Schultz in Olive Branch, Mississippi, that had a fairly large swine operation. The following Sunday, Jack and Sam started up the big Ford truck and drove south out of Memphis, found Highway 178, then headed to Olive Branch to look at Schultz's hogs. If they liked what they saw, they would inquire about purchasing a few.

Ivan Schultz was a large, jovial fellow with an accent that sounded all too familiar to the two war veterans. During their introductions, Jack mentioned that they had been in Germany during the War. Schultz quickly informed the brothers that all members of his family were proud American citizens, having immigrated to the United States ten years before the War.

Schultz had two types of swine, Poland China, which were black and white with semi-erect ears, and Durocs, which were red pigs with drooping ears. Both types had plenty of length and height, with very large hindquarters. Schultz and the brothers walked among the pens discussing the care and management of farrowing sows. They talked about the length of gestation, which was 111 days, the average number of piglets, which was ten, and the amount of time from birth to weaning, which was seven to eight weeks. Schultz recommended that the male pigs be castrated at three to four weeks and raised to a weight of 250–300 pounds before slaughter, which usually took ten to twelve months. Sam decided he wanted to buy six sows and one boar of each type, and he wanted mild-tempered sows with at least fourteen teats each. Prices were negotiated, sows and boars selected and the brothers loaded six Duroc sows on their truck and headed for Nut Bush.

The brothers arrived an hour later at the farm they had leased a mile north of Jimbo's Grocery. The farm consisted of ten acres of land with a large, tin-roofed shed. Two rows of seven farrow pens were added underneath the shed. There was also a nice-sized corncrib and a storage building located on the property. The owners of the farm lived in the house and were going to work for the Cooper Brothers. The family had experience in both breeding and growing of hogs.

After leaving the farm, they drove a half a mile away to the building site of the slaughterhouse. Sam had bought raw lumber from a sawmill near the community of Bucksnort. The lumber had been delivered the week before and a crew of four men had erected the frame and boarded up two sides of the building. The pump house for the water well was already completed. One of the locals, recommended by Jimbo, had witched the location of the well with a divining rod made from a forked limb of a maple tree. A local well-driller brought in a cable rig to do the drilling. A large underground stream of water was located forty-five feet down the hole. The driller described it as very strong water supply with rapid recovery to tap. Sam was relieved; plentiful water was crucial to operating a successful slaughterhouse. The brothers spent a couple of hours going over the layout, checked the building construction that had been completed, and then headed back to Memphis and dinner at City Pitt Barbeque.

Freddie Clanton was happy to see both Jack and Sam. He treated them to a free dinner and pulled up a chair to shoot the bull. Freddie did most of the talking while the brothers ate their meal. Freddie stated that he was a little concerned about his brother because he believed he was drinking and gambling too much. He was afraid that Slick owed a great deal of money to some loan sharks who had little tolerance for unsatisfied debt.

Jack said, "Freddie, I've heard rumors from a couple of bars that Slick has been playing a lot of high-stakes poker and losing. Supposedly he has been borrowing money from a guy named Franco Marcelli."

Sam chimed in, "You know this shit could affect our liquor business and our relationship with your brother. But I don't want it to ruin our friendship."

Freddie asked, "Could you two come back here tomorrow night? I'll try to get Slick over here and maybe we can talk some sense into him."

The next afternoon Sam went home to wait on Jack, so they could go together to the meeting. When he arrived, he checked the mailbox and, to his delight, he found a letter from Adelle. He grabbed a cold soda pop from the fridge and sat down at the kitchen table to read the letter. Her letter smelled of sweet perfume. He was aroused as he remembered their lovemaking and the wonderful feelings they had shared that night in Paris. He finished reading the letter. Adelle had booked passage on the *Queen Mary* and would arrive in New York City on December 23rd. She requested that he meet her there so they could celebrate Christmas together. She said that she had not booked return passage to Paris and would be open to a trip to Memphis if he were in agreement. Sam decided he would write her a letter tomorrow and agree to all of her wishes.

Jack arrived home and Sam shared the content of her letter. Jack slapped him on his shoulder and said, "Sam, that sounds great!" Smiling, he teasingly said that he had always wanted to see New York City.

Sam looked at him quizzically. Jack laughed and hurried to say, "I'll be more than happy to take care of things around here. It's a good time for you to be gone because our produce business will be slow in midwinter. Now that we have that settled and out of the way, come on, let's go talk to Slick and straighten his ass out."

Jack and Sam arrived at the barbeque joint to find Slick and Freddie sitting outside at a picnic table. They sensed tension, but Slick put on a false front and acted as if he didn't have a problem in the world. Freddie ordered a round of cold beer and two slabs of dry-rubbed ribs.

During the meal, Jack, being his normally blunt self, asked, "Slick, how much do you owe these bastards and how long have you got to pay them off?"

Slick, looking like he had eaten sour grapes, replied, "I owe 'em a little over $3,000 and they've given me until Friday to pay them off or they'll send some goons to break my legs or maybe even kill me."

Sam butted in, "Look, Slick, you done got your ass in a bind, but if Jack will agree, we will loan you the money, provided you will sign an agreement putting up an additional 33% of your part of the business. You will also agree that, should something happen to you, we can pay your brother $3,000 more and own the entire business."

Slick, not having a better option, agreed to the deal. Sam said, "I'll draw up the agreement tomorrow morning and meet you back here in the afternoon. After you sign, I'll give you the money." Sam, being a man of his word, returned the next afternoon with the money and the agreement. Slick arrived, smelling of the liquor that provided his income. Freddie acted as a witness to William Clanton's signature.

After he signed, Sam handed Slick the money and offered a bit of advice, "Slick, we're business partners and I consider you a friend. You've got to pay off this loan tonight. Don't wait until Friday. Then you should get yourself to Nashville and bring us a load of whiskey. Jack and I will pay you for your gas and the whiskey, but first, you need to get straight with the loan shark."

Slick shook hands with Sam, then gave Freddie a hug before leaving.

When Slick was gone, Freddie looked Sam in the eye and said, "I've got a bad feeling about this."

Sam had the same feeling, but said, "Oh hell, Freddie, Slick will do the right thing and this will all be over soon."

CHAPTER 8

Slick Clanton was missing, disappeared without a trace. No one had seen him for three days. Freddie was distraught, vacillating between anger and sorrow. He had called the police and they said, out of respect for Freddie, they would do what they could, but they too were aware of Slick's reputation. Jack and Sam had spent time driving around town and asking their friends and customers if anyone had seen or heard from Slick. The negative results were disheartening and they feared for the worst. Sam asked Freddie what he knew about Marcelli. "Would he really do such a thing, like snuff someone for an unpaid debt?"

Freddie said, "Never met him, but I hear he runs with a fast crowd and keeps some tough guys on his payroll."

Meanwhile, the company was running low on whiskey and Jack was forced to make the trip to Nashville on Friday in order for Cooper Distribution to make deliveries on Saturday. Life must go on, including the search for Slick, as well as consideration for some sort of retaliation against Marcelli. Sam wanted to err on the side of caution—the last thing he wanted was to bring unwarranted attention to his brother and himself.

On Sunday, Sam went back to Olive Branch to pick up the other load of sows from Schultz. If everything went as planned, he would have time to return in the afternoon for the two boars.

Jack stayed at the apartment to rest up. He had taken a date out on the town for a night of drinking and dancing. He had inquired about Marcelli at several of the local honkytonks he visited during the evening. The only thing of importance he discovered was that Marcelli lived downtown on the top floor of the Fountain Hotel, located on Union Avenue.

When Sam reached Olive Branch, Schultz was busy attending his hogs. That gave Sam time to look around in the pens for barrows old enough to slaughter. He counted around thirty barrows and twenty-five gilts. Sam believed the slaughterhouse would be completed within the next two weeks and he wanted to begin supplying his pork to a select group of his favorite customers. His target group was going to be high-profile barbeque joints like City Pitt.

Sam spoke to Shultz about the possibility of his supplying enough hogs to get the business up and running. Schultz said he could help some, but he had his own customers to take care of. However, he knew of a couple of other growing operations in Mississippi and he would check with them. Schultz helped load the sows and Sam headed for Nut Bush to drop them off. During the drive, he considered alternatives for bolstering their supply of hogs ready for market. The trip and delivery went as planned and he returned for the boars. Everything was now in place for their hog breeding operation.

Early Monday morning, Sam went to the port offices to talk to Dave Hinkle about the possibility of shipping hogs using a river barge. He also needed to find sources for fresh vegetables to supply his customers through the winter months. The two men started their visit with a cup of fresh strong black coffee and a couple of fried apple pies that Dave's wife, Pat, had made the day before. The pies were delicious and Sam asked Dave to pass on his compliments to Mrs. Hinkle. Sam asked Dave if he could tell him where the people of Memphis got their vegetables during the winter months. He described his customers and let Dave know he was worried that he might lose their business if he could not supply them year-round. He then told Dave that he needed a source of live hogs ready for slaughter. He wondered aloud about the feasibility of shipping them from other river communities by barge.

After considering what he had heard, Hinkle said, "Sam, you've come a long way in a short time and I'm proud of you. Now first, let's address shipping hogs on the river. Shipping should be by truck—the river is too unpredictable and a moving cargo adds to the danger. There are hog farms down in Rosedale, Mississippi, and over in Marianna, Arkansas, but someone would have to haul them to the barge, load 'em on, off load 'em, and truck 'em to your slaughterhouse. It'd be much safer and simpler to truck 'em to start with. You can use your own trucks, or get the farmers to haul them to you, or hire Henson's Trucking Company to haul 'em for you. No matter what you choose, you're gonna be deadheading one way. You should ship something on the empty truck, like cases of whiskey, for instance."

Always expansive with good advice, Mr. Hinkle continued, "As for the fresh vegetables, the majority are grown in South Texas, Florida and California and shipped east and north by truck or rail into the other states. You should send telegraphs to the Agricultural Growers Associations in each of those states and get lists and information about their growers. If you're in a hurry, go to Nashville and check with a produce supplier named Hawkins. He's an ex-riverboat captain and has been in the produce business for years. And, one more thing, you'll need more warehouse space, so rent more and distribute everything from there. Several men have tried this in Memphis before, but have failed for various reasons." Sam felt almost overwhelmed with all the information Mr. Hinkle seemed to always have right at his fingertips. In a mood of contemplation, Sam thanked him sincerely and headed off to his day's work.

Sam and Jack looked at a couple of empty warehouses the next day. One had three loading docks, two offices, and enough warehouse space for both the whiskey and the produce. Leasing this warehouse would give them more privacy at home. They could use the one they owned as a garage for all of their vehicles. The owner's wife, Nancy, had shown them the warehouse, and Sam told her they would let her know for sure right away. She said her divorced sister, Rose, was an experienced business secretary and looking for a job. She said Rose's ex-husband had been a real go-getter. He would take Rose to work and then go get her. The brothers laughed at the joke and asked if she and Rose could meet them at the warehouse on Friday, and she agreed they would. Sam went to Nashville on Thursday to pick up a load of whiskey. While he was there, he met with Captain Hawkins and offered him a deal if he would share his out-of-state produce suppliers. Sam offered him a 2% commission on anything they bought from his suppliers for one year and Hawkins agreed to the terms. He said they should receive their first shipment the following week, delivered to the address that Sam gave him. He asked Sam to give his best regards to his old friend, David Hinkle.

On Friday, the brothers met Nancy and Rose at the warehouse and signed the lease and hired Rose to work as their secretary. She would share one of the offices with Jack. Sam would use the other office. The brothers spent another couple of hours with Rose, going over their lists of customers for both the whiskey and produce businesses. They explained their income and expenses, adding that there was another business in the works. Sam gave her the name of their bank and loan officer, telling Rose that she would be responsible for billing customers and paying bills for the company. They also discussed buying office furniture and equipment the next day, as they all wanted her office ready by Monday.

Sam and Jack asked their two employees to clean the new warehouse Saturday morning while they bought and delivered the furnishings for the offices. While shopping, they came across a used double-door floor safe and Sam bought it as well. By the end of the day the new warehouse, renamed *Cooper Brothers Distribution Warehouse # 2*, was swept clean with cases of whiskey stacked neatly along one wall. Sam stood looking at the name on the cases. It was a known name and a quality product, but he knew they should expand to carry other brands, maybe some Kentucky bourbon, a line of imported wine, and a brew of beer.

Jack interrupted his thoughts, "Let's get crackin', big brother, I've got a hot date tonight!" Sam laughed as they turned to head home.

He also had a date, with pen and paper. He was going to write a letter to Adelle and finalize the trip to New York. He had been working seven days a week so that he could take a week off without causing undue stress on Jack. His plan was coming together; their business was growing, and their customers depended on them for good service. Sam wrote for over an hour, doing his best to communicate his feelings. He wanted to express his excitement and desire to see her again. It was hard to believe that it had been more than two years since he had last held her in his arms. He wondered if she had changed—would she recognize him? He knew he had changed. He was stronger now and his body had filled out since leaving the military and Arbuckle Island. He had grown a moustache. He remembered that many of the French men had worn facial hair, so maybe she would like it. Yes, he knew he had changed, maturing emotionally and physically. Having returned from the War to the loss of his parents and their homestead, then to the chaos of the flood, all causing him to meet challenges for not only survival, but for successes, so far, in business ventures. Yet, he had not changed in his longing for the passion he and Adelle shared. He wanted to hold her, to taste her lips and feel her body next to his. He had met other women around town, but not a single one had interested him. They would be together soon and he would join the woman of his dreams, hopefully forever. She was all he wanted. He and Jack, as brothers, were soul mates of one kind, but she, as a different sort, was as vital to his life as the air he breathed.

Sam and Jack went to the building site on Sunday afternoon to check on the progress of the workers. The building was complete with the butcher tables in place. All that was needed were the accessories. The knives and meat hooks were on order and would be ready for pick up by midweek. They agreed that they could start a week from Monday, since all the required inspections had been made and permits were forthcoming in the mail early in the coming week. Their projects and plans had been submitted to both the City of Memphis and the state of Tennessee and approved without fault. Sam would need to hire another man to help Jordan with produce deliveries. He would need another truck and crew for delivering the meat. But most importantly, he needed more hogs now to start the business. If they were going to make this work he had to have the supply to meet the demand. Jack and Sam knew they needed to replace themselves on the delivery trucks. One of them would be needed in the office to supervise shipping and receiving, making sure a steady supply of products remained available. The other would need to remain out on the road, calling on customers and overseeing the deliveries.

Sam packed an overnight bag and left Memphis on Monday. He wanted to locate all large hog farms in Northern Mississippi, from around Tupelo in the east to Clarksdale in the west. Schultz had given him names of a few people that he knew and had spoken with. The first stop in the search was near Holly Springs, not far from Tupelo, where he met Alonzo Harding, a friend of Schultz who owned a small breeding operation but was looking to grow. Sam agreed to buy everything he could produce as long as he sold exclusively to Cooper Brothers.

Alonzo gave him directions to Riley Farms, near New Albany, which was the largest operation that Sam had ever seen. Several families working together grew enough corn to feed over 300 head of hogs. They stored the corn in grain silos located centrally to three large sheds containing sixty farrow pens. They were currently selling hogs to the Pilgrim Brothers in Memphis and to meat suppliers in central Mississippi.

Sam convinced them to sell Cooper Brothers a minimum of ten hogs a month, starting the following month. At the end of the day, he rented a cheap motel room in Tupelo. Sam enjoyed a meal of meatloaf and fresh vegetables at a local diner recommended by the motel clerk.

The following day he traveled to Clarksdale with several stops around Oxford, home of the University of Mississippi. He was impressed with the beautiful campus of Ole Miss, as the locals called it. Maybe, in the future, if he was lucky, his children could attend college there.

After his last stop of the day in Clarksdale, Sam had dinner at a café where the specialty was fried catfish and pinto beans. The day had been a success. He had found three growers that seemed interested in selling their hogs commercially. Sam ate enough to feed a family. After finishing his third glass of iced tea he headed for the cash register, and that was where he saw the missing person poster. What he read caused his heart to skip a beat: the name of Bobby Pascal and a description of his boat appeared right in front of his eyes. There was a $200 reward for information leading to his whereabouts. Sam paid for his supper and then asked if he could have the poster. The cashier said it was fine by him. The poster had been there for over a month.

Sam returned to his motel to consider what was to be done with this new information. He had hoped that Bobby Pascal was buried and forgotten, but that obviously was not the case. Sam had an idea that could solve the problem, but it was a long shot at best.

CHAPTER 9

Sam read the poster again when he got to his room. The boat description was too accurate to go unnoticed if it was seen by anyone at the Port of Memphis. The boat had been covered with a canvas tarpaulin since they had moved it into the warehouse. No one of late had seen the boat. Obviously Pascal's body had not been found. Sam's idea depended on it never being found. Unless another skeleton was found and misidentified, the bodies of the river pirates could play an important role in the scheme that he was hatching in his mind. The name of notification at the bottom of the poster was Duke Pascal and the address was 212 Pelican Avenue in Algiers, Louisiana. Sam wanted to discuss his finding of the poster and the implications of his idea with Jack before they put any plan of action in motion. He would be home the next night after making a few more stops on behalf of the hog-processing operation.

Of the stops made during the trip, Southaven, Mississippi, had the most potential. Sam had met with three different growers;

their interest and proximity to Memphis offered mass potential for the company. The growers were all related. They were transplants from Iowa and their ancestors had developed and perfected the art of raising swine. Together, they had almost fifty hogs ready for market. Fortunately for the brothers, they had not booked the animals with any other processor. Therefore, prices were negotiated and present and future commitments were made. The plan was to begin shipping hogs within two weeks with the numbers to be dictated by the demand.

Jack was happy to see his brother when he returned. He was full of good news and anxious to share the news with Sam. Jack grabbed a couple of beers out of a bucket of ice and they sat down at the picnic table outside. Jack reported that the first shipments of produce from South Texas had arrived and the condition and quality of the vegetables exceeded what they had expected. Rose was very organized and knew the majority of their customers. She had ridden in the delivery truck on her second day of employment and had spoken with some of the customers. She said her day out of the office had given her a personal feel for their business.

The other good news, Jack relayed, had to do with the beer they were drinking. The produce hauler from Texas had brought it with him. The beer was made in Mexico and the distributor from San Antonio was looking for companies farther north to distribute the beer locally through franchises. The driver said there were at least three brands available, all best when served with a slice of lime. The stock prices were less than domestic beer. Moreover, rumor has it, according to the truck driver, that the imported beer franchises were wide open to states east of the Mississippi River. There was a good chance, if they acted quickly, to secure the distribution rights for all of Tennessee and Mississippi, maybe more if they got their foot in the door. Last but not least, the workers at Nut Bush were ready to kill hogs.

Sam said that was great news and that he had good news to share as well; he told Jack about his trip and how he had located new growers, the good news of finding market-ready hogs and his preference to start with Schultz and the growers in Southaven. Sam asked, "Have you spoken to Freddie or any other operators of the barbeque joints? Have any of the restaurants agreed to give us any orders?"

"Freddie is ready for his first order and so are two other joints. They'll take whole hogs, excepting the bacon cuts. Three restaurants are ready, but all they want are loins, hams, slabs of bacon and sausage," answered Jack. He added, "I think we should wait a few more weeks before we sell sausage to the restaurants. We could start with loins, hams and bacon. The sausage-makin' needs to be perfected and approved by us first. We could have Jimbo give away samples at his store and see what his customers have to say."

"Jack, that sounds like a good plan to me, but first we need to fill in the final pieces of the puzzle. We have to buy two more delivery trucks and move Jordan into the warehouse full time and give him a raise. The color of his skin is and probably will continue to be a problem for some of our closed-minded customers, and I personally worry about his safety. I have seen how nasty it can get, and he deserves better. He'll be a big help in the warehouse. We need to hire and train four more men for delivery this week so we can be ready for the following week. You need to oversee the whiskey and produce delivery until we can hire or promote someone as supervisor. What about Chuck? Is he ready for the supervisor's job?"

"Chuck has done everything I've asked. He knows the liquor side of the business very well, but he lacks experience on the produce side. Rose says she knows a couple of guys with experience. If we offer 'em more money than they're making now, they'd probably come to work for us," Jack explained.

Sam mulled over Jack's information. "That all sounds like a workable idea to me. Tell her to make the offer. Right now, I have something else we need to talk about." Sam pulled out the poster and laid it on the table.

Jack read the poster and swore, "Hell, that ain't good news! What are we gonna do?"

Sam was ready to share his plan with his brother. "This is what I think we have to do. We'll contact Duke Pascal and tell him about Slick's disappearance. We'll tell him Slick was our business partner and was murdered by Franco Marcelli for what he knew about the disappearance of Bobby Pascal. Our story is that Slick, for a while, was tight with Marcelli and borrowed money from him to pay off gambling debts. We'll tell him Slick bought a pistol off one of his bodyguards, who told him that he took it off of a man he was ordered to kill near the mouth of the Arkansas River. Then, he and another of his men stole the man's boat, which we can describe, and delivered it to Marcelli. We can tell Pascal that Marcelli came to town with a big mouth and bodyguards, throwing around a lot of cash. We'll say that we believe he killed Slick, or had him killed, when Slick couldn't pay off his gambling debts and tried to play what he knew to keep Marcelli off his back."

Sam continued, uninterrupted by Jack. "On Sunday, when no one's there but us, we'll have Pascal come to our new warehouse. We'll show him the gun, which he will recognize and want back, and tell him that Slick left it in his desk drawer the night he went to see Marcelli. The same night he disappeared forever.

"The reward is two hundred dollars, but we'll tell him we want a thousand. That will be our motivation and give us more credibility.

"Finally, we'll let him know that Franco Marcelli lives at the Fountain Hotel with his bodyguards. We can emphasize that he is extremely dangerous and can't be trusted.

"So, Pascal gets rid of Marcelli and goes back to New Orleans satisfied that he has avenged his brother's death, or Pascal is eliminated by Marcelli. We will benefit from either result."

"Sam, that's a brilliant plan. There are some risks, but I believe it will work. We just have to make sure that we act out our parts and make damn sure we keep him away from our apartment and anyone on the docks that might connect us with the boat."

The brothers were up early and had breakfast at the diner where Jack was popular with the waitresses. They talked about business, but avoided discussing the Pascal situation in public. After eating, they went to Warehouse #2 to find several new men looking to be hired. Jack interviewed the new men while Sam talked with his current employees. He described the new roles they would have with the company and offered them all a small raise in pay. Jack recommended hiring all three of the new men. All were experienced drivers with previous experience in the food industry.

Sam asked Jack to hang around the warehouse while he went looking for another truck. After looking at several trucks at different dealerships, he found exactly what he was looking for. It was a 1943 GMC ton-and-a-half military ambulance with a long wheelbase. He thought the inside of the ambulance could be reconfigured to carry hanging meat. Their business logo could be added to both sides, giving them more name recognition. There was no demand for military ambulances, so the dealer offered to sell at a price that Sam would have been foolish to pass up.

He returned to the warehouse, picked up a driver for the ambulance and followed him to a welding shop. He told the welder what alterations he wanted, and then headed to City Pitt Barbeque to talk with Freddie.

Sam wanted to deliver their first pork on Wednesday of the following week. The holding pens at the slaughterhouse were complete, everything was in place and the first hogs would be delivered on Monday. The slaughtering business was tough men's work. Men came to work in bib overalls and scuffed work boots. They provided meat for fine-dressed men and women who would rather not think about where their beloved bacon came from. Sam had heard his daddy say, "Slaughtering hogs is not a job for men in short britches."

The thought of his father caused a moment of sadness. He wished that his father were still alive so that he could ask his advice and hear bits of his hard-earned wisdom. He knew he was fortunate to have a brother to share his troubles with, and a great brother, as Jack was. They rarely argued, and Jack allowed Sam to make most of the decisions, content to offer only advice.

Freddie Clanton was busy smoking meat when Sam arrived. Greetings were exchanged and Sam got himself a bottle of pop and took a seat at the picnic table. When Freddie joined him at the table, Sam asked if there was any word of Slick.

Freddie said, "Sam, I haven't heard a thing and all I think about these days is cutting the heart out of Marcelli. I know the bastard is responsible for my brother's disappearance."

Sam felt he should tell his friend of the plan involving Duke Pascal, and maybe later he would, but not now. "Freddie, sometimes things just have a way of working themselves out. Be patient for a little bit longer and don't forget, I'll always be on your side." At that he changed the subject. Sam said, "Freddie, I need to know your order for next week, you'll be our first delivery and I want to be sure I have what you need."

Freddie replied, "We usually need four to five hogs per week. Bring me two on Monday and three on Thursday. That should cover the weekend." Sam told him about the new delivery truck that he had just purchased and his plans to modify the interior of the cargo area. Freddie was impressed as he heard Sam's descriptions of the modifications. His previous supplier had only had a flat bed truck that attracted swarms of flies and was open to the eyes of the public. Sam explained to him how the slaughtered hogs would be hung overnight in the shed that they had converted into an icehouse. Also, the delivery truck would have two boxes of ice to keep the temperature low in the cargo area. Freddie was fascinated by Sam's description and said, "Sam, I see big things in your future. You think through all the necessary details and you always think ahead. I have little doubt that you will be very successful one day."

Heartfelt compliments sometimes embarrassed Sam, so he said, "Thanks, Freddie," and left the joint.

Sam returned to the apartment to write a letter to Duke Pascal, a letter that could have serious consequences for several people, especially Sam and Jack. His letter was very short and to the point. It stated:

I have information on your missing brother. He was robbed and murdered by a very dangerous man in Memphis, Tennessee. My business partner was also murdered because of what he knew about your brother's murder. You should meet me at our warehouse in Memphis one week from Sunday. I will supply you with the name and address of the man responsible. Do not come alone. I suggest you bring several men with you because armed bodyguards surround the man I speak of. The reward you have offered is not enough for the danger I will face for giving you this secret information. If the information I give you proves to be helpful in solving the death of your brother, I want you to pay me a reward of $1,000.

Sam included the address of their warehouse and took the letter to the post office. He needed to mail it before he changed his mind.

The next week went by quickly for both brothers. The new employees were a godsend. Without them, deliveries would have fallen behind. Jordan and Chuck had proven invaluable in their new roles at the warehouse. Jack was dividing his time between the warehouse and the delivery drivers. Sam spent two days at the slaughterhouse overseeing the operation from the initial processing to the first deliveries. He learned there was an art to hog killing so that they bled out completely, ensuring the best flavor of meat. Schultz had brought in the first load of hogs and hung around to make suggestions as they were processed. A black man named Abraham Martin was selected by Sam to run the slaughterhouse. Schultz suggested that from now on, while working at the slaughterhouse, Abraham would be called Ham, an appropriate name and easier to remember. Abraham laughed, and said he thought that Schultz would become a good friend. At the end of day the processed meat was hung in the cooler, ready for delivery the next day. Sam accompanied his drivers as they made deliveries on Tuesday, observing the way they communicated with the customers and personally thanking the customers for their business.

The converted ambulance was a major success. The customers really appreciated the idea of iceboxes in the back of the delivery truck. The boxes were big enough to hold two 50-pound blocks of ice. The ice kept the compartment cool and the meat fresh. Sam was proud of the alterations as well. The racks on both sides of the compartment left the middle open for easy access. The drain tubes in the bottom of the iceboxes allowed the melting ice-water to drain onto the street, keeping the meat compartment cool but dry. By Saturday the entire operation was running like a fine-tuned engine with a four-barrel carburetor, and the customers were singing their praises.

CHAPTER 10

The brothers woke up early on Sunday morning, had breakfast at the Beale Street Diner and attended morning church services with Dave and Pat Hinkle. Pat had made a picnic lunch and after church the four of them returned to the apartment where Pat unveiled the goodies in her picnic basket. First she spread a red-checkered tablecloth over the picnic table. She had prepared fried chicken, potato salad, seasoned green beans and corn muffins. Jack poured four glasses of sweetened sun tea that he had set out to brew before church. The friends enjoyed the food and fellowship with ample compliments bestowed upon Mrs. Hinkle's cooking. The men were delighted to find that she had prepared an apple cobbler for dessert.

After a couple of hours, Dave and Pat said goodbye and headed home. Sam went inside and retrieved the .45 caliber Colt from under the bed. This, he would use as evidence for convincing Duke Pascal of his personal knowledge of Bobby Pascal's demise.

Sam was going to take one of the delivery trucks to the warehouse alone to await the arrival of Pascal. Jack would arm himself with the shotgun and other pistol. He would park the Ford pickup in the parking lot of the building behind their warehouse. He was to remain there until he was sure Pascal had arrived. Then, if possible, he would slip inside, concealing himself behind the cases of whiskey. Plan B was for him to hide outside below a window that Sam would open at the back of the office.

Jack gave Sam a brotherly hug and urged him to proceed with caution. There was a possibility that the gang from New Orleans had already arrived. Sam slipped a slim hunting knife inside his boot as a last line of defense should he need it. Sam headed to the warehouse with anxious anticipation, combined with the determination to succeed that he had learned in the military. He had faced danger before and lived to tell about it; he intended to do just that again today.

When Sam arrived at the warehouse there was no one there. He unlocked the front doors and raised the cargo doors. While he waited, he kept his mind busy by taking inventory. He used the opportunity to restack the cases of whiskey in a way to provide adequate cover for Jack. It was nearing sundown when Sam completed the inventory. He had gone into the office to check the inventory against the purchase tickets when he heard a car drive up.

He walked to the front of the building just as all four doors of a black Cadillac Fleetwood swung open. Five men spilled out of the vehicle: a driver, three tough-looking Creoles, and a large, dark-complexioned man that had to be Duke Pascal. He wore a three-piece suit with a bowler hat, his shoes were two-toned brogans made from alligator skin, and he carried a walking cane that would double as a formidable weapon. Sam noticed as they came face to face that Pascal had a facial scar that extended from the corner of his left eye to just below his left ear. He carried himself with an air of superiority, the trait of a man who had never known fear. Sam felt a tingling sensation run up his spine—hairs stood up on the back of his neck and his arms were covered with goose bumps—this evil looking son-of-a-bitch was a devil incarnate and if he wasn't the devil, he was close kin.

He walked up to Sam and demanded, "Who the hell are you and what do you know about my brother?"

"I'm Sam Cooper, and what I know about your brother was told to me by my partner who's been missing for almost a month. I believe my partner was murdered by the same man that killed your brother and I think that he was killed because of what he knew about your brother's murder," Sam replied, as bravely as possible.

Sam paused for a few seconds, then added, "I have a pistol in my office that I think belonged to your brother. Do you want to see it?"

Pascal's crew had spread out in a semi-circle, with Sam and Duke in the center. Sam asked Pascal if he wanted to step into his office and have a seat and a glass of whiskey. Duke, without speaking, pointed at two of his crew and then nodded toward the office. They immediately searched both offices, making sure there wasn't any danger to their boss. Sam stepped into the office, followed closely by Pascal. The driver and the other Creole stopped at the door and turned facing the front of the warehouse. Sam opened the desk drawer and Pascal stepped behind the desk and removed the pistol, inspected it carefully, then pointed it toward Sam's chest.

Pascal growled, "Where did you get this pistol? And don't lie to me, Mr. Cooper."

Sam, doing his best to appear calm, set two glasses on his desk, poured a shot of whiskey in each, and handed one to Duke Pascal. He said, "Please take a seat and I'll tell you everything I know."

"First of all, a week and a half ago, I was in Clarksdale, Mississippi, when I saw this." Sam placed the poster on the desk. "This was the first time I had a name to put with the story my partner, Willy Clanton, told me. Willy was a man who loved to drink and gamble late at night with a tough group of men, some known to be bodyguards of a local mob-boss, Franco Marcelli. Willy came to me one morning after being out all night and he handed me this gun and asked me to hide it. He said he'd won it in a poker game and what he had heard that night was worrying him."

"Marcelli's man was running low on money, so he put this pistol on the table to cover his bet. Drunk, he spilled his guts, and told Willy the pistol had been a gift to him from his boss, for killing a Louisiana man. He said they intended to steal the guy's really nice boat and get rid of his body somewhere near the mouth of the Arkansas River, but after they found two suitcases filled with money, they placed your brother's body in the boat's cabin and sank the boat."

Pascal interrupted the story, "Why would he be worried, if he already knew these guys and won the gun without cheatin'?"

"Well," Willy said, "another man in the gang told the shooter he'd better shut the hell up, or the boss man would have him gutted and thrown in the river."

Pascal was impatient. "Where's the damn money now?"

Sam knew his life depended on the rest of the lie. So without hesitation, he said, "Marcelli keeps it in his room on the top floor of the Fountain Hotel down on Union Avenue. At least, that's where Willy went to borrow money after I refused to advance him any more. The last day that I saw Willy, he said Marcelli had threatened to kill him if he didn't pay off his loans in three days. So, I changed my mind and gave him the money. But, instead of paying off what he owed Marcelli, he got drunk and lost it all in another poker game. He was overheard there talking bad about Marcelli, and I haven't heard from him since."

Pascal became the interrogator: "How do I know that you're not the one who killed your partner and my brother? How do I know that this Marcelli still has the money, and who else knows about all this?"

Sam, still outwardly calm, took a drink of his whiskey, thinking that this could all go wrong at any minute. He promised himself that the last thing Pascal would ever see would be the knife as he stabbed it in his left eye. He hoped Jack was somewhere safe and ready to lend assistance.

Sam finally answered Pascal's question, "I am just a businessman, not a murderer. The police were notified and Willy's brother is my friend. I don't know for sure if Marcelli has your money, he's not a friend of mine. My brother and I are the only two people that know you are here. Most importantly, why the hell would I write you a letter and invite you here if I was involved? If you don't want to handle Marcelli, give me a thousand dollars and I'll pay somebody else to handle him." He saw anger flash across the face of Duke Pascal. Sam had questioned his nerve.

"Don't you dare question my resolve, farm boy, maybe I will kill you first! Then, I will kill this Marcelli and take back my money. How do you like that idea ,Mr. Cooper?" Pascal asked with a sneer.

"I don't like it at all, and neither will my brother. He's waiting in a room at the Fountain Hotel. If I don't call him after you leave, he'll have someone tip off Marcelli that you're coming and he'll be ready for you. I believe you would prefer to have the money instead of my blood on your hands." Before Pascal could reply, Sam, bluffing, added, "Just in case you decide to come back for me later, I'm telling you now, I've written three letters describing your involvement in all this. The sealed envelopes are in the hands of three of my friends who will go to the police if something should happen to me or my brother. So why don't you do us both a favor? Go kill Marcelli and get your money."

Sam was poised to kill Duke Pascal if he felt the least bit threatened, but he was doing his best to appear at ease. Pascal finished off his whiskey and told his driver to go start the car. He stepped away from the desk and pointed at Sam with his cane. "You'd better not be lying to me, Mr. Cooper. If I kill that man and his bodyguards, I will be doing you a favor and that will be your reward. No money will be coming to you. Consider your life a gift that I can take back any time I feel like it."

He turned, motioned his crew to the car and then he was gone. Sam sat where he was and poured and tossed back another shot of whiskey.

He watched the tail lights of the car pull away and called out for his brother. Jack stepped inside the front door. He had not made it into the warehouse, but he'd been outside below the window and had heard everything.

Jack said exactly what Sam was thinking, "We can't let that evil bastard live. If he takes care of Marcelli, we have to kill him and his crew before they leave town. If we don't, he'll come back later to kill us."

Sam slowly shook his head, "I'm all out of ideas, little brother. You got any?"

Jack answered, "Yes, I do. It came to me while I was standing below the window listening to that crazy bastard. Come on, I'll explain on the way to Slick's house. There's something useful in the shed behind the house and he'll get the chance to reach up out of his grave, wherever that is, and give us a hand. Grab that roll of piano wire and I'll get the truck."

When they got to the shed, Jack grabbed a crowbar and pried the door open. There, sitting in the back corner under some gunnysacks, was a box of U.S. Military "pineapple" hand grenades.

Sam was totally amazed. "Where in the hell did Slick get these?"

Jack said, "Who knows? He said he bought 'em from a couple of soldier boys who stole 'em from a military base and he gave 'em fifty bucks for the entire lot." Jack grabbed the case, carefully placed it in the bed of the pickup and crawled in behind it. He told Sam to hand him the piano wire and a pair of pliers, and to drive toward the Fountain Hotel. He began cutting the wire into five-foot lengths, attaching one end to the pins of four of the grenades. Before they reached the hotel, he yelled for Sam to pull over and he jumped in the passenger seat. Jack explained that he intended to wire the grenades to the frame underneath the seats of Pascal's Cadillac, then tie the pin wires to the inside of the wheels.

Sam asked, "How are we going to know if and when he takes care of Marcelli?"

"I don't know. Just drive to the hotel, and we'll locate his car, and figure it out from there."

Pascal's car was parked a block away from the hotel, facing the front entrance. The driver was leaning back against the front grill and smoking a cigarette. He appeared to be watching the windows on the upper floor, maybe waiting for a signal from someone. The brothers parked their truck down the block and watched too.

Sam said, "Jack, we can't do this here. There're too many innocent people around. They could get hurt. Besides you can't do it with that driver close like he is. He'll see you and all hell will break loose." Jack agreed, the location wasn't good, but part of the plan might still work. If he could wire the back wheels next to the gas tank, the explosion might be enough to kill them all, but before he could do anything, Sam whispered, "Look who's comin'."

Duke Pascal and two of the Creoles were walking toward the car. Duke was in the lead with two of his men following closely behind. They were carrying duffle bags, which they loaded into the trunk of the car. They joined the driver at the front end of the car and waited. What were they waiting for? Soon Jack and Sam saw the other Creole jogging down the street toward the Cadillac. The driver started the car and the final thug hopped into the backseat. The car headed up the street, then turned left on Front Street. The brothers followed at a safe distance, trying to avoid being noticed. Pascal's driver turned toward the Port of Memphis. They could not follow safely, so they drove to their apartment and parked their truck.

Jack ran inside and grabbed a canvas duffel bag. He placed the grenades in the bag and they continued their journey on foot.

Pascal's car was parked in the shadows of the dock offices. The driver, as earlier, was leaning against the front grille of the car, smoking another cigarette while keeping a lookout.

Both brothers slipped behind the building and worked their way closer to the dock. Jack was the first to spot movement near one of the moored boats. He held up his hand to warn Sam. Duke Pascal and two of his men appeared to be waiting for someone, and as before, one of the Creoles was missing. The brothers couldn't move safely until they knew his whereabouts. Jack, using hand signals, indicated to Sam to look at the top of one of the docked tugboats, which had an extra hump in the outline of the roof. Several minutes passed before they saw the slightest movement. Pascal's scout appeared to be facing downriver, watching for something or someone. The distant sounds of a boat engine could be heard and it was coming up the river toward the port. The scout whistled to alert Pascal that a boat was approaching the dock.

Sam whispered to Jack, "You stay here. I'm going to work my way above them. They're going to wait on that incoming boat and there's an empty slip behind them." Jack nodded and Sam slipped away. He eased along the building and then ducked under the docks, hoping that he would not be snake-bitten. He climbed a wooden ladder to reach the deck of a boat three slips down from the empty slip. He hid in among the cargo and waited for the boat that was docking. He could see two men on the bow of the boat ready to tie her off.

Once the boat was secured, Franco Marcelli climbed out of the cabin onto the deck and headed to the port side of the boat to disembark. One bodyguard was still mid-ship and the other was securing the stern when Pascal and two of his crew stepped from the shadows to confront Marcelli.

Duke spoke first, "Hold up there and state your name." Both bodyguards reached for their weapons, but halted when the other Creole appeared on the deck of the adjacent boat and shouted, "Arrête toi!" while aiming a shotgun in their general direction. They may have not known the exact meaning of the order spoken in Cajun French, but they did understand the shotgun.

Marcelli shouted in anger, "What is the meaning of this? Get away from my boat!" He continued to rant, "You men are making a mistake. I'm Franco Marcelli and I will make you regret this day."

That was before he got a close look at Duke Pascal. What he saw struck fear into the depths of his soul.

Pascal spoke evenly, "Mr. Marcelli, I came here tonight after traveling many hours to recover money taken from my family and to avenge the death of my baby brother. I have visited your hotel already and have recovered the money you stole from me. Now, I intend to kill you and your worthless bodyguards who have failed to do the job for which they are paid. I will take your boat downriver and feed your bodies to the fish, as you did to my brother."

Marcelli spoke in a trembling voice, "I did not do these things that you accuse me of. I beg you to reconsider your actions. I make a lot of money and I will give half of it to you if you let me live." Marcelli pointed at the nearest bodyguard and said, "If it's blood you want, kill those two."

At that moment, one bodyguard turned to leap into the river, but was blown back toward Marcelli by the blast of a shotgun. He tried to breathe with lungs that were rapidly filling with blood. He made one final gurgling sound, as if to speak, and died.

The Creoles dragged the living bodyguard on board and forced him to kneel near the bow, using rope to secure his hands behind his back. Marcelli was also told to kneel near the bow, but unlike his somber employee, he continued to cry and beg for his life. Pascal boarded the boat and ordered his men to prepare to cast off. Two men released the tie-downs from the cleats and the third took the captain's chair. They waited for word from Pascal, but he was busy. Duke Pascal was performing a cultural voodoo ceremony, speaking in French Creole while standing behind Marcelli, holding in his hands a small cloth bag containing bones. This was his voodoo amulet, which he called *gris-gris*. He hung the bag around his neck and pulled apart his cane, revealing a long, narrow blade. At this point, the Creoles began chanting in their Cajun tongue. Pascal raised the blade above his head as his voice joined the chant of the Creoles. In a downward thrust, he drove the blade into the base of Marcelli's neck and down through his heart. Marcelli squealed, not loud but focused in tone. Pascal withdrew the blade from Marcelli's neck, stepped behind the bodyguard and, with a quick slash, cut his throat from ear to ear. He touched the tip of his tongue to the blade, tasting the blood before wiping it clean on Marcelli's back.

He turned and gave the signal to cast off. The Creole driver started the boat and backed out of the slip, allowing the stern to drift downstream.

This is where fate intervened once again: if he had backed the boat upstream, his life might have continued in the manner he was accustomed to. Instead, the boat drifted directly in front of where Jack was concealed. As the boat was throttled up and began to move away, Jack pulled the pin on one hand grenade and dropped it into the bag with the other three. He tossed it without ceremony onto the back of the departing boat. In less time than it took Jack to count to ten, the boat exploded with a deafening boom into a bright ball of fire. All of the men on board were killed instantly. Duke Pascal was sent straight to hell, joining his brother in Satan's court.

Sam was shocked at the sudden turn of events. He had seen and heard everything and had been prepared to deal with Pascal when the boat returned. He was sure the driver of the Fleetwood would abandon his post and now come running. He slipped off the boat and hid behind a mooring post. He removed the .32 caliber pistol from the shoulder holster and racked a shell into the chamber. As he had expected, the driver appeared and stopped directly in front of Sam, staring at the burning wreckage as it sank below the surface. Sam extended his arm and fired one shot just behind the driver's right ear. He dropped onto the dock, where Sam rolled him over and shot him again between the eyes. Sam searched his pockets and found both his car keys and his wallet. He wanted to make sure all of his identification was removed before dumping him into the river. Jack joined Sam and together they threw the body as far they could into the river, where it slowly sank while heading downstream.

Sam and Jack raced to the Cadillac, jumped inside, and Sam drove quickly away from the port to their apartment. They drove the car into the warehouse and parked it next to the Chris Craft. They were accumulating nice vehicles from one particular New Orleans family. Sam was pretty sure that there were two more bags of money in the trunk, but this time they had provided fate some assistance.

CHAPTER 11

Sam lay in bed, exhausted but wide awake, adrenaline still coursing through his veins. He could not stop reflecting on the events that had just taken place. Everything had happened so quickly. Even the best of plans often played second fiddle to the windows of opportunity and last night Sam and Jack had taken full advantage of the opportunities that had been presented as the course of events took an unforeseen turn.

Only time would tell whether they had rid themselves of future threats from the Pascal family. The two bags under the bed contained a little over $32,000. That, combined with the $15,000 hidden in the wall, presented a problem that needed to be dealt with sooner rather than later. Then there was the big black Cadillac sitting in the warehouse. Tomorrow, he would buy a canvas tarp to conceal the car as they had the boat.

In the trunk of the car, they found an Enfield .30 caliber rifle with a variable scope, a .32 caliber Beretta, and two .38 caliber

Smith and Wesson semi-automatic pistols, and enough ammo to start a small war.

He and Jack were certain that they had heard sirens heading toward the port soon after they arrived home. They knew there would be an investigation by the local law enforcement, but fortunately there was very little evidence left to find. David Hinkle would know whose boat was missing within a day or sooner, depending on what the police found at the Fountain Hotel.

The following morning, they went to work as if nothing had happened. All of the employees were busy doing what they were paid to do. Jordan and the drivers were loading the trucks for the day's deliveries, while Rose was on the phone taking new orders. Jack knew that Sam wanted to talk to Mr. Hinkle at the boat docks, so he volunteered to check on the slaughterhouse operation and left with the drivers. Sam remained at the warehouse for another hour before leaving for the docks. On the way he stopped at Farris Mercantile to buy a large tarp to cover the Cadillac. It was something he needed to do before meeting with David Hinkle. The Cadillac stood out like a diamond in a rat's ass, and needed to be hidden from prying eyes.

After he stopped by the warehouse to cover the car with the tarp and disguise the shape as well as he could, Sam headed to the port. Upon his arrival he walked toward the office, but stopped short when he saw Dave and several of his crew standing in front of the empty slip where last night's massacre had taken place. Sam walked toward the group of men and was acknowledged by Dave.

"Good morning, Sam. Come on over, something unusual happened here last night. We're trying to figure out what it was. Maybe you can help us."

Sam replied, "I'll be glad to try if you can give me a clue."

Hinkle began by telling Sam what they knew and what they had found. "The local police came by last night because one of their patrolmen heard a loud noise that he thought was an explosion near the docks. He looked around, but saw nothing unusual, and left. This morning a couple of officers came by the office and informed me of what the patrolman had heard, so we came down to have a look. We found bloodstains on the dock by this empty slip and there are some pieces of debris on the decks of two of these boats. It appears as if the debris was from something that was afire. There are scorched spots on the boat decks where it landed. Did you or Jack hear anything unusual last night?"

"Well, I woke up once and I thought I heard a clap of thunder, but I went back to sleep. Jack didn't say anything this morning, but during the War we learned to sleep through a lot of terrible racket. Are any boats missing that you know of?"

Hinkle said, "Yeah, Franco Marcelli had this slip rented, but he was seen leaving down the river yesterday afternoon. I guess we'll have to wait and see if he returns, and if he does we can question him. The blood on the dock might be from a fish that was caught and cleaned here, or might be from a muskrat that was shot for its pelt. I hope the answer is as simple as that. What can I do for you today, Sam?"

Sam explained, "I need to make a trip to New York City the week before Christmas and I'm looking for information. If I drive, I need a map and directions. If I take a train, I need advice on the best route and the length of time it'll take to get there. Why don't I come back in a couple of days when you're not so busy?"

Hinkle agreed and told Sam that he should come back on Wednesday. That would give him time to gather the information that Sam requested. Sam thanked him and headed for City Pitt Barbeque to talk to Freddie Clanton. He wanted to tell him parts of the story, but just how much he wasn't sure.

It was getting colder now, the mornings especially. Neither Sam nor Jack owned any winter clothing and they needed to do some shopping. Thanksgiving was next week, and then a month later, there was Sam's trip to New York. He wanted to buy some new clothes in Memphis and Christmas presents in New York. He'd use money and suitcases supplied by the Pascal family.

Then, there was the engagement ring for Adelle. His mind was made up. He was going to ask her to be his wife. He hoped and believed she would say yes. He needed a woman in his life. He wanted a home with a woman's touch and a woman's smell. He loved his brother and he would miss living with him, but it was time each had a place of his own. Sam hoped that Jack would meet a special woman soon, and giving him more privacy was a good first step.

Sam parked the truck in front of City Pitt and found Freddie in his office paying bills. Clanton looked up and smiled at Sam. "Hey, my friend, perfect timing. I was just paying your invoice, so have a seat. My customers love the taste of your pork and my sauce. Business is growing right out the door, which means I need more space or a second location."

Sam congratulated him on his success and thanked him again for his business. Then, very seriously, Sam asked Freddie to stop what he was doing.

"Freddie, I've got something you need to hear. Franco Marcelli and several of his bodyguards were killed last night on his boat. We can't bring your brother back but we are rid of the man that was responsible for his death."

Freddie stared in disbelief. "Are you sure he's dead?"

Sam nodded and replied, "I could not be more certain unless I had done it myself. A very dangerous man came up from New Orleans to settle a score and, as it turned out, gave us the revenge that we've been looking for. That's all I can tell you for now and you need to keep that information to yourself. There will be more information available soon, I'm sure. The cops are already conducting an investigation and will probably show up here within the next few days. Please be careful what you say to them about Jack and I. We don't want to be drug into this investigation. I know you would like to ask a lot of questions, but for now, I want to discuss a different matter."

As to the different matter, Sam said, "Jack and I would like to pay you for the rest of Slick's interest in the liquor business. We agreed to pay an additional three thousand dollars after we loaned money to your brother. However, because of our friendship and your assistance in our pork business, we're willing to pay you five thousand instead. It's up to you how you use it, but maybe it will help you expand this building or open another store. There's a building for sale on Second Street across from the Fountain Hotel. It's double the size of your current location, in a great spot and right next to the biggest hotel in town. You could raise your prices, as you'd have patrons with more money."

Freddie remained quiet for a few minutes, thinking about what Sam had just told him. He was glad that Sam and Jack had become such good friends. A year ago, he didn't even know them and now they were a big part of his life. The loss of his brother had been less difficult having them to talk with. He wondered how much involvement they had had with the killing of Marcelli. He figured Sam would share that information when he was ready to do so and decided not to press the issue for now.

"Sam," he said, "I can't thank you enough for what you've done for me and my brother. The extra money isn't necessary, but is certainly appreciated. I heard about the building downtown all right, but I wasn't sure I could afford it. Do you think the owners might lease it out?"

"You don't want to lease, trust me. It would be a waste of money. If you can't swing the loan by yourself, Jack and I will be your partners in the building, but not the barbeque business. The business will remain a hundred percent yours. We're leasing our second warehouse for our business now, and Jack and I would like to own that building or one similar. We can talk to Mr. Dunn at the bank, if you want. But first, you should go look the Second Street building over. If it's good enough for you, it's good enough for us."

Freddie said he'd go the next day and have a look at the building. Sam headed back to the new warehouse. He needed to keep his part of the business running smoothly. On Wednesday, the radio news announcer reported that two dead bodies had been found on Tuesday morning in the Fountain Hotel. Robbery was the apparent motive. This confirmed what Sam and Jack thought; the Creoles had killed the two bodyguards who were in the hotel room when they stole Marcelli's money. The police would now put two and two together and conclude that the explosion at the dock was tied to the two dead bodies.

Sam and Jack were still in the clear unless someone started asking questions about the Cadillac. Sam told Jack to keep everyone away from their original warehouse, if possible. He had decided to drive the Cadillac to New York City when he went to meet Adelle at Christmas. While he was there he would get rid of it somehow. If he falsified a bill of sale and got a new title before he left, he could either sell or trade the car. If not, he would drive it to the city anyway, park it and walk away.

Jack went along with almost everything Sam had decided, except for trading the car. He told Sam, "I'm afraid for you to take the car to a dealership, or for that matter, for you to try and get a title. We don't want anyone tracing that car back to Duke Pascal and then asking how it came into our possession. Sell it to an individual for cash, or park it. Take a train back to Memphis. That will give you a chance to relax and enjoy the time you spend with Adelle."

Next, Sam addressed the idea of buying a house. He had been thinking of how best to approach Jack without hurting his feelings.

He loved his brother, but he wanted his own place with more privacy for himself and Adelle. So, he just laid it all out and hoped for the best. To his relief, Jack was in total agreement with the idea.

Jack said with a laugh, "I've been thinking the same thing, big brother. There are several young ladies in this town that would like to spend a little private time with me. You know what they say: 'All work and no play makes Jack a dull boy.'" Jack gave his brother a big hug and told him that Dave had called the office to say that Pat was cooking Thanksgiving Day dinner and they were invited. Jack had said they would be there and that he would like to bring a date. Dave thought it would be great and that Pat would enjoy having some female company.

The rest of the workweek was busy, but normal. All phases of the business were growing and they had hired several more employees. On Saturday, Sam and Jack went shopping for clothes. Jack had invited a young lady to join them. Her name was Gina and she advised them on what did and did not look good. They each bought a couple of suits along with several pairs of pants, shirts and shoes. Finally, they completed their wardrobe with nice overcoats, and even an everyday work coat. Gina was rewarded with drinks and dinner for services rendered.

Sam could tell that she and Jack shared a mutual attraction for one another, and that made Sam happy. It seemed that she was more than a passing fancy for Jack. Sam believed that any man could be the king of his castle, but successful kings had one thing in common—they had a good queen by their side. Their father had not had much, but what he did have was a wife who loved and supported him and, when she passed away, he lost his queen and his will to live.

The day before Thanksgiving, Jack and Sam gave all of their employees a smoked ham and encouraged them to enjoy a day off with their families. The brothers were certain to enjoy spending the day with Dave and Pat. They were as close to family as the brothers had, and Pat's cooking was as good if not better than their own mother's!

On his way home, Sam had stopped by a liquor store and bought two bottles of wine for the dinner. One was a rich, red Bordeaux and the other, a Sauvignon Blanc, a crisp white. The wine, a few fresh vegetables and a ham would be their contributions to the Thanksgiving Day dinner. Sam knew beyond a shadow of doubt that he and Jack had a lot to be thankful for.

CHAPTER 12

Thanksgiving Day dawned clear, but cool. The leaves had gone from yellow and red to a light brown and the air had that certain smell of fall, both clean and crisp.

The brothers showered and shaved, using a new aftershave picked out by Gina.

"Jack, we smell like a couple of coconuts with a hint of lime. I betcha this is how it smells every day in the islands of Hawaii. Maybe you ought to get Gina one of them little grass skirts we saw the island girls wearing when we went to the picture show."

Jack laughed and replied, "Yeah, you're right. When we put on these new clothes and shoes, we're gonna be a couple of dandies, that's for sure. Gina would look damn nice in one of those grass skirts doing a little hula-hula dance. While we were in Germany, I met a nurse named Shelli James. She had been based in Pearl Harbor, working in one of the field hospitals. She told me the island of Oahu was pure paradise before the Japs attacked. She

said there were palm trees, white sand, bright blue water and all the fresh fish that you could eat."

The brothers, dressed in their new clothes, loaded the box of goodies they were taking to the Hinkles' Thanksgiving feast into the bed of the truck and headed to Gina's house. She also looked festive, dressed in a pumpkin-colored pantsuit with a white scarf and her dark hair pushed back with a twisted pearl headband. She wore matching pearl earrings and a pearl necklace that accented her dark complexion. Jack told her that she was sure a sight for sore eyes. She flashed a beautiful smile and said that she thought the brothers just might be the most handsome men in Memphis.

Gina sat between them as they completed their journey to the Hinkle home, which was a quaint brick house with white pillars supporting a porte-cochère, originally used as a carriage porch, built over a cobblestone driveway. They were greeted at the front door by Dave, who invited them inside a home saturated with the wonderful aromas of Thanksgiving dinner. Dave and Pat were introduced to Gina and pleasantries were exchanged between all. After paying numerous compliments to Sam and Jack, Pat took Gina under her wing and headed for the kitchen. Jack followed with the box of food, leaving Sam and Dave alone in the living room.

Sam pulled the cork from the bottle of red wine and poured two glasses. Dave went to his roll-top desk and retrieved a map of the eastern half of the United States and a sheet of paper with handwritten notes. He and Sam took seats on the sofa and spread the map out on the maple coffee table. Dave had outlined a route that went north through Louisville, Kentucky, continued across Ohio and turned east just south of Pittsburg, Pennsylvania. The route would then cross the Allegheny plateau, pass through New Jersey and end in New York City.

This, Dave thought, was the fastest route, but he suggested a slight detour that would take Sam to Lexington, Kentucky, where

Dave's brother lived and worked. Dale Hinkle was the broodmare manager at a prominent thoroughbred farm and would be able to show Sam that farm as well as a couple of stud farms. Dave insisted that Sam should spend one or two days in the area and enjoy the beauty of the bluegrass state. Sam agreed that it was a good idea. It would give him a break from the long drive and allow him to see what Dave liked so much about horses and Kentucky.

They were called into the dining room, where vast amounts of food had been placed on the table. After they were seated, Dave said the blessing and dishes were passed around. There was turkey and dressing, ham, sweet-potato casserole, mashed potatoes and gravy, green beans, fried okra and dishes of sliced fresh vegetables and yeast rolls with butter. This was all washed down with glasses of Luzianne sweet tea. Sitting across the room on the baker's rack were pumpkin, apple and chocolate pies for dessert.

Sam poured everyone a glass of the Sauvignon Blanc wine and proposed a toast to good friends and prosperity. All of the food was delicious and large amounts were consumed amid enjoyable conversation. After dessert, Pat served coffee and Sam was asked to elaborate on his upcoming trip to New York City. He told them about his planned meeting with Adelle, the circumstances of how they had met, and his feelings for her. He told them that she was the woman he wanted to marry and that he intended to buy an engagement ring once he reached the city where he would ask her to be his wife. He admitted that he was nervous and afraid she would say no.

He planned to stay until after New Year's Day and, if everything worked out as he hoped, they would come back to Memphis by train. The purchase of a home was brought up and Pat told Sam of a house nearby that was for sale. It belonged to a nice couple who was moving to Florida. She thought it had three bedrooms, a nice kitchen, large bathroom and plenty of room for children should they choose to expand their family. She gave Sam the names, address and phone number of the sellers and she told Sam that he should call soon because of the popularity of the neighborhood. Sam assured her that he was very interested and would make contact as soon as possible.

The socializing lasted until almost dark. Gina, Jack, and Sam thanked Dave and Pat for a wonderful day and left. Jack said he was staying at Gina's, so Sam dropped them off and went home to write a letter to Adelle. The last letter she had sent him had included the details of her trip. She would depart France on the fourteenth of December and arrive in New York City on the twenty-third. He decided that he would leave Memphis early on the fifteenth and go to Lexington for a couple of days. He should reach his destination by the twenty-first, in time to buy the engagement ring and a few Christmas presents. He included his itinerary and the address of the Waldorf Astoria where they would be staying.

After he completed the letter, he went outside and sat at the picnic table. He needed some fresh air and some time to think. He took the cellophane wrapper off of a new pack of Camel cigarettes, grabbed an ashtray and lit a smoke. Here he was, sitting with a full belly, planning a trip to New York City. He would be driving a new Cadillac and staying at one of the world's most famous hotels, to meet the love of his life. Just eight months ago, he and his brother were living off the land with barely enough to eat. He prayed that their good fortune would continue.

The next day, Sam drove to the Hinkle residence and picked up Pat, who was going with him to look at the house she'd told him about. The owners, Russell and Sarah Basham, were happy to show Sam their home. Russell was a medical doctor who wanted to retire and spend the rest of his life in a warm climate near an ocean. The house was red brick with a large screened-in porch on the back. There were three bedrooms that shared a large bathroom. The kitchen was very nice and there was an additional bathroom near it that contained a lavatory and commode. The living and dining rooms were large, with a fireplace on the living-room end and pot-bellied stove on the end nearest the kitchen. Mrs. Basham had maintained both a flower and a vegetable garden at the back of the house. Everything was perfectly maintained.

Sam took Pat back home and returned to negotiate a transaction with the Basham family. They were willing to sell at a lesser price if Sam could pay them quickly. Sam offered them an all-cash payment within two days and the deal was done. Dr. Basham promised they would be gone before Christmas and asked Sam if he would be interested in any of the furniture. Sam was interested and purchased most of their furniture, plus the lawnmower and gardening tools.

Over the next two weeks, Sam worked hard every day, mostly at the slaughterhouse. He wanted to do everything he could to ensure the businesses ran smoothly in his absence. His slaughter-house manager, Abraham, was in complete control of the employees. He had already fired a couple of workers and had replaced them with better employees. The meat business was growing every week and so far, with the help of others, like Schultz, the company was meeting all demands with a minimum of complaints.

Jack had worked out pricing on the Mexican beers. In February, they would begin supplying three brands: Tecate, Dos Equis, and Corona. They hoped to have the exclusive distributorship for eastern Arkansas, western Tennessee and northern Mississippi, with options on the entirety of all three states. Domestic beer sales were also on the future agenda, along with a selection of bourbon, rye and wine. Those were items that would have to wait until Sam was back in the office and he or Jack had time to make trips to the different distilleries and breweries around the country.

Two days prior to leaving for New York, Sam was given the keys to the house and the Bashams left for Florida. That night, Sam and Jack moved the Cadillac into the garage of the new house and closed the garage door.

The following day Sam packed his bags for the trip and moved the rest of his personal belongings to the new home. Everything was falling into place for the trip and Sam was excited that he would be leaving before daylight the next morning. Jack was also excited that he had the apartment to himself and relieved the Cadillac was going away. Gina could spend some time at his place and that was just fine with Jack.

Sam was on the road at five o'clock the next morning, heading north toward Nashville. He thought about Adelle; he hoped she was safe on the *Queen Mary* and headed to New York. Would she say yes when he asked her to marry him, and would she want to live in America? A lot of questions would be answered soon enough.

Late in the afternoon Sam reached Louisville and decided to spend the night. He knew that the Four Roses Distillery was located here and he wanted to pay it a visit. He drove downtown near the Ohio River and checked into the Brown Hotel, a sixteen-story building, which was the largest hotel Sam had ever stayed in. The restaurant on the first floor served a delicious meal that included a spicy stew called burgoo. It was a dish that Sam had never heard of but truly enjoyed.

The next morning he drove to the Four Roses Distillery, hoping to work out a business arrangement, giving Cooper Brothers the distribution rights for their renowned bourbon and rye in Memphis and points further south. Upon his arrival he discovered the Four Roses Distillery had recently been purchased by the Seagram Company and were not adding any distributorships at this time. Sam left his name, address and phone number and asked to be placed on a list for future business.

His next stop was the broodmare farm near Lexington, where he would spend time with Dave Hinkle's brother, Dale. The first few things he noticed on the drive were the rich greens of the grasses, the beautiful white wooden fences and the fields full of magnificent thoroughbred horses. Dale worked at Dearborn Farm near historic Midway, Kentucky, just ten miles east of Frankfort, the state capitol. Frankfort was also the home of Frankfort Distilling Company, another company recently purchased by Seagram.

Dale was just as friendly as Dave and welcomed Sam into his home. He lived in a three-bedroom house located on the backside of the farm near the foaling barn. The two men sat on the front porch for a while, listening to the sounds of the farm and enjoying a glass of Kentucky bourbon while they got to know one another. Finally, Dale announced it was his bedtime and told Sam to be ready by six o'clock in the morning and they would have a big breakfast in town before starting the farm tour.

To Sam, the guest bedroom looked very inviting and he was ready to hit the hay. He was looking forward to learning more about the racehorse business from someone he believed he could trust. The city of Midway served as a railway station and was divided down the middle by the railroad track. Dale and Sam had breakfast on the south side of the track at the Furlong Restaurant. It was filled with people involved in the thoroughbred industry. Dale explained that it was a slow time on the farms. Foaling season would start in January, breeding season would start in the middle of February, and the public horse sales were finished for the year.

Dale spent time explaining the breeding and foaling aspects of the business. Sam was amazed at the amount of work required to produce a live and healthy foal. The broodmares were put in well-lighted stalls every night starting in December. The lights were turned off at ten o'clock by the night watchman. According to Dale, horses were referred to as "long-day breeders" because they came into heat as days increased in length in the spring. The exposure to fifteen hours of continuous light, both natural and manmade, stimulated the mare's reproductive cycle by simulating the amount of daylight later in the spring. A successful breeding was followed by eleven-and-a-half months of worrying while waiting on the birth of a live foal. Sam noticed the word "lucky" was used often when talking about racehorses.

Dale switched the conversation to his brother and his sister-in-law, wanting to know how they were doing. Sam placed his cigarette in the ashtray and proceeded to tell all that he knew about Dave and Pat. He heaped praise on both of them and told how helpful they were to Jack and him. Dale told Sam that Dave and Pat had had a son who had been killed in a boating accident on the Ohio River. That had been their primary reason for relocating to Memphis. Sam was deeply touched by their loss and he felt a great sadness because he knew what great parents they must have been. Dale insisted on paying for breakfast and then they headed for the farm.

The barns were beautifully constructed and were clean and nice enough for anyone to live in, safer than most residential homes. The stalls were filled with heavy-bodied mares and high-spirited weanlings, all begging to be turned out for the day. Sam watched as the grooms walked the horses to their prospective paddocks and released them to run and play. The weanlings were released into the smaller paddocks in groups of three and four and separated by gender. The mares were turned out together in greater numbers in the larger fields.

Dale drove to the other side of the farm, explaining that the farm sat on 1,200 acres of rolling hills with ten horse barns, three hay barns and a large equipment shed. There were four houses on the farm. The farm owner's plantation-style home sat at the end of a driveway lined with a cannonade of oak trees. The farm manager's house, the broodmare manager's house, and the yearling manager's house were strategically located around the farm. The yearling barns were separated by gender, the fillies in one and the colts in the other. As they were released in groups of four, Sam watched in awe. Their grace and athletic ability were simply sensational.

Dale explained the importance of confirmation, bone density and pedigree, and how all of it related to the value of the individual horse. He talked about the importance of the limestone base and the natural spring water gathered in concrete tanks across the farm. The limestone was responsible for adding natural calcium to the grass and the water, which in turn led to the growth and development of the growing horses. Sam listened to every word, learning all he could about the thoroughbred business from an expert with a lifetime of experience. The next stop would be a stallion farm, where the leading runners of a prior generation offered their genetic contributions for a fee.

Today they would visit Calumet Farm, located less than ten miles away. Tomorrow they would visit the very famous Claiborne Farm in Paris, Kentucky. The Wright family, who had just sold Calumet Baking Powder Company to General Foods for $40,000,000, owned Calumet. Their homebred Whirlaway, winner of the 1941 Triple Crown, had accelerated their farm's success. Whirlaway retired to the farm as a five-year-old and shared breeding duties with a stallion named Bull Lea, a son of Bull Dog. Bull Dog had been a French thoroughbred racehorse and was the leading North American sire of 1943.

Sam was introduced to Calumet's trainer, Ben Allyn Jones, and his son, Jimmy. Dale had arranged for a short tour of the farm that started with the showing of both stallions. Sam was allowed to pet a Triple Crown winner, who was held by his groom, and to feed carrots to both stallions. He loved touching and watching these powerful animals.

On the way back to Dearborn Farm, Sam was a regular chatterbox, rambling on about all that he had seen. That night he bought dinner at the Chop House in Lexington for Dale and the yearling manager, Tom Hirshe. They each drank a glass of Four Roses bourbon on the rocks before dinner. Sam explained that he and his brother were in the liquor business and would like to become a distributor for some of the finer Kentucky bourbons. The steaks were grilled to perfection and provided a perfect ending to a very fine day.

The following morning, Dale and Sam drove to Claiborne Farm, owned by Arthur "Bull" Hancock, a man famous for his brilliance and his determination to improve the American thoroughbred racehorse. This farm had more natural beauty than Calumet, with a beautiful stream of crystal-clear water and a verdant landscape of rolling hills.

Sam was allowed to see Blenheim II, the sire of Whirlaway and former winner of the Epsom Derby, and a fine representative of his breed. The next stallion he saw was Sir Gallahad III, a successful sire of the Triple Crown winner Gallant Fox. He was also the sire of several other Kentucky Derby winners and, despite being twenty-seven years old, Sir Gallahad III was still a fine-looking stallion. The next horse was a magnificent animal named Princequillo, who was brought to Claiborne Farm in 1945, where he was bred to many of the nation's top mares. The farm manager told Sam and Dale that Mr. Hancock was attempting to purchase a European stallion named Nasrullah. He said that Mr. Hancock believed Nasrullah would be one of the greatest stallions of his generation and he was determined that he would stand at Claiborne Farm.

Sam went to sleep that night thinking about Adelle, wondering what she was doing and if she was thinking about their future together. He hoped that someday the two of them could come back to Kentucky so that she could see what he had seen and experienced. Maybe they could have their own thoroughbred horses one day. The next two days would be filled with anticipation as he completed his journey to New York City.

He said a prayer before going to sleep and asked God to keep an eye on Adelle and Jack, the two most important people in his life.

CHAPTER 13

Sam drove as far as Pittsburg, Pennsylvania, before stopping for the night. The trip had gone smoothly and he had seen interesting parts of the country for the first time. The Cadillac was a very comfortable ride and he had to admit he enjoyed the respect and admiration shown by fellow travelers. He was going to regret giving it up. But for their safety, it had to be done. Now that Adelle, he hoped, was going to be part of the family, he couldn't afford to take any chances.

After checking in to his hotel, Sam asked to speak with the manager and was shown into his office. He introduced himself and asked Mr. Bergman if he knew of any reputable jewelry stores in New York City that specialized in engagement rings. Bergman said, "I have a relative on my wife's side of the family that has a store in the diamond district. His name is Robert Hernreich and the name of his store is the Diamond Center. He's a diamond buyer and specializes in loose stones that he can place in any setting you choose. His diamonds are of the same quality as the stores on Fifth Avenue, like Tiffany's, but half the price. Just tell him personally that his cousin Hugo sent you."

Sam thanked Mr. Bergman and was given directions to Hernreich's business located on 47th Street.

Sam struggled with the heavy traffic as he approached the city. It seemed there were a helluva lot of people trying to get to the same damn place. The cab drivers were the worst, constantly honking their horns and yelling. On several occasions Sam gave them the universal sign of annoyance with his middle finger. After what seemed an eternity, Sam turned onto 47th Street and entered the diamond district. Parking was a pain in the butt as well. Finally he parked the car, entered the Diamond Center, and asked to speak with Mr. Hernreich.

Robert was a handsome fellow with a great smile and he soon put Sam at ease with his quick wit. The two men spoke at length about diamonds, money, and the woman that would be wearing the ring. Sam shared as much of the story as he dared, but did unintentionally mention Camp Chaffee in Fort Smith, Arkansas. Sam was shocked when Hernreich mentioned that his relatives owned a jewelry store in Fort Smith. Sam was quick to add that he now lived in Memphis and steered the conversation in that direction.

After an hour of looking at diamonds through a jewelers' loop, a decision was made to purchase a two-carat, radiant-cut diamond that reflected the light back in a brilliant display of fire-like sparkles. Hernreich guessed that Adelle would need a size six. He suggested giving her the engagement ring first and then returning for the wedding band. That way if the engagement ring needed sizing, it could be done at that time. Sam agreed with the suggestion, knowing there was still the possibility that Adelle might decline his proposal. Sam paid the price they had agreed upon and Hernreich said that he would deliver the ring to the hotel personally the following day at six o'clock in the evening and suggested they have a drink to celebrate the occasion. Sam confirmed the time and place, thanked Hernreich for his help and headed for his car.

Upon his arrival at the Waldorf, Sam handed the bellman his keys after a promise that his luggage would be brought to his room. Sam signed at the front desk with the last name of Cooper; he told the clerk that he had been in France during the War and that a young lady might ask for Sam Mantooth, which was how she knew him in Paris. The clerk made a note and winked, acting as if he had heard this type of story before. Sam found the bellman and they took the elevator to the fourth floor, where he was shown into his assigned room. Sam tipped the bellman ten bucks and thanked him for his help. The bellman thanked him for his generosity and returned to the lobby.

Sam took stock of the outstanding and tasteful furnishings, baskets of toiletries and all of the amenities that the hotel supplied at his expense. He had heard someone say, "Money can't spend itself," and this week he would definitely aid and abet the spending of many dollars. He still had Christmas presents to buy and train fare to purchase. But maybe, if lucky, he would sell the Cadillac for a fair sum.

Sam had decided to dine in the hotel restaurant and was seated next to a table of four well-dressed men. During the meal he heard the men talking about racing horses at Aqueduct Racetrack. He heard bits and pieces of the conversation, enough to believe they owned the horses they were talking about. Sam told the waiter that he would like to buy a round of drinks for the four men. When the drinks were delivered, the men turned and thanked him, but did not ask him to join their table.

Sam finished dinner and was waiting to sign for his meal when two of the men left. One of the remaining men motioned for Sam to join them. Both men stood and shook his hand. The first man to introduce himself was Bob Kleberg from King, Texas. He introduced his friend as Warren Wright of Lexington, Kentucky. Sam took a seat and told Wright that he and his friend Dale Hinkle had visited Calumet Farm just two days earlier and had heard his name mentioned as the owner. Wright confirmed that he was the owner of Calumet and that Kleberg was the owner of King Ranch in South Texas. Sam told Kleberg that he and his brother owned a supply company and bought fresh produce grown in that part of Texas. Wright asked him if he owned any horses.

Sam said, "Mr. Wright, I don't own any horses at this time. I would like to some day, and I want one of them to look like Whirlaway."

Wright laughed and replied, "Bob here might take offence to that remark. He owns Assault, last year's Triple Crown winner. He plans to run him at Aqueduct next week. One of the two men that just left is his trainer, Max Hirsch, and the other fellow is the owner and trainer of his competition. His name is Hirsh Jacobs and his horse is Stymie, the 1945 North American Champion and the leading money-earner of all time."

The three of them ordered another round of drinks. Sam was asked why he was in New York City. Sam told them the story about his journey to find Adelle after the War and the circumstances surrounding their introduction in Paris. Both men were surprised that this would be the first time that he had seen her since the War. The conversation lasted for another hour before they all decided they needed to retire for the evening. Before leaving, Kleberg invited Sam to come to the races at Aqueduct on January third for the Jerome Handicap. As they separated, Kleberg turned and said, "Be sure and bring your friend, Adelle. We'd all like to meet her."

Sam waved and replied, "Thank you, I will."

Sam awoke to the sight of snow falling outside his window and the sound of horns honking on the street below. Today was December twenty-first, just two days before he would finally hold the love of his life in his arms again. He picked up the phone and waited for the operator and asked for room service. He ordered coffee, eggs and bacon to be brought to his room. He showered, shaved and dressed while he waited for breakfast to arrive.

After he ate and smoked a cigarette, he went downstairs to talk to the concierge. He needed directions to the port where the passengers on the *Queen Mary* would disembark. He also asked for any suggestions on where to shop and where to take a date on New Year's Eve. The concierge gave him an address and directions to the port, suggested a few stores for shopping and insisted that Times Square in midtown Manhattan was the place to be on New Year's Eve. He also saved Sam a trip to the port by placing a phone call to the booking agent for the *Queen Mary* and asking for the ship's manifest. He was given confirmation that Adelle Devaux was booked into a first-class cabin and should arrive before noon, day after tomorrow.

Sam spent several hours strolling in and out of retail shops, acting like any other tourist. He purchased a few gifts before returning to the hotel to await the arrival of Hernreich and to inquire about placing the ring in the hotel safe.

Sam was waiting in the lobby and was irritated because Robert Hernreich was thirty minutes late. He stepped outside to cool off and saw Hernreich trying to extricate himself from the arms of a pretty, long-legged brunette. They were standing outside a cab and upon further review, Sam decided Hernreich wasn't trying very hard after all. Finally the brunette gave him a big kiss and returned to the cab. Hernreich waved goodbye to the girl, turned and waved hello to Sam. They entered the lobby together and sat down in two leather chairs in front of a marble-topped table.

Robert had already apologized for being late and with a smile, blamed it on the brunette, whom he described as a very happy customer that just wanted to show her appreciation. He produced a black, satin-covered jewelry box and opened it for Sam's examination. The ring was stunningly beautiful, even catching the eyes of two well-dressed ladies standing nearby.

Looking at Sam, one of the ladies said, "Young man, that is a gorgeous ring and it will be worn by a very lucky lady. If she says no to your proposal, let me know and I'll leave my husband in a New York minute."

Sam laughed, "I'll keep that in mind, but I must offer it to my lady first."

When they walked away, Hernreich told Sam that the lady's husband was one of the owners of the Yankees, the city's professional baseball team, and very well off. Sam acknowledged Hernreich's comment but stayed focused, watching as the very important ring was placed in the hotel safe and waiting until he was given a claim check.

Then he turned to Hernreich and said, "This is your town, so you lead and I'll follow."

They had dinner at Delmonico's Steak and Seafood House. Sam had steak and lobster and decided he had just eaten the most flavorful food of his memory. He would have to bring Adelle here for dinner as well. In the course of the evening, there was a lot of camaraderie between the two young men. Hernreich asked Sam to call him Bob or Bobby. Robert, he said, sounded too formal for friends.

Sam offered Bob a smoke after dinner, but he cordially declined. Rather seriously, he said, "Sam, smoking tobacco will make you old and dead before your time. If you love this woman enough to marry her, you should do her a favor and quit smoking. That's just a suggestion that you can think about later. Tonight we're going to a few of my favorite jazz clubs and you can consider this your bachelor's party."

While riding in the cab, Sam told Bob that he had an almost new, black Cadillac sedan that he had driven to New York and would like to sell it so that he and Adelle could take the train back to Tennessee. Bob told him that he knew someone who would likely be interested and that they would probably see him tonight.

The first club was the Royal Roost on 47th Street, where Billie Holiday was performing. She put on a hell of a show and they stayed for about an hour before grabbing a cab to 52nd Street. There, clubs lined both sides of the street and the sidewalks were crammed with people dressed to the nines moving from club to club. They went into the Famous Door where they watched and listened to Charlie Parker and Dizzy Gillespie perform a popular new style of jazz called bebop. This was Bobby's favorite club and Sam could see why—he knew and was known by a large number of patrons, especially women. They were seldom alone as a constant parade of young women graced their table. Sam had learned from an earlier conversation that Bobby had a young daughter. However, he was currently separated from her mother.

Sam enjoyed the drinks, music, the newfound friendship and all of the female attention, but he never once lost sight of his primary mission. He had come to New York to reunite with his future bride and that was what he intended to do. Everything that he enjoyed was something he wanted to share with Adelle. He and Bobby ended their musical adventure at the Three Deuces, where they enjoyed the final set of music performed by Miles Davis. Sam was a musical novice and Bobby had to explain to him that in one night they had seen most of the top jazz musicians outside of New Orleans. Sam stated that there were a few jazz and blues clubs in Memphis, but nothing like these in New York... yet.

The cab dropped Sam off at his hotel first. During the drive, Bobby had made Sam promise to introduce him to Adelle, so that he could see the diamond ring on her finger. Sam acquiesced to the request, not sure of what Adelle would think of his association with a New York playboy. Sam was unaccustomed to being out until two o'clock in the morning. Moments after sliding between the sheets, he was sound asleep.

The following morning, he called the office and talked to Rose and she gave him an overview of the businesses. According to her, everything was going smoothly and Jack should be back in the office around noon. Sam gave her the hotel phone number and his room number and asked her to have Jack give him a call. He also asked her to remind Jack that New York was an hour ahead of Memphis. She promised that she would do that and wished him well. Sam showered and went downstairs. He badly needed some food in his belly.

Jack called around one o'clock and Sam was really glad to hear his voice. Jack was his rock, always there when he needed him, both as a brother and a business partner. They talked for almost an hour, sharing stories and laughing at their outcome. Jack knew that tomorrow was an extremely important day for Sam and he told him the one thing he needed to hear, that Adelle was crossing the Atlantic Ocean with a one-way ticket to be with him, and that was a major commitment from her. Jack encouraged his brother to relax, to stay strong as always, and reassured him that everything was fine in Memphis.

Sam had his laundry taken to the cleaners by room service, and he spent a quiet afternoon walking around the city. He found a barbershop and had his hair trimmed. He ate an early dinner and retired to his room with a copy of the *New York Times*. He perused the entire paper looking for things to do that he thought Adelle might enjoy. In addition, he found several articles on the national economy. If you believed what President Harry Truman was saying, the country was on an upswing. He wanted to raise the minimum wage to sixty-five cents an hour, encourage building projects for low-cost housing for returning veterans and the general population. He also wanted to restart rural electrification and other programs put on hold due to the War. Increasing government benefits to the poor and promoting more foreign aid to war-torn Europe and Japan was high on his list of priorities. Sam wondered where the hell Mr. Truman was going to get the money to pay for all of that, but that was not Sam's problem, nor what was of most interest to him.

There were several articles about horse racing in the sports section. Armed, a horse owned by Calumet Farm, had just been voted American horse of the year. Calumet also had the male two-year-old champion, Citation, and the two-year-old filly champion named Bewitch. They also had Coaltown, another successful two-year-old colt, who was second in the voting behind Citation. One article spoke about the Golden Age of horse racing, the popularity of the sport nationwide, and the incredible success of Calumet Farm and their father and son trainers Ben and Jimmy Jones. There was something about horse racing that attracted Sam, but there was still so much he didn't know.

There was one thing that he knew for sure—he was looking forward to seeing Adelle tomorrow. The plan was to wake early, go to the port and stay there until he saw Adelle. Sam said his prayers, asking God to bless and protect his friends and loved ones.

CHAPTER 14

Sam was awake before daylight and full of anticipation. After he showered, brushed his teeth, shaved, and trimmed his moustache, he dressed in one of his new suits and applied some cologne recommended by Jack's girlfriend, Gina. Finally, after checking in the mirror one last time, he grabbed his overcoat and headed for the hotel restaurant. He dined on pancakes and bacon washed down with three cups of strong coffee.

Outside, the sun had risen without a single cloud to obscure the beauty of the eastern sky. The temperature was in the mid thirties. The bellman hailed a cab and told the driver to take Sam directly to the passenger ship terminal. The route took them down 52nd Street, past the jazz clubs he had visited two nights before. He thought of Hernreich and how he might call him in a couple of days and introduce him to Adelle.

When the Hudson River came into view, he began looking for large cruise ships and spotted one docking at the southern pier.

His heart skipped a beat and he told the driver to hurry. Sam paid the cab fare and headed toward the shipping terminal. He stopped a porter and asked him if that was the *Queen Mary* being towed in. The porter said that it was not and that he should check with the port authority because one of their patrol boats had just come up the river and was now docking. Sam walked down to the pier and asked one of the disembarking patrolmen if he had seen the *Queen Mary* on his way up the river. The older man looked Sam up and down before he answered, "Yes sir, the ship is about an hour out of port and I bet you're waiting on a woman."

"Yes, I am, but how did you know?" Sam asked, puzzled.

"Well, you're dressed like a Sunday preacher and you smell like you just left a bawdy house. Besides, you're not the first lovesick beau that I've ever met. You need to stay away from the coffee and find yourself a seat inside. She'll be here soon enough and then you can make up for lost time."

Sam shook his hand, thanked him and headed for a warm spot inside.

After what seemed like hours, he spotted a large cruise ship with tugboats both fore and aft. Sam watched in amazement for the next half hour as the tugs expertly maneuvered the large ship to a perfect docking.

Another hour passed before passengers began to disembark. He searched a sea of faces looking for Adelle and jumped every time he saw someone wave. The porters were unloading the baggage and Sam noticed that many of the trunks required two men to carry them to the carts. He thought those probably belonged to Adelle. Several hundred passengers passed by him without any sign of her. He thought of the Babe Ruth expression, "Every strike brings me closer to the next home run." That was when he caught a glimpse of a pretty dark haired woman who had just stepped onto the pier. She was talking to another woman who was carrying a child. Adelle was probably helping the lady off the boat, Sam thought. She turned and looked in his direction; their eyes met and she waved happily.

At that moment, Sam began to make his way toward her. When he heard a wolf whistle, he turned to see where it came from. It was the patrolman and he was watching Adelle. He looked toward Sam and gave him a thumbs up. Sam waved and continued pushing his way toward Adelle. She broke free of the crowd and ran into his arms. Sam grabbed her around the waist and lifted her off the ground. His face was buried in her thick dark hair and her scent filled his heart with joy. He could feel her sobbing as she called his name over and over. Several moments later, he leaned back so that he could look into her eyes and what he saw there removed any doubt forever from his mind. She loved him as much as he loved her and it showed. She placed her hands on his cheeks and said, "My handsome Yankee gentleman."

Then she kissed him and he kissed her back, again and again. Her lips tasted like sweet cinnamon and her breath smelled of sangria. He finally choked out the words, "I love you."

She answered back, "Oh, Sam, I have missed you so much and I love you more!"

Sam was aroused by her accent; it was so damn sexy. He finally set her feet back on the ground and took her hands in his. That was when he noticed that the lady with the child was standing nearby and watching with a smile. Sam also noticed for the first time that the little girl somehow looked familiar. She had dark hair and big blue eyes. She looked like a smaller version of Adelle, but she had high cheekbones and a dimple in her chin, just as he did. Sam continued to stare at her as reality forced itself inside his befuddled brain. He turned and looked into Adelle's eyes.

She softly said, "I want to introduce you to a very special little girl. She is our daughter and her name is Samantha Devaux."

Adelle waited for her words to gain full effect, and then she added, "She is two years old and has been waiting a long time to be held by her father."

With tears streaming down his face and weak at the knees, he moved toward his daughter. He reached for her with trembling hands—with only a slight hesitation she allowed him to take her into his arms and when she said, "Papa," Sam's heart melted. With that single little word she had taken control of his heart and soul.

Sam said to her, "Your papa loves you and I'm so very happy to see you."

Adelle stepped close and said, "Sam, I would also like to introduce you to Nathalie, Samantha's au pair."

Sam transferred his daughter to one arm and shook hands with the young lady, who said, "Bonjour, Monsieur Sam!"

Sam continued to carry his daughter as the four of them made their way to the baggage claim. Adelle and Nathalie left Sam to speak with a porter. With his help they located their bags along with two black trunks secured with leather straps and buckles. Sam was unsure how the trunks were to be transferred to the hotel, but the porter solved that problem. He whistled at a man sitting in a delivery truck and the two of them loaded the trunks and a couple of large bags onto the bed of the truck. Sam hailed a cab and Nathalie got in the front with the driver, leaving the backseat to Adelle, Samantha and Sam. The cab led the way to the hotel and the truck followed close behind. Sam pointed out the jazz clubs as they made their way back up 52nd Street. Samantha was quite content nestled between both of her parents.

When the cab reached the Waldorf, Sam spoke with the bellman and made arrangements for the bags and trunks to be transferred from the truck. Sam paid the cab fare and the delivery driver before going inside to secure an additional room for Nathalie. The hotel was almost full, but there was an available room down the hall on Sam's floor. It was mid-afternoon when everyone and everything were in their appropriate places. Sam and Samantha were getting along well, but she was tired and Nathalie took her to her room for a nap. When they were finally alone, Adelle and Sam laid down on the bed to rest and talk. Soon, they were wrapped in one another's arms. Adelle started to speak but Sam placed his finger on her lips and began to kiss her. He had waited years for this moment and he was going to take full advantage of the opportunity. For the next hour they made love. They started slowly, rediscovering each other's secret pleasures, and then escalated rapidly to a maddening level of lustful sex.

After they cooled down, Adelle explained to Sam her reasons for keeping her pregnancy and Samantha's birth a secret. She had been afraid of what might have happened to Sam. She had moved back in with her family while she was pregnant. Her mother had been supportive during her pregnancy, but her father had been upset until he held his granddaughter for the first time. She had written Sam several letters after the birth of their daughter but they were all returned over a period of months. When she was sure that Sam had returned to the States, she feared she would never see him again. It was only after receiving his letter that hope was rekindled. She had been learning to be a mother and helping her family restore their winery to its pre-War status. In the end, she had decided to keep Samantha as a surprise. If Sam had not wanted the both of them, she would have returned to France without him to raise her daughter alone. Sam kissed her again and told her that everything was perfect. He was a very happy man, but he needed to run downstairs for a few minutes.

When he returned to the room, he went to the side of the bed, got down on one knee and asked Adelle to marry him. With tears in her eyes, she said, "Yes." Sam opened the ring box and slipped the ring on her finger. Her mouth opened in complete surprise.

"Oh my," she said. "It is so beautiful and so big. How are you able to afford such an exquisite diamond?"

Sam winked at her and said, "There has been so much that has happened in the last year, and I'll tell you all about it in due time. Tonight, I just want to enjoy spending time with my daughter and my fiancée. Why don't we get dressed and all go out for dinner, Nathalie included?" Adelle wanted to shower first and Sam went to retrieve his daughter. Samantha was awake and playing with her doll when Sam knocked on the door. She came eagerly to Sam and he picked her up and gave her a hug and a kiss. He did his best to explain to Nathalie that she should dress for dinner, but then gave up. He'd have Adelle call her with details. He then took his daughter downstairs to look for a new toy in the gift shop. They looked at a basket of stuffed animals and Samantha chose a pretty little pony with a pink bow. Sam couldn't have been more pleased. It was obvious they shared similar interests. The maître d' at the Waldorf had suggested they dine at La Famiglia Ristorrante Italiano. It was family owned and served original recipes. The warm fragrances emanating from the kitchen made their mouths water immediately after walking through the door. Samantha was especially fond of the stuffed ravioli and was doted on by several members of the staff and the owner's wife. The adults shared bowls of spaghetti and meatballs, linguine with clam sauce, and a plate of delicious veal chops. Sam and Adelle shared a wonderful bottle of Illuminati Riparosso, a full-bodied red wine from the Abruzzo region in central Italy. Adelle was a wine connoisseur, with a highly refined taste for fine wines and a vast knowledge of wine-growing regions around the world. The more he learned about his fiancée, the more impressed he became. Sam knew that he was truly blessed. Adelle had been his guardian angel during the War and now she was going to be his wife and soul mate for life.

They spent the morning of Christmas Eve shopping for presents, bought lunch from a street vendor, and in the evening they attended church services at St. Patrick's Cathedral in Manhattan. Adelle was Catholic and wanted to raise their daughter in the Catholic Church. Sam didn't have any objections. He had attended Riverdale Free Will Baptist Church on several occasions, but did not feel a strong affiliation with a particular church.

Christmas morning was full of laughter and joy. Samantha was the center of attention and Sam enjoyed his role as Santa Claus. Late in the afternoon, they took a cab to Rockefeller Center to view the Fifteenth Annual Christmas Tree adorning the plaza. Samantha squealed with delight when the lights were turned on at dusk. It was a magnificent sight for everyone involved. Sam's thoughts drifted back to Arbuckle Island and he wondered if electricity had come to the community. It didn't seem fair that this tree was decorated with 30,000 lights, yet many rural communities around the country had not a single electrical light. His mind filled with memories of his mother and father. Gifts had been rare at Christmas time, but love had been plentiful. He hoped to return someday soon to the graves of his parents in Arbuckle Island Cemetery. There was also a debt owed to Jack Dunn and his father's gold watch to reclaim for his brother and himself.

During the next few days they were typical tourists, visiting Central Park, the Central Park Zoo, and the Statue of Liberty, which had been a gift to the United States from Adelle's home country of France. Sam had called Robert Hernreich and brought him up-to-date on all of the recent events, especially his newfound fatherhood. Bob wanted to meet Samantha and then take Sam and Adelle out to dinner and to the jazz clubs. Sam discussed this with Adelle and she thought that the night before New Year's Eve would be the best choice. Nathalie would keep the baby at the hotel, giving them a chance to enjoy the New

York City nightlife. On that chosen night, Hernreich arrived at the hotel bearing gifts and immediately charmed all of the ladies, including little Samantha. He brought her a gold necklace with a Saint Christopher medallion, which he adeptly placed around her neck. She surprised him with a kiss upon his cheek and he became charmed instead of the charmer. Bobby took Adelle by her left hand and admired the engagement ring he had helped to create, telling her how lovely it was and how lucky she was to have Sam as her man. Adelle, Sam and Bobby took a cab to Le Poisson, a seafood restaurant with a French chef. Adelle chose the wine, a Sauvignon Blanc from her region of France. It was a bottle of Domaine de la Devaux, produced from green-skinned grapes grown on her family's vineyard. She explained the grape got its name from the French word *sauvage*, meaning "wild", due to its early origins as an indigenous grape in the southwestern region of France. Dinner was as impressive as Adelle's knowledge of wine. After the main course was consumed, Adelle ordered dessert, a slice each of clafoutis, a black-cherry pie covered in a thick butter-based batter, and three small bowls of crème brulee. Sam's only contribution was his wit.

He told them, "If my hogs were raised on food served in New York City, they would all wear blue ribbons and march in the Macy's Day Parade." Bob laughed and said, "I'll have to stroll around Central Park a couple of times this week myself or all of this delicious food will make me as fat as one of your Tennessee hogs."

While Adelle was in the ladies' room, Bob told Sam that he had a buyer for the Cadillac. If the car were as nice as Sam had described, the buyer would give him $2500 in cash. Sam thanked Bob and asked if he could have the buyer come by the hotel at around ten o'clock the next day and they would finalize the deal.

Adelle enjoyed the performances of Dizzy Gillespie at the Onyx Club and Miles Davis at the Three Deuces. This was all new to her but she hoped to experience it again soon. She was amused by Bobby's popularity with all the pretty ladies. At the end of the evening, Sam and Adelle bid Bobby goodnight and he left with one of the young ladies in a cab headed back to his apartment. Sam and Adelle hailed their own cab and returned to the hotel, where they made love well into the early hours of the morning.

Sam was summoned downstairs at a little after ten o'clock the next morning to meet a well-dressed black man who introduced himself as Maurice Jackson and a friend of Mr. Hernreich. Sam had the bellman call the hotel valet service to bring the car around and he and Maurice went for a drive. During the drive, Jackson asked Sam numerous questions, one being where and how he obtained the car. Sam told him that he had taken the car from a dead criminal who had lost his life fighting over stolen money. Jackson told Sam that he was in the process of opening a new jazz club in Harlem and he needed the car as a status symbol. He needed to impress the established musicians to come and play at his club. When they returned to the hotel he pulled a wad of money from his pocket and told Sam to count it. Sam counted twenty-one hundred-dollar bills and turned to face Jackson, who said, "That's all that I have; you can take it or leave it." Sam took it and the Cadillac was driven away.

The rest of the day Adelle and Sam rested and played with Samantha. Everyone was going to Times Square tonight to watch the glass ball drop, signaling the beginning of a new year, 1948. They dined early and returned to their rooms to rest and prepare for the evening's main event. Adelle had purchased a new baby carriage for the journey to Times Square. Cabs couldn't be counted on this evening because there were too many people who wanted to go to the same place at the same time. The walk would be a little less than a mile and the weather was good. At nine o'clock they left the hotel. The streets were busy with honking cars filled with partygoers. The sidewalks were crowded with people from every race and creed, some old and some young. A few of the young groups were rude and took more than their share of the sidewalk, but Sam managed to avoid trouble by walking in front of Samantha's carriage while the women took turns pushing. The crowd at Times Square was large and rowdy. Musicians were playing and street vendors were selling beads and party hats. Sam bought some beads for the girls and hoisted Samantha up on his shoulders. Ten seconds before midnight the crowd began the countdown and, when the ball dropped, Sam gave Adelle a big kiss. Nathalie had caught the attention of a couple of sailors who talked her into sharing quick kisses. Of course, last but not least, Sam and Adelle each gave Samantha kisses. It was a wonderful evening overall and the walk back to the hotel was made without any problems.

As he walked, Sam once again reflected on what had taken place in 1947. He was hoping 1948 would be a little less violent. He just wanted to get back home and enjoy his family. He would take everyone to the horse races on Friday and then board the train for Memphis on Saturday. It was time to go back and turn the new house into a home.

CHAPTER 15

The train left Penn Station at 1:00 p.m. on Saturday with everyone on board. Sam leaned back in his seat and closed his eyes but did not sleep. Instead, he thought about the last few days. Everyone had enjoyed the races, including Bobby, who had joined them for their last day in town. Calumet's three-year-old colt, Coaltown, won the Jerome Stakes in 1:36 flat and Sam and Samantha were allowed in the win picture. He remembered the story that Warren Wright had told him before the race. The Jerome Stakes was named after Leonard Walter Jerome, a grandiose figure who lived in New York City during the last half of the nineteenth century. He had made and lost a fortune in the stock market and was heavily involved in horse racing. Jerome had been adored by thousands of people and, as one reporter wrote, "He did not enter high society, he created it." In 1865, he bought 250 acres in the suburbs of Manhattan for a large sum of money and built his own racetrack named Jerome Park, which many have called the birthplace of organized racing. The first stakes race that was run at the track was aptly named the Jerome Stakes. The racetrack was torn down four years later, after it was sold to the city of New York for a much larger sum of money than Jerome had originally invested. The land was then used to build a badly needed water reservoir for the city and the stakes race was moved to Morris Park and then years later to Aqueduct.

While at the races, Adelle had surprised Sam with some interesting news of her own. She told him that her father had owned a few racehorses in France. He had been a partner with a couple of friends, but that had been before the War. She and her family had been attending the races since she was a little girl. The local racecourse, Bordeaux-le-Bouscat, was only six kilometers from her family's vineyard. Both flat racing and steeplechases were held at the track. She and her father had also attended the races at Longchamp, home of the most important races that were run in France, the most notable being the Prix de l'Arc de Triomphe which, she said, was usually attended by royalty from both France and England and attracted the best turf horses from around the world. Sam was impressed and slightly embarrassed that Adelle knew more about horses and horse racing than he did. She told Sam that racehorses were expensive to maintain and that it cost just as much to train a cheap horse as it did to train a champion. Her advice was simple, "Buy the best and hire the best or go broke chasing dreams."

Later, Sam had called Jack and wished him a happy new year. During the conversation he had told Jack about Samantha. Jack had handled the news like the great brother that he was, as always. Sam asked him if he, Gina and Rose could fix up a room for Samantha before they returned to Memphis. Jack said that they would be happy to help with the essentials for Samantha, but would wait for Adelle to decorate the house. Jack was also very happy to hear that the Cadillac had gotten a new home. Sam finally drifted off, lulled to sleep by the staccato sounds made by the wheels passing over the railway.

The following morning Sam was seated in the dining car awaiting the arrival of the women in his life. He had slept the best that he could in the passenger car, while Adelle and Samantha had shared the sleeping car with Nathalie. During the night, the train had traveled through Pennsylvania and Ohio and was now in northern Kentucky. He had been awake drinking coffee when the train crossed the Ohio River into the Bluegrass State. Sometime today he wanted to tell Adelle about the flood and all of the events that had followed. She needed to know all of the circumstances surrounding his and Jack's lives since moving to Memphis, with the exception of a few gory details. Her life would be filled with new experiences in a new culture with strange customs, and inevitably, a certain degree of homesickness. His thoughts returned to the moment at hand when Samantha came running down the aisle calling him Papa. He gave her a big hug and kiss and seated her next to him, close to the window, where she could see the rolling hills covered in large stands of virgin hardwood timber. Adelle followed, also with hugs and kisses for Sam, and a pleasant greeting to boot.

"A man could certainly get used to all this attention," said Sam.

Breakfast consisted of bacon, eggs, fresh fruit and delicious pastries. Sam pointed out the window and made Adelle aware that the train was passing through Kentucky. She thought the country was pristine, and hoped that they could visit the area one day soon.

Late in the morning Adelle and Sam found time to be alone while Samantha took a nap. Sam told Adelle the story of his father's death and the brothers' arduous life on Arbuckle Island, including the details of the flood. He told her about finding the boat and the suitcases filled with money and their decision to keep it, and as a result the changing of their last names. He explained their reasons for moving to Memphis, and he told her about the friends they had made, and a little about the businesses they had started.

Finally, he told her about the encounter with Duke Pascal, Pascal's murder of Franco Marcelli, and the subsequent explosion that took the life of Pascal. Adelle listened patiently with occasional looks of shock and concern. She expressed her relief that Sam and Jack had survived the flood and the violent encounters with criminals. She told Sam a story she had heard about a pirate when she was a schoolgirl growing up in France. The story went that there had been a bloodthirsty pirate who, for years, attacked cargo ships traveling the seas of coastal European countries, including France, Great Britain and Spain. The reward offered for the pirate's capture became so large that he feared a mutiny by his own crew. He fled the area and was never heard from again. His name was Jacques Lafitte Pascal. Adelle wondered if Duke Pascal could have been part of the same family, possibly his son or grandson.

Sam said, "Adelle, I don't know who his ancestors were, but he was the most evil man that I have ever met. I believe that he could have given Adolf Hitler a run for his money. I sincerely hope that we've seen the last of that family."

Adelle nodded her agreement. She had heard enough about the Pascal family and the name alone created fear in her heart.

Adelle had a few secrets of her own and was unsure when and how she should share them with Sam. She loved Sam with all of her heart and soul. Yes, he was tall, dark and handsome, but that was not all. The first night that she met him, she had sensed that he was both a tough man and a gentle man. He had been sincere and kind to her, but that awful War had forced him to be someone who killed to keep from being killed, someone who seized an opportunity and made the most of it. When she lay in his arms she felt safe as well as loved. What Sam did not know and would never have considered asking about was how wealthy her family was. Her family money was old money that had been passed from one generation to the next. The vineyard had been in the family for over 200 years, along with several hundred acres of prime farmland. Her father, along with his brother and his sister, owned several buildings in Paris and homes in the city of Cannes on the French Riviera. Adelle was a born romanticist—the money was nice, but she loved living in the country and living a more simple lifestyle. She had dreamed of meeting a prince who would ride up on a fiery-eyed stallion, sweep her off her feet, and carry her off to his castle. Well, Sam was her prince, the father of her daughter, and he was taking her to his home in Memphis, Tennessee. She could tell that he was infatuated with thoroughbred horses and in time, if he wanted, they could buy a horse farm in Kentucky and raise their children in open spaces away from the noise of the city. For now, she would simply explain that she had money of her own and wanted to help pay for some of the expenses. She would never do anything to take away his pride because that was part of what made him the man she loved. She had confidence that Sam would succeed where others had failed. If there was a mountain in his path, he climbed it. If there was a river in his way, he crossed it. And if there were problems in his life, he solved them.

The rest of the day flew by—Sam playing with Samantha, and Adelle explaining to Nathalie some of the American geography and history as she knew it. The porter announced that they would be arriving in Memphis in an hour, on time at 6:05 p.m.

Sam had asked Jack to meet them at the station with a couple of employees and two trucks to transport the luggage and trunks from the train to the house. Sam and the girls would grab a cab and head to dinner, where they would wait for Jack and Gina to join them. Sam wanted to meet somewhere quiet so everyone could start getting acquainted. The most important people in his life were about to be in the same room and he hoped that they all liked one another. Jack and Gina were waiting on the station platform when Sam stepped off the train, holding Samantha in one arm, and Adelle holding his other arm. Jack waited for the proper introductions and then hugged everyone but Nathalie. He was certainly glad to see his brother and thrilled about the happiness that he saw in Sam's eyes. Adelle also looked content; her beauty was more than he remembered, and her face glowed with confidence. Samantha was a very pretty little girl and there was no denying that she was Sam's daughter, the resemblance was too great. Gina, after exchanging pleasantries, was making an effort to befriend Nathalie despite their language barrier.

After the luggage was identified, Jack told Sam to head on to the Dixie Café and he and Gina would meet them there within the hour. Sam was happy to oblige—he was looking forward to eating and sharing some Southern-style cooking. Perhaps he would order a plate of fried chicken and a bowl of mashed potatoes with gravy that he could share with Samantha. After their meals were served, it quickly became obvious that Samantha was a big fan of fried chicken, the drumsticks especially.

The diner was a little out of Adelle's comfort zone, but she adapted quickly. She and Nathalie enjoyed a salad and baked fish with rice pilaf and drank iced tea for the first time. Sam and Jack, joined by Samantha, ate almost everything fried. Gina settled for a hamburger and fries and a bottle of Coca Cola. Conversation flowed around the details of the trip that had started in France. Jack was curious about the post-War reconstruction and the overall attitude of the French civilians, many of whom had lost almost everything during the War. Adelle assured him that the citizens of France were strong-willed as a whole. She reminded

Jack that France had been involved in wars for hundreds of years and that the French were accustomed to starting over. She went on to explain how, fortunately, the countryside had recovered with only a small amount of visual evidence of the previous destruction. The cities, on the other hand, were still rebuilding with the financial aid of the United States. She said that there was a lot of hope pinned on the Marshall Plan that was currently being discussed by the United States Congress. It would offer loans primarily to the United Kingdom and France, and would be directed to industry and infrastructure, which most Allied nations knew to be essential for the European revitalization and reintroduction to the world economy.

Jack came away from his discussion with Adelle realizing that she was not only a beauty, but also a highly informed and intelligent person. He was again pleased and at ease with Sam's good fortune. After dinner was complete and the conversations reached a pause, Sam thanked Jack and Gina for all of their help and called for a cab to take his family home. Unpacking would wait until the following day so that everyone could get some much-needed rest. Samantha was delighted with her room but decided she would like to sleep in the room with Nathalie. Sam and Adelle stayed awake talking about the house and what needed to be done in order of importance. Sam told Adelle he would introduce her to Pat Hinkle because he was sure Pat would be helpful in steering her to stores in town that had items, large and small, needed to fill out their home. The very first thing that needed to be done was to replace the Cadillac with a satisfactory family vehicle. Adelle told Sam that the car should be his decision and that she would be happy with whatever he decided as long as he promised to give her driving lessons. Early the next morning Jack stopped by to give Sam a ride to work, leaving Adelle and Nathalie at home to unpack.

Jack, after telling Sam what a lucky man he was, wanted to know what Nathalie was doing traveling with Adelle. Sam explained that she was an au pair or, in America, a live-in babysitter. Of course Jack thought she was cute and liked her accent. Sam told him that she was off-limits for now and would be for a while! Jack brought Sam up-to-date on the businesses and reported that everything was going well and the demand for their services had continued to increase during the brief time he had been away. He asked about the chances of getting Kentucky bourbon any time soon. Sam explained about the recent sale of the distilleries and the temporary hold placed on new business and that it would be a couple of months before he could return and speak to the owners. When Sam walked into the warehouse, he was greeted as if he had been away for years. Rose brought him a fresh cup of coffee and a stack of papers to review. She let him know that she was happy he was back. It felt good to be back in a comfortable environment where he was in control and he dug into the paperwork.

Later in the morning, Sam called the Buick dealership and asked if they sold a car that would seat six people comfortably. The salesman told him that they had just received a new Buick Roadmaster sedan convertible. It was burgundy with a white convertible top and matching burgundy interior and easily seated six adults. The price was $2,300. Sam asked the salesman if he would bring the car down to the warehouse so that he could see it. The salesman said that he would be there within the hour. Next, Sam called Dave Hinkle and brought him up-to-date on his personal life and asked if he could bring Adelle and Samantha to the Hinkles' house to introduce them. Dave was obviously eager to meet them because he suggested that they come over around twelve-thirty for lunch. Sam thanked him and said they would be there.

He had just hung up the phone when the new car was driven into the warehouse parking lot. Sam liked what he saw and asked if he could drive the car to his home and show it to his fiancée. The salesman got into the passenger seat and Sam headed home. He liked the way the car handled and Adelle liked it because it was big and beautiful and perfect for their new family. Sam and the salesman drove back to the dealership and negotiated a price of $2,100 and Sam paid for the car with the cash that he had received from the sale of the Cadillac. After going back by the house to get Adelle and Samantha, Sam drove to the Hinkle residence. Pat had prepared more than enough homemade soup and sandwiches for everyone. She adored Samantha and was impressed with Adelle when she saw that she was a caring and compassionate person. During lunch the two women discussed furnishings and decorating trends, while the two men talked business, except when they were busy entertaining Samantha. The women made plans to shop the next day and then said goodbye. Dave shook Sam's hand and gave him an approving wink.

After a brief stop at home to turn Samantha over to Nathalie for her afternoon nap, Adelle rode with Sam in the new car to check on the hog operation in Nut Bush. Sam had thought he would never feel better than he had when he and Jack had bought the Ford pickup truck, but he'd been wrong. Riding in the new car with the woman he loved had just taken over first place.

Adelle stayed in the car while Sam talked business with Abraham, toured the facility and watched his employees work. The pork operation was now producing sausage for restaurants and small grocers, as well as cracklings and pickled pig's feet for the bars and honkytonks. Sam had a chance to visit with Jimbo when he stopped by to pick up his order of sausage and cracklings for the grocery store. Sam thanked him for all his help and took him to meet Adelle and show him the new car. After his introduction to Adelle, Jimbo broke into a big smile and told Sam that he had very good taste in women and cars. He also said the citizens of Nut Bush were very happy with the current arrangement they had with Cooper brothers and wanted to do more business in the future.

Sam put his arm around Adelle and pulled her close as they drove back into Memphis. He felt like the luckiest man in the world. She was beautiful and smart and, moreover, he felt as if he could talk to her about anything and she would always offer her own well-thought-out and unselfish opinion. Their conversation turned to the topic of their upcoming marriage. Sam suggested that they marry in Memphis in May. Adelle agreed, saying that planning for a May wedding would give her family time to make proper travel arrangements. Her mother, father and brother would definitely come and maybe other relatives as well.

Sam said, "On my side it will just be Jack, a few friends and business associates from around town."

Sam told her what he knew about the Catholic churches around town, which wasn't much. Adelle said she would choose one to attend this Sunday and they could go to a different one each week until they had visited them all. She also had a plan to personally meet soon with the appropriate church officials at the Memphis diocese office to learn more about wedding ceremony requirements. She would write a letter to her family telling them of the wedding date. She had, of course, written them from New York and told them of her safe arrival, her engagement to Sam and how much he loved their granddaughter. There were many things to do in her immediate future. Turning their house into a home and planning a wedding were at the top of her list.

CHAPTER 16

Jean Pascal was drinking iced tea and smoking a cigarette on the screened-in front porch of his mama and daddy's two-story house on Pelican Avenue in Algiers, long considered a part of New Orleans, but sitting on the west bank of the Mississippi River in Orleans Parish. His family had lived here for forty years and was both respected and feared. The New Orleans police were well paid to stay on their side of the river and let Algiers take care of its own problems. There were many nights that Detective Flint of the N.O.P.D. had dined in their house. He would come to eat their boudin and their crawfish etouffee and then he would leave with his pockets stuffed with wads of their money.

That arrangement worked well for everyone; for years his family had taken money from bank robberies across the South and Midwest and invested in legal and illegal business ventures. The profits made from the investments were divided proportionately and placed in different family bank accounts. This arrangement had been developed and perfected by his aunt and uncle. Mostly his Uncle Frank, who had been a getaway driver for a gang of bank robbers before he was injured. That was whom he had recently gone to see in Arizona, fully prepared to kill them both if he had believed they were responsible for the disappearance of his younger brother. They had been the last known people to see Bobby alive. However, his Uncle Frank's story had been very convincing. He confirmed that Bobby had left Oklahoma during the early stages of a major flood. The general consensus had been that the boat had sunk and Bobby had drowned in the swollen river.

But that was before the letter had arrived, proclaiming knowledge of Bobby's death. Prior to that Duke had practically given up on finding their little brother. So, without waiting on Jean to return, and in a moment of blind rage, Duke had taken his father's car and three of his mother's Creole relatives and headed for Memphis with blood in his eye. Jean had just returned from Memphis and was preparing to tell his father that he had not found his brother nor did he have any solid leads as to his whereabouts. Duke had been missing for over three months now and Bobby had been missing for almost a year. Jean had stayed in Memphis for a week after New Year's. He had gone to every hotel and motel in the area. He had gone to bars and restaurants, showing Duke's picture to bartenders and waitresses, and absolutely no one had seen him. There had been a story about a loan shark that had gone missing around the same time as Duke. There were some who believed that his boat had exploded near the Port of Memphis, killing him and everyone on board. Jean wasn't sure whether he should tell that story to his daddy. Jacques was a man who did not like bad news. He was a mean old man who still scared the shit out of Jean, who considered himself to be a tough man. Duke had been the older brother and the only one that didn't fear their father. That's because Duke had become a worshipper of voodoo and believed that he was protected by strong spiritual powers.

Duke had been in charge of finding Bobby and now that he was missing, the job to find them both belonged to Jean. His mother, Leona, was a Creole his father had married when he moved to the United States from France. The Creole families were very close-knit, and his mother was grieving over the loss of her two sons. That just made his father angrier and meaner. Jean knew that Duke had traveled to Fort Smith, Arkansas, by boat, looking for Bobby, and the only clue that he had was from a dockhand in Little Rock named Clarence, who said Bobby's boat had stopped there for fuel while heading downriver. He said it was driven by two men who looked to be in their twenties and dressed like farm-hands. So far that information hadn't helped, because the damn boat had disappeared into thin air. Jean couldn't wait any longer to talk to his daddy. He stepped inside the house and faced the wrath of his scowling father.

Jacques asked, "Do you have any news that will help find your brothers?"

Jean told him, "No!" but that he was not done; he wanted to go back to Memphis and offer rewards for information about the boat or the car. On his first trip he was looking for his brother, now he would be looking for his brothers' trail.

"Do you think your brothers are still alive? That is all that I want to know."

Jean answered truthfully that he did not believe that they were alive. Jacques nodded in agreement. "Neither do I," he said. "I'm going to have my detective friend call the Memphis police and ask them some questions. I'll tell him that my car was stolen and he can have the police in Memphis search for it. You will stay here and help me run our business until we hear something from Flint." That was good news for Jean because he had missed the nightlife in New Orleans. He had an apartment in the French Quarter, just a block off Bourbon Street, and he rarely had to sleep alone. New Orleans was blessed with a large number of beautiful women that were attracted to his money and lavish lifestyle.

Jean visited with his mother for a while before leaving. She was heartbroken over her missing sons. No matter what her sons had done, she still loved them. Jacques Pascal was an experienced criminal and the head of the family, but Leona's connection to her Creole family had opened many doors. When something illegal needed to be done, the Creoles were always there to help. Two of the men that went to Memphis with Duke had been her nephews, sons of her dead brother. Jean left the house to catch the five o'clock ferry that would take him across the river, where he would catch the trolley to Bourbon Street. He thought about all that had happened over the last few years and considered what would happen now that his brothers were gone. He wondered if his father would replace the missing money that had been lost along with his brother. His uncle Frank had told him that there had been a little over $52,000 on that boat. That meant that 70 percent of that money belonged to the Barker and Davis families in Oklahoma. Frank had also told him that it had been the last of the money; there wouldn't be any more money coming down the river. That was why he and Esther had left Oklahoma and moved to Arizona. They had wanted to distance themselves from a dying business.

The money from bank robberies had dwindled over the past five years. The majority of bank robbers were either in jail or dead. Jacques knew from his own personal experience that the bank robbers had reached the end of an era and the family needed a new business. As a result, the Pascal family had begun dealing in the nefarious business of human trafficking. Men were occasionally shanghaied and sold as slaves to work in South American mining operations, but the men were more difficult to deal with and their value was limited.

Women became the Pascals' specialty, especially young women, but never any of the local girls. The Pascals made sure of that, besides, there were hundreds of women who came to New Orleans every year looking for work or running away from their families and wouldn't be missed until well after they were secured onboard a slave ship. The Pascal family paid their network of abductors to drug the women and secretly deliver them to one of their warehouses along the waterfront in Algiers. The women were then taken to an island located in a bayou sixty miles down the river from New Orleans. The Pascal family had supplied the money for the building of screened-in sleeping quarters that looked like an ordinary fishing camp. Miles of marshland surrounded the island and the camp was closely guarded by the Creoles. Every two months a slave ship would anchor off the Louisiana coast and the captain would come to the island in a skiff to inspect his cargo. The Creoles would then deliver the women to the ship, where they would be taken abroad and sold as sex slaves. Jean especially liked this business—he was actively involved in the abductions and enjoyed taking trips to the slave camp, where he was treated as the patron by the Creoles and pleasured by the women of his choosing.

Jean missed his little brother Bobby—the two of them had been very close—but not his older brother Duke, whom his father had chosen to take his place as head of the family business. Jean knew that with the disappearance of his older brother, he would sooner rather than later become the head of all family business. His mother and father were old and seldom left Algiers. When he returned to Memphis this time, he would do his best to find the truth about his brothers' disappearance. If he could revenge their deaths his father would be impressed and Jean would be given respect and rewarded with more power. This time he would check out the Port of Memphis. That would have been where the boat would have come ashore after Bobby's death, if there were any truth to that story. It was also where the reported explosion had taken place involving the loan shark's boat. There was a good chance that one of the dockhands had seen something. He would travel to Memphis by boat and take a couple of men with him. When he docked the boat, he would ask if anyone had seen his brothers. Then he would describe the missing boat and offer cash for any useful information; if that didn't work then he would pass around a bottle of whiskey and see if that would loosen their tongues. He knew damn well that somebody on that dock knew something. Jean would wait until his father had talked to his friend Detective Flint. Maybe Flint would find out something from his Memphis counterparts, but Jean thought it was unlikely.

CHAPTER 17

Sam and Jack had worked hard all morning and were now headed to lunch at Freddie Clanton's new barbeque restaurant in the heart of downtown. Freddie had secured a loan from Mr. Dunn down at First National Bank and bought the building across from the Fountain Hotel. The new restaurant, named The Rib Palace, occupied two floors of the building. Freddie's new menu included dry rubbed ribs that were cooked slowly over a charcoal pit.

On the way to lunch Sam asked Jack if he knew what day it was.

Jack answered, "Well, Sam, I think today is the ninth of April, a week after my birthday that you must have forgotten, again, but I think you were referring to the date of last year's flood."

Sam retorted, "Damn it! I did forget your birthday, but let me know what I can do to make amends. You're right about the flood though. It was one year ago today that we found the boat and the money that forever changed the course of our lives. That's why I invited you to lunch, sort of a private celebration for just the two of us."

Freddie spotted the brothers when they walked in the door and came forward to greet them.

"Hi guys! How the hell are you?" he asked as they exchanged handshakes.

Sam said, "We're doing good, buddy. This place looks great and the tables are full, business must be booming."

Freddie couldn't help but smile. "We've been really busy since the day we opened and in the evenings there's usually a waiting line outside the door. I can't thank you enough for suggesting this place."

Jack interrupted, "Hey Freddie, have you heard that my brother is getting married?"

"I've heard a rumor to that effect and I couldn't be happier, I also heard that he is a proud new father. You guys are becoming well known around town and the good news has preceded you."

Freddie showed them to an empty table and told them he would be back. The brothers ordered a rack of ribs that they shared. The meal came with baked beans, coleslaw and a cold glass of sweet tea. Freddie rejoined them as they were finishing up the meal. Jack was the first to compliment him on the great-tasting food. Sam told Freddie that he would like to come back on Friday night and bring the rest of his family. He was sure that Adelle had never eaten barbeque. Freddie welcomed the idea and said he was looking forward to meeting some new friends. When Sam and Jack offered to pay, Freddie refused to take their money. He said it was the least he could do. Freddie walked outside with them and pulled Sam off to the side and said, "I just wanted to tell you something that I heard while you were gone. An old friend of my brother told me that there was a Louisiana Cajun in town asking questions. He was in a nightclub showing a picture of his brother and asking if anyone had seen him. He said that his brother had been missing for several weeks. Do you think this has anything to do with my brother's disappearance?"

Sam swore, "Well, shit! I hoped that we were through with that family. The answer to your question is yes, it does. The man that killed Franco Marcelli is probably his brother."

Freddie asked if he could help in any way, and Sam told him to keep his ears open and call him if he heard anything.

Sam and Jack got in the car and headed back to the office. While on the way Sam told Jack everything that Freddie had said.

"I think I really messed up when I sent the letter to Duke Pascal. I should have left well enough alone," Sam added.

Quickly, Jack replied, "If it makes you feel any better I thought that you did the right thing. I still have the missing person's poster rolled up and hid in my closet. I thought that it could come in handy some day because it has Pascal's mailing address listed on it. Do you think we might have to pay them a visit?"

Sam thought a minute before he spoke, "I would rather not do that right now. Sometimes it's better to let a sleeping dog lie. I don't know shit about New Orleans, but if you will bring me that address I will see if David Hinkle has a map of the area and figure out what part of the city they operate from. I'm beginning to think these guys are like a sore throat, unpleasant and hard to get rid of." Sam told his brother the story about the pirate by the name of Pascal that Adelle had read about in school. The subject was dropped when they reached the office, and Jack said he would bring the address to Sam.

At the end of the day, Sam drove home and was glad to see Pat Hinkle's car in the driveway. It was important to Sam that Adelle had a new friend to help her make their house a home. Samantha was the first to greet him when he walked through the door and she rewarded him with hugs and kisses. Food cooking in the oven made the house smell great and it already was beginning to feel like home. The women stopped what they were doing and welcomed him home. On his way out the back door to take Samantha to swing in her new tree swing, he asked Pat to please check with David and ask him to bring home a map of the New Orleans area if he had one to loan. She nodded a yes to him as Samantha pulled him out of the door. After a dinner of a delicious stew served over a thick but flaky crust, a dish Adelle called shepherd's pie, Nathalie took Samantha to give her a bath and ready her for bed. Sam helped Adelle clean up the kitchen and she asked him why he needed a map of the New Orleans area. Not wanting to cause her undue worry, he said that it was just information that he needed for his delivery business. He changed the subject by asking her about her day and whether she had heard from her parents. She said that she hadn't received a letter yet, but had plenty to say about her day.

Together, they put the baby to bed. Adelle then smiled seductively at Sam and asked him if he would like to practice making more babies.

He laughed at her innocent wit and said, "I can't think of anything that I would rather do, my dear."

On Friday, Sam and Adelle met Jack and Gina at The Rib Palace. The girls were favorably impressed with the décor and the number of people waiting in line for a table. While they were waiting, Adelle and Gina had a glass of wine. Jack and Sam each had a cold bottle of Corona, the Mexican beer that Cooper Brothers now supplied throughout Memphis. Jack pushed a slice of lime into his bottle, but Sam didn't because he wasn't sold on the idea of putting fruit in his beer.

Adelle was not familiar with the taste of barbeque, but became an immediate fan. She had a slice of smoked brisket with a side salad, while everyone else dined on smoked ribs and all the "fixins," which, Sam explained to Adelle, was the Southerner's way of asking for accompaniments that were served in addition to the main dish. Freddie came to the table and was introduced to Adelle. He expressed his pleasure in meeting her, but voiced his disappointment that Samantha was not with them. Sam promised to bring her the next time they came for dinner and also laughingly reminded Freddie that most adults occasionally needed their own night out.

As they were leaving the restaurant, Jack and Gina suggested that the four of them go to one of the local movie theaters. There were three within walking distance. Just a few doors down the street was the Loews Station Theater, where *A Foreign Affair* with Marlene Dietrich was showing. Jack thought that was funny and told Sam and Adelle that they had already starred in that one. Sam jokingly told him to watch his mouth. The next choice was the Princess Theater, featuring Humphrey Bogart and Lauren Bacall in *Key Largo*. The final choice was at the Malco Theater where *Fort Apache*, a western, starring Henry Fonda, Shirley Temple and John Wayne was showing. The ladies voted for *Key Largo*. Sam and Jack preferred *Fort Apache*. Adelle and Gina told them that *Key Largo* was a movie about a World War II vet who goes to Florida to visit his buddy's widow and has a conflict with mobsters who are trying to take over her hotel.

Sam really preferred the western but he wanted to keep his fiancée happy so he voted with the girls. The night was filled with firsts, Adelle's first barbeque and first American movie, and Sam's first movie since the end of the War. On Saturday, Nathalie was up early and prepared breakfast. Adelle told Sam to eat hearty because she had a long list of outside projects to complete and he was going to star in his own movie. The weather outside was sunny and cool, perfect for building flowerbeds and tilling a small vegetable garden. Samantha thought playing in the dirt was a great idea. She made mud pies and served them to her parents and by the end of the day she looked like a real farm girl, covered in dirt from head to toe.

David Hinkle stopped by to drop off the map Sam had requested, giving Sam a chance to take a break and drink a glass of iced tea with him. When he asked Sam why he needed a map of New Orleans, Sam avoided answering the question and said he would explain later. Dave hung around long enough to give Sam some gardening advice, push Samantha in her tree swing, and spend time talking with Adelle, getting to know and appreciate her more than ever.

Sunday morning found Sam, Adelle, Samantha and Nathalie sitting inside the chapel of Saint Peter Catholic Church. It was a beautiful display of European architecture and art, and Sam was in awe. This was the first time that Sam had attended Catholic church, and he was filled with inspiration from the majesty of the church, yet humbled by its sanctity and tradition. Arbuckle Island's Riverdale Freewill Baptist Church had been filled with local friends and great fellowship but Saint Peter Catholic Church in Memphis, Tennessee, was filled with the power of God. Adelle remained after the service to introduce herself to the parish priest, asking him questions about the church's educational system. She was most interested in their primary education and the requirements for joining the local parish. Nathalie, as usual, was quiet around Sam, but she was always speaking French and laughing with Samantha. Samantha was amazingly, naturally, bilingual. Her French flowed better than her English, but her English was improving by the day. He knew she would be a great little student. Once again, Sam realized how blessed he was to have Adelle and Samantha in his life.

On Monday, Sam took the New Orleans map with him to work. He planned to go with Jack to their old apartment in the afternoon and search for the exact location of the Pascal residence. He wanted to know just how close they were to the Mississippi River, and the best way in and out of their neighborhood. If he was going to battle them he wanted to plan as if he were still in the Army.

While in Germany, he and Jack had helped plan numerous successful reconnaissance missions and raids. Sam preferred attacking during the night when they could dress in dark clothes and blend into the darkness. They could camouflage their faces and approach the target virtually undetected. The key to any successful raid was speed and stealth, surprising the opponent while they were sleeping or at least unprepared. Sam kept a hidden pistol at his new home and one in the safe at work. All of the other arms were stored at Jack's apartment and needed to be properly cleaned and oiled. Their old staff sergeant would say, "Listen lads," as he held his rifle in one hand and his crotch in the other, "this is my rifle and this is my gun, this one's for fighting and this one's for fun." Sam remembered well how important the weapon could be. He had fought in hand-to-hand combat before. Up close, he preferred his trench knife with a double-edged blade on one end and skull buster on the other. The hilt had a knuckle-duster hand guard with four striking points that provided maximum effectiveness when striking an opponent. In addition, Sam was quite sure that Jack still had a part of the box of pineapple hand grenades that could be used for multiple targets.

In the afternoon, the brothers met at Jack's place and completed an inventory of their weaponry. Jack promised that he would start an inventory of their ammunition later that night and the next day would buy whatever bullets they needed. They studied the map and marked the approximate location of the Pascals' house in Algiers. While cleaning their guns they debated whether to attack the remainder of the Pascals, or wait until one or some of them returned to Memphis so the two brothers could confront them on their home turf. Jack was up for either place; whatever Sam wanted to do was fine with him. Sam's gut feeling was to attack, but his heart told him to stay put and protect his family. There was a glimmer of hope that the problem would go away and they could avoid further bloodshed. At the end of the day he went with his heart and headed back home to be with Adelle and Samantha. That was where he knew for certain he could find peace and happiness.

CHAPTER 18

The residents of Memphis enjoyed beautiful spring weather during the month of April, with the exception of a few late-night thunderstorms. Adelle, being unfamiliar with tornadoes, snuggled close to Sam when the thunder and lightning filled the Tennessee skies. She had read an article in the local newspaper about a tornado that had destroyed a couple of houses and a barn over in Brinkley, Arkansas, killing a man and his wife. To allay her fear, Sam had reassured Adelle of their safety and told her what to do and where to hide in the house if she felt in eminent danger. The joy of spring fever, however, dominated the fear brought about by the thunderstorms. Adelle worked in her gardens daily and persuaded Sam to help her when he could. Samantha loved playing outside and kept Nathalie too busy to help in the gardens, but that was all right. Adelle didn't mind because Nathalie was now a very important part of the family and Samantha loved her dearly.

Adelle had received a letter from her family describing their plans and providing an itinerary for their transatlantic voyage and the subsequent train travel from New York to Memphis. They would arrive a week before the wedding and stay for a week after, allowing them to spend some quality time with Samantha, while Sam and Adelle enjoyed their honeymoon. Adelle was keeping the honeymoon destination a secret from Sam, but assured him that he would be very pleased with her decision. The wedding date was Saturday April 24th at Saint Peter Catholic Church. Sam had happily acquiesced in order to honor the wishes of his future bride.

Together they spent multiple evenings assembling a guest list, hoping anyone desiring to attend would not be forgotten. Rose was in charge of making dinner reservations and preparing a guest list of business associates. She prepared a list of mailing addresses of Cooper Brothers' customers, along with the names of city officials whom she thought should be invited. Pat Hinkle was helping Adelle select the wedding cake and a list of menu items to be served at the rehearsal dinner. Sam had given her permission to reserve an entire restaurant for the rehearsal dinner and to spend whatever it took to make the night a total success. Gina had been tasked with looking for a band for the rehearsal dinner because Adelle wanted Gina to be involved in their wedding and for their guests to enjoy dancing after dinner.

The Lucky Millinder Orchestra was traveling from Chicago to Memphis that week to perform at the Ellis Center on Saturday night. Gina spoke with their agent and he agreed to allow the band to play two hours of music after the rehearsal dinner on Friday. The orchestra played big band swing with a touch of rhythm and blues. Lucky Millinder had been born and raised in Alabama, but now lived in Chicago and traveled the big band circuit. Adelle gave her blessing, knowing they were very fortunate for the opportunity to hire such a popular band.

Sam had made a habit of stopping by the Port of Memphis in the mornings and having a cup of coffee with Dave Hinkle. Dave was a very good source of sage advice, and Sam needed his wisdom and calm judgment at this time in his life. Sam wished that he could confide in Mr. Hinkle, telling him the story of the flood and the subsequent events that followed, but he feared that he would lose Mr. Hinkle's respect and the friendship that he cherished as a son would a father's.

Dave was still concerned with his lack of knowledge of the events that had taken place on his docks on the night of the explosion. He shared his gut feeling with Sam. He believed something very wrong had taken place that night, but he had little proof to back it up. Finally, one day, Sam told Dave the story he had shared with Freddie Clanton, about a gangster from New Orleans who was looking for his missing brother, and about the poster that he had seen while traveling in Mississippi. He intentionally left out the part of the story concerning the missing boat. Dave considered the new information and thought there was a possibility the two events could be connected. Maybe two bad men had eliminated each other on that fateful night and the world was a better place without them. Sam quickly concurred.

Late one afternoon Sam and Jack left work and stopped at The Rib Palace for a cold beer and conversation. They found two empty bar stools at the end of the bar and took up temporary residence. The upcoming wedding became the primary topic of conversation. Jack wanted to plan a bachelor party for his brother, but Sam was opposed to the idea. He saw nothing good coming from a wild and crazy night out in the Memphis bars and bawdy houses.

Freddie came down the stairs and joined the two brothers. Sam engaged Freddie in the ongoing debate and, much to his surprise, Freddie was in favor of having the bachelor party.

Freddie said, "Hell, Sam, this should only happen once in a lifetime; it's only fair that you give your friends one last night out with their buddy before he gets hitched—besides, you'll be paying for the drinks. We can start here and work our way over to Beale Street and finish out the evening at my favorite joint, the Republic Nightclub. They always have good musicians playing on the weekend."

Sam lowered his head in defeat. "Oh hell, why not! But just remember if you can't run with the big dogs you'd better stay at home on the porch." Jack and Freddie slapped Sam on the back, laughing, happy with their victory.

Jack was quiet for a moment, looking first at Freddie and then at Sam. "Big brother, you're gonna have to tell Adelle, I don't want to be the one that makes her mad and if you have to, tell her it was Freddie's idea." Sam assured them both that it wouldn't be a problem. He was confident that Adelle would understand. Before leaving, Sam told Freddie to call him if he heard any news of the Pascal family returning to Memphis.

Freddie responded, "You'll be the first to know."

Saturday morning, Sam lay in bed with Adelle wrapped in his arms and his face buried in her beautiful brown hair. The bedroom windows were open and the cool, fresh spring air created a mild chill in the room. Birds were singing in the oak trees that surrounded the house, serenading another beautiful sunrise. Adelle and Sam had been awake for over an hour; their early-morning lovemaking had been both slow and tender. Adelle had brought him to the edge of sexual bliss several times as she sat astride his manhood but each time she had slowed her movements, making him wait until she was ready. Just when he thought he couldn't wait any longer her movements and breathing quickened as she arched her back and cried out as they climaxed together. After rolling off of Sam and onto her side, she waited until her breathing had returned to normal before she said, "I love my beautiful American man." Sam started to speak, but instead pulled her into his arms and kissed her.

Adelle sat up, grabbed her robe from the foot of the bed, and sat back down on the side of the bed facing Sam. The serious look on her face caused Sam concern and he responded by asking, "What's wrong, sweetheart?"

She looked him in the eye and said, "There is something that I want to tell you. There is nothing wrong, but there is something that you need to know."

Sam intertwined his fingers and placed his hands behind his head, expecting the worst. "What is it? Please tell me."

"My family will be here in a couple of days and you really don't know anything about them. It's important to me that you like my family and for them to get to know you and love you as I do."

Sam smiled, "If that's all you're worried about, just relax, we'll get along fine."

She placed her hand on his chest and took a deep breath before she spoke, "Sam, my family is quite wealthy, as were my grandparents and their parents before them. It's old money, money and land that have been passed down from one generation to another. Please don't assume that my parents are lazy and spoiled, they are just the opposite. They are very proud and work hard, making sure that our vineyard is producing the finest grapes to be used in the production of our world-class wines. The art of making fine wine has also been passed down from one generation to the next. Someday they will leave everything to my brother, André, and me. He will be left in charge of the business, but I'll have certain responsibilities for the rest of my life, as will our children. Once or maybe twice a year we will need to return to my home to see my family. My father would like to expand his sales into the United States and he would like for both of us to help. With my help, you could learn the business and help us establish a distribution network. I have little doubt that my father will see the business that you already have and ask you to become personally involved in our export business." Adelle stopped and waited for Sam to say something.

Sam thought before he spoke and, after careful consideration of his answer, he said, "I really appreciate your honesty and thank you for sharing more of your family history. It's obvious that you have class and that you're well educated. Since you haven't asked me to pay for any of your travel expenses and haven't asked me for any money since you arrived, I had to assume that you and your family had money. Jack and I have planned in the near future to stock and distribute both imported and domestic wines. Jack is very focused on our wholesale liquor business and wants to expand our list of products and broaden our sales territory. If you and your family want us involved in the importation and distribution of your wine, then we will be happy to help."

Adelle looked relieved, "Oh, Sam, you have made me very happy. I was so worried about all of these things."

Sam explained that he was primarily in charge of the pork business and that it took a lot of his time, something that he would have to change. He added, "The Pilgrim brothers, owners of the City Meat Market, have let it be known that they are interested in buying part or all of our pork business and when the time is right, I will give that idea further consideration."

Adelle shared more of her family's itinerary. They were already in New York and were staying at the Waldorf. They had called from the hotel yesterday to let her know that they were safe and on schedule. They had spent most of the day shopping before going to dinner with Bobby Hernreich. They would board the train in the morning and arrive in Memphis on Monday. She had booked three rooms at the Peabody hotel for a week and two additional rooms for the weekend. She had made reservations at various restaurants and scheduled a tour of Memphis for the middle of the week. She told Sam that her mother, father and brother would join the two of them for the last few days of their honeymoon, but refused to divulge the location. Sam attempted to reach and grab Adelle to tickle a confession out of her, but she was quick and ran out of the bedroom, heading to the kitchen to make coffee.

Sam lay in bed thinking about everything Adelle had shared with him. One week from today he would be her husband and a new member of her family. He wondered what her family would think of him. He was just a country boy from Arkansas without any formal education. He was street smart and war-hardened but definitely not a wine connoisseur. He was sure that wine from France would be shipped to New York, where it would be warehoused, sold and distributed. Memphis could be a distribution hub for the South, but they would also need hubs in the East, West and the upper Midwest. That would require a considerable amount of time and travel. He and Jack would need to think seriously about selling the pork business or hiring a general manager.

He would talk to Jack about that on Monday morning. They would need to make sure their employees and the citizens of Nut Bush were taken care of, as well as their growers and suppliers. The first question that needed to be answered was: How much was the new business worth and how could he establish its value? The smell of frying bacon and the sound of Samantha's laughter brought him back to reality. He was hungry and needed to get out of bed and get dressed for breakfast with his daughter.

CHAPTER 19

It was a quiet Sunday morning in New Orleans and Jean Pascal had slept late. He was not alone in his bed—one of his regular girls, a local named Tera Borel, had accompanied him home after a night of heavy drinking and raucous behavior. She was one of his favorites, never asking for more than he offered, even helping him select and seduce young women for his human trafficking business. He paid her a reasonable fee for helping him and treated her to food and drink when she was with him. She liked rough sex and last night had been especially wild, at least the parts he could remember. This morning his head hurt from too much alcohol and his guts were rumbling. He needed food, but that would require too much of an effort, maybe he would wake Tera and send her out for food. He got out of bed, took a piss, and threw on a pair of pants before going out on his balcony to smoke a cigarette.

The previous week he and two Creoles had taken three women downriver to the slave camp, where he had stayed for a couple of days. There were eleven women in the camp now but he needed at least twenty before the slave ship arrived. The ship had come in March and would return sometime in May. In March they had sold thirty-one women into slavery, most of them kidnapped during Mardi Gras in February. March had always been a successful month: hundreds of women came to Mardi Gras every year, and drinking and partying made them easy prey. Farm girls from the Midwest were usually the most gullible, followed by spoiled little rich girls from Georgia and Florida who enjoyed a dare. In the past his brother Duke had wanted to sell a few of the wealthy ones back to their families for a costly ransom, but Jacques had refused; he feared their secret trade would be exposed and brought to an end by federal agents who couldn't be bought. Then there were always a few who either died in the swamps trying to escape or caused so much trouble that they were killed in front of the others to set an example. There had been an attempted escape just last week, but she had been caught a mile from the camp. Jean had been there to administer her punishment. She had been stripped naked and tied to a tree, where instead of whipping her, which would have left unsightly scars, she was sexually abused repeatedly by the entire band of Creole guards. She would be broken and mentally scarred for the remainder of her life, but still a saleable asset.

Duke had been missing now for six months and it had been three months since Jean had been to Memphis. His father had reported Duke as a missing person and the Cadillac as a stolen vehicle to the local police, who had subsequently contacted the Memphis Police, telling them that Memphis was his last known location. At least that was what Detective Flint had told his father and mother. Last week he had gone by their house and told them there hadn't been any news about their son or the missing car and the case was officially closed. Jean didn't believe the cops had made any effort to find his brother. They were too involved with the family's illegal business and didn't want to involve any outside police. If anything were to be done, he would have to do it himself. Shit, he didn't want to go back to Memphis. He didn't know a damn soul up there and somebody had already killed both of his brothers and that had been no easy task. Who in the hell were they dealing with, and did he really want to know? His father would make him go back, along with a couple of Creoles who would report directly to his mother. He would have to make an effort, but maybe they wouldn't find anyone and he could return home in a few days. Jean liked being second in command, knowing that someday soon the business would be all his.

Jean opened the door and yelled, "Tera, get your ass out of bed and go get us a couple of po'boys and some red beans and rice, I'm fuckin' starvin'! Don't fool around, I mean it!"

"All right already, stop yelling at me. You're makin' my head hurt," Tera replied as she went out the door, slamming it behind her.

Thirty minutes later Tera was back with the food and Jean wasted little time taking it out on the balcony, where they sat at a green wrought-iron table with two matching chairs. Very little was said as they ate their food like two shipwrecked sailors. When they finally came up for air, Tera told Jean that she had scored several girls names from last night and the hotels where they were staying.

Jean smiled, "Sounds good, ma chérie, let's take two tonight. I'll bring the knockout drops and you slip the Mickey Finn into their drinks. Let's do one at a time. Get one of them off by herself and I'll be watching; when I drive up, bring her to my car and help her into the backseat and I'll take her from there. After I leave, wait thirty minutes and drug the next one. I'll be back in time to pick her up and drop her off. When I return we'll go have us a few drinks to celebrate a good night's work. Now go on home, I gotta go see my mama and daddy."

Jean crossed the bridge into Algiers, turned left on Verret Street and then right on Pelican Avenue. He pulled his car into the backyard and parked under the big oak tree. His mama was sitting on the porch, drinking her ice tea and peach brandy. She usually started drinking around noon and drank until she went to bed. Jean figured that was how she coped with his old man. It was a wonder that she hadn't cut his throat years ago. Jean walked up the steps to the porch and kissed his mother on the cheek and asked her how she was doing.

"Not so good, I got the rheumatiz and my knees and back hurt like the devil."

Jean offered her his sympathy. Then he asked, "Where's Daddy? I come by to tell him that I'm gonna take the boat and a couple of men and head to Memphis next week. I want to see if anyone on the dock can remember seeing our boat. If there's not any new information, I'm coming back home for good."

Leona answered contritely, "Yo' daddy's in the house and he's been in a black mood ever since that cop told him they was gonna quit lookin' for your brothers. I just want to lay my sons to rest where they was raised. I worry their spirits are lost and won't never rest till they're home." Jean patted his mama's hand and walked away, knowing there was nothing he could say to make her feel any better. Jean's visit with his daddy was even worse. Jacques ranted and raved, his speech laced with profanity and unfounded accusations. Jean slipped out the back door while his daddy carried on, unaware that his son was gone. Jean thought that his daddy had finally gone mad—he had always been an evil bastard, but now, in Jean's opinion, he was as crazy as a run-over dog.

Jean parked the car near the corner of Toulouse and Bourbon streets, while he waited for Tera to bring their first mark. Within a few minutes Tera turned the corner onto Toulouse Street, leading a young brunette who walked unsteadily and, without the support provided by Tera, would have undoubtedly fallen to the pavement. Jean opened the rear door and the two women got in the car. He drove a block south, turned right on Royal Street and pulled to the curb where Tera got out of the car and started walking back toward Bourbon Street.

Jean crossed the bridge into Algiers and drove to a warehouse on Morgan Street. He knocked three times on the door and two Creoles came to carry the now-sleeping victim inside to be locked away on the third floor. Jean turned the car around and returned to the French Quarter. After an hour of waiting Jean was mad and it was getting worse by the minute. He hated waiting. It just increased the chances of something going wrong.

Suddenly, Tera and a very pretty blonde came walking down the street holding hands and chatting like best friends. Jean was surprised when Tera opened the passenger door and slid across the seat, followed closely by the blonde, who said, "Hi! I'm Veronica Chandler, but just call me Vicki."

Tera said, "Miss Vicki is in town with some of her friends from Georgia, who she believes to be boring and, in her words, 'regular old fuddy-duddys.' I was telling her about my handsome beau and how great he was in bed and she said she had heard about a ménage-à-trois and wanted to know if we were interested."

Jean's interest was piqued, "Is that right, Miss Vicki? You're interested in a three-way with me and Tera?"

Vicki replied boldly, "Only if you think you can handle it, big boy. I'm away from home and looking to take a walk on the wild side." She solidified her intentions when she turned and kissed Tera on the lips and placed her hand between Tera's legs and slowly caressed her upper thighs. Tera responded with passion and Jean drove rapidly to his apartment.

The three were busy removing clothes as they climbed the stairs to the bedroom. Jean finished undressing Vicki when with both hands he tore away her panties and pushed her back on the bed. Tera, not wanting to be left out, pulled Jean's pants down and placed her mouth around his manhood. Vicki lay naked on the bed, watching with keen interest. Jean pushed Tera back onto the bed and lay on his back between the two women, kissing one and then the other.

Over the next two hours it became a free-for-all. All three sexual partners participated recklessly in a scorching love triangle. When the three stopped to catch their breath, Jean persuaded Vicki to let him tie her hands to the headboard with colorful silk scarves. Thinking this was a part of the sexual experience, she also allowed him to tie her feet to the bedposts, leaving her totally vulnerable. Tera straddled Vicki and begin kissing her neck and breasts while Jean went into the kitchen. Vicki was experiencing sexual ecstasy when Jean slipped the needle in her vein and pushed the heroine into her bloodstream. Vicki looked at Jean with surprise but Tera drew her attention back by licking and fondling her until she screamed with delight. Jean liked the power he now held over her and pushed Tera to the side. He penetrated Vicki with a hard thrust, pumping harder and deeper with every stroke. Vicki was aware of an intense pleasure she had never felt before. At times, she felt as if she was floating above the bed with Jean deep inside of her, touching very sensitive places, and then she began to climax, over and over, each orgasm growing in intensity, one becoming continuous with the next until it seemed they would never stop. Her pleasure spun out of control, becoming almost unbearable, and finally she reached nirvana. Her mind was overcome with an imperturbable stillness free of desire, aversion and delusion, and then she slept.

Jean rolled off Vicki and lay on his back, totally exhausted, thinking it was too bad he couldn't keep this one for his very own. Vicki was in a deep sleep and Tera was sitting naked on the balcony drinking a glass of wine. Jean knew that Tera wasn't sexually satisfied and that after he rested she would want him again, this time with his full attention on her pleasures only. He had given Vicki a large dose of heroine and she would stay asleep until at least midmorning. He would keep her drugged in the apartment until he and Tera grew tired of using her. After that, maybe he would ship her to the slave camp with the others.

Something she said earlier remained in his mind. She apparently was the only daughter of a very wealthy businessman from Atlanta, Georgia, who owned part of a very large soda pop company. Maybe he could convince her to marry him. Being a part of the family would allow him to live a very comfortable lifestyle while they waited to inherit millions of her daddy's money.

CHAPTER 20

Monday morning started out very similar to Sunday; Sam found himself alone in bed again. He could hear the rattle of pots and pans in the kitchen and the enthusiastic voices of Nathalie and Adelle conversing in French. He dressed for work and went to the kitchen for a cup of coffee. Adelle was in a joyous mood. Sam knew it was because her parents were arriving today. The kitchen was filled with the wonderful aroma of fresh-baked bread and cake.

All Sam received was a kiss, his coffee, and a sheet of paper listing the time of arrival for the train and names of her family, including two girl cousins. She patted him on the butt as he went out the door and reminded him once again of her family's arrival time. Sunday had been filled with a flurry of activity as well. Adelle and Nathalie had begun baking and cleaning house at seven o'clock in the morning, then went to mass at Saint Peter Catholic Church at eleven. It had become Sam's responsibility to get Samantha dressed and ready for church. After returning home from church, Adelle asked Sam to call and reconfirm the hotel reservations at the Peabody and call the train station to see if her family's train had left New York City on time. Sam realized that a lot of the flurry was brought on by Adelle's need to make their wedding and their home perfect for the exciting time. He wanted her to be happy and was willing to help in any way that he could. He spent all afternoon taking care of and playing with Samantha while Adelle and Nathalie hung new curtains in every room of the house.

Sam knew he had failed terribly in acquiring knowledge and understanding of activities surrounding weddings. He had previously thought that a man and a woman showed up at the church with a few friends and a preacher, got married, and lived happily ever after. That was dang sure not the situation he now faced and it was a little too late to change his mind. He was glad it was Monday and he was heading to work where everything would be close to normal. He had a routine that he was accustomed to following and right now he wanted and needed to be busy doing the things he understood.

He had promised to call Bobby Hernreich some time after noon to confirm his itinerary and find out if he was bringing a date to the wedding. He was looking forward to seeing his friend again and felt honored that he would travel this far to attend his wedding. Sam wondered if Bobby and Jack would behave themselves in the presence of all of the women who would be at the wedding. He needed to find out if Bobby would be in town for the rehearsal dinner.

At noon Sam and Jack drove to David Hinkle's office in the Ford pickup. Sam had called David earlier and invited him to lunch. Being his typical self, he said Pat had made him a sack lunch and he should probably stay at work. Sam refused to take no for an answer, and David finally caved in to the pressure. He was waiting in the marina parking lot when they arrived. Sam scooted over next to Jack, making room for his friend, and the three of them were on their way to the Dixie Café.

Sam immediately asked Dave for some fatherly advice. He started with some "What if?" questions. Soon Dave and Jack were laughing at Sam's fear of the unknown. The normally cool and confident husband-to-be was having a pity party and it lasted until they were seated in the café.

A bit more seriously, Dave asked, "What's got you the most worried, Sam? You know that when it's all said and done, very little will change except Adelle and Samantha's last name."

Sam gave the question careful consideration before he answered. "I guess it's her daddy. I soiled his daughter's reputation by getting her pregnant and leaving the country without asking her to marry me. If the same thing happened to me, I would think long and hard about cuttin' the balls off such a man."

Jack said, "Hell, man, you didn't know you had gotten her pregnant and I know that even before you knew about Samantha, you were hoping to marry her someday. You need to get that bullshit out of your head, big brother."

Dave added, "Jack's made a good point—you didn't know, but you do know that it takes two to tango. You and Adelle were two consenting adults. I think her father should be proud to have you as a son-in-law. I advise you to walk up, look the man in the eye, and shake his hand like the proud man you are."

"Thanks, guys. I guess I need to tell you more, because there's something else I haven't told either of you. Adelle's father is a wealthy man. He comes from old money and enterprises that have passed from one generation to the next for over a hundred years. I'm just an uneducated farm boy, born from generations of poverty and heir to nothing but hard times. If he thinks that I'm not good enough for his daughter, then he's probably right."

"Sam! Sam, you're overreacting. You might have been born to a family with little coin or material possessions, but you inherited character and determination. I see it in you every day. You're building a business here and you're doing it with integrity and hard work. Stop degrading yourself and start acting like the man you've become. I say this as your friend, and it's your friendship that I value."

Those kind words spoken by Dave Hinkle meant more to Sam than he could verbally express. He remained silent for a period of time before he spoke. "Thanks for your confidence in me. You're right, I have been doubting myself, but from this day forward, I promise I will act like the proud father I am and the husband I want to become."

With that, Sam signaled for the waitress and said, "Let's order lunch before Jack dies of starvation."

Jack laughed with relief, saying, "Thank God for the small things, and by the way, you're paying for lunch."

During lunch, Sam passed around the paper Adelle had given him before he left home. He hoped talking about them would help him remember the names. Her father's name was Adrien, her mother was Claire, and brother, André, all with the surname Devaux. The name of her unmarried cousin was Danielle Devaux, and the married cousin was Sasha Babineaux. Jack asked Sam what he knew about them and if the girls were as pretty as Adelle. "That's been part of the problem. I know very little about any of them. Adelle doesn't elaborate about her family problems, if there are any. By the way, Jack, you're coming with me to the train station. You can decide for yourself if her cousins are pretty while you're carrying their luggage."

They had dropped Dave back at the Port of Memphis a couple of hours ago and had returned to their warehouse, hoping to get a little work done. Sam failed to accomplish very much. He called Bobby and enjoyed a spirited conversation about his personal life and his plans. He would be arriving, by himself, on Friday afternoon. Sam looked at his watch constantly, still nervous with anticipation. He and Jack needed to leave soon. He would drive the Buick to the house and pick up Adelle and Samantha. Jack would bring the pickup truck to the station for hauling luggage. He stuck his head in Jack's office and told him he was leaving.

"Don't worry, big brother. I'll be there when the train rolls in."

Sam was standing on the platform of Memphis's Grand Central Station. He was holding Samantha when Jack walked up and asked where Adelle was. Sam told him she was in the diner getting Samantha a soda pop. He had been reading a plaque on the side of the building and started telling Jack about what he had learned: "This place was built as a central station in 1914 and it serves trains running north and south, and then there is Union Station two blocks north, which serves trains running east and west. There are seven different railways using this station and we're waiting on the Louisville and Nashville Railroad. Also another bit of information is that the trains stopping here can unload and keep going in the direction of their next destination. The trains at Union Station have to stop up the track and back in."

"Wow, Sam, you're just full of valuable information. I'll be sure and keep that in mind the next time I need to go somewhere."

Adelle returned with a bottle of Orange Crush soda, Samantha's favorite. After greeting Jack with a hug, she thanked him for coming to help.

"It's my pleasure. A team of horses couldn't keep me from this."

Samantha spotted the train first. She pointed and said, "Choo-choo," as everyone laughed.

Adelle kissed her on the cheek, saying, "Yes sweetheart, that's mémé and papi's choo-choo and they're coming to see you."

Samantha's eyes lit up even more. "Comin, mémé and papi, on the choo-choo twain." Soon the train clanged to a screeching halt, causing Samantha to cover her ears.

Passengers began to get off the train in large numbers and Adelle searched for familiar faces in the crowd. Soon, she yelled with delight and began running toward a group of well-dressed passengers. Sam followed her at a distance, still holding Samantha in his arms. As he came close to the group, Samantha started squirming and wanting down. He sat her down and she ran to a middle-aged woman whom he assumed was Claire, Adelle's mother. Sam stopped and waited, watching the reaction as his daughter became the focal point of their attention. The family had many things to say, but Sam understood only a word of the French here and there. Finally, he was acknowledged by a handsome fellow close to his own age, who stepped forward with his hand extended in greeting. The moment had arrived: it was time to meet the family. Sam shook his hand and he introduced himself in English as André Devaux. Next, Adelle introduced Sam to her mother and two cousins.

Sam said, "Hello! Nice to meet y'all."

Smiling, the ladies, replied, "Bonjour!"

Adelle took his hand and turned toward her father, who was holding Samantha. She said, "This is my father, Adrien Devaux."

Looking him directly in the eye, Sam stepped forward, extending his hand, and said, "Hello, Monsieur Devaux. I'm Sam Cooper, the proud father of your granddaughter and, with your permission, the future husband of your beautiful daughter. Thank you for coming."

Adrien Devaux shifted Samantha to his left arm, and shook Sam's hand.

"*Merci pour ma petite fille*, or as you Americans would say, thank you for my granddaughter. She is very important to me. You and I have much to talk about, but let's find a more pleasant setting. Shall we leave this train station? I'm ready to see more of your city."

As expected, Jack had already made acquaintance with the two younger women of the group. Adelle introduced him to her parents and all together they proceeded to the suitcases that had been unloaded.

An hour or so later, after Adelle's family was comfortably situated in the Peabody hotel, Sam invited André and Mr. Devaux to go with Jack and him to the warehouse to see that part of their operation, and to sample a glass of Tennessee whiskey. This would give the women time to visit and get dressed for dinner.

The next few days were carbon copies of one another: during the mornings, Sam would take the men to breakfast at a different diner each day, and then show them around the Memphis area. One day he had taken them to Nut Bush to see the slaughterhouse and meet Jimbo. The next day they met Dave Hinkle and toured the port. They would return home for lunch with the women, squeeze in a nap and then take the women wherever they wanted to go.

On Wednesday night, Freddie Clanton treated the entire family to dinner at The Rib Palace as part of his wedding present. It was a huge hit with the nouveau Americans. When dinner was served, Freddie was on hand to cheerfully wish everyone "*Bon appétit.*" Sam told the Devaux family that all of the pork served at dinner came from Cooper Brothers and quite possibly was grown on one of the farms in Nut Bush. After dinner, Mr. Devaux complimented Freddie on his fine cuisine, thanked him for his excellent service and wished him great success in the future. Jack and Gina acted as late-evening hosts for Danielle, Sasha and André. They listened to jazz on Beale Street, mingled with the locals, and soaked up the Memphis atmosphere.

Thursday night the entire wedding party was driven to Anderton's Restaurant and Oyster Bar on Madison Avenue for dinner and drinks. With the exception of a few tables near the front, Rose had reserved the entire restaurant, knowing from experience that it served fresh seafood and was within walking distance of the Peabody. The first course served was fresh oysters on the half shell, a delicacy that neither Jack nor Sam had ever tried before. After a fair amount of coaxing and teasing, Jack was the first to down a raw oyster and was followed shortly by an extremely reticent groom, who was coerced without humility by his beautiful bride-to-be. Sam, after washing it down with a slug of cold beer, offered an opinion, "The first person in history that ate a raw oyster was either on the edge of starvation or a very brave soul indeed." He was rewarded with a round of applause and a kiss from Adelle.

The main course was boiled shrimp, lobster and crab legs, fried shrimp, grilled red fish and grouper, served with boiled potatoes and corn on the cob. After dinner the ladies headed back to the Peabody to take food to Samantha and Nathalie. All of the men headed to Beale Street to celebrate Sam's bachelor party. Sam, if given a choice, would have preferred to go home, but this was a tradition and he didn't want to disappoint anyone. The first stop was the Tap Room and Adelle's father bought a round of tequila shots; Freddie Clanton bought a second round and the party was off and running. After an hour of laughing and drinking Sam decided to buy drinks for the members of the band that had been singing the blues. The band appreciated the gesture and dedicated a song to Sam's upcoming marriage. They sang a T-Bone Walker song titled, "Mean Old World" and were rewarded with a round of tequila shots, courtesy of André, who, as it turned out, could play piano. When the band came back from a session break he was allowed to play a song with the band. It was the Robert Johnson song "Sweet Home Chicago" and Sam and Jack were also invited on stage to sing along. They were joined by all of their friends and practically everyone else in the bar as the band played an extended version of the rowdy song.

Everyone in the bar seemed to be having a great time when fate intervened and Earl, the redneck cook from the now-defunct Mack's Burgers, walked in and recognized Sam. He hadn't learned his lesson from his previously broken jaw and decided to start running his mouth, threatening Sam with a broken beer bottle. Sam at this point was feeling bulletproof and fully intended to kick the redneck's ass again, but was denied the opportunity when Jack seemed to come out of nowhere and poleaxed Earl with a roundhouse punch that started below his knees and ended on the side of the redneck's head. Earl was out like a light, never knowing who hit him. The bartender, in a gesture of goodwill, suggested they leave before the cops showed up and hauled them off to jail.

As a group, they thanked the band and the bartender and headed for The Black Diamond nightclub down the street to drink a toast to Jack's first-round knockout. After congratulatory backslaps and a hip, hip hooray, drinks were finished and cabs were called to take everyone home.

Friday night was the wedding rehearsal night at Saint Peter Catholic Church. The rehearsal started at six o'clock and lasted for about an hour. Sam and Jack felt like two fish out of water, but managed somehow to satisfy both Adelle and the rather pedantic priest in attendance. All of the men, except Bobby, were nursing hangovers and Jack's right hand was bruised and swollen. Sam noticed that Bobby was focused on Danielle, flashing his best smile and flirting with her whenever he got a chance. Hell, maybe he would fall for her and become part of the family.

Adelle was watching Sam with loving eyes and thinking of the previous night. She had been highly amused at Sam's lack of sobriety when he returned home from the bachelor party. She found him to be funny and highly agreeable to all of her suggestions. She suspected something out of the ordinary had happened but Sam remained mum, just smiling to himself. After helping him undress and get into bed he became sexually persistent and Adelle had humorously called him a horny Casanova. She had pretended to resist his advances but, in the end, hadn't been able to resist her own desires.

Sam was also thinking about last night. His memory was lacking in detail, but he distinctly remembered the highlights and they made him smile. He had awakened Friday morning with a headache, concerned that Adelle might be upset with him for coming home drunk. After making coffee, taking two aspirin and drinking a large glass of water, he had fixed her breakfast in bed. She was surprised, but pleased, and didn't seem upset with him after all. As they ate, she told him how wonderful and helpful Pat, Gina and Rose had been. They, with the help of her mother, had taken care of all the last-minute details surrounding the wedding, allowing her to spend precious time with her family. She showed him Samantha's little dress. It was the same color as the rose petals she would carry down the aisle. Sam, knowing how much time and effort she had put into the selection, had assured her it was beyond beautiful.

Sam had taken Adelle, Samantha and Nathalie to the Peabody on his way to pick up Bobby Hernreich at the railway station. After the rehearsal dinner they would spend the night in the extra rooms at the Peabody—Adelle had assured him that it would be more fun if the anticipation of the wedding and the honeymoon were spiced up by a brief separation.

Bobby had arrived in his fashionable splendor, carrying a long, wrapped box in one hand and a shopping bag in the other. Sam had taken him to lunch at Freddie's place. Over lunch they swapped tales. They both had a big belly laugh when Freddie told his version of the bachelor party highlights, witnessed live with his own bloodshot eyes. After lunch, Sam had dropped Bobby off at the Peabody for a nap and a shower. Sam asked him to be dressed and ready by five o'clock. Before leaving for the church he wanted to calm his nerves with a stiff drink from the hotel bar. After the rehearsal, everyone returned to the Peabody for dinner in the ballroom. The only empty tables were those reserved for the wedding party. The remainder was filled with friends, customers and a handful of city officials, all listening to the music of the Lucky Millinder Orchestra.

The orchestra played soft music during dinner, stopping only when Sam tapped his glass with a spoon and asked for every-one's attention. He gave a short, but heartfelt speech and thanked everyone for coming and then asked the orchestra to resume playing. Adelle and Sam danced to a couple of songs, the first after dinner and the last song of the evening. The time in between was spent meeting and greeting their guests, thanking them for coming to dinner and encouraging them to attend the wedding ceremonies the following day. Sam did not really want to be away from his fiancée and daughter for the night, but this was Adelle's plan and she had carefully and thoughtfully worked to make certain the wedding would go smoothly. He kissed her goodnight in front of the hotel and told her he would see her tomorrow.

The plan was for the men of the wedding party to meet at Sam's house around noon for lunch. Rose and Pat, who had been so sincere and helpful throughout the week, came by to prepare a delicious lunch for the men. The tuxes had been delivered to their house the day before and the men would dress for the wedding there and leave for the church together. A little before noon all of the men arrived at the house for lunch. Bobby was carrying the long box under his arm. Sam was curious as to what it contained but he didn't have to wait long to find out. After lunch, Bobby presented the box to Adrien Devaux, and the very surprised father of the bride opened the box to find a new 12-gauge Winchester pump action shotgun. The joke was obvious to all of the American men, but Mr. Devaux was confused by the gift. Bobby explained that it was an anecdotal colloquialism in this country that the father of the pregnant daughter use an "age-old custom" whereupon he forces a shotgun wedding on the man who had taken liberties with his daughter. This was to ensure that the daughter's social honor would be restored and the unborn child would have both parents.

Adrien, still unsure of his role, asked, "Am I really supposed to take this gun into the church?"

Bobby replied, "No, sir, but we can use it to make sure Sam doesn't have a change of heart at the last minute."

Finally, everyone, including Mr. Devaux, laughed at Sam's expense. A sense of honor compelled Sam to try and explain, but Adrien stopped him and said, "I will be very happy to have you as my son-in-law, but I am going to keep this beautiful shotgun just in case you ever stray from your vows."

The flower-filled church with glorious organ music was magnificent. Little Samantha preceded her mother and grandfather, tossing pink rose petals down the aisle as she led them to the altar. Adelle looked beautiful in her delicate pink gown as she walked down the aisle. Sam, dressed in a handsome black tuxedo, waited proudly. He felt like his heart would burst with happiness, especially when Samantha squeezed between her mother and him. With a happy little smile she handed him her last two rose petals. The homily by the priest was a bit heavy on dogma, but well received by the bride and groom outside the main altar. The vows were those that were part of the marriage rites of the Church. Sam placed the wedding ring on Adelle's finger and she in turn placed a beautiful wedding band on his. Finally, they were pronounced man and wife and Sam kissed his bride.

After a receiving line, the wedding party and those guests who wanted to attend gathered in the narthex of the church for the cutting of the four-tiered wedding cake and a glass of champagne.

Adelle tossed her bouquet, which was caught by Gina. Sam and Adelle exited the church, surrounded by throngs of well-wishers tossing rice. They were headed to their home to be alone and enjoy their wedding night. Tomorrow they would leave on their honeymoon and only Adelle knew the destination.

CHAPTER 21

Sam and Adelle slept late on their first morning as man and wife. They had enjoyed having the entire house all to themselves on their wedding night. Spontaneous lovemaking had taken place in the living room shortly after returning home from the wedding, with Adelle still wearing her wedding dress pulled high above her waist and Sam taking only enough time to drop his pants around his ankles. Sam held his climax longer than he thought possible but lost all control when Adelle began biting and sucking on his neck, raking his back and shoulders with her long fingernails and matching his rapid thrusts with her own enthusiasm. Adelle wrapped her long, slender legs around Sam's waist and felt the deep penetration of his rock hard shaft before crying out as she experienced the intensity of her first orgasm of the night. More orgasms soon followed after they stripped each other naked and moved their lovemaking into the bedroom, teasing and pleasing each other for hours while declaring over and over their everlasting love for one another.

Around midnight they had wandered naked into the kitchen looking for food and refreshment. After eating a piece of pie and drinking a glass of wine at the kitchen table, Adelle began rubbing Sam's crotch with her bare foot as she leaned back in her chair with her eyes closed, and slowly running her tongue back and forth across her lips. Sam responded like a young stud, pulling her to her feet, placing her back against the cool metal of the refrigerator before lifting her up and penetrating her slowly as she cooed with pleasure. They made love slowly, sharing deep passionate kisses, and then, to Adelle's surprise and ultimate delight, Sam bent her over the kitchen table and took her hard and fast, driving his hard shaft back and forth against the tiny bud of pink taught flesh nestled in its hidden crevice, creating within her the strongest sexual arousal of her memory. Adelle climaxed with an orgasm so powerful she was left too weak to stand and remained laying across the table until Sam gathered her in his arms and carried her to their bedroom. She fell asleep cradled in his arms, smiling and very happy that this wonderful man was her husband.

In the morning, Adelle lay in bed listening to a local jazz station on the radio. She could hear Sam whistling a tune while taking a shower. Sam was her soul mate; she had known this since the first night they met. He made her feel safe, he made her happy, and most of all she could tell that he loved her as much as she loved him. When he came into the bedroom with a towel wrapped around his waist and his dark hair wet and combed back, she thought he was the most handsome man she had ever seen. She asked him to sit down on the bed—it was time to share their honeymoon destination.

Adelle took Sam's hand and asked, "Sweetheart, do you want to know where we're going today?"

Sam smiled his slow southern smile and winked at her, "Well, it might help me choose the right kind of clothes to pack. But, as long as you're going with me I don't really care where we go."

"Well, you should pack for the Kentucky Derby, because that's where we're going."

Sam jumped to his feet and exclaimed, "You're teasing me, aren't you?"

"I'm not," she said as she smiled. "We're taking the 4:10 train to Louisville. Bobby and Danielle are going to be on the train with us. They are going on to New York for a few days and returning to Louisville on Friday for the Derby. My parents and brother are going to drive our car and meet us in Lexington on Thursday."

"How are we going to get around when we get there tomorrow and who's going to take care of Samantha if your family leaves? " Sam queried.

"We have a car rented from Hertz Rail-Drive and it will be waiting on us when we get off the train. The first few nights we'll be staying at the Hotel Lafayette in Lexington. You said that you wanted to talk to a couple of bourbon distilleries and I thought that you might want to look at a few horse farms that are for sale. Sasha and Nathalie will stay with Samantha and Gina and your brother will help as well. Mr. and Mrs. Hinkle have also pledged their help if it's needed."

With a puzzled expression, Sam asked, "What did you mean when you said we can look at horse farms for sale, and do we have tickets for the Kentucky Derby already?"

"Yes, we have tickets for the Derby. My father has always wanted to go to Kentucky on the first Saturday in May, so with the help of David Hinkle, he reserved a box that seats eight people. He's also interested in purchasing some land in the States. I told him of your new fascination with racehorses and he wants to look at horse farms that are for sale."

All of the good news had Sam's head spinning, so he sat back on the bed to let it all sink in. Finally, he asked if her parents were moving to Kentucky.

"No, but they would like to come to Kentucky once or twice a year to visit their grandchildren."

Sam was really confused now. "What do you mean when you say 'visit their grandchildren' in Kentucky?"

"Well, sweetheart, I missed my period this month. I don't know for sure, but I could be pregnant with our second child," she said as she studied his face, waiting for a reaction. She continued, "I also hoped you would consider turning over the day-to-day business operations to your brother and spend some time raising our children on a horse farm."

"How long have you known about all of this and why are you just now telling me?"

"I may or may not be pregnant, that's why I haven't said anything before now. Going to the Kentucky Derby is a wedding present from my family and they wanted it to be a surprise. And finally, my family and I have only had the last few days to discuss buying a farm and unless you've forgotten, we've had a very busy week."

"Damn it, Adelle, that's a helluva lot of information and I need some time to think about what you've told me!"

"Sam, I know this is a lot for you to consider, but we can discuss it further when we get on the train. Let's eat some lunch and get ready for our trip. I love you and whatever you decide is fine with me. Now kiss me and get dressed, we have a train to catch."

Jack arrived a little after two o'clock to drive them to the train station. As always, Sam was glad to see his brother and invited him into the house.

"I hear you're going to Kentucky to watch a big ole horserace," Jack said and winked at Adelle.

"Well, it seems that everyone around me knew before I did. But, I may be more excited than anyone else because Citation is running and he's my favorite racehorse. While I'm there I intend to secure us a line of Kentucky bourbon, maybe two or three. I'm going to go see Seagram, the distillers of Four Roses and Jim Beam, Brown-Forman, the distillers of James E. Pepper Bourbon and the Ripy brothers, who make Wild Turkey."

"Sam, that sounds good and I hope you get it done. We really need a line of Kentucky bourbon to sell our clients. But let's stick to the business at hand—I have a thousand dollars in my pocket and I want you to bet it on the nose of the horse you think will win. Now, let's get all of the bags loaded and get you and Adelle to the train."

Laughing, Sam said, "Damn, little brother that's a lot of money to bet on a horse race. I hope like hell that I don't get robbed by some Kentucky hard boot."

When Sam and Adelle were finally on board the train and seated next to Bobby and Danielle, Adelle leaned over to kiss Sam on the cheek and she whispered, "I think Bobby may have fallen in love and I know Danielle is infatuated with his good looks and charm."

Sam had noticed the same thing. Bobby and Danielle were holding hands and acting like a couple of lovebirds.

After dinner he took Bobby into the smoking coach for an after-dinner cigar. When they were alone, Sam said, "Hey old buddy, you're acting like a love-smitten teenager. So, what have you got to say for yourself?"

Bobby blushed at the question and his answer was surprisingly sincere. "Man, I don't know. I've never met a woman like Danielle before and she's got my heart in her hands. She's beautiful, smart, classy and the best damn romance I've ever had and I don't want to go anywhere without her."

Sam put his arm around Bobby's shoulders and said, "I know the feelings you're talking about. I felt the same way about Adelle after just one night of being together. It must be something that runs in the family's bloodline. They're so damn sexy and never afraid of telling you how they feel. I'm gonna buy us a couple of glasses of bourbon and we're going to drink a toast to the charming Devaux girls."

Sam told Bobby about Adrien Devaux's plans of buying a horse farm and Adelle's desire to raise their kids in the bluegrass state. Bobby thought it sounded like a great idea and promised to come visit. After talking for a while they retired to the sleeping car where their ladies were waiting.

The trained arrived in Louisville soon after the couples had finished breakfast. Bobby and Danielle got off the train to stretch their legs and wish Sam and Adelle a safe and prosperous week. After promising to return for the weekend they boarded the train and Sam went to find the luggage while Adelle went to pay for the rented car.

Adelle returned shortly with the keys to a Chrysler Town and Country four-door sedan, a car large enough for their luggage and adequate room for seven passengers. After loading the car and receiving driving directions Sam took the wheel and headed for Lexington.

The route chosen took them close to Lawrenceburg and the Seagram office located at the Four Roses distillery. Sam suggested they stop and tour the facility and Adelle agreed. Sam parked in front of a Spanish mission-style stone building and he and Adelle went inside where Sam introduced himself as a Tennessee liquor distributor looking to add a line of Kentucky bourbon to his inventory. They were shown into the office of E.W. Davidson, the director of sales. After introductions, Sam told him about Cooper Brothers' distribution business and his desire to sell Four Roses Bourbon in Memphis. Mr. Davidson asked several business questions related to volume of sales, age of the business and Sam's financial credibility.

When it looked as if Cooper Brothers would be turned down due to the short amount of time they had been in business, Adelle interrupted and said, "Mr. Davidson, Sam and I are here on our honeymoon and have taken time out of our schedule to visit your facility. My maiden name was Devaux and my family owns a vineyard and winery in the South of France and my father is, at this moment, making arrangements for our wine to be shipped Stateside with Cooper Brothers being the sole distributor. This will undoubtedly increase the sales volume of my husband's company and give he and his brother international credibility. I am asking you to consider this when making your final decision."

Davidson broke into a smile, winked at Sam, and said to Adelle, "I am familiar with your wine and know a little of your family's history. I admire your sense of purpose on behalf of your husband's company and with you by his side I am sure the company will continue to grow and prosper. It would be my pleasure to supply our bourbon to Cooper Brothers for resale in Memphis and any other regional markets you can service west of the Mississippi River."

Sam, beaming with pride, stood and offered his hand, "Adelle and I would be proud to do business with you and sell what I believe to be the finest Kentucky bourbon made. I thank you for this opportunity and, with my wife and brother's help, I believe it will be a successful venture. My wife and I are going to the Kentucky Derby this weekend and would be honored to have you as our guest."

Davidson thanked him for the invitation, stating that he had made prior arrangements with a group of friends that attended the Derby every year. In turn, he invited Sam and Adelle to bring their friends and family to a large party to be held in Louisville the evening before the Derby, proclaiming it to be the best of the best and assuring them it would be attended by many celebrities, dignitaries and people of interest. He wrote down the address in Louisville and handed it to Sam. Adelle thanked him and she and Sam left the office and headed for Lexington.

The Hotel Lafayette, a twelve-story hotel, was located on Main Street in downtown Lexington and within walking distance of several fine restaurants. After checking into the honeymoon suite and resting for an hour, Sam and Adelle dressed for dinner and walked a brief distance to the area's newest restaurant. Columbia's Steakhouse had opened in February and after only two months had become a Lexington institution and the local hangout for public officials and police.

Both Sam and Adelle enjoyed the Diego Salad and the beef tenderloin that was served with a dollop of garlic butter melting on top. Sam watched and listened as his wife and the headwaiter discussed the available wine selection and together agreed upon a bottle of Château du Cèdre 1944, a Malbec wine of dark color produced in the French Bordeaux region and, according to Adelle, served primarily with red meat and often referred to as the "black wine of Cahors."

The headwaiter suggested they retire to the back room after dinner, where they would find an array of gaming tables and complimentary drinks. He told them that the gaming room was available by invitation only and even though gaming was illegal in the state of Kentucky, it was overlooked by the local police who themselves enjoyed the gambling and free booze. Sam thanked him and told him they would give it a go.

Sam's winnings were offset by Adelle's losses, but by the end of the night they had become acquainted with two judges, the chief of police, the county sheriff, a bank president, several lawyers and a real estate broker named Bill. If they bought a farm, most of the people they met could be very helpful in one way or another. Bill had promised to pick them up at ten o'clock the next morning and show them two farms that were for sale. One farm was between Versailles and Midway and the other was between Versailles and Frankfort, both located on a limestone ridge that ran from the south of Versailles to the north of Midway. The farms were reported to have very fertile soil and an ample supply of artesian spring water.

Bill was eating breakfast in the hotel restaurant when Sam and Adelle came downstairs the following morning. He invited them to sit at his table and told them they should eat hearty because they would most likely miss lunch. During breakfast Sam told Bill about his liquor business and his desire to meet the sales director of Brown-Forman distillery. Bill informed them that one of the farms they were visiting would be located less than a mile from Brown-Forman and that he knew several people that worked there. Sam asked him if they could stop by the distillery after they looked at the farms and he said he would be happy to oblige.

The first farm was located a few miles south of Midway and contained 155 acres surrounded and divided by four-plank wooden fences. There was a main house and three employee houses, three horse barns, one hay barn and large equipment shed with a repair shop. The entire farm was mowed and manicured and the main house was well landscaped. Sam and Adelle toured the main house and decided it needed a great deal of renovation. Bill said the owners lived out of town and came only a few times during the year.

The second farm was a couple of miles northwest of Versailles near the end of a county road. There were 260 acres of rolling hills and large oak trees and beautiful fields of lush green grass dotted with grazing thoroughbred mares and foals. It was love at first sight. Adelle loved the large colonial style mansion that was the focal point of the tree-lined driveway. Sam loved it all but felt drawn to the beautiful creek that flowed through the middle of the property. Bill told him the creek was called Glenn's Creek and it was the water source used in making bourbon at the Brown-Forman distillery. There were two matching stone bridges that crossed the creek and it was obvious a very skilled stonemason had constructed them. The creek itself was narrow in width but carried a sufficient amount of flow bolstered by numerous artesian springs. Bill noticed Sam's focus on the creek and assured him that as far as he knew the creek ran continuously, even during the driest months of the year. He quickly pointed up the creek where several doe and fawn could be seen grazing on the bluegrass. The five horse barns were also built of native stone and each was a mirror image of the other. The barn roofs were adorned with one large cupola in the center and one smaller on each side and every stall had a window facing outside. Bill told them there were three employee houses on the west side of the farm along with two large hay barns, one large barn used for housing the farm equipment, and one tobacco barn. He further explained that all of that and a forty-acre field used for growing tobacco were hidden from sight of the main residence by the rolling hills.

The house was beautifully furnished and all of the rooms were large and well-lit by natural light during the day. A winding staircase led them upstairs to five spacious bedrooms. The master bedroom opened onto a balcony with a distant view of the Kentucky River flowing northwest toward the Ohio River. Both the living room and master bedroom had hardwood floors and large natural stone fireplaces. The kitchen floor was constructed of carefully laid stone and a large handcrafted carving table stood in the center. The sink was on the outer wall beneath a large window that offered a view of the pretty creek and stone bridges. The dining room and study completed the eastern side of the home and both opened onto a large stone porch that would be perfect for Sam to sit and drink coffee in the mornings as he watched the sun rise in the eastern sky.

Adelle felt at home and didn't want to leave. She told Sam that she believed this farm was one of the most beautiful and pleasant places on earth and offered her family peace and tranquility along with a degree of safety. Sam felt the same and knew that this was the farm they would attempt to purchase.

Bill drove them past the old Oscar Pepper distillery, now known as Brown-Forman, but it was late and Sam decided to come back the next day. He knew Adelle would want to return to the farm for a second look at the house and tour the employee houses and all of the barns. Sam wanted a quiet evening with his wife to discuss their future and the changes they would have to make in their life should they buy the farm. He missed Samantha and before dinner he would call home—hearing her sweet little voice was just what he needed right now. She had brought a joy into his life that he could never have imagined a year ago.

When they returned to the hotel Adelle headed to their suite to freshen up while Sam made reservations for dinner at the hotel restaurant. When he reached the room he could hear the shower

running so he picked up the phone and called the hotel operator and asked her to place a call to his residence in Memphis.
André answered the phone and Sam spoke with him briefly before
asking for his daughter.

He relaxed as soon as he heard her say, "Hello papa! Can you
come home now?"

Sam laughed and talked with her until Adelle came out of the
bathroom wrapped in a towel and reached for the phone. He lay
back on the bed and listened as Adelle talked to Samantha and
then her father. She told him about the farm and how wonderful
it was. He told her they would leave Memphis a day earlier than
planned and arrive in Lexington on Wednesday evening. She
asked him to make sure that Nathalie and Sasha had everything
they needed before leaving and he assured her he would and that
everything would be fine. She spoke briefly with her mother and
brother while Sam changed clothes for dinner.

Dinner was reasonably quiet but pleasant and the two of
them had a chance to converse seriously. Sam let Adelle know
that regardless of the final decision on the farm purchase, he had
responsibilities and obligations in Memphis that would require his
personal involvement. She understood and said she believed that
once her father saw the farm he would have to decide whether he
wanted to purchase it and, if so, it would take at least two months
to complete the transaction. She also suggested that they investigate the possibility of hiring a farm manager to take care of the
farm and the horses they were going to eventually purchase. That
would allow them to continue living in Memphis for the time-
being and come to the farm during the holidays. They would also
need to attend the broodmare sales in the fall and assemble a group
of experienced advisors before purchasing their future bloodstock.

Sam jumped at the chance to mention Dale Hinkle and the
possibility of hiring him away from Dearborn Farm. It would be

a promotion from broodmare manager to farm manager and Sam expressed his belief of Dale's honesty and integrity.

Adelle smiled at his enthusiasm and said, "As you Americans often say, let's not get the cart in front of the horse. My father would need to meet your friend, but first he will decide if he likes the farm as much as we do. Tomorrow we can return to the farm and meet the current manager. We will ask him of his future plans after the farm is sold and meet the rest of the employees under his tutelage."

Sam replied, "That's fine by me. We will go back to the farm tomorrow and after we look at the barns and farmhouses, I'll go to the distillery while you conduct your interviews. For now, I would like to invite you up to our room to enjoy the privileges of matrimony."

"Well, Mr. Cooper, I thought you would never ask."

The next morning they had a casual breakfast and drove out to Oak Lawn Farm, where they met Bill. He told them that he had talked to the owners and they had given their permission for Sam and Adelle to spend time on the farm without him. He told them he had other clients in town for the Derby and needed to spend some time with them. Sam told him that it was fine and that they would be in touch. Adelle reminded him that her parents would be in town tomorrow and would want to see the farm for themselves. Bill promised that he would make the arrangements and drove away.

CHAPTER 22

Jack had been very concerned by the news he had received from Charles Lacella, one of his most trusted employees, and the fact that Sam was on his honeymoon in Lexington some 400 miles away added to his worries.

After making all of his deliveries Chuck had returned to the warehouse, come into Jack's office and closed the door. He had shared some disturbing information that he had learned from his brother Carl, who worked at the Port of Memphis. Carl had been working on the docks yesterday morning when the owner of a boat from New Orleans came to him and asked if he had seen a particular boat arrive in the last few months. He had described the boat belonging to Jack and Sam to a tee. Chuck had said that his brother lied to the stranger by telling him that he'd never seen such a boat in Memphis.

Jack had asked, "What else did he say about this stranger from Louisiana, did he know his name?"

"The man's name was Pascal. Carl said there were a couple of Creoles traveling with him and that they had been in port for a couple of days. He also said two of the three port employees that moved the boat still worked there and would remember the boat. One of the two workers is visiting his family over in Missouri and left before the arrival of Pascal. The other worker, Jude Lawson, recently lost his wife and has started drinking regularly at several of the bars close to the port. Carl believes that Lawson will tell everything if he's approached by Pascal while he's drinking."

Jack had thanked Chuck for the information and asked him to thank his brother for his discretion.

Chuck had stood and looked Jack straight in the eye. "Boss, me and my brother grew up in a rough part of town and we ain't scared to get our hands dirty, if you know what I mean. I just want you to know that I appreciate everything you and your brother have done for me and I'll always have your back."

Jack had been moved by Chuck's declaration of loyalty and decided to share a little more information. "The Pascal family members are known to be involved with other crime families and should be considered armed and dangerous. My brother and I became indirectly involved purely by accident. Tell your brother to let me know if he hears anything interesting and I'd like to know where Pascal is hanging out—I also want to know what the son-of-a-bitch looks like."

"You can count on us and we'll do anything we can to help out," Chuck had promised.

Jack sat back in his chair, trying to decide what he should do. He decided he was not going to bother Sam. He wanted him to enjoy his honeymoon and he was sure that he could manage the situation. He had to decide whether he would kill Pascal himself. Was it worth the risk? The answer was yes. The question was how?

Sam's in-laws had left town this morning and would be in Kentucky by now. He didn't want to scare Nathalie and Sasha but he would feel better if he locked up his apartment and moved into Sam's house until the situation was resolved. He would keep Samantha safe or die trying.

It was time to get a move on; he told Rose he was leaving early and headed toward his apartment. Gina had been living with him for the last month and she would be home soon. He would ask her to go with him to Sam's and tell her he was just being cautious.

After Chuck left the warehouse, he drove to the port to meet up with his brother. Carl was waiting for him down at the dock with two fishing poles and a cricket cage.

Chuck asked, "What are you doing with those dang fishing poles? We need to be out looking for that Louisiana feller and his gang of thieves."

"That's what we're gonna do, little brother. That's their boat right over there and they'll be back here directly. I've got us a couple of bottles of suds tied to a string and chillin' in the river. We won't be suspected of spyin' if we're just sittin' here fishin' and drinkin' beer and when they head back to town we'll follow 'um. When we find out where they're goin', you can go and get Jack."

"That's a helluva plan and maybe we'll catch a mess of fish while we wait. Give me one of them poles and hand me a cricket."

Jack reached the apartment ahead of Gina. He had enough time to put a pistol in the glove box and the sniper's rifle behind the seat of his truck. He also pulled up his pants leg and slipped an Arkansas pig-sticker into his boot. He was packing a suitcase when Gina arrived; he told her Sam had called him at work and asked if the two of them could stay at Sam's house until he returned. Gina thought he could have asked her first but agreed to go along and began packing her own suitcase. Jack hated lying to her, but didn't want to tell her any more than he had to about the Pascal family. He told Gina that he would like to stop by Freddie Clanton's Rib Palace and pick up enough barbeque to feed everyone at Sam's house. She thought that sounded good and they threw their suitcases in the truck and headed downtown.

Gina sat down at the bar and ordered a glass of wine and Jack went looking for Freddie. He found him in his office and told him Jean Pascal was back in town and asking questions about his missing brother. Freddie asked what he could do to help.

Jack replied, "For starters I need enough barbeque to feed five people. I'm moving into Sam's place until he gets back. I also need you to call me if you hear anything that involves Pascal."

Freddie went into the kitchen and returned shortly with a box full of food. He handed the box to Jack and told him he would make some inquiries and call if he had any worthwhile information. Jack thanked him, collected Gina, and headed to Sam's house.

Chuck and Carl had caught a few small-mouth bass and several large crappies and were trying to add to their haul when Pascal and his crew walked up. Without so much as a hello, he asked them the whereabouts of a good restaurant. Chuck, thinking quickly, sang the praises of The Rib Palace. Pascal asked for directions and Chuck supplied them. Pascal walked away without thanking them and the Lacella brothers began putting away their fishing gear.

Carl was the first to speak, "That's a rude bastard and I don't like him. Why don't you go find Jack and I'll take care of the fish. When I'm finished I'll mosey on down to The Rib Palace and wait across the street until you and Jack get there."

Chuck agreed and drove to Jack's apartment, where he found the place locked up tight, so he headed to Sam's house. Jack's truck was parked in the driveway and several lights were on in the house. When Gina answered the front door, Chuck asked to speak with Jack. She told him Jack was on the back porch playing with Samantha. As he passed through the house he exchanged greetings with Nathalie and Sasha, noting their natural beauty. Jack was surprised when he looked up and saw Chuck standing at the back door. He asked Gina to take Samantha inside and invited Chuck to take a walk with him.

Chuck waited until they were far enough away from the house that the women couldn't hear their conversation and then proceeded to tell Jack what was going on with Pascal.

He said, "Pascal is having dinner at The Rib Palace tonight and my brother is going to meet us there. He should have arrived by now and will be watching the entrance from across the street. If we leave soon, Pascal should still be inside the restaurant where you can get a good look at 'im under the lights."

Jack told him to drive on ahead and he would be there soon. "I want to say goodnight to everyone in the house and I'll meet you at the bar and you can point him out to me. Thanks for your help! I owe you!"

Jack told Gina he had to run an errand. She looked into his eyes, wanting to ask questions, but kissed him instead and asked him to please be careful. He gave Samantha a hug and a kiss, told

Nathalie and Sasha goodnight and reminded the ladies to keep the doors locked until he returned and not to let anyone they didn't know into the house.

Chuck was drinking a Corona at the bar when Jack arrived. Jack ordered the same and took a long pull from the bottle. Chuck told him that Pascal and his crew were sitting at the last table near the window. Jack slowly looked over his right shoulder and observed a dark-complexioned man that looked to be about thirty years old sitting with two other men. He didn't look as big or as evil as his brother but Jack decided he still looked like a dangerous man.

"Chuck, I want you and your brother to go on home now. This is something I need to handle myself and I don't want him to see us together."

Chuck protested, but Jack insisted they leave. Jack waited for a few minutes and went to his truck and drove to his apartment. He shoved the pistol into his belt, grabbed the rifle and walked to the port. He needed to find an elevated location with a good view of Pascal's boat. He wanted to be close enough to shoot Pascal but far enough away to escape the Creoles and outrun them back to his truck. The maintenance shop looked about right, if he could get onto the roof. He found a wooden stepladder behind the office and carried it behind the shop. Once he reached the roof he climbed carefully to the peak. The tin roof was a little slick but the ridgeline of the roof offered a natural gun rest. Now, all he had to do was wait.

Almost an hour passed before he saw one of the Creoles step out of the shadows and board the boat. Jack's pulse quickened and he took a couple of deep breaths to calm his nerves and steady his hand. Soon he saw a group of men approaching. There were more men than Jack expected—he recognized Jude Lawson and Jean Pascal, but there was another white man he didn't recognize and two Creoles.

His first impulse was to take the shot, but then he hesitated. Under his breath he uttered, "Shit!" He knew it was too damn risky and he could see that Jude Lawson was drinking and would probably tell Pascal about his and Sam's arrival in his brother's boat. Right now he wished Sam was here to help him decide what to do. He watched them board and decided now was the time to quietly exit and go home. Maybe he would have another chance tomorrow.

He eased onto the ladder, climbed down and began walking toward his apartment. As he walked he had the eerie sensation he was being followed. The hairs on the back of his neck stood erect and his sense of survival kicked in. He ducked behind a storage building and eased into a recessed doorway. Once again, he took a couple of deep breaths and tried to slow his breathing. He was sure he heard a quiet footstep as someone placed his or her foot carefully on the loose gravel, then nothing.

Finally, he sensed movement, then he saw a shadow moving his way. As the shadow became a person he stepped forward, slamming the butt of the gun into the side of a Creole's head. The man went down hard but scrambled to his feet, wielding a wicked-looking knife, and charged in Jack's direction. Jack stepped to the side, turned his body, grabbed the Creole's arm and, with a rolling hip lock, tossed him hard to the ground. The Creole wasn't done; he rolled over and prepared to get back on his feet.

Jack hit him hard, pounced on his back, and shoved his face into the gravel. Without hesitation, Jack pulled the pig sticker from his boot and thrust it into the stranger's neck at the base of his skull. "Kill or be killed" was the motto that had been drilled into his brain by his commanding officers during the War and his training had taken over. Jack stood and looked around, wondering if the dying Creole was alone. When he saw no one else, he took one last look at the Creole, who was convulsing in the agonal throes of his untimely death.

It was time to get the hell out of Dodge—Jack sprinted to his truck and turned the key, praying it would start. Luck was on his side as he left the apartment in a cloud of dust, slinging gravel as he sped away. He wanted and needed to get to Sam's place and protect the women who had been placed in his care for safekeeping.

As he drove, he decided he needed more help. Chuck was an employee and a friend and Jack appreciated his help, but tomorrow he would talk to someone else and suddenly he knew whom it would be. He was going to Nut Bush to confide in Jimbo. He would tell him about the Pascal brothers and seek his advice and his help. Jack sensed a particular strength in the big and quiet man. He knew very little about Jimbo's past, but he thought of him as a friend and believed he would be a valuable ally. He felt good about his decision and breathed a sigh of relief as he pulled into Sam's driveway.

CHAPTER 23

Sam and Adelle were downstairs at their hotel waiting for Adelle's mother, father and brother to join them for dinner. They had arrived an hour and a half earlier and gone to their rooms to rest. Sam had gone to the old Eliza Pepper distillery in the afternoon while Adelle remained at the farm going over details with the farm manager. To obtain bourbon from Brown-Forman, Sam was required to pay up front for any deliveries that were to be made for the next three months. If Cooper Brothers' distribution company was successful in selling their bourbon and rye over that period of time, credit would be extended to a limit of $1,000. Sam had given the distiller $500 as a security deposit and gone back to the farm. On the trip back to the hotel Adelle bubbled over with excitement. She couldn't wait to share the details with her family tonight and show them the farm in the morning.

Sam was excited about the farm as well, but was beginning to feel the early stages of Derby fever. Post positions had been drawn around noon and there were only seven horses entered in the 1948 Kentucky Derby. Citation and Coaltown were coupled as a single betting interest and Eddie Arcaro was riding Citation. He believed that Citation's biggest competition would be his stable-mate, Coaltown, who was blessed with plenty of early speed. Unfortunately, Calumet Farms' Bewitch was out of the Kentucky Oaks due to a case of sore shins and she was the only three-year-old filly that Sam was familiar with. Maybe he could call Dave Hinkle and get a tip on who to bet on in the Oaks. That would be a job for tomorrow. He could see Adelle's family coming down the stairs and for now he needed to focus on being a good son-in-law.

Adrien, Claire and André joined them at their table and, after greetings were exchanged, the maître d' brought the first bottle of wine that Adelle had ordered earlier. Adrien complimented his daughter on her selection of wine and proposed a toast to a wonderful weekend of racing with family and friends.

Sam asked about their impression of Kentucky so far and Adrien replied, "This is a beautiful country, somewhat sparse in population, but the hills covered in trees and the meadows full of blooming wildflowers are simply majestic. We especially enjoyed the last hour of our drive, passing the beautiful horse farms with their rich green fields and elegant thoroughbreds."

Sam said, "The last, large farm you passed on the left with the white fences was Warren Wright's Calumet Farm. His horses, Citation and Coaltown, will be the favorites running in the Kentucky Derby. I visited the farm last December with my friend Dale Hinkle and saw Whirlaway and Bull Lea, the sire of Citation and Coaltown."

"Yes, we saw the farm and I'm envious of your visit to Calumet. My daughter has mentioned your friend as a possible candidate for farm manager if we should decide to buy a farm here. I look forward to meeting him and I promise to give him proper consideration. Tell me what you think of the farm that we will look at tomorrow."

Sam talked enthusiastically about the farm throughout dinner. He shared his opinions, and confirmed everything that Adelle had told her father previously. He inquired about Samantha, Nathalie and Sasha, and was told they were fine and that his brother Jack would be checking on them daily. The food was good, the service was excellent, and after dessert everyone returned to their rooms— the plan was to get an early start in the morning and complete a thorough tour of the farm.

Bill met them at the farm the next morning and, like any real estate agent worth his salt, he smelled a possible sale. He stayed by Adrien's side throughout the morning and explained all of the reasons he should buy the farm. Sam used the phone in the main house to call Dave Hinkle. Dave answered the call at his office and was happy to hear from Sam. After answering several questions related to their honeymoon trip, Sam asked Dave if he liked any of the fillies entered in the Kentucky Oaks.

Dave replied, "Well, Sam, I don't want you to bet all your money on what I'm going to tell you but I've talked to a couple of my friends that hang around Churchill Downs and I've got two fillies for you. One black groom named Sketch is touting the filly Back Talk and an Irishman named O'Toole really likes a filly named Challe Anne. O'Toole knows the trainer Ridenour and he says she's training through the bridle."

Sam thanked him for the information and asked him how things were going at work. Dave told him there had been some men from New Orleans hanging around the dock asking questions and spending a lot of time drinking with one of his employees. This morning he had given the boat owner, a fellow named Pascal, a forty-eight-hour notice to remove his boat from the docks and he should be gone by Saturday night. Sam's heart skipped a beat and he knew he needed to talk to his brother immediately. Sam told Dave he would call him later and wished him luck getting rid of his problem.

Sam called his office and asked to speak to his brother. Rose told him that Jack wasn't in the office right now, but she would have him return the call later. Sam told her to have him call the hotel and gave her his room number. He was compelled to ask about business and Rose gave him a positive report on everything except a delivery truck that had been taken to the garage for repair. Sam thanked her and told her he would be back in the office on Monday.

He called his house next and Nathalie answered. She told him everything was fine and that Jack and Gina were staying at the house. Sam told her to have Jack call him and asked if he could speak to Samantha. Nathalie asked if he wanted her to wake the baby from her afternoon nap and he said, "No, I'll call back later when she's awake."

Adrien, Adelle, and Bill walked into the house and joined him at the kitchen table. His wife looked at him, smiled and asked him if he had seen any problems with the farm.

"No, I haven't, I'm happy with everything I've seen. I believe that this farm is a small slice of heaven here on earth."

"Good! My father is ready to make an offer on the farm if you're okay with it."

Sam looked at his father-in-law and nodded.

Adrien turned to Bill, who was already filling out an offer and said, "My offer is for everything on the farm, including all of the farm equipment, all of the furniture and furnishings. I am willing to look at the mares and foals, but that will be a separate offer and, should we come to an agreement, a separate contract as well."

Bill never stopped writing and said, "That was not the way the farm was listed, but I believe I can convince the owners to accept your offer along with your contingencies."

After the offer was completed, Adrien read it over and signed it. Handshakes were exchanged and Adelle gave Sam and her father hugs and kisses. Bill told them he would try to have an answer by Saturday and headed to his car. Sam suggested they all head back to the hotel for celebratory drinks and dinner at Columbia's Steakhouse. In unison, everyone agreed and headed for the door.

Dinner was a grand celebration. Caesar salads were followed by perfectly cooked steaks, either fillet or ribeye, topped with roasted garlic butter. Adrien brought a wine carrying case containing three bottles of wine, all French Bordeaux with a specific vintage. He told Sam that the French were superior in the vinification of Bordeaux wines, starting with the selection of grapes and ending with the bottling of finished wines. Each bottle was opened and allowed to breathe and then placed in a bucket of ice for ten to fifteen minutes to allow the wine to reach the optimum serving temperature. The first bottle was a Lafon-Rochet, Saint-Estéphe, Bordeaux '44, followed by a bottle of Le Bon Pasteur, Pomerol, Bordeaux '43 and finally a bottle of Duluc de Branaire-Ducru, Saint Julien, Bordeaux '39. Adrien explained that the weather conditions of each growing season determined the quality of the grapes for that particular vintage and that these were bottles from his own private cellar that had gone undiscovered by the Nazis. He had originally brought them to drink at the wedding but then had decided to save them for a private family celebration during Derby week.

Jack had called and left a message at the front desk and Sam had intended to call him back, but the effects of the wine and the sultry glances from his lovely bride changed his course for the rest of the evening. There were too many good things happening all at one time and he did not want to ruin the moment. He decided he would rather make love to his wife tonight and call Jack in the morning.

After a night filled with passionate lovemaking the newlyweds slept late. Sam awoke to the sound of Adelle's voice as she talked on the phone to someone about a Derby party. He heard her say, "Thank you, Mr. Davidson, for the invitations and we will see you there." Adelle leaned over and kissed Sam good morning and headed for the shower.

Sam called Rose at the office and asked to speak with his brother. Jack answered and Sam skipped the chitchat and asked him what was going on with Jean Pascal.

Jack wasn't sure how Sam knew but answered the question as directly as he could, "Pascal has been at the Port of Memphis all week drinking with the locals and asking them questions relating to the boat and his missing brothers. I'm sure he knows about us by now and Gina and I have moved into your house to protect Samantha. There is something else that I need to tell you that you're not gonna like. The night before last I went to the dock to spy on Pascal and evaluate my options. When I was leaving I was followed by one of Pascal's Creoles who was armed with a nasty-looking blade, and I killed him before he could kill me. There's been nothing on the radio about a dead man found at the docks. I think Pascal found the body and disposed of it himself."

"Jack, I want you to go back to my house now and do not let Samantha out of your sight until Pascal has left. Dave told me he has given Pascal notice to leave the dock by Saturday. Do not try to take him on by yourself. As soon as he leaves town I want you to put our boat in the water and get it ready for a quick trip to New Orleans. I'll be back Monday and you and I are going on the offence. I intend to put an end to this shit once and for all."

Jack agreed and Sam finished, "Call me if you need me! I'll call you again tomorrow and, Jack, thanks for everything."

After eating an early lunch everyone loaded into the Buick and headed to Louisville. Adrien wanted Sam to drive directly to

Churchill Downs to see exactly how long the trip would take. He considered this a trial run for an event he had dreamed of for years and didn't want to be one minute late the next day.

Everyone was fashionably dressed for the Barnhill-Mason Derby Gala that started at six o'clock and that meant they would have about three hours to do whatever they pleased. Highway 60 was a straight shot from Lexington to Louisville and took them through Frankfort, the state capitol. The distance from their hotel to Churchill Downs was a little over eighty miles and it took them almost two hours to drive. Once they arrived and parked in view of the twin spires, Derby fever took full effect and the decision was made to attend a few of the afternoon races.

Adrien wished to check out the view from tomorrow's reserved seats and purchase a few Derby programs. On the way in, Sam heard a man hawking tip sheets for the Derby and Derby under-card. He thought the man had an Irish accent and went to investigate a hunch. His hunch was correct and he introduced himself to Paddy O'Toole and told him of his friendship with Dave Hinkle.

O'Toole flashed a smile and praised Hinkle as a very fine man he had met shortly after arriving in the United States from County Kildare, Ireland. He took a pencil and circled the horses on his tip sheets for that day and the next that he felt had the best shot at winning and handed it to Sam. Sam offered to pay, but O'Toole refused the money and said, "Any friend of Dave is a friend of mine and I don't take money from friends unless they win." Sam thanked the jovial Irishman and continued inside to find his wife and family and see the location of tomorrow's seats. As a group they watched and wagered on three races, winning two out of three.

The Derby gala was underway at the old Barnhill Mansion. Sam, Adelle, her parents and brother had arrived a few minutes early and met the hosts, Andrew Barnhill and George Mason, and their wives, Molly and Susan, respectively. A local band was playing soft music and the bar areas were the gathering places for many of the prominent guests, all of them dressed to the nines. The governor of Kentucky, Earle Chester Clements, was pandering for future votes in one area and several owners of tomorrow's Derby entrants were answering questions for the local newspapers and radio stations in the other.

Adelle found E.W. Davidson and introduced him to her father and mother. He took them to meet his wife and introduce them to other prominent guests. There were several young women in attendance and André wasted little time making a move. He joined a trio of what appeared to be single young ladies and was warmly welcomed with smiles and curtsies. Sam got himself a drink and began touring the mansion, taking time to look at the paintings of past Derby winners and bronze sculptures of Whirlaway, War Admiral, and Count Fleet. When he laid his hand on the sculptures and closed his eyes he could visualize the horse running in the Derby, moving powerfully, his sides heaving as he inhaled and exhaled the huge volume of air required to sustain the oxygen level in the blood pulsing through his veins.

His thoughts were suddenly interrupted when someone said, "It appears you have been affected with the love of horses and suffering from the effects of not owning one." He became aware of Adelle's presence and was slightly embarrassed to have been caught daydreaming. She was standing with her father and mother.

Adrien smiled and placed his hand on Sam's shoulder, "That's a problem that we are going to solve very soon, young man. I also yearn to own a classic American racehorse and dream of it frequently." He added, "If we continue to have success betting on the horses suggested by Mr. O'Toole as we did today, we can use our winnings to buy our first horse. Why don't we eat dinner and head back to Lexington so we can get a good night's sleep and be ready for tomorrow?"

Derby day dawned cloudy and cool with rain in the forecast, but it did not dampen the spirits of Sam, Adelle and the rest of the Devaux family. It was a big day in the bluegrass state. During breakfast at the hotel there was a buzz amongst the patrons. Most of the conversations were centered on Citation and Coaltown. The connections of Galedo had scratched him from the race, leaving a field of only six horses. The Kentucky Derby was scheduled as the seventh race, to be run at 4:32 in the afternoon, and because of the short field there wouldn't be any place or show wagering.

The plan was to meet in the lobby at nine o'clock and leave at nine-thirty. The men came down first to give the ladies a little private time to complete their ensemble. They were dressed in smooth broadcloth suits with crisp white shirts and colorful ties. Accessories included matching fur felt fedora hats with Nunn-Bush tieless slip-on shoes. Adrien and André both wore wine-colored suits, while Sam had chosen a fashionable navy blue. Adelle and her mother came down the stairs together and were noticed by almost every man and woman in the lobby. They were both dressed in the latest European fashion. Adelle wore a navy blue taffeta dress with a low neckline and full back-pleated skirt. Her wardrobe was completed with a two-tone plaid, flared back topcoat and suede pumps with ankle straps. Claire wore a tailored, dark green silk suit with a brown satin stole and matching satin pumps. The women also wore gloves with ruffled cuffs and close-fitted berets accented by colorful feathers. Each wore strings of pearls knotted at the throat and carried slender suede handbags.

Sam kissed his wife and told her how beautiful she and her mother were and that it would be his honor to drive them to the Kentucky Derby. The road from Lexington was already crowded with traffic headed to Louisville. Everyone was very excited; their dreams of attending the Derby were soon to be fulfilled and by the end of the day there was a good possibility they would have a signed contract to purchase a prestigious thoroughbred farm. Bill had left a message at the front desk stating the offer had been verbally accepted and hopefully would be signed by the end of the day.

Bobby Hernreich had called earlier to let them know that he and Danielle had arrived late the previous evening and would meet them at the box seats. Sam told him the box was in the grandstand just past the sixteenth pole and high enough to be under the cover of the roof, which would help keep everyone dry if it rained.

The rain held off and they made it to their seats an hour before the first race. The grandstand and infield were filling fast and Sam decided to go ahead and place his and his brother's bets on the Derby, and his bet on the Kentucky Oaks. He matched Jack's $1,000 and bet it all on the entry of Citation and Coaltown. In the Oaks, he bet $500 to win on Challe Anne, going with Paddy O'Toole's information again. When he returned to the box Bobby and Danielle had arrived and Danielle was wearing a stunning engagement ring. Congratulatory handshakes and hugs were bestowed upon the happy couple and Bobby told them the wedding date was June 13th, which coincided with the Belmont Stakes. The ceremony would be on Sunday afternoon the day after the third leg of the Triple Crown.

By the end of the second race it was announced that the attendance for the seventy-fourth running of the Kentucky Derby was a new track record for Churchill Downs. Every seat in the grandstand was filled and the infield was packed with well-dressed patrons waiting for their chance to see the promising three-year-old colt named Citation. The citizens of the United States were looking for a post-War hero and this dark bay colt had captivated their hearts. Sam was thrilled when Challe Anne won the Kentucky Oaks with Back Talk a distant third. The winner paid $8 for a $2 win ticket and Sam collected $2,000 from the betting window and bet another thousand on the Calumet entry in the Derby.

It had been raining lightly since the third race, but after the fifth the skies opened up and it poured down. Amazingly, almost no one left the races. People had come to see a great race and a rainstorm was not going to change their minds.

The track condition was listed as sloppy when Citation walked onto the track. He had drawn the one hole and was the first horse in the post parade. He stopped and looked at the crowd in the infield with his ears pricked forward and waited as if he were posing for pictures. The crowd began to chant "Big Cy" and he pranced alongside the pony horse, arching his neck and showing off his well-muscled body that glistened from the light but still steady rain. Coaltown was next and he also looked fit, confident and ready to run. Escadru, Grand Pere, Billings and finally My Request, the horse Arcaro had originally committed to ride in the Derby, followed the Calumet entry of 1 and 1A in order.

Everyone in the grandstand was on their feet, cheering as the horses approached the starting gate. André was watching the race from a different box with one of the young ladies he had met at the gala and her family. Sam affectionately squeezed Adrien's shoulder and thanked him for making this all possible. He then took Adelle's hand in his, leaned over and softly kissed the back of it. Claire was holding Adelle's other hand as she stood motionless, her senses captivated by her surroundings. He turned to look at Bobby and Danielle. Bobby, wearing his ever-present smile, gave him a wink. Sam took a deep breath, hoping to relax and slow the beating of his heart as it pounded inside his chest. He also felt the urge to pee, but that would have to wait—the horses were now loading and the race was only moments away.

The gates opened and the crowd roared in unison. Citation and Coaltown broke on top and Coaltown quickly took the lead. Grand Pere broke into Billings at the start, causing him to interfere slightly with My Request. Arcaro took Citation off the rail where the mud was deepest and took a light hold, allowing Billings, Grand Pere and Escadru to pass him on the inside. Escadru was forced to take up when in close quarters as the horses entered the backstretch. Coaltown continued to set the pace and before reaching the half-mile pole had established a six-length lead and was showing no signs of tiring.

Sam shouted, "Damn it! Coaltown is going to steal the race! Why isn't Citation running faster?"

The words had barely passed his lips when Citation began to make his move. By the three-eighths pole he had gone from fifth to second and was within three lengths of Coaltown. At the quarter pole they were running in tandem—Citation looked Coaltown in the eye and began to pull away.

Again the crowd roared their approval and Adelle shouted, "Oh Sam! Citation is going to win."

Arcaro smacked Citation one time with the whip and then hand-rode him to the wire for a three-and-a-half-length victory over Coaltown, who was three lengths in front of My Request. Grand Pere and Escadru tired badly and were beaten by twenty plus lengths. Everyone in the box screamed with joy and the crowd began chanting "Big Cy" over and over. Adelle jumped into Sam's arms kissing him on the lips. Bobby and Danielle were also kissing and Adrien was hugging Claire as she sobbed with joy.

Sam said, "We won't make the Preakness, but thanks to Bobby and Danielle, we'll damn sure be at the Belmont."

Everyone in the grandstand remained in their seats until well after the trophy presentation. Citation was draped with a blanket of roses as the winner's pictures were taken. Governor Clements made a short speech before handing the trophy to Warren Wright, who quickly proclaimed Citation as the greatest racehorse in America. The crowd yelled their affirmation as Citation was led from the winner's circle and returned to his barn. America had a new hero who walked on four legs and gave hope to the common man of better things to come.

Sam cashed his and Jack's tickets and, with a fist full of hundred dollar bills, a slight smirk on his face and a touch of bravado in his voice, boldly stated, "I'm buying dinner!"

CHAPTER 24

Jean Pascal had only made the return trip to Memphis as a favor to his mother. She wanted to know where her other boys were and what had happened to them, so he had brought two Creole brothers, Nello and Rollo, son's of his mother's close friends, with him to Memphis.

As he sat in the front of the boat smelling the muddy water of the mighty Mississippi River, he vowed that this would be the last trip that he would make in search of his missing brothers. He and the two Creole brothers had departed New Orleans the day before and were now just downriver from Memphis. Jean and his father both knew they were dead and gone but his father wanted revenge. He wanted to wash his hands in the blood of those responsible, but was too damn old to do it himself. Jean was living large and had no intentions of killing anyone, but the Creoles might if an opportunity presented itself. Jean planned to stay for a week, if necessary, but that was all he was willing to do. He would dock the boat at the Port of Memphis and ask anyone he could find about his brothers, the missing boat and the missing Cadillac.

The slave ship was due to arrive in less than two weeks and Jean had twenty-two young women in his camp. This trip to Memphis would prevent him from adding to that list. Unless! Unless! Yes, that's what he would do. He had an epiphany; he suddenly realized he could kidnap a couple of women here and take them downriver. This trip wouldn't be a waste after all; he had drugs and help, now he just needed to find the women.

Jean stood, turned and shouted to his companions, "*Plus vite, mes amis!*" He was ready to get off the damn river and find a decent place to eat and meet some of the local women. Twenty minutes later they pulled into the Port of Memphis and Jean went to the office to pay. He paid for a week and returned to the boat to direct his crew to the assigned slip.

A dockworker came to the slip to check on their progress and told them his name was Jude Lawson. He added, "If you need anything just ask for me, I'm here all day."

Jean took the bait. "Mr. Lawson, can you find me good food, fine wine and beautiful women?"

"Mister, if you've got the money, I've got the time and I can find you any damn thing this city has to offer. By the way, Mr. Lawson was my old man's name, so just call me Jude."

"Jude, when you get off work, come on back and we'll have a drink and see what my money can buy."

Jean sent one of the crew in to town to pick up supplies, including the liquor he would need to loosen Lawson's tongue. He wanted several bottles of wine and rum, and a bottle of Tennessee whiskey for himself. While he waited he unpacked his suitcase and changed into clean clothes. Since he would have his own personal guide he would go out on the town and check out the availability of the local women.

Jude returned at five-thirty looking mighty thirsty and Jean poured him a cup of rum. He sipped on a glass of whiskey and watched as Lawson guzzled the rum. After serving him his second cup he started a casual conversation and asked a few exploratory questions. Lawson answered the questions without hesitation and Jean knew that he had found his huckleberry. He suggested they use Jude's car and head into town for a meal and more drinks, if and only if he could drive. Lawson laughed, sounding very much like a braying jackass, and said, "I don't give a shit who drives, but if you wreck it you buy it."

Rollo stayed behind to guard the boat while Nello rode in the backseat of Lawson's car. His job was to discretely watch his boss man's back and he was very good at his job. Their first stop was the Arcade Bar and Grill, known for its burgers and fries, ice-cold beer and cheap whiskey. Jean enjoyed it all while Jude passed on the food and focused on the whiskey. The waitress, who said her name was Heidi, smelled of cheap perfume and talked too much while chewing on her bubblegum, but was cute enough to make the list of possible candidates for a boat trip down the Mississippi. Jean asked her if she wanted to come back to his boat after work and have a drink and casually mentioned she could bring along a girlfriend if she liked.

Her response was just what Jean wanted to hear: "Mister, if I decide to come visit you at your boat you won't need no one else. After midnight I turn into a real she-cat and I'll be more than you can handle. Whether I come or not depends on how big a tipper you are. If you leave me a thirty-dollar cash tip and cab fare I'll be there for sure, if you catch my drift." She turned around to walk away but purposely dropped a napkin on the floor and bent over to pick it up. She took her sweet time letting him enjoy the view of her tight little ass and then winked as she walked away.

Lawson enjoyed the view as well and said, "If you want my opinion, I'd say the mouse done took the cheese."

"Jude, I don't give a rat's ass about your opinion. What I want from you is information. I want to know if you have seen my missing brother or my stolen boat at your dock. My brother was a big, dark-haired mean-lookin' son-of-a-bitch, probably well dressed and driving a big black Cadillac. My boat was a beautiful twenty-one foot Chris Craft, possibly driven by a couple of farm boys. That would have been in April or May of '47. Does any of that ring a bell?'

Lawson, feeling somewhat offended by his new friend, replied, "I don't remember seein' your brother or a big black Cadillac around the dock. And I damn sure don't remember seein' any farmers drivin' a fancy boat."

Jean didn't like the answer or the attitude but he had plenty of time, after all this was just his first night in town.

A black band, three men and two women, took the stage and introduced themselves as Crow Didley and The Happy Flappers. One man played the piano, another the saxophone, the lead singer played the guitar and the two women sang backup and danced. The band began to play a style of music that Jean liked but wasn't familiar with. He asked Lawson about it and he said it was a new form of rhythm and blues. It had started here in Memphis and some people were calling it rhythm music and others were referring to it as rockin' music. Jean understood the rockin' part because the music made him move and sway, nod his head and tap his foot to the beat.

Heidi returned to bring the check and whispered in Jean's ear, "My lovin' is a lot like this music you're listening to. Once I get the rhythm I'm going to rock your world and all you got to do is keep the beat." Jean liked what he was hearing and left Heidi a thirty-five dollar tip and took a cab back to the boat, leaving Lawson to his own demise. He sat on the deck of his boat and pondered his next move. Heidi arrived around twelve-thirty. She was dropped off by one of her co-workers, but didn't offer to return the cab fare. That was all right, though; Jean knew she would need it when he was done with her. He didn't want her to stay any longer than she needed to. She hadn't lied about being all that he could handle. She was wild and insatiable and enjoyed the rough sex that Jean liked as well. She was going to be perfect for the trip down South.

The sun was shining bright on the waters of the Mississippi when Jean crawled out of the small bed in the boat's cabin. He was alone and feeling a little rough around the edges. Heidi had left some time during the night and he was glad she was gone. It was Sunday morning and the docks were quiet. There was only one dockworker that he could see and he was busy working on the engine of a boat a few slips down. Jean slipped on his pants and walked down to introduce himself and make a few inquiries. The worker's name was Carl—Jean asked him the same questions he had asked Lawson the previous evening and Carl gave him basically the same answers. Jean thought he saw Carl flinch when he asked him about the boat. He couldn't be sure but he thought Carl knew more than he said he did. Around lunch Carl closed his toolbox and left for the day, leaving Jean and his crew alone on the dock. The Creoles prepared food for the three of them and Jean sat on the back of the boat, eating alone, brooding, pissed off at himself for even coming back to Memphis.

Monday wasn't any better. Thunderstorms, strong wind and heavy rain started just before noon. Jean spent the afternoon stuck in his boat's cabin and decided he would give it only one more day. If he didn't discover anything significant by the end of tomorrow he would leave on Wednesday morning and return to New Orleans.

Jude Lawson came to the boat early on Tuesday morning and announced his arrival by rocking the boat with his foot and shouting that he had remembered something. Jean came out of the cabin wiping sleep from his eyes.

"What have you remembered, Lawson? And this better not be a waste of my time."

"It's not going to be a waste of your time, but I want to know what my information is worth to you. If I help you find what you're looking for I want to be paid and paid well."

He had piqued his curiosity and so Jean asked, "What do you know and what do you think it's worth? Speak up! Don't make me wait all damn day!"

"I want five hundred dollars before I tell you anything. That's my decision and that's my price!"

Jean lied, "That's all the money I have with me and if I give it all to you I won't be able to get back to New Orleans. Here's what I'm willing to do: If your information is helpful, I'll give you two hundred dollars now, buy you all the rum you can drink and write you an IOU for two hundred more, I'll pay you cash for the IOU when I come back."

Jude was getting more money than he had thought he would get, so he replied, "I guess that's fair enough. Can I come on board? I don't want anyone else to hear what I've got to say."

Jean nodded and his crew stepped off the boat as Lawson stepped on board and walked to the back of the boat.

"What I'm about to tell you could get me fired because the men involved are brothers and real good friends of my boss. A little over a year ago, two well-dressed men showed up in a boat that sounds like the one you described. They rented the small warehouse and apartment up on the hill between here and Main Street. I helped move the boat into the warehouse myself. I don't know if it's still there or not. I haven't seen it since that day. Their names are Sam and Jack Cooper and they own a liquor distribution company. One of 'em still lives in the apartment but the other one lives in my boss's neighborhood. As a matter of fact, he just got married a few days ago and is probably on his honeymoon. Just so you know, these men are a couple of war veterans and I've heard they're damn tough in a tussle."

"You let me worry about how tough they are. You need to come back here after work and show me exactly where they live and then we'll go to town and have some food and drinks. I'll give you your money when you come back. Thanks for the information, but right now you need to go back to work before you get fired."

Jean was excited about finally uncovering information regarding his little brother and the missing boat; now he had to do something about it. The missing money would be almost impossible to recover, so he would take something that belonged to them. First he had to find out if the men had anything of value. If they didn't, maybe he would burn down their houses and haul ass back home.

Lawson returned as the sun was approaching the western horizon and immediately asked for a bottle. Pascal poured him a cup of rum instead and handed him his two hundred dollars.

"We have work to do before you get drunk. After our work is done I'll give you two bottles and you can do whatever you want. I need to see where these men live and decide what I'm going to do."

Jude threw back the swill left in his cup, grabbed both bottles of rum off the table and headed for his car with Jean and his crew following. Jean rode in the front as they headed for Jack's apartment. As they approached they saw a black Ford pickup driving away.

Lawson exclaimed, "That's Jack's truck right there and it looks like he's leaving! If you want to look around, now would be the time."

Jude stopped near the apartment and Jean motioned for Rollo to check it out. He rolled down the car window and looked around. The building was constructed of wood, 2 x 12 rough-cut lumber that looked strong and secure. He saw one entry door, a pair of hinged warehouse doors and at least one window in the apartment. His man returned and told him the doors all had padlocks and the windows had metal bars and thick curtains. He believed with the use of a crowbar and plenty of time, he could break in the window on the backside of the apartment. Jean would consider that later but he wanted to see the other house first and told Lawson to head out.

Jude drove across town to Sam's neighborhood and then slowed down as he passed Sam and Adelle's house. Pascal told him to go down the street, turn around and drive back by the house. Jude did as he was told and, after passing the house, Jean asked him to stop near a grove of oak trees lining the road. He quickly spoke to Nello in French and the Creole jumped out of the car and disappeared into the trees. Pascal motioned the car forward and told Lawson to drive around for half an hour. Lawson took them back into town and showed him Cooper Brother's Warehouse #2. This time Jean got out of the car and looked up at the windows in the warehouse office that offered possible access. There were three delivery trucks parked outside that could be hotwired and rammed through the warehouse doors if it came to breaking and entering. He returned to the car and told Lawson to head back to the neighborhood.

Lawson stopped near the same grove of trees and Nello slipped from behind a large oak and climbed into the backseat.

He addressed Jean in his Cajun-French dialect, and Jean's face broke into a smile.

He slammed his fist into the palm of his other hand and yelled, "Hell yeah! Finally some good news, I won't have to leave this place empty-handed after all." Lawson looked questioningly at Pascal, but Jean offered no further explanation. Instead he gave the order to drive past the house and head back to the port. As they passed the house Jude noticed that Jack's truck was parked in the driveway and he wondered what had Pascal so excited.

When they reached the docks, Jean and his crew got out of the car and Jean told him to be back in the parking lot around ten-thirty and walked away. That was fine with Jude—he had money, two full bottles of rum and a couple of friends he enjoyed drinking with.

Nello had given Jean mostly good news; only one piece of information concerned him, but overall he was both pleased and excited. The good news centered on the two young and pretty women and a little girl living in the house. They were all he needed to pay for the trip. Those two women plus Heidi would be excellent prospects for the slave trader and he could hold the little girl for ransom. The bad news causing him concern was the fact that the brother and his woman appeared to be staying at the house as well. He might let his crew kill the brother and take his woman as an additional captive. He would rather not have to deal with the man. Murder was a serious crime that carried the death penalty, whereas kidnapping was often overlooked.

As he walked toward his boat he noticed the dock's mechanic and another man fishing in one of the empty slips and decided to engage them in conversation. He asked them to recommend a good place to eat and was surprisingly pleased with the answer from the stranger. He had recommended a barbeque joint called The Rib Palace, said it was the best around. Jean had eaten barbeque before, but hadn't had the opportunity to eat it very often.

He washed up, changed shirts and he and his crew walked into town to eat. He figured walking would give him time to think and they could take a cab back to the boat after dinner. As he walked he thought about his plan. He knew his daddy didn't like asking for a ransom, but in this case maybe he would approve. When he sold all twenty-six women to the slave trader, he would collect between $35,000 and $40,000. That should make the old man happy, if that was even possible. His father was an unappreciative asshole and getting worse ever day.

The Rib Palace was better than he expected. The food was excellent, the atmosphere was good and the bottle of wine helped him relax. Nello and Rollo ate like two ravenous wolves, barely speaking a word during the entire meal. He thought he detected someone looking at him and when he glanced up he saw two men turn back toward the bar and one of them looked familiar, like the fisherman that recommended the restaurant. He took another bite of food and a sip of wine before looking back toward the bar. Both of the men were gone, nowhere to be seen. He finished his meal and paid the bill for he and his crew. They caught a cab back to the dock, where Lawson and another man were waiting.

Jude was drunk and with slurred speech introduced his friend as Ralph Hutchins, a farmhand from West Memphis. He was also drunk and wearing a stupid grin on his face. Jean invited them to join him on his boat for a drink. He didn't need Lawson anymore but he had promised him rum and it was to his advantage to keep him in the fold for now. Out of the corner of his eye he saw Rollo whisper something to his brother and then disappear into the shadows.

He asked Nello where his brother was going and he replied in his poor English, "He think maybe dat he see something and he go to check."

Jude and Ralph stayed for an hour and would have stayed longer but Jean told them he was tired and needed to go to bed. Rollo still wasn't back and after the two men left, he told Nello to go and find his brother. Soon, Nello returned carrying the lifeless body of his brother. He had tears in his eyes, something Jean had never seen before. Jean told him to lay his brother on his back on the boat's deck. He didn't find any frontal wounds, so he rolled him over on his side. There was only one small stab wound on the back of his neck. Whoever did this was obviously a formidable fighter based on the location of the wound and the fact that he had so easily killed such an experienced tracker. Now the question was what to do with the body. Nello wanted to take his brother home, but Jean finally convinced him to start the boat. They would take him a few miles down the river and dig a grave; that was the best they could do for now. The loss of Rollo was going to make their job much more difficult. Who had killed Rollo and why were questions that needed to be answered, pronto. Someone in Memphis presented a serious threat to his plan and he needed to step up his game if he was going to win.

His only other idea was to offer Jude a large sum of money to help them kidnap the women and promise him more money and liquor when they reached New Orleans. He, of course, would never reach New Orleans. Somewhere around Baton Rouge, Jean would get him drunk and have Nello kill him and dump his body into the river. He would be doing him a favor, Jean reflected. He was destined to die anyway and cirrhosis of the liver was not a pleasant ending for anyone.

It was almost daylight by the time they returned to the Port of Memphis. Nello had grieved long and hard at his brother's gravesite. Jean practically had to drag him onto the boat and upon their arrival he crawled into his bunk and slept for most of the day.

That evening he made his proposal to Lawson and found the task of convincing him to participate much more difficult than he would have imagined. He had to raise his offer from $1,000 to $2,000, swear that he would buy him a case of Tennessee whiskey before they left Memphis and promise him a couple hours alone with each of the women once they reached New Orleans. Jean told him they would need the use of his car during the day, starting tomorrow, and he would be expected to help them as soon as he got off work each day.

The next day Jean drove Nello to Sam's neighborhood and dropped him off beside the tree-lined road. He had given him instructions to watch the house but stay out of sight. He wanted to know how often the one brother came and went. He also wanted to know if the women spent time outside with the child. As he left he drove past the house and saw the Ford truck parked under the porte-cochère near the front door. He drove around Memphis killing time until he ran low on fuel. He stopped at a Mobil filling station and told the attendant to fill it up with gas and check the oil. He bought himself a bottle of Coke and a bag of peanuts. He poured the peanuts into the bottle of Coke and sat on a bench near the garage.

His mind wandered, and he thought about the girl from Georgia. What was her name? He was pretty sure it was Veronica or Vicki, and he wondered how she was handling her captivity. He and Tera had used her for their personal entertainment for several days before shipping her downriver to the camp. She was a pretty little thing and he wished she were here. If she were, he would have gone back to his boat and spent the afternoon with her in bed. Instead he paid for the gas and drove to the Arcade Bar and Grill, hoping to see Heidi.

He was disappointed to find she was not at work. The bartender said she should be in around six o'clock and worked until midnight.

Pascal asked if he knew where she lived or if he had a phone number for her and he answered tersely, "Nope, I sure don't!"

Jean ordered a hamburger and took it with him back to the boat, where he waited for Jude to get off work. Some old man who said he was one of the dock owners came down to his boat and had the audacity to deliver him a notice to vacate the premises by Sunday. He wanted to know why and the old man told him it had been previously reserved for next week. Being told what to do pissed him off but he bit his tongue and said he would be gone by Sunday. Later, when Lawson showed up, they drove back to pick up Nello, who was waiting behind the same oak tree. He told them that the man and a woman left early in the morning but the man returned shortly afterwards and he and the child had come outside a couple of times during the day but not for very long. He had left again in the afternoon and returned with the woman from his morning trip. The two other adult women had sat on the back porch for a while, but were never far from the house. He added that no one had been home all day at a house nearby and he had hidden in some bushes behind that house where he had a view of the back of Cooper's house.

Jean informed Lawson that he would buy him a meal and one drink at the Arcade and then he would be dropped off to scout the house until midnight. Jude complained, but was cut short by being reminded of his future payday. Heidi was their waitress and Jean made arrangements for her to meet him at the boat the next afternoon. After dinner Lawson was dropped off at the empty house and told to stay there until they returned to pick him up.

Jean spent several hours at the bar of the Fountain Hotel while Nello slept in the car. He enjoyed putting on a front and telling strangers he was a successful shipping magnate from New Orleans, making up lies about his work and his family business.

He left in time to retrieve Jude from the night-watch and found the dumbass standing out in the open by the road.

Jean growled, "What in the hell are you doing standing out here?"

"Hand me that damn bottle of rum and after I've had a slug I'll tell you."

Jean reached under the seat and handed him the bottle. Lawson grabbed it, turned it straight up and drank like someone dying of thirst. "Everyone around here turned off their lights and went to bed a couple of hours ago and I damned near walked back to town. Here's what you really need to know: Jack and his girlfriend took the little girl and left around seven o'clock. They were gone for about an hour and when they came back the girl was lickin' on an ice cream cone. They left them other two here by their selves and I peeked in the window hoping to see some skin. They are a pair of fine-looking women and they talked like you do when you're talking to that Creole."

Jean thought, "They're pretty and speak French, what a stroke of luck." He quickly finalized his plan but kept it to himself. Lawson was too busy sucking on the liquor bottle to give a shit what he was thinking anyway. He would slip Heidi some knock-out drops after she had given him his carnal satisfaction and tie her up in the cabin and gag her. Then, he and Lawson would drop Nello off in the woods and park the car in front of the empty house and wait for Cooper to leave. If he didn't leave, he would send Jude to the front of the house to tell him his car had broken down, and when he stepped outside Nello would have to kill him. They would use chloroform on the women, tie them up, load them in the car and haul them back to the boat. He would have the boat ready to go and leave immediately.

Saturday morning came too quickly. It was cool and cloudy and Jean had struggled to sleep, thinking and planning for a busy night of crime. He wanted to stay away from the neighborhood until it was time to make their move. He worried that Lawson's car had been in the area too often already. He and Nello walked into town and ate breakfast and drank coffee at a bakery that made pretty good donuts, but Jean missed the beignets from Café du Monde and their strong chicory-flavored coffee. The café was only two blocks from his apartment and located next to beautiful Jackson Square, where Jean enjoyed sitting and watching New Orleans wake up.

Heidi came to the boat shortly after noon. Jean was drinking a glass of wine and insisted she have a glass as well. It wasn't long before they were both naked and engaged in sexual foreplay. That was how they spent the afternoon, hardcore sex and then a glass of wine while they caught their breath. It was in her fourth and fifth glasses of wine that Jean slipped the drugs. She told him she needed to close her eyes for a minute and slipped into a state of unconsciousness. Jean had plenty of time to tie her hands and feet securely before gagging her with a pillowcase.

Jean dressed, placed the chloroform, rags, ropes and cotton into a paper sack. He walked toward the parking lot and Nello appeared from the deck of a tugboat parked nearby. Jude Lawson met them in the parking lot and told them he had just quit his job and collected his earnings. He was ready to take care of business and head down South. He wanted to know if they could strip the women naked while they traveled and maybe have sex with at least one of them on the way. Jean said that Heidi was already naked and he would let him abuse her one time after they were several hours downriver from Memphis. Jude was as happy as a kid at Christmastime and sped toward the Cooper house. Once they arrived at the vacant house, Nello disappeared into the woods and Jean and Jude took cover where they could watch the front and back of the targeted house.

They could see movement in the house, but couldn't identify anyone specifically. At around seven o'clock Jack stepped out the back door and carefully scanned the surrounding area. Both Jean and Jude lowered their heads behind the bushes where they knelt, hoping to remain undetected. Several minutes passed before Jean cautiously peeked through the leafy limbs and found that Jack was gone. Within moments the front door opened and Jack appeared carrying a small child, followed closely by a woman that Jude identified as his girlfriend. The three of them got into the Ford truck and drove slowly toward town.

Nello crept behind the house and flattened his body against the wall between the back door and a window. He motioned for Jean to join him. Jean told Lawson to wait five minutes and then go to the front door and knock. He was instructed to tell whomever answered the door that he was a friend of Jack Cooper and was delivering a box of groceries. Jean sprinted toward the back of the house, running as low to the ground as possible while maintaining his balance. As soon as he reached the back of the house Nello stepped to the window, inserted a thin bladed knife and unlocked it. They were hidden from anyone inside the house by a set of thick velvet curtains. They waited until they heard Jude knock on the front door and identify himself.

They also heard the women talking to each other and then one of them said, "We were not told about any grocery delivery and you should leave and come back later when Jack is here."

Nello raised the window, cupped his hands, and motioned for Jean to go in. Jean quickly placed his foot in Nello's hands and was vaulted through the window. The Creole placed his hands on the windowsill and, with a powerful leap, dove into the room. Jean helped him to his feet and together they moved quickly through the door into the living room. The women screamed and tried to run but were not quick enough to avoid being tackled to the floor. They struggled and thrashed, but this was nothing new for Pascal, he had the process down pat. Jean chloroformed the one he held and then the other while her arms were pinned by the Creole. He opened the front door and told Lawson to hurry and bring the car to the front of the house. Once the women were bound and gagged, Jean and Nello carried them to the car and dumped them in the backseat. Jean went back through the front door and locked it. He picked up a small table that had been knocked over during the struggle and straightened the living room rug. He slipped back through the open window, pulled it closed and sprinted to the car. Lawson hit the gas before Jean's ass hit the seat.

The women were still unconscious as the car slid to a halt in front of the boat dock. Jean and Nello lifted them onto their shoulders and carried them to the boat while Jude moved the car. Heidi was awake and thrashing around on the bed when the cabin door was flung open and the women were dumped on the floor next to the bed. Jean started the engine while Nello released the ropes from the tie-downs. The boat was backing out of the slip when Jude jumped on board. Moments later they were headed downriver with their valuable cargo safe inside the cabin.

Jean breathed a sigh of relief; the hardest part of the job was over and it had been a success. He didn't have the kid and wouldn't receive any ransom, but that was ok, she would've required extra care and added stress to the journey. He would have to deal with Lawson, who was already drinking heavily and ogling the captives, but Nello would solve that problem soon enough. His old man would be happy with him for dealing a blow to his perceived enemy. Men he had never met but men who, in his mind, had stolen from him and done harm to his family. He would lie to him and swear he had spilled the blood of his enemy. He would lie to his mother also, and tell her that her sons were dead and properly buried. Most importantly, he was returning home to New Orleans free of his family's burden. Free to enjoy his ill-gotten gains any damn way he pleased.

CHAPTER 25

Sam backed up his boast and paid for dinner at the Blue Moon Steak and Seafood Restaurant located less than a mile from Churchill Downs. The atmosphere was as good if not better than the food and the food was delicious. Practically everyone in the restaurant had been to the Kentucky Derby and witnessed the great performance of Citation, who was at the moment the primary topic of conversation.

Sam sat between Adelle and Bobby, laughing and joking, enjoying life. He was glad that Bobby was going to marry Danielle; she and Adelle were very close friends and the two couples would be spending more time together. Sam was excited to be going back to New York, first for the final leg of the Triple Crown and then for their wedding.

Bobby was pleased that Sam and Adelle would be living on the farm in Lexington. Currently, he was not interested in owning racehorses, but who knew, he might change his mind. He did tell everyone that if he were reincarnated he hoped to come back as Citation. He would be an American hero, a superior athlete, and would get laid twice a day.

Everyone was having a good time but it was getting late and Sam and his family had a two-hour drive ahead of them. Farewells were made and Sam pointed the car toward Lexington. Adrien believed they would have a signed contract waiting for them at the hotel and would soon own a thoroughbred farm in the heart of the bluegrass.

Adelle shared some exciting news with her parents. She told them there was a good chance she was pregnant again and her mom sassed her for not telling them sooner. Her dad predicted the new baby would be a little boy and the conversation turned to children and grandchildren. Sam thought about Samantha and wished she were here; he missed her terribly.

When they arrived back at the Hotel Lafayette, Adrien went straight to the front desk to check for messages. He returned with a broad smile and a signed real estate contract. He first gave Adelle and his wife hugs and shook hands with Sam and André before exclaiming, "We have a deal! My dream has finally come true and the contract has a closing date thirty days from today. We will own the farm together and Sam and Adelle can represent us at the closing. The rest of us will be back home by then. I will have the money sent to an account at a local bank that I will select tomorrow and show them a carbon copy of the signed contract. I'll be sure and make them aware of the surrounding circumstances. Oh Sam, by the way, there is a message for you to call Jack."

Sam excused himself and headed to the room to place the call. With the help of the operator the call went through and Jack answered.

Sam said, "Hello, Jack, and don't worry, I've got your money. Citation was a man amongst boys today."

Jack hesitated before answering, "Sam I'm glad to hear it, but that's not the reason I called. I think we have a problem."

Sam's heart jumped into his throat, "Is Samantha okay? Has something happened with Pascal?"

"Samantha's fine! She's sitting right here on the sofa. But, Gina and I took her to get an ice cream cone down at the diner because she was tired of being stuck in the house. We were gone for about an hour and when we got home Nathalie and Sasha were gone. All of their stuff was here and the doors were locked. I thought maybe they had gone outside for a walk, but that was over two hours ago. Since then, Chuck Lacella came by and told us that Pascal's boat is gone. He also said that Jude Lawson quit his job at the port and told a couple of people he was going to New Orleans."

"This doesn't sound good, Jack. Did you look around the house to see if there were any other clues?"

"Sure I did and the only thing I found was a window in Nathalie's room that was unlocked."

"Lay the phone down and take a light outside and look for footprints underneath that window."

Sam waited for several minutes, which seemed much longer, before Jack returned with bad news.

"Sam, there's footprints all right. It looks like two different tracks; one's larger than the other. I'm sorry I didn't think to look earlier."

"Don't worry about it. There's no doubt in my mind that one set of those prints belong to Pascal and I'm gonna kill that son-of-a-bitch for this. I'll leave here before daylight and head home. Is our boat ready for the water?"

"Not yet, but it will be by the time you get here and I'll have everything else ready as well. Weapons and munitions, food and water and anything else you can think of. Chuck Lacella will go with us and so will Jimbo."

"Jimbo?"

"Yeah, I talked to him for quite a while the other day in case I needed help here. He's originally from Metairie, Louisiana, and he's somewhat familiar with Pascal's operation. You know how it is, he knew people that had some dealings with Pascal's people. Before he moved here he killed two men in a bar fight with his bare hands and that's the reason he left Louisiana and dropped his last name. He told me it was in self-defense and he wasn't charged by the police, but was worried that he had put his family in danger and they left town in the middle of the night."

Sam was surprised that Jack had gotten that much information out of Jimbo. Having someone from the New Orleans area that knew the lay of the land would certainly be helpful. "All right, Jack, we're gonna need some help, but you need to let 'em know that there's going to be a lot of bloodshed and killing once we get there. I've got to tell Adelle and her family what's going on. I'm sure she will be very upset and want to come with me, and Jack, thanks for taking care of my baby girl. I hate that this happened, but we're going to find Nathalie and Sasha and bring them home." Sam hung up the phone and took a deep breath before heading downstairs.

When Sam walked up to the table Adelle and her family were still in a joyous mood, drinking wine and making plans. Sam hated to spoil the party so he took a seat and waited for the right moment to break the bad news. Adrien told Sam that he was going to contact Dale Hinkle and set up an interview and at the very least pay him to help evaluate the horses on the farm for possible purchase. He and Claire would stay in Lexington for the rest of the week and André wanted to go back to Memphis.

Sam saw this as his opportunity to interrupt and he told them about the missing girls and that there was a suspect, albeit a suspect that was headed down the Mississippi River toward New Orleans. Adelle and her mother were devastated. Sam told them that he needed to leave for Memphis before daylight and André and Adelle promised to be ready to go. Sam convinced Adrien and Claire to stay in Lexington and take care of the unfinished business there. He promised to keep them abreast of the situation as it unfolded and swore on his honor that he would find Nathalie and Sasha.

The drive to Memphis started at four-thirty in the morning and ended at two o'clock in the afternoon. The 425-mile trip was completed without incident, with only three stops for refueling and a quick lunch break in Jackson, Tennessee. Sam had kept his foot on the Buick's gas pedal, passing cars when he could. Twice oncoming cars had flashed their headlights, warning him of patrol cars ahead. Sam had driven directly to their home and he and Adelle rushed inside to see Samantha while André and Jack unloaded the luggage. After holding and kissing his daughter, he told her how much he loved her and went back outside to talk to Jack.

It was obvious that Nathalie and Sasha had not returned and Jack confirmed that there hadn't been any news, so far, of their whereabouts.

He had taken the boat to the marina early in the morning and Carl Lacella had drained the old gas from the fuel tank and refueled with new, changed the oil and filters and tuned up the carburetor. The extra fuel cans were full and the boat was parked in a slip and ready to go.

Dave Hinkle was aware of the missing women and was furious that his former employee might have played a roll in the kidnapping. He had refused any payment for the work done on the boat. He wanted to join the search but had given Carl permission to go in his stead. He supplied them with a coil of hemp rope, kerosene lanterns and a couple of smudge pots to keep them warm. Chuck and Jimbo were at the apartment, cleaning and organizing the guns and ammunition. Jimbo had seen the map and location of Pascal's residence and was somewhat familiar with the Algiers area. He knew a few people who used to live there and possibly lived there still.

During their drive from Lexington, Sam had convinced André to stay in Memphis and watch over his sister and niece. André had fought with the French Resistance during the War and considered himself an excellent marksman. He asked Sam to supply him with a pistol and extra ammunition and to rest assured that his family would be safe in his absence.

Adelle was worried about Sam and wondered how he would find the missing girls, but chose not to question his means or his methods. She detected a cold fury raging within her husband and knew there would be a reckoning when he found the Pascal family. This chapter of Sam's life needed to end and she never doubted for a moment that he was totally capable of handling the situation. If these curs only new Sam and Jack as she did, they would have known that hell was coming and bringing his friends.

CHAPTER 26

Jean Pascal was not enjoying his trip home like he had thought he would. Jude Lawson was drunk, rude, and a huge pain in the ass. Nello was always quiet, but he hadn't said a word all day. He was constantly turning and looking back upriver. Maybe he was missing his brother and felt bad about leaving him buried so far from home or maybe, like Jean himself, he was worried about the Cooper brothers. His kidnapping of women had always been done under the cover of darkness. Secrecy was and had always been his ally. He was certain no one would think twice about Heidi missing work for a few days. The French girls, however, were a different story. They would be missed immediately and someone would come looking for them and those someones would be the ex-military fuckers that had killed his very dangerous brother Duke and Rollo, one of his best trackers.

Damn it! He had screwed up royally. His entire operation could be exposed to the outside world. Only a handful of people, including a few local cops, knew exactly what he was doing and they were paid to keep their mouths shut. There had been others in the past who suspected what his family was up to but couldn't prove it, and if their gossip or inquiries became too persistent they paid a price, sometimes the ultimate price.

Jean needed to move quickly and that meant getting rid of Lawson sooner than he planned. Jean had allowed him to give the women a drink of water earlier and he had roughly fondled Heidi's naked breasts. She had cussed him like a sailor and spit in his face.

When he raised his hand to strike her, Nello had grabbed his wrist, squeezed hard and told him, "No!" Lawson had backed away but stood at the cabin door making vulgar gestures toward the French women, frightening them to tears. They had already crossed into the state of Louisiana and Jean decided it was time to eliminate the uncouth bastard. He had served his purpose and now he was just excess baggage.

Jean told Nello to bring Heidi out of the cabin and tie her hands to the railing, exposing her pretty little derrière for all to see. He turned to Jude and said, "I made you a promise and there she is. You've got twenty minutes to get it done." When Lawson looked toward his prey, Jean looked at Nello and drew his finger across his throat. The Creole nodded that he understood and stepped to the back of the boat. As soon as Jude dropped his pants and grabbed Heidi around the waist Nello picked up a large pipe-wrench from the floor of the boat, raised it above his head, stepped forward and slammed it into the back of Lawson's skull, ending his worthless life.

Jean stopped the engine and let the boat drift with the current. He untied Heidi from the railing and shoved her back into the cabin while Nello stripped the rest of the clothing off of Lawson. Together they dragged the dead body to the front of the bow and Jean returned to the helm. Once the boat reached cruising speed he yelled, "Now!" and Nello pushed the body overboard. There was a sickening thump as the prop eviscerated the torso, passing through it like a knife through butter. The body would now sink to the bottom of the river and become dinner for the turtles and catfish.

Jean estimated they were somewhere around Natchez, the original stomping ground for riverboat pirates. The town had a history of violence and one more dead body in the river wouldn't raise any alarms. If Lawson's body were found, it would be buried in a paupers' grave in the potter's field outside of town.

They were only a few hours from Algiers with Nello at the helm. Jean wanted to delay their arrival until after dark; they would be less conspicuous when they took the women off the boat and into their warehouse. He needed to find a spot to kill some time and the captives were about to bust a bladder. Approximately thirty miles north of Baton Rouge he spotted a sandbar in the middle of the river with a small thicket of trees at one end and motioned for Nello to head to the west side while he scouted for a safe place to tie up. He spotted a partially submerged log and pointed it out. The trees would provide cover from anyone passing by and shade from the bright afternoon sun.

Once the boat was secure, he grabbed Lawson's denim shirt off the deck and went into the cabin. He tossed the shirt at Heidi's feet and told her he was going to untie her hands and if she did anything stupid she would end up like Jude. When her wrists were free she put on the shirt to cover her nakedness and climbed off the boat without saying a word. Jean turned his attention to Sasha and Nathalie. He spoke to them in French and told them they could leave the boat for a little while and he would bring them some food and water. While he was removing the ropes from their wrists, Sasha told him her family had money and they would pay him if he let her and Nathalie go. Jean told her he would think about it.

The meal was sparse—a loaf of bread, a jar of grape jam, three cans of peaches and a bottle of red wine—it was all he had on the boat. The women were starving and ate what was offered. During the meal he told Sasha that he would set them free if he were paid $30,000 in cash. She seemed encouraged and felt certain her family would pay. He told Heidi that she now worked for his family and her first job was to watch over the other two. His art of deception had been honed to perfection over the years. His ability to lie with a smile and a straight face was second to none. He just wanted to get them locked away in his warehouse and then tomorrow he would make a decision about the ransom.

They loaded onto the boat and departed the sandbar when the sun was low in the western sky. The remainder of the trip was uneventful and they arrived safely in Algiers under the cover of darkness. The women were all taken upstairs to a room with bunk beds, given a jug of water, a box of cookies and a chamber pot to share. The door was closed and padlocked from the outside. There were four Creoles staying downstairs: three male guards and a female cook. Jean loaded his belongings in his car and headed for his apartment. He wanted to take a shower and sleep between clean sheets with Tera. He was tired and needed sleep but first he wanted a bowl of gumbo, a glass of wine and a blowjob, in that order.

He awoke the next morning to find Tera gone. He lay in bed knowing that he needed to get up and pay a visit to his parents but he had to decide what he was going to tell them. His mother needed closure on her missing children and his old man wanted money and retribution. An eye for an eye was what he believed. Tera returned with a thermos of hot coffee and a sack of warm beignets and he joined her on the balcony for breakfast.

He told her he was going to take two of the women down to the camp after lunch. He had decided to keep one of them here to make the call for the ransom money. If it didn't work out he could keep her at the camp until the slave ship returned in two months. It was a chance worth taking. He wasn't going to tell his father and the $30,000 would be his to keep.

Tera wanted to go to the camp with him, but he told her he needed her to stay and he would take her next time. The real truth was he didn't trust the slave trader he was dealing with. If he decided he wanted Tera for himself, an argument could turn into violence and screw up everything. She did her best to change his mind by teasing him with her body and exposing her finest assets but he wasn't going to change his mind. He felt an emotional attachment with this girl and didn't want to lose her. They took a shower together, taking turns pleasing each other until all the hot water was gone and their bodies were covered in chill bumps.

Jean dressed in jeans and hiking boots in preparation for his trip downriver. He kissed Tera goodbye and left the apartment for a quick trip to his parents' house. On the way he stopped by the warehouse and told the guards to have the women and the boat ready to leave within the hour.

He left his car at the warehouse and walked the short distance to his family's residence. He entered without knocking and heard his parents arguing in the kitchen. They stopped talking when he entered the room and his mother stood and hugged him tight. His father was the typical ass that Jean had come to know all too well. Immediately he wanted to know if Jean had extracted blood from his son's killers. Jean decided to lie about everything and tell them what they wanted to hear.

"Yes, I did. My men and I killed the man responsible for Duke's murder. He is now fish food on the bottom of the Mississippi

River and I kidnapped two women from the family of the men responsible for stealing our boat and money. I am taking them to the camp this afternoon and within a couple of days they will disappear forever."

His father clapped his hands together in celebration of the revenge he so coveted. He said, "I might make a man out of you yet and teach you to run the family business as I would."

Jean held his temper in check and told his mother that Duke was buried in Memphis and Bobby's body had been found and buried in Fort Smith, Arkansas. She put her hands together and closed her eyes, apparently thanking her savior for this small bit of good news.

Jean asked his mother to walk with him outside and he told her about the Cooper brothers and warned her they could be following him. He said, "Mama, these men are tough and dangerous. If they show up here, throw Daddy to the wolves and act as if you know nothing. I'll see you when I get back."

He returned to the warehouse and brought the French girl named Sasha downstairs to make her phone call. He told her what to say and gave her instructions for when and where the money was to be delivered. He dialed the phone number and when a woman named Adelle answered it, he handed Sasha the phone. She told Adelle what he had instructed her to say and pleaded for her help.

Jean took the phone away from her and gave Adelle one final demand, "You have five days to deliver the money and if you don't you will never see your friend again." He hung up the phone, marched Sasha back up the stairs and locked her in the room by herself. He walked away when she began crying and pleading to be reunited with Nathalie and Heidi.

It was time to leave and take the other two down to the camp where they would be sold along with the rest of the captives. He was ready to collect his money from the slave trader for this group of women and lay low for a while. Maybe he would take Tera to the Florida panhandle for a working vacation and enjoy her pleasures on the white sandy beaches.

CHAPTER 27

Sam and Jack were loading weapons and supplies into the boat early Tuesday morning when Chuck and Carl arrived. The two of them pitched in and by the time the sun appeared in the eastern sky the boat was ready to go. Jimbo and his son Jordan came walking down the dock carrying a couple of boxes of groceries, accompanied by Dave Hinkle. The groceries were loaded onto the boat and Jimbo told Jordan to get on back to the grocery store and help his mother open for business before going to his own job. Dave took Sam aside and told him Pat would be spending part of every day with Adelle and Samantha until he returned. He then handed him a card with the name and phone number of the director of the FBI office in New Orleans. He recommended that Sam give them a call rather than the local police if he ran into trouble. Sam shook his hand, thanked him for his help and walked back to the boat. He took the helm, checked to see if everyone was ready and shouted, "Cut her loose, we're losing daylight!"

Once the boat was headed downriver and everyone had settled into their seats, Jack took a hard look at his brother. He hadn't seen Sam this intense since before the end of the War. Before battle, his brother would grow quiet as he stared out over a battle-field somewhere in the heart of Germany, working up the courage to kill another human being. That was how he looked now as he stared down the muddy Mississippi River with his jaw muscles clenched and a look of total determination on his face.

Jack closed his eyes and thought back on their childhood, remembering his brother as they sat in the back of their father's old truck, listening to the baying of coonhounds as they followed the scent of their prey. His dad's favorite old hound, the one they called Boots, was easily distinguished from the rest of the mob by his deep-throated howl. Sam was always the first to jump out of the truck and run toward the dogs when their howls changed to barking, telling the world they had treed a coon. After the hunt they would return home full of excitement, rushing into the house to sit around the kitchen table eating a slice of their mother's homemade pie while telling her stories of their night's adventures. That was a long time ago and a helluva lot of water had run under the bridge since then.

Sam was deep in thought, mindful only of the hum of the engine and the sound of the water as it parted at the bow and rushed alongside the boat. His mind was focused on the task at hand, but he was tired of violence and wished to live his life in peace with his family. Those damned Pascals couldn't leave well enough alone and now they had forced his hand. He didn't have a choice, recovering Nathalie and Sasha was his duty and to end the threat of violence toward the rest of his family was an obligation. It was hard to make a plan when venturing into unknown territory, but he felt confident in the team of men his brother had assembled.

Chuck and Carl were carefully loading ammo into all of the guns brought on board and Jimbo was using an Arkansas whetstone to sharpen the blades on two hatchets and a long-bladed knife he had brought with him from his grocery store. Jack was dozing, his hat pulled down over his eyes, resting and waiting his turn to drive. Everyone was fully vested in the mission and was trying to do something to help while passing the time.

Around noon Sam pulled the boat over to the riverbank, aiming for the shade of a couple of large cottonwood trees. The boat needed fuel and he figured everyone, including himself, could use a break. This would be a good time to plan their strategy for when they reached their destination. After the boat was safely secured, the Lacella brothers stayed on board to empty one of the fuel cans into the gas tank while the other three crew members carried food and drinks to the base of one of the large trees. The two brothers completed their task and joined the others for a working lunch. Sam asked everyone to share their thoughts on how best to succeed in finding the missing women and return them to safety.

Chuck and Carl didn't have any ideas but promised to do everything possible to help save the victims.

Jimbo said, "I made a couple of phone calls to old friends in the last couple of days to inquire about the whereabouts of another old friend who lives in the swamps a few miles outside of New Orleans. His name is Boudreau and he's a friend of several Creole families that make a living hunting and fishing near his camp. I was told that he rarely comes into town anymore, but spends time at Gaston's Trading Post located at the mouth of Bayou Sauvage. He may know what's going on already, but if he doesn't, he can find out. I also found out the Pascals live in a house on Pelican Avenue in Algiers and own a warehouse at the end of Verret Street, near the river. There are those living in the neighborhood that believe the family has been dealing in human trafficking, women in particular."

Sam was both impressed and disturbed with the content of Jimbo's information and opened his map to share what little he knew of Algiers. He and Jack had marked an "X" on the map indicating the approximate location of the Pascals' home. He quickly found Verret Street on the map and showed the others that the residence and warehouse were only a few blocks apart. Jimbo took the map and pointed to the area on the river where he thought the trading post was located. The bayou was a few miles past Algiers, which would give them an opportunity to pass by the city during daylight hours.

Sam looked at Jack and asked, "What do you think we ought to do, little brother?"

Jack answered, "Why don't we stop at the trading post and give Jimbo a chance to talk to his friend, if he can be found? We can leave him there and the rest of us can return to Algiers and do some scouting, then go back and pick him up before we make our move. Jean Pascal may have seen me and I know for certain he saw Chuck and Carl, so we have to wait till it's dark to put boots on the ground. Chuck and Carl can stay and guard the boat while me and you do our reconnaissance."

Sam liked the plan and said, "Sounds good to me. Let's load the boat and get the hell out of here."

Jimbo didn't like the idea of being left behind, but agreed to do it, only if they promised to wait until he was with them before attacking. Sam assured him they wouldn't do anything without him unless they were forced to. With that understood, Jack took the wheel, started the engine and resumed their journey down the river.

Late in the afternoon Jack swung the boat to the west side of the river and pulled into a small marina in St. Francisville, Louisiana. Sam wanted to fill up the two empty fuel cans and top off the tank. He asked the attendant if there were any good camping spots down the river. He was told that on the west side of the river just above Port Hudson there was a long island that created a large amount of still water on the backside with a flat riverbank. Everyone else had gotten out of the boat to stretch their legs and use the outhouse behind the marina. Sam did the same and returned to the boat and paid for the fuel. The attendant asked where they were headed and Jack answered, "We're going on a hunting trip somewhere down around New Orleans."

"What are you all a huntin' for down that way?" he asked.

"Skunks," replied Sam as they pulled away, leaving the attendant scratching his head in bewilderment.

The edge of darkness was upon them when they spotted the recommended camping area. Before getting off the boat Sam was adamant that no time should be wasted; he wanted Carl to secure the boat and help Jimbo unload the cooking supplies, then light the smudge pots. He needed Chuck to dig a fire pit while Jimbo got the food ready to cook. He and Jack would unpack the sleeping gear and gather firewood. The entire crew was efficient in their duties and within an hour supper was ready. Jimbo had broiled two steaks for each crewmember. In a cast-iron skillet he fried potatoes that he had peeled and sliced since leaving St. Francisville.

While they ate, Sam told them he wanted everyone to get to sleep because as soon as the moon was high enough in the sky they would resume their journey. He and Jack would take turns driving, but he needed one of the other three to take turns acting as spotters. He didn't want a tired crew so he strongly suggested those not working should get some additional sleep in the back of the boat.

The meat and potatoes disappeared quickly with Jimbo receiving an abundance of praise for his cooking. The trash and spoils were buried in a hole and supplies were returned to the boat. Shortly thereafter, everyone was bedded down and most were fast asleep.

Around midnight Sam rolled out from under the tarp and filled the coffee pot with fresh water and three heaping spoons of coffee. He sat the pot on the glowing embers to boil while he checked the boat. Jack was next to come to the fire and he filled two cups with steaming hot coffee.

Jack told Sam it had been way too long since they had shared a cup of coffee around a campfire and Sam agreed and added, "Our lives have changed a lot since our first trip to Memphis and when this is over, many things will change even more. Adelle thinks she's going to have another baby and wants us to be living in Kentucky when it's born. Jack, I really like Kentucky, but I don't want to leave you in Memphis by yourself dealing with all the business problems. I'm willing to stay or sell out my part, I'll leave it up to you."

Jack replied, "I appreciate your concern, big brother, but let's wait and worry about that after we get these girls back. I'm really worried about not knowing where they are and what might happen to them. We'll have a long boat ride back to Memphis, hopefully with both girls in tow, and we can talk more about our future. Let's wake the rest and get back on the river."

The night driving was slower but significant progress was made. They had passed through Baton Rouge just before daybreak and were now twenty miles or so past the lights of the city. Everyone needed to get off the boat for a little while and Sam pulled into a cove surrounded on three sides by cypress trees. This would be the last stop before reaching what Jimbo called the "Big Easy" and Sam wanted to get them fed and watered. As soon as they landed and the boat was tied off, everyone hurried into the woods for some much-needed privacy.

Breakfast was a generous portion of fried ham on toasted bread, washed down with fresh water and strong coffee. Sam rolled a smoke and everyone but Jimbo, who didn't smoke tobacco, followed suit.

Chuck spoke his mind by saying, "The first time I met Pascal I didn't like him, but after sittin' in a boat for two damn days following his ass down the river, I now hate the son-of-a-bitch." His comment helped ease the tension and everyone managed to laugh a little.

"He deserves your wrath and ours as well. He comes from a bad family and I believe deep down that he would have kidnapped little Samantha if she hadn't been with me. It's time to put an end to all this bullshit, I'm damned tired of sleeping with one eye open," Jack added.

"Jimbo, how many of the Pascal family are left?" Sam inquired.

"As far as I know there's just the middle son, Jean, his evil old man and his equally wicked mama. Nobody knows for sure where 'Big Jack' Pascal came from or exactly when he came to south Louisiana, but he's cut a wide swath over the last ten to fifteen years. He bought and sold stolen property, financed illegal operations and punished anyone that blocked his path. In certain circles his name has been whispered in connection with many of the mysterious deaths in the area. If we kill them all we will be doing this area and the rest of the world a big favor."

"Do you mean his mama too? I'm not sure we should do that—killing a woman is something I've always said I'd never do," Sam broke in.

"His mean old mama's kin are the ones doing all of the stealing, kidnapping and killing. She's the one that whelped all them evil sons and her Creole kin would never have gotten involved with

Jacques Pascal if she hadn't married him. I say kill the old bitch," Jimbo added emphatically.

Jack stood and said, "Let's get out of here and back on the river, we'll cross that bridge when we come to it."

Around noon they began to pass through the New Orleans area. Jimbo was the only crewmember that had been there before and the rest were caught up in the moment, staring at the sights of the famous old city. Only Jimbo's eyes were focused on the other side of the river looking for old landmarks, recalling his previous life there and the ghosts that haunted his past.

As the boat drew even with the French Quarter, Jimbo shouted, "There's Algiers on the right and pay close attention when we get around the bend. Tonight you should probably dock the boat there on the right, tie up under that freight dock and climb out on the left side. Verret Street is gonna be coming up purty quick now and right after that is the Pelican Avenue area. That three-story building could be their warehouse or maybe the one next to it, I'm just not sure."

Sam and Jack were studying the details of the area and looking at the windows in the building, wondering if the girls were in one of the rooms. Jimbo told them the trading post was just a couple more miles ahead and on the opposite side of the river. Jack spotted a building with a couple of boats tied out front and headed in that direction. He passed by slowly, turned back up the river and eased over toward the floating dock. Once the boat was secure everyone disembarked and walked inside. They immediately smelled the wonderful aroma coming from the big pot sitting on the wood cook-stove.

The owner took a look at their hungry faces and said, "Dat's gator and venison gumbo, made fresh today, cost each of you two bits for a bowl and another nickel for a cup of da brown rice. Soda pops in da cooler cost a nickel too."

He looked closer at Jimbo and his mouth opened in surprise, "Good Lord have mercy, is dat you, Jimmy?"

"Yeah, Leo, it's me all right."

"Well I d'éclair! I never thought I'd see you again."

Jimbo grinned and said, "Set some bowls out for my friends and come on out back and let's talk a while. Fellas, he makes a mean pot of gumbo and it's got quite a kick to it, so you better get something cool to drink first. I been knowin' Leo a long time and he sho do like his peppers. The day after I eat his cookin' I have to soak my asshole in the cold river water." He laughed loud and walked out back to talk to his friend.

The rest grabbed a pop and a bowl of gumbo and took a seat at the picnic table on the front porch. The gumbo was delicious and no one spoke a word until the bowls were empty.

Chuck's face was covered in sweat when he said, "That's some good shit, but hotter than the bowels of hell!"

Suddenly the loud ringing of a dinner bell broke the silence. Startled cranes and pelicans took flight, vocalizing their displeasure. Sam jumped up and headed to the back of the store.

When he spotted Jimbo, he asked, "What the hell is going on?"

"That's how Leo sends a signal into the swamp. Lets them know that he has a message and needs a runner to come to the post. It won't be long until you see a pirogue coming up the canal."

"A what?"

"A pirogue. It's a flat-bottomed canoe made from a hollowed-out cypress tree. Works well in the shallow waters of the swamp unless you're as big as I am. My big ass won't fit in them skinny little canoes and them old gators seem to prefer dark meat to white," Jimbo said with a smile.

Before long Sam spotted an Indian paddling steadily toward them. Leo shouted out that he needed Boudreau to come to the post pronto. The Indian stood up, turned around and began paddling in the other direction.

Leo turned to Sam and said, "Dat's gonna cost you one silver dollar. You can't take no paper money into the swamp cause the swamp rats will eat it while you're sleepin'. Y'all make yourselves comfortable, it's gonna be a while. There are some bottles of wild honey and a few jars of mayhaw jelly on the top shelf in case you was to get a sweet tooth. They're two bits apiece," Leo added before walking away.

They whiled away the rest of the afternoon sitting in the shade of a large live oak tree that was draped in Spanish moss. Jimbo gave them a lesson on the many uses of the moss, including its use in the water cooler he used in his grocery store. Leo fed them red beans and rice for supper that was almost as spicy as the gumbo they had had for lunch. Sam paid him for the food and drinks and left a silver dollar for the runner.

He had waited as long as possible, but it was time to see where and how the enemy lived. Jimbo walked them to the boat and warned them there would be Creole guards at the warehouse and maybe the house as well. Sam thanked him for his advice, hit the throttle and headed toward Algiers.

Sam eased the boat under the freight dock and tied off to one of the support posts. He and Jack stuck pistols in their belts before quietly climbing over the side and dropping into the muddy water.

Sam told Chuck and Carl to remain armed and alert, in case he and Jack were running from trouble when they returned. He asked Chuck to hand him a bottle of whiskey from the cabin; he needed a prop for the action he and Jack were about to undertake.

Sam led the way as they climbed the muddy and slick embankment. Once they reached higher ground they walked toward the warehouses, walking together in the middle of the road with Sam's arm around Jack's neck, giving the appearance of two friends who had been out drinking away their sorrows. They walked down Morgan Street acting jolly as they moved toward the buildings at the end of Verret.

Jack was the first to spot a guard sitting on the front steps of a three-story building. As they drew abreast of the building, Sam pulled his brother closer to the steps and attempted to engage the guard in conversation. He appeared to be Creole and spoke to them harshly in his Cajun French, motioning for them to continue on. The brothers did as they were told and turned right on Verret Street, walking south toward Pelican Avenue.

Jack waited until they were out of sight and beyond hearing distance before he finally spoke, "I looked up while you were talking and saw another Creole looking out an open window on the second floor. That has to be Pascal's building and I bet the girls are inside."

Sam shushed him and said quietly, "I agree, but let's wait until we're past the Pascal residence before we discuss it. I think that's their house ahead on the right, so keep up the act and watch for guards."

As they walked past the house they observed an elderly woman sitting on the porch drinking from a mason jar. She was sitting in what appeared to be a cane-bottomed chair, swatting at mosquitos, underneath the glow of a coal oil lantern hooked to a chain hanging from the ceiling. She watched them closely until they passed out of sight and turned right onto Pelican Avenue. They looked at the back of the house but saw no one else outside and picked up the pace as they worked their way back to the boat.

Carl and Chuck helped them onto the bow of the boat and together pushed it from under the dock and out into the current of the river. Sam whispered for everyone to remain quiet until they had floated past the buildings. He pointed out the suspected building and watched the backlit windows, looking for movement inside. After they had reached a point far enough away, Sam started the boat and returned to the safety of the trading post, hoping Jimbo had new information to share.

Jimbo was waiting and caught the side of the boat as it eased along the dock and secured it to the cleats. There was an older man sitting in a chair observing the docking process. Jimbo introduced everyone to Boudreau Guillory and he simply nodded his head in acknowledgment. He was casually dressed, wearing light cotton trousers and a pullover shirt. His long hair was pulled into a ponytail and when he walked away he moved with the grace of a cat. He quickly returned, bringing them each a bottle of beer. Sam reached back into the boat for the bottle of Tennessee whiskey, pulled the cork and handed it to Boudreau. He took a pull directly from the bottle, smacked his lips loudly, and said, "*Merci beaucoup!*"

Jimbo asked everyone to sit down and proceeded to tell what he had learned from his old friend. "Jean Pascal is selling women into the sex slave business. They are usually kidnapped around New Orleans and taken to the warehouse across the river until he can ship them bout' forty miles downriver to a camp he had built in Bay Denesse, where they are held until a slave ship comes, every other month, to pick them up. Boudreau told me that two days ago three women were brought to the warehouse after dark and yesterday afternoon two of the three were taken down to the camp. He says there are five or six Creole men living at the camp, hunting and fishing to feed the women and dishing out punishment to those that try to run away. He has never been to the camp himself but has a friend that has been there a couple of times and he told Boudreau how to get there."

Leo had been listening to the story and offered a place of refuge and his personal protection for the female captive in the warehouse if she was found alive.

His disgust with the situation spilled out when he said, "We don't treat our women dat way down South, we treat dem like ladies. I never trusted dem Pascal boys, they was always sneaking around, coming and going at all hours of the night. I know they've killed people that got in their way; especially da older one dat dabbled in voodoo and human sacrifice. The bad people always get their comeuppance in the end and their end is near. I will drive da boat right this minute if you want to go and get dat poor little girl."

Sam considered what he had just heard from Leo. He couldn't think of a good reason to wait so he stood and said, "Let's do it! Carl, you and Chuck get the weapons out of the boat's cabin and arm everybody. We'll use the soot off the smudge pots to darken our hands and faces. Jack, I want you to take the rifle with the scope and go ahead of us when we get there and set up across the street from the warehouse. The rest of us will get close and then storm the warehouse on my cue. Be careful firing your weapons inside, we could accidentally hit one of our own. Fist, knives and clubs would be safer unless you don't have a choice."

When everyone was ready to go, Sam took a moment to go over the final details and then passed around the whiskey bottle and said, "For luck!"

Leo drove past the target area and the freight dock, then turned the boat around and angled slowly toward the riverbank. When the water became shallow, Jimbo eased over the side of the boat and held it steady while Jack joined him in the water. Sam handed him the rifle and he vanished into the darkness. When the rest of the crew members were safely on dry land Jimbo pushed the boat back into the current and joined them. As a team they slipped across the street and continued without stopping until they reached the end of the warehouse.

Sam whispered, "Jimbo, you and Chuck go to the back door and wait until you hear me whistle. As soon as you hear my signal I want you to kick in the back door and give 'em hell. I'll see you inside."

Sam and Carl waited five minutes, giving their friends time to get in place, and then together moved to the edge of the building. Sam placed his thumb and forefinger in the corners of his mouth, whistled loudly and charged the front door with Carl on his heels. Sam watched the guard stand and point a pistol in his direction. He heard the shot and anticipated the bullet's impact, but saw the Creole slammed down instead. He mentally thanked his brother just before crashing through the front door. The first thing he saw was Jimbo tossing another Creole into the wall like a sack of flour. The man's head hit the wall with a terrific force, bouncing off a wooden beam and leaving little doubt of his final fate.

He heard a woman scream from the other room and motioned for Carl to check it out. Sam hit the stairs on the run and made it as far as the second floor before a bullet whistled past his head. He ducked behind a wall and waited. Chuck came up the stairs and dove through the doorway, drawing fire from the shooter, who inadvertently exposed himself long enough for Sam to aim and fire. The final Creole went down writhing in pain from the bullet wound in his knee. Sam and Chuck charged up the final flight of stairs ready to confront any further resistance. The wounded guard lay in front of a padlocked door and Chuck grabbed his wrists, roughly twisting both arms behind his back.

Sam searched the shooter's pockets and found a key that he used to unlock the door. Sitting on the bed crying was Adelle's cousin Sasha Babineaux. Immediately recognizing him, she jumped to the floor and ran into his arms. Sam held her close while she sobbed uncontrollably. Finally catching her breath, she said, "Monsieur Sam, poor Nathalie has been taken away from me."

Sam assured her that everything would be fine and assisted her down the stairs and out the front door. He handed her off to Jack, who was waiting on the front porch with the rifle slung over his shoulder. Sam turned and went back inside, intending to gather information from the wounded Creole. He, however, was incommunicado, refusing to speak, even though Jimbo was crushing the bones in his hand and standing with a foot on his wounded knee. The excruciating pain caused the Creole to faint and Sam turned to the female cook Carl had found in the kitchen. Her fear was odoriferous, possibly from the voiding of her bowels. Sam asked her the whereabouts of the other two girls and she confirmed what Sam had heard from Boudreau.

Sam looked straight into her eyes and said, "Tell your people to leave me and my family alone or I will come back with more men and kill them all." She quickly nodded her head in agreement with his directive.

Sam looked at the destruction caused by his men and concluded there were two dead Creoles and one with a wound that would prevent him from ever walking normally again. He told Carl to tie the cook's hands, gag her mouth and lock her in the room upstairs before leaving. Jack and Sasha were waiting for him at the bottom of the steps and without hesitation he gathered her in his arms and moved quickly toward the riverbank with Jack and Chuck guarding his flank. After reaching the river, he saw Leo manipulating the boat toward the riverbank and Chuck wading into the water to intercept and halt its movement. Jack handed Leo the rifle, climbed on board, turned and reached out his arms to take Sasha from Sam.

Sam turned to check on the whereabouts of Carl and Jimbo and to his absolute amazement he saw the big man dragging a dead body with each hand. He continued to watch as Jimbo reached the river and with a mighty heave tossed one body into the river and then the other. Sam and Carl climbed aboard the boat and helped the tired and weary giant of a man climb onto the bow, where he lay exhausted, gasping for breath. Chuck pushed the boat back into the current and boarded from the rear, completing a dangerous but successful mission.

Boudreau was waiting when the boat arrived back at the trading post. He helped Sasha out of the boat, placed his arm around her waist and softly said, "*Mon Dieu!* What has happened to you? Let this old man help you inside, *ma chérie.*" Leo followed them inside to prepare food and drink for Sasha and her saviors.

CHAPTER 28

Sam and Jack were sitting on the dock drinking coffee flavored with chicory and admiring the sunrise as it painted the clouds in the eastern sky a variable array of soft yellow and pink colors. The journey to complete their mission and save Nathalie from Pascal would resume again today, but first they needed to get Sasha to a telephone. Last night, before succumbing to much-needed sleep, she told them the entire story of the kidnapping and the trip down the river. She told them about being locked in the warehouse with Nathalie and a girl named Heidi. How the other two were taken away while she was kept behind and forced to make a phone call to Adelle demanding $30,000 of ransom money for her release.

Sam, of course, needed to let Adelle know what had happened. According to Sasha's story, Nathalie was still in the company of the girl named Heidi, a young woman from Memphis who also had been abducted by Jean Pascal. The total number of women in the camp was estimated by Boudreau to be more than twenty.

He had helped draw a detailed map of Bay Denesse and marked the location of the camp as it had been described to him by one of the friendly Creoles. Sam had offered to pay for a guide but Boudreau had pointed out the possible consequences for local folks getting involved.

Eventually, the rest of the men joined them on the dock. Leo and Boudreau had heated water over an open fire and carried it inside to fill a number three washtub for Sasha to bathe in. Being true to their Southern roots and acting as gentleman should around a lady, they hung blankets to give her privacy and ran all the menfolk out of the post. Boudreau expounded on the information he had supplied the previous night. He felt sure that there would be at least a half a dozen men besides Pascal at the camp, and the best time to attack would be before midnight while they were under the influence of alcohol.

He wasn't sure who the slave trader was but gave his opinion anyway, "His description fits a Puerto Rican trader named Enrique Balthazar, a distant relative of a Caribbean pirate named Don Miguel Enriquez. Balthazar is a modern-day pirate known for trading in illegal drugs, prostitution and stolen property. Once the women are taken on his ship and sailed into international waters, they're never heard from again. Time is not on your side and the sooner you reach the camp the better. You must leave here by noon; the entrance to Bay Denesse is through Bayou Tortillen that is easiest found during the day and the bay is large enough for you to remain out of sight during the remaining daylight hours. The bayou is several miles long and you'll enter on the western edge of the bay. Pascal's camp is located in the northeastern corner and looks like a typical hunting or fishing lodge. After dark you can spot the cook fires burning and use them to locate the camp."

Sasha came out of the trading post drying her dark hair with a well-worn towel. She looked refreshed after her bath and announced she was ready to travel into town and call Adelle. Leo suggested using his flat-bottom boat and taking only Sam and Sasha. He knew the location of a phone booth in the French Quarter area that was fairly close to the river. Sam was ready and liked the idea of using a different boat to travel past Algiers; after all, the Pascal family owned the boat he was using.

The trip to town was short and uneventful. Leo stayed with the boat while he and Sasha made their way to the payphone. Sam made the collect call and was relieved when Adelle answered on the third ring. He told her how glad he was to hear her voice and she responded in kind, declaring her love and concern. He told her Sasha was safe before giving her an abbreviated version of what had happened and explained that he needed to speak with her again after she had spoken with Sasha. He handed her the phone and listened while she spoke rapidly in the French vernacular of the Bordeaux region. He couldn't understand what she was saying but knew it was an emotional conversation exemplified by the tears streaming down her cheeks. Knowing time was short, she ended her conversation and handed back the phone.

Sam told Adelle he had some important information and asked her to get pencil and paper. First, he gave her the name of the trading post where they were staying, followed by the addresses of Pascal's home and warehouse in Algiers, and then the phone number of the local FBI office. He asked her to wait until after lunch the following day to make the call and to tell them about the kidnappings. A detailed map showing the location of the slave camp would be left for them at Gaston's Trading Post.

Finally, he asked her to phone Dave Hinkle immediately: "Tell him what I have told you and ask him to bring his car to New Orleans as soon as possible. Ask him to come to the Hotel Monteleone and I will meet him there. If he gets there first, tell him to rent a room and wait for me." Adelle confirmed the information he had given her, before pleading with him to find Nathalie and bring her home to Samantha. She hung up after a tearful goodbye and Sam led Sasha back to the boat.

Jack had their boat ready for departure when they arrived back at the trading post, but Boudreau had prepared a meal of boiled shrimp and brown rice and insisted everyone eat their fill before leaving. It smelled delicious and no one wanted to argue, knowing this would be the last hot meal they would have for a while.

Sam looked around the table at his crew, appreciating each and every one of them for giving up a part of their life to assist him in accomplishing his mission, and wondered if they would all make it back alive. The next phase of this operation, when measured against previous experiences, was going to be a mile shy of a good time. Jean Pascal was going to be present, along with a group of his seasoned veterans. They also had the advantage of defending their native land; a territory they were familiar with versus his small group of ragtag warriors that had never seen the area before. During the last World War the United States was forced to fight Germany's finest soldiers in the forests and on the beaches of their homeland and kicked their Nazi ass. Sam and Jack had been a part of that victory and he believed they would be victorious again, but would his crew suffer casualties as they had in the real War?

The ultimate question was whether to rely on stealth or come in with guns blazing. The safety of the women in the camp had to be considered; stray bullets could wreak havoc and injure or kill the very ones they were risking their own lives to save. He needed to create a diversion that would allow his men to get inside the compound and cash in on the element of surprise. He had an idea that just might work if they had Slick's hand grenades in the boat. He believed they had but he needed to know for sure, so he asked Jack.

Jack confirmed there were six left, stored near the front of the boat's cabin. He stared at Sam with a questioning look and his answer was, "We need a diversion away from our point of entry into the compound. We'll talk more on the way down and develop a plan of attack. If anyone needs to use the head, do it now, it's time to take this show on the road. There's some women that need to be saved and we're gonna go save 'em."

Three hours later they were near their destination, moving slowly and watching for landmarks on the eastern side of the river. The river grew wider and wider the farther south they went; the river-banks were almost non-existent, allowing the river to spread into the marshland, creating the swamps and bayous that were home to vast varieties of wildlife. The bayou Sam was looking for would be coming up any time now and he didn't want to miss it. Jimbo spotted an opening in the tree line a couple hundred yards down-river and alerted the rest of the crew. Within a few minutes they were motoring down a bayou they believed to be Bayou Tortillen, the gateway to Bay Denesse.

Alligators lurked along the tree line looking for their evening meal, turtles lay on ancient cypress logs sunning themselves before slipping into the brackish water as the boat approached, and multiple species of waterfowl launched themselves into the air and circled overhead emitting a cacophony of squawks, quacks and honks. Wild hogs and whitetail deer were prevalent and could be seen grazing and rooting for food on the many small islands dotting the landscape.

Jack spoke the words Sam was thinking when he said, "I'd like to come back here someday under different circumstance – fishing and hunting here must be great."

Once they reached the end of the bayou and entered the bay their focus returned to the mission of freeing the women from bondage. Sam kept the boat close to the northern shoreline, hoping to remain undetected by anyone at the camp. He found a small island with enough elevation to provide a dry camping area large enough for his crew to spread out and relax. Sam warned them to remain vigilant for any impending danger, especially poisonous snakes indigenous to the southern swampland. Snakebites from a Cottonmouth, Copperhead, or Canebreak Rattlesnake out here in the wilderness could lead to a painful death for the unlucky victim. He also told them not to light a fire or strike any matches after dark. Dinner would be fresh water and cold sandwiches, poor fare for possibly one's last meal.

Jimbo took one of his very sharp hatchets and felled two small water oak saplings, removed all of the limbs and solved a stealth problem that had been bothering everyone. The water in the bay was shallow and a man on each side of the boat using the poles could propel the boat quietly forward without using the motor.

After a cold supper and prior to the sun setting completely, Jack climbed back aboard the boat. His goal was to sort through the supplies and offload anything that wasn't needed for the night's operation. The rest of the crew pitched in by forming a human chain from the side of the boat to the center of the little island. Unneeded supplies were passed from hands to hands and several hundred pounds of weight was removed in a short amount of time. Besides their cache of weaponry, all that was left on the boat was one fuel can, several jugs of water, an army medical kit and a box containing three carbide lamps and two dry-cell-battery powered flashlights.

Before leaving the island Jimbo asked his comrades to gather for a moment of prayer. He asked God to keep them safe and give them the strength to succeed. He asked that they be granted the wisdom to understand and defeat their enemy and the will to protect the women and keep them out of harm's way. He concluded the prayer with, "In God's name we pray," and together in unison the rest joined him in saying, "Amen!"

Without another word they boarded the boat. Sam took the helm and guided the boat away from the shoreline and proceeded toward the middle of the bay where they could see the cook fires and plot their approach. Sam knew the sound of the boat would carry across the water and the Creoles would know someone else was in the bay. Maybe, if they were lucky, the camp guards would think it was just someone on a fishing expedition. Jack was the first to spot the glow of a cook fire on the distant shore and Sam pulled back on the throttle and turned the bow toward the north. A second fire was spotted and Sam looked skyward to find a guiding star that bisected the distance between the two fires. Sam had already told everyone to speak quietly if at all; the sound of their voices could easily carry across the water and alert Pascal or the Creoles.

It would now become a waiting game, the cook fires would eventually burn out and most of the guards would go to sleep. Darkness was their ally and Sam wanted to wait until the fires had been reduced to embers before beginning their approach. He hoped that would happen before the light of the waning moon illuminated the entire landscape.

Finally, Sam gave the go-ahead. Jack and Jimbo manned the poles, slipped them quietly into the water and pulled the boat forward. The process was repeated over and over as both men found their rhythm. The distance to the tree line marking the shore diminished with each pole placement and, after reaching the mid way point Sam told them to stop. He listened for any new sounds coming from the camp and heard none. Whispering, he told Jimbo and his brother to stand down and hand the poles to Chuck and Carl.

Sam retrieved the bag containing the hand grenades, removed the two on top and handed them to Jack and said, "I think we should come ashore at the right side of the camp and offload. Once everyone is on shore we'll move quickly. You'll go ahead of us until you reach what you believe to be the middle of the camp and throw one grenade as far past the camp as possible. Most of the Creoles should run in that direction and when you get them in a cluster throw the other one. Everyone except me will join you to finish off the ones that are left. I'm going inside to find Nathalie."

Jack's response was quick and to the point, "I hope it works out that way, but it rarely does. You know Pascal will be armed, so stay sharp and keep your head down."

The boat ran aground and everyone jumped ashore with weapons in hand. Jack dashed forward, pulling the pin on the grenade as he went – sliding to a stop, he heaved the grenade into the darkness and dropped to the ground. Much to Sam's chagrin, only one guard took the bait. He came running around the corner of the building and was hit by gunfire from several directions. Suddenly gunfire erupted from the edge of the clearing and bullets sounding like angry bees began zipping past Sam and the rest of the crew. Everyone scattered into the brush as more guards opened fire from the windows of the main building. Women were screaming and crying inside, reminding the saviors to hold their return fire.

Sam yelled, "Damn it to Hell, we've got to get inside."

The Creole guard firing from the clearing suddenly screamed as Jimbo split his skull with one of his wickedly sharp hatchets. Jimbo picked up the dead body and, using it as a shield, began walking slowly toward the back door of the cabin. The remaining guards focused their efforts on stopping the big man. Sam saw his friend stumble and his heart skipped a beat, but Jimbo kept coming.

Sam saw this as an opportunity to charge the front door and with a rebel yell he led the rest of his men inside. Several shots were fired in their direction and he saw Carl go down right beside him. Sam reacted by charging straight into the face of danger. He used his skull crusher to deflect the barrel of a gun away from his face and thrust upward with the Arkansas pig sticker. He felt it penetrate the flesh under his assailant's jaw and he shoved hard. The tip of the blade passed through the man's tongue and into the roof of his mouth. The man wailed as Sam pulled out the blade and stuck it between the Creole's ribs.

Jack was in a knife battle a few feet away: sensing he had met his equal, he jerked the pistol from his belt and slammed it into his opponent's mouth, knocking out several of the man's teeth, and pulled the trigger. Blood, bits of bone and wads of brain matter painted the wall behind him as he dropped to the floor. Jack turned and joined his brother as they moved toward the sounds of more fighting down the hall.

Chuck was down on one knee fighting for his life and Jimbo was standing behind him facing two very determined enemy combatants. He was keeping them busy, attacking with hatchets in both hands and paring counter thrusts from their blades. Sam stepped forward and with all of his might threw the skull crusher into the face of one, knocking him backwards, giving Jimbo the opening he needed to end his life with a fatal blow to the throat.

The big man focused his attention on his remaining opponent and the man began to wither from the intensity of the blows.

Jack had saved Carl's ass by making a diving tackle that took the remaining fighter to the floor. He managed to secure the man with a chokehold, rendering him unconscious. Sam helped Jack tie his hands behind his back and then turned back to check on his wounded men. Carl had been shot through the thigh, but was conscious. Jimbo had been shot through the calf of his left leg and had several cuts on his arms and chest. Chuck had been stabbed in the side and was bleeding the worst of all. Jack had a few superficial cuts and a large bruise under his left eye but was ready for more. He asked the obvious, "Where's Pascal?"

Sam answered, "I haven't seen him but he has to be here somewhere." He shouted, "Ladies, we're here to help you! I need some of you to come out here and help my wounded men. I'm looking for Jean Pascal and a girl named Nathalie that just arrived. If you know where they are, please tell me and you won't have to worry about him ever again."

A young woman who said her name was Molly spoke up, "He has a private cabin out back and that's where he takes the new girls. We've all been there and all of us would like to see him punished for what he's done to us."

Several women had come out of the rooms and were attending to Carl and Chuck. Jack ran to the boat and came back with the medical kit and handed it to the women. He told Jimbo to stay and get his wounds treated but he shook his head no.

Sam, Jack and Jimbo went out the back door and headed straight toward Pascal's cabin. The door was locked but that wasn't a problem; Jimbo kicked it once and shattered the doorframe. The door flew open and standing inside was Jean Pascal, holding a skinning knife to Nathalie's throat and smiling an arrogant smile. There were two other women on the bed behind him that Sam didn't know, but it appeared they were also captives. One was very frightened of the situation, the other not so much. Jack stood to Sam's left and Jimbo was on his right, both ready to charge.

Pascal sensed the same and issued a stern warning, "Throw down your weapons or I will cut her throat. Take out all of your weapons and toss them toward me now."

Sam said, "Let her go now and we will let you live. If you harm one hair on her head I will pluck out your eyes and cut off your tongue. Then I will let my friends have you and they won't be so friendly."

"You don't scare me, Mr. Cooper. I owe you for killing my brothers and stealing our boat, which I'm going to drive out of here very soon. I am going to keep this girl as my hostage just to make sure you don't try to follow me. Now throw down your weapons! This is my final warning!"

Sam told his brother and Jimbo to do as they were told and he would do the same. Together they tossed their guns toward Pascal's feet.

Pascal demanded they also toss their knives and he told Jimbo to toss his hatchets as well. Jimbo noted the defiant look of the less-frightened girl, Heidi, and tossed his boning knife a little harder. It slid close to her feet and she glanced down and then looked into Jimbo's eyes. He blinked twice and she nodded her head slightly to let him know she understood.

Sam spoke up, "We didn't kill your brother or steal his boat. We found it on the flooded Arkansas River. I didn't kill your older brother either, but I did meet him, and as far as I'm concerned whoever killed him did you a favor."

Jean laughed, "You may be right about that, but I'm going to make you pay for the trouble you've caused me and my family. You and your brother have cost us a lot of money and screwed up my entire operation. I'm going to take these girls and as many others as I can load in the boat and get the hell out of here. Did you kill all of my men?"

Jack's answer was laced with venom, "All but one."

"Well, maybe I'll let him drive my other boat and we can take more of these lovely women with us. I'm going to sink any boat that I can't drive and leave your asses stranded here. What do you think of that, Mr. Cooper?"

Before Sam could answer, Heidi grabbed the knife at her feet, stood and plunged it into Pascal's back. His shock caused him to release Nathalie and turn to look for his attacker. When he saw Heidi jump away, he hissed, "You little bitch," and raised his knife to kill her.

With unbelievable quickness Jimbo charged forward, grabbing Pascal's arm and twisting with all his strength. Jimbo broke his knife-wielding arm and dislocated his shoulder all in one motion. Pascal screamed in agony and reached for the pistol stuffed in his belt, a move that sealed his own fate. Jimbo jerked him forward, wrapped his big hands around Pascal's head and snapped his neck. The last son of Jacques Lafitte Pascal fell dead at his feet.

No one moved for a moment and then when it appeared Nathalie was on the verge of collapsing, Jack reached forward and wrapped his arms around her, whispering, "It's ok, you're safe now."

Jimbo turned and walked out the door, leaving Sam alone to deal with the other two women. Sam introduced himself and asked their names.

Heidi, still staring at the lifeless body of her abductor, looked up and said, "I'm Heidi and that's Veronica; I live in Memphis and she's from Atlanta. She's been here for a few weeks but I just got here night before last. I was on the boat with Nathalie and another French girl that's still locked up in a warehouse in New Orleans."

Sam told her that Sasha had been rescued and was safe now. He invited them to come with him back to the main building.

Veronica finally spoke up, "I know I don't look like it, but I'm from a wealthy family and I know my mother and father have been looking for me. Please take me with you when you leave."

Sam assured her that he would take her with him and Heidi as well. He led them both outside and Jack followed with Nathalie in tow. When they entered the main building he was surprised to find Chuck and Carl laying comfortably on cots, drinking wine, surrounded by women asking a continuous string of questions. He hated to interrupt such a happy gathering but he needed to make a plan for tomorrow.

"Ladies, can I have your attention, please? I need for one of you that's been here a while to step forward and tell me how many women are here. I need a few of the other women to help get some food for my men."

One lady stepped up and introduced herself as Cathy. She said, "I've been here for six weeks and, counting those three with you, there's twenty-four women here." She pointed to a group of women and told them, "Go to the kitchen and fix some food for our heroes and bring us another bottle of wine."

Sam addressed Cathy and the rest of the women present, "We have a transportation problem. Tomorrow I am going to take two boats and as many women as I can fit in them back to New Orleans. The local branch of the FBI should be coming in the next couple of days. When I get back, I'll call their office and bring them up to speed. Afterwards, we'll come back to get more of you. Jimbo, Chuck and Carl will stay here and recuperate until we make our last trip. We'll leave them plenty of weapons in case they need to protect you. These three women with me are going on the first trip, so talk amongst yourselves and decide who else is going and who's staying."

Jack and Sam walked back outside to look for Jimbo and found him near the boat dock. He had been busy; seven dead bodies were stacked together and covered with a tarp. He had found the keys to the other boat in Pascal's cabin and had been contemplating hauling the bodies away and dumping them into the swamp so the women wouldn't have to see them again. Sam thought it was better that the FBI didn't see them either but suggested they wait until morning. He wanted to eat and find a place to sleep; the adrenaline rush from earlier had left him exhausted.

Someone inside called out the window, telling them the food was ready, and Sam turned to go back inside, saying, "Damn, I'm hungry, let's eat."

The sun was shining brightly when Sam was awakened by the sound of voices. He raised his head to peer over the side of the boat where he had slept to see what was causing the commotion. He looked, blinked his eyes, and looked again at six naked women bathing and washing their hair in the water of the bay. The women saw him and laughed at the surprised look on his face. None of the women bothered to cover themselves and Sam forgot to turn his head. They giggled and waved and he waved back. One asked if he would like to join them and he said, "I would like that very much but I'm a married man and my wife wouldn't understand." He lay back down because he couldn't get out of the boat if he wanted to. The swelling inside of his pants was a dead giveaway that his male hormones were working well and could cause him to make a bad decision. He loved his wife and didn't want to stray from his nuptials despite the voluptuous temptations.

Jack walked out of the building and whistled his approval. The girls laughed heartily; they were very happy to be free of their captives and able to do as they pleased. Jack told Sam that Chuck and Carl were being waited on hand-and-foot by several of the very appreciative women and had no intentions of getting out of bed. He asked Sam if he had seen Jimbo leaving in the flat-bottomed boat just after daylight. Sam shook his head no and rose up to look out across the bay. The women were out of the water and in various stages of dress, some already returning back to the lodge. Sam pointed to the east where he could see what he believed to be the boat moving in their direction.

Ten minutes later Jimbo eased his boat to a stop next to the brothers.

Sam asked, "Where've you been, Jimbo?"

Jimbo grinned and replied, "I been feedin' the local gators and they sho' was hungry this morning. After I eat a bite I'll take the rest of them ole boys to a different spot and make some other gators happy."

A yell from inside announced breakfast was ready and they headed for the kitchen. The women had outdone themselves this morning. There were platters of steaming hot food sitting on the wood tables in the dining room. The room was filled with joy and laughter in stark contrast to the evening before. They had found Pascal's private stash of wine and were freely partaking again this morning.

Sam, Jack and Jimbo declined the wine, drinking cups of black coffee instead. Everyone had eaten their fill when one of the girls spotted a boat coming across the bay and alerted the rest. The three healthy men walked outside with weapons in hand to see what they were facing. What they saw as the boat drew closer shocked them all.

Sitting in the front of a fishing boat was Leona Pascal, matriarch of the Pascal family. She was being escorted by two of her Creole relatives, who were unarmed and showing no signs of aggression. Sam stepped forward to meet the boat as it came to a stop against the shoreline. He wasn't sure what to say, so he said nothing and waited for her to speak.

"We didn't come here looking for trouble and don't want none. I've come to get my boy and take him home. Can you bring him to me?"

Sam answered, "Ma'am, he's dead."

"I figured as much. I still wanna take his body home and put it in a proper grave so I can visit him from time to time."

Sam looked at Jimbo and he, in turn, pointed at the tarp-covered bodies.

Sam asked Jack to get a blanket and said, "Jimbo, help him wrap the body in the blanket and load it on her boat." He looked back at the sad old lady and told her there was one of the guards still alive and tied up in the shed out back.

"I'd like to take him too. I'm done with all this shit and you don't need to worry about any of my people ever bothering you again."

"That all sounds good to me, but what about your husband? Is he going to stop harassing us and kidnapping innocent women?"

"You don't have to worry about him anymore. I cut the old bastard's throat with a straight razor while he was sleepin' last night. He cost me three sons and any chance of grandkids. We sunk his body in the river about halfway down here. I'm gonna bury my boy proper and then I'm gonna disappear for a while. Consider those boats and that lodge as spoils of war. You can have it all or burn it down; it's just going to bring back bad memories. I want you and the rest to leave me alone from now on and let me die naturally."

Jack and Jimbo loaded her boy's body on the boat and went to get the guard.

Sam asked her one last question, "When is the slave trader coming here to pick up these women?"

Her answer was, "I don't rightly know the answer to that question, but I'll ask your prisoner." She spoke harshly to him in his native language and after several minutes turned her attention back to Sam. "He says they usually show up around the middle of the month. It could happen any time in the next three or four days."

Jack helped the guard into the boat, leaving his hands tied. He pushed the boat back into the water and watched, along with everyone else, as it gradually disappeared across the bay.

Jimbo loaded the remaining three bodies into the flat-bottomed boat and told Sam, "I'm gonna get rid of these dead ones and you need to get those other boats and some of the women ready to leave so you and Jack can take them to New Orleans and get back down here before dark. I want to get this over with and go home to my family."

CHAPTER 29

Sam's boat was approaching Gaston's Trading Post with Jack following close behind in Pascal's other boat. Six women had crowded into each boat, ready to experience a normal life again and anxious to notify their family and friends of their safety. Sam had given each one of them $25 in cash to use as they needed. He and Jack would leave this group of women – with the exception of Nathalie – at the trading post with Leo, and pick up Sasha. He would take her and Nathalie to the Hotel Monteleone to meet Dave Hinkle, assuming he was there.

Leo, Boudreau and Sasha had seen the boat coming up the river and were there to meet them. Nathalie was the first one out of the boat and ran straight into the arms of her ecstatic friend. While she and Sasha were celebrating their reunion, the rest of the women, with the assistance of Leo and Boudreau, disembarked from the boat. Jack had docked behind him and the unloading process for the women in his boat was duplicated. Sam had a quick conversation with Leo, briefing him on the events that had taken place at the camp. He told him he would give a more detailed version later. Veronica wanted to go with them but he told her she would have to wait until they returned, but promised she would be safe where she was.

He asked Jack to drive the boat while he explained the details of their plan to Sasha. Once they reached the French Quarter he jumped ashore, asked the girls to follow and headed for the hotel. Dave wasn't there so he rented a room for the girls and used the phone to call his house. Gina answered the phone and told him that she and Pat were taking care of Samantha while Adelle and André followed Dave to New Orleans in the Buick. She told him they had left early this morning and then asked about Jack. He told her he was fine and would call her in the next couple of days. He hung up and told Nathalie and Sasha that Adelle was on the way and asked them to remain at the hotel until she arrived and to tell her he had gone to pick up the rest of the women and would return in the morning.

His next call was to Ron Moquett, the director of the New Orleans FBI office. A secretary asked his name and told him to hold while she checked to see if he was available. Sam waited impatiently until a voice on the other end of the line answered, "Moquett."

Sam told him who he was and began telling him the details of the kidnappings. When he reached the part of the story that involved the slave camp in Bay Denesse, Moquett interrupted.

He said, "I've had numerous reports of missing women filed in my office over the last eighteen months but my investigations have always reached a dead end. I have an open file on my desk right now involving a young lady from Georgia who went missing in the last thirty days. Is there a chance that you've encountered someone at this camp by the name of Veronica Chandler?"

Sam answered, "Yes, sir, I have. She is waiting at Gaston's Trading Post, where I took her and ten other women about an hour ago. I wanted to talk to you first before I brought them into town."

Sam continued his story, trying his best to emphasize the importance of a rapid response to a small window of opportunity. He told him that he had to get back to the camp before the slave trader came for the other women. He ended the conversation by reminding Moquett of the map he had left at the trading post. Sam was told that he should wait until the agency could mobilize a team of agents to oversee the rest of the operation.

Sam said, "I can't do that." And he hung up the phone.

Sam returned to the boat and told Jack he had talked to Gina and what she had told him about Adelle and André. He reminded him to call her when they got back the next day. He quickly told him about the call to the FBI and then dropped him off at the other boat. It was mid-afternoon and they would have to hurry to reach the camp before dark. Sam didn't wait around – he was anxious to get back and get the rest of the women to safety. He figured the men could fend for themselves.

When he reached the Bayou Tortillen he glanced over his shoulder and saw Jack in the other boat trailing approximately a quarter of a mile behind. Sam wasted little time traversing the bayou and reached the cabin as the sun disappeared below the western horizon. Jimbo was waiting when he pulled up to the dock and as soon as they finished securing the boat, Jack arrived. Sam hadn't looked in a mirror lately, but if he looked anything like Jack, with his scruffy beard and windblown hair, he knew he needed a shave and a haircut.

Jack tied off his boat, grabbed a knapsack from under the seat and stepped ashore. He asked, "What's for supper?"

"After you left this morning I shot and skinned a young buck and picked some wild onions. The girls made a very fine venison stew and we been waitin' on you," Jimbo answered. "What's in the knapsack?"

"Leo sent a few things – there's hard rock candy and peppermint sticks for the girls, smoking tobacco for everyone but you and some antiseptic salve for anyone that needs treating. The salve is some bad-smelling shit so it must be good."

Jimbo replied, "That's good that Leo did that. Carl was runnin' a low fever today according to one of the girls. That bullet wound might be infected so after supper we'll doctor him good whether he likes it or not. You two need to get the rest of these women out of here early tomorrow and come back and get the rest of us."

Jack smiled and said, "All right already, if I don't eat soon I'm gonna starve. My stomach already thinks my throat's been cut. I promise to get the girls out of here early, but if you don't let me eat now I may not come back for the rest of you."

Jimbo looked like he was upset. He stared at Jack for a minute and then started laughing, "You're right, Jack, if you don't eat you ain't never gonna get big and strong like me. Come on, let's get you fed."

The stew was very good, a little spicy, but good, and there was plenty of it. Chuck was feeling well enough to join them for dinner; his wound had stopped bleeding and his appetite was improving. Carl was still feeling a little rough and stayed in bed. After dinner Jack took the salve into his room and made sure he slathered plenty on his wounds. Carl told them not to worry, he'd been hurt much worse when he wrecked his bicycle as a kid.

Late in the evening a heavy band of thunderstorms rolled in off the gulf, forcing everyone inside. The thunder and lightning lasted for over an hour and it rained buckets well into the night. Jimbo had repaired the door on Pascal's cabin so that it now closed completely. He invited Sam to come in out of the rain and share the warmth, away from the noise and temptations of the main lodge. Sam accepted the offer and left instructions for the girls to take turns night-watching the camp.

He brought a bottle of red wine to drink while they discussed what to do with their so-called spoils of war. There was the 24-foot Cabin Craft transport boat, a flat-bottomed boat and motor, the lodge itself that had most likely been built on untitled land, a plethora of weapons and various other sundries. Sam had little desire to go through the rigmarole of deciding who got what. He had already given all of the money confiscated from Pascal and his guards, plus some of his own, to the women of the camp. He wanted to do more: they certainly deserved it for all of the pain and suffering they had endured during their captivity. Sam suggested each of the men choose a gun and knife to keep and give the rest to Leo and Boudreau for all of their help. If the women wanted a weapon for their personal protection they could choose first. He asked Jimbo to discuss the future ownership of the boats and lodge with Chuck and Carl after he and Jack left with the remaining women. Jimbo said he would be glad to help and told Sam he appreciated being included.

They were up before dawn and rousted everyone but Carl out of bed. Carl's fever had broken during the night and he woke up hungry, which Sam took as a good sign. He told Molly that Chuck would rustle his brother something to eat; her job was to get the women down to the boats and get them loaded. He told Chuck to take care of his brother because they hoped to be back around mid-afternoon and would need him to be ready to travel.

The trip was a repeat of the day before. Sam did his best to interact with the women, learning their names and where they were from. The three-hour trip went faster when he had others to talk with. Something seemed wrong, though, when he pulled up to the trading post dock. There weren't any women there to greet their friends, just Leo and Boudreau.

His question was fraught with angry overtones, "Leo, what have you done with the other girls? They were supposed to stay here with you until we got back with the rest."

"Whoa! Ease up, Sam, before you blow a gasket. The damn Feds showed up yesterday afternoon on a Coast Guard cutter and took them to the Navy barracks up by Metairie. Weren't shit I could do about it! I told 'em you was bringing more this morning and they said they'd be back before noon today to pick 'em up."

"I'm sorry, Leo, I'm a little bit on edge right now. I need you to tell the Feds that I've gone back to pick up my men and there's a damn good chance Balthazar, the slave trader or pirate or whatever you want to call him, will be there in a day or two and if they want to arrest him on American soil they need to get their ass down to Bay Denesse. Help these women off the boats while I fill up my gas tank. The girl named Molly is the leader of this bunch and she will be the one the Feds need to talk to. I need to piss and get me and Jack something to eat before we start back."

There was no need to take both boats back so the Cabin Craft was left behind. Sam loved their Chris Craft and appreciated its dependability. Something about the boat enhanced his sense of security and made him comfortable in his own skin. He and Jack talked a lot on the way back. They talked about the camp and the possibility of turning it into a real hunting and fishing camp that could be shared by all of them. If someone wanted to stay there and work hard, the lodge could become a profitable hunting and fishing operation. They were curious to see what the rest of the crew had decided while they were gone. After reaching the end of the bayou they motored to the island where they had stored their supplies. Other than a couple of boxes of crackers that had got wet, everything was just as they had left it. They reloaded everything onto the boat and continued their short trip to the camp.

Carl was sitting in front of the lodge in a wooden chair when they arrived and he hollered, "Welcome home, boys! Get out and stay a while."

They tied off the boat and joined Carl, whose health looked markedly improved, and within moments Chuck and Jimbo came from behind the lodge to complete the gathering.

Jack asked if they were ready go and Carl said, "We're ready, just need to load the weapons on the boat. Chuck stored most of the knives and pistols in some old army ammo boxes; the rifles and shotguns will have to go in the boat's cabin. Jimbo, tell 'em what you found this morning."

"I took the flat-bottom into the swamp behind the lodge and did some lookin' around. There are two more small cabins on separate islands not far from here. One has a lean-to shed on one side with a couple of canoes underneath and the other is used to store trapping gear and has a woodworking table where someone has been making duck calls out of wood from local bois d'arc trees. There were a dozen or so already completed so I brought them back here. I tried one and it sounds real good." He handed one to Sam and told him to give it a try. Sam blew on it a few times and handed it back. "What have you got in mind?"

Jimbo gave him a big smile. "Glad you asked. The three of us talked while you were gone and we think all of us should own this place and the boats together as equal partners and turn it into a business. Carl wants to live here year-round and I believe my old friend Boudreau would move down here and help him. During the off-season they can use these duck calls as patterns and make more to sell to the hunters. What do you men think of our idea?"

Sam answered, "I can't speak for my brother, but it's fine with me. I can help with start-up money but I won't have any time to help with the day-to-day business."

Jack agreed the idea sounded good but, like Sam, money was all he could offer to the partnership. He added, "Let's discuss the details while we're traveling up the river. Come on, get your stuff and get it loaded on the boat. I want to get back and check on the girls, the Feds took them into custody. We'll tell you the rest of the story on the way."

Just prior to casting off, Jimbo alerted them there was a boat headed their way. Everyone looked up to see a Watson lifeboat about forty feet long with five rough men aboard and it was coming directly toward them. Sam was in their boat and quickly armed himself and handed pistols to the others. There wasn't enough time to take cover so they turned around and faced the intruders.

The driver hit reverse and halted the boat about twenty yards out. One man stepped to the front of the boat and demanded to know the whereabouts of Jean Pascal. Sam answered for his crew, "He's dead, killed by the United States Federal Bureau of Investigation. Who are you?"

"My name is Captain Balthazar and I've done business with Mr. Pascal in the past. Where are his men and what are you doing here?"

Sam took a hard stance and pressed forward with his answer, "His men are all dead. My friends and I have bought this place for hunting and fishing and if you're not interested in catching fish you need to get the hell out of here."

Balthazar's face flushed with anger and his reply echoed those feelings. "What if I don't want to leave? Maybe I will take this place for myself and take you and your men as my prisoners!"

Jack lost his temper and aimed his pistol at the pirate's head. "My friends and I have faced tougher men than you and we're still free. I'll shoot you between your fucking eyes if any of your men so much as move a muscle. Now get the fuck out of here and don't ever come back!"

Balthazar was still processing the threat when another boat appeared on the horizon and it was moving fast, coming their way. It was approaching from Balthazar's blind side and he was totally unaware until he heard the sound of the speeding engine. His reaction was too slow to avoid the threat of the incoming boat. Sam recognized the boat as belonging to the Coast Guard and there were numerous men on board armed with automatic weapons. Sam told his men to get down, fearing incoming fire.

The Coast Guard fired a warning round from a .50 caliber machine gun mounted on the bow of their boat. The pirates were caught between a rock and a hard place – if they tried fighting their way out of the situation, they would be caught in a deadly crossfire. They surrendered peacefully and several men wearing jackets, emblazoned with the FBI shield, boarded their boat and ordered the pirates to get on their knees. They were quickly hand-cuffed and forced to lie face down with their hands behind their back. The man in charge, dressed in army fatigues and wearing combat boots, came ashore to tell Sam and his crew to stand down and holster their weapons. He introduced himself as FBI Deputy Director, Ron Moquett, and asked to speak to Sam Cooper.

Sam stepped forward, shook his hand and introduced his brother and the rest of the crew.

Moquett looked them over before saying, "I appreciate what you men have done for these women, freeing them from the clutches of these heinous bastards. I want you to know that thanks to your bravery, all of them are safe and will soon be reunited with their families. I cannot, however, condone your actions in the course of this operation. You operated outside the laws of this country and should have been arrested."

Jack interrupted, "We came here to save two members of our family and didn't know where they were or whether they were dead or alive. Once we found them, we didn't have time to come find you."

Moquett retorted, "Please don't interrupt me. Here's the way this is going down. My office has ordered the Coast Guard to send a patrol boat into the Gulf and capture the mother ship belonging to Balthazar. The FBI will take all of the credit for his capture and the death of Jean Pascal. We will also take the credit for finding and freeing the women who were enslaved here. You will not be punished for any of your actions, and you will be financially rewarded. The family of one of the missing girls has offered a reward of fifty thousand dollars for her safe return and her father insists on personally giving you the money tomorrow morning at the Hotel Monteleone. Unless one of you has a problem with that scenario, I'm taking my men and my prisoners out of this godforsaken place. Good day, gentlemen!"

Moquett took possession of Balthazar's boat and ordered the Coast Guard to escort them back to New Orleans. He was barely out of earshot when Jack said, "That arrogant prick needs his ass kicked."

Sam laughed at his brother and said, "He ain't all that smart anyway. He doesn't know about the Cabin Craft or the flat-bottomed boat that belonged to Pascal and didn't think about the financial possibilities of this godforsaken place. Somebody tie that flat-bottom to the back of our boat and let's get out of here. My wife is waiting on me and she don't know it yet, but she is gonna reward me tonight for being faithful yesterday."

The five new partners discussed the future of their hunting and fishing venture while traveling up the river. They agreed to use half of the reward money as operating capital and split the rest amongst themselves. Carl wasn't going back to Memphis with the rest. He wanted to return to Bay Denesse and start the cleanup and renovation of the lodge and cabins. The Cabin Craft would be used to transport hunters to and from New Orleans and the flat-bottom would be used for local hunting. Sam suggested they use part of the reward money to purchase another boat specifically for fishing. Everyone hoped Leo would benefit from the new enterprise, selling supplies and gear to the clients, and that Boudreau would join the team as a paid employee. His knowledge of the area and its people could be a valuable contribution to the overall success of the operation.

When they reached New Orleans, Sam and Jack were dropped off near the hotel and Jimbo took the boat back to the trading post. Sam was anxious to see his wife and sleep in a comfortable bed. Jack wanted a hot bath, a good meal, and a good night's sleep. He would call Gina in the morning after he had checked in with Rose at the office.

The next morning Sam and Adelle were having breakfast in the hotel restaurant. The previous night's lovemaking had required a lot of energy and left them famished. There were a lot of things to discuss between the two, but for the moment the conversation centered on finding a nanny for Samantha. Nathalie had told Adelle she wanted to return to France with Sasha and spend some time with her family. The kidnapping had left her mentally traumatized, and she didn't want to return to the house in Memphis where the entire ordeal had begun. Adelle thought she could possibly return once they were living in Kentucky but that wasn't certain. Adelle was going to need help packing for the move and even more help with Samantha once the new baby was born in December.

Sam told her a little bit about the new business venture and some of the tentative plans the partners had made. He told her that he would be traveling back with her, Nathalie, Sasha and André in their car and Jack was going to ride back with Dave and one of the other kidnap victims, a girl from Memphis named Heidi. Jimbo and Chuck were going to drive the Chris Craft back to Memphis, and Carl would stay behind to help get the new business started.

They had just completed their meal when the waiter informed them there was a family in the hotel lobby asking for Mr. Cooper. Sam asked the waiter to pull another table next to theirs while he went to find the inquiring family.

Sam introduced Adelle to Jay Chandler, his wife Bonnie and their daughter Veronica. Jay Chandler was a true Southern gentleman with abundant charm and polite wit. He and Bonnie were overjoyed that their daughter had been found and returned safely. He asked many questions about the history of the Pascal family and the kidnapping operation. Sam answered some of the questions that he was more comfortable with, and some he avoided answering by playing dumb.

He diverted the conversation away from the past and told of their plans to use the reward money to start a commercial hunting and fishing operation in the marshlands of Bay Denesse. Mr. Chandler was very impressed that Sam, whom he knew had masterminded the rescue mission, was going to share the reward with his four companions. He told Sam that he had many business associates who loved to hunt and fish, but he would personally like to be their first client. He would bring a group of his key employees as soon as the camp was open for business.

Sam thanked him for his support and told Veronica that he and Adelle wished her well. She gave him a hug and thanked him again for her rescue.

Jay set a leather case on the table and said, "There's fifty thousand dollars in cash in that case. Please tell your companions how grateful we are. I hope we see you soon and please be safe."

After he and his family left the table, Sam took Adelle's hands in his and told her he was ready to go home. As they were walking away Adelle asked him if he had noticed the pretty dark-haired girl with the almond-shaped eyes sitting nearby in the restaurant and Sam told her he hadn't really been paying much attention, but that he had noticed a young lady. He stopped and turned to look back, but she was gone.

The young lady they had seen was already heading out the back door of the hotel. Leona Pascal, with a knife at her throat, had told her where to find Sam Cooper. Her name was Tera Borel and she was seeking revenge for the death of her lover and partner in crime. Jean Pascal had meant a lot to her—his devilry allowed her to live out her own twisted fantasies and somebody was going to pay for taking him away from her. Perhaps she would change her appearance and travel to Memphis. After all, she had just overheard the Coopers talking about hiring a nanny and she was looking for a new line of work.

DAN WHITE was born and raised in rural Arkansas. He was educated at the University of Arkansas and Baylor College of Dentistry in Dallas, Texas. He currently lives outside of Lexington, Kentucky, in the heart of the Bluegrass on a thoroughbred farm where dogs and horses rule.

Made in the USA
Charleston, SC
24 December 2016